MY LOVELY EXECUTIONER

Jimmy Gallivan is only three-and-a-half weeks from his prison release for trying to kill his wife's lover seven years ago. But fellow-inmate Rand has other plans for Gallivan. A break-out is engineered, and now they're hiding out in a sanitarium. But the whole set-up seems suspicious. Rand's boss wants Gallivan to help him with his drug operation. But is that all there is to it? Because it begins to seem like the whole escape was engineered just for him. And what about Jesse? Where does she figure in all of this? Is she the bait—or has she become Gallivan's new jailor?

AGREEMENT TO KILL

Punching Dixon had gotten Jake Spinner thrown in jail, but now that he's out all he wants is a fresh start back on his farm. Suddenly Dixon is dead and Spinner in on the run, escaping town in the getaway car with Dixon's assassin in the back seat! He knows the cops won't believe his innocence. He knows his only chance is to keep the cold, clubfooted little killer known as Loma with him. Because Loma is his ticket to a new life. His respectable life shattered, Spinner figures that the only ones who'll take him in now are the guys who hired Loma. The choice is easy— until he meets Ann.

PETER RABE BIBLIOGRAPHY

From Here to Maternity
  (1955)
Stop This Man! (1955)
Benny Muscles In (1955)
A Shroud for Jesso (1955)
A House in Naples (1956)
Kill the Boss Goodbye (1956)
Dig My Grave Deep (1956)*
The Out is Death (1957)*
Agreement to Kill (1957)
It's My Funeral (1957)*
Journey Into Terror (1957)
Mission for Vengeance (1958)
Blood on the Desert (1958)
The Cut of the Whip (1958)*
Bring Me Another Corpse
  (1959)*
Time Enough to Die (1959)*
Anatomy of a Killer (1960)
My Lovely Executioner (1960)
Murder Me for Nickels (1960)
The Box (1962)
His Neighbor's Wife (1962)

Girl in a Big Brass Bed
  (1965)**
The Spy Who Was Three Feet
  Tall (1966)**
Code Name Gadget (1967)**
Tobruk (1967)
War of the Dons (1972)
Black Mafia (1974)

As by "Marco Malaponte"
New Man in the House
  (1963)
Her High-School Lover (1963)

As by "J. T. MacCargo"
Mannix #2:
  A Fine Day for Dying (1975)
Mannix #4: Round Trip to
  Nowhere (1975)

*Daniel Port series
**Manny deWitt series

My Lovely Executioner

Agreement to Kill

By Peter Rabe

Stark House Press • Eureka California

MY LOVELY EXECUTIONER / AGREEMENT TO KILL

Published by Stark House Press
2200 O Street
Eureka, CA 95501
griffinskye3@sbcglobal.net
www.starkhousepress.com

ISBN: 1-933586-11-7

Book design by Mark Shepard, WWW.SHEPGRAPHICS.COM
Proofreading by Joanne Applen

*The publisher wishes to thank Chris Nielsen and
Max Gartenberg for all their help in the production of this book.*

First Stark House Press Edition: November 2006

0 9 8 7 6 5 4 3 2

CONTENTS

A PERSONAL RECOLLECTION
By Max Gartenberg

I did not think the first impression would last. It was 1950—we were both grad students (I in English and he in psychology) at a midwestern university and Peter did not look like a writer. It took me some time to learn that writers have no particular profiles.

Four years later, I was setting up as a literary agent when I was visited by Claire Rabe, Peter's wife, who actually looked more like my idea of a writer than Peter did. So I was not a little surprised that she wanted me to place a novel—but one by Peter.

Since I didn't have much business at the time, I decided to take the novel on, particularly as Peter had saved me the work of submitting the manuscript to the publisher directly.

I called the publisher and told him of the circumstances and was surprised to learn that the publisher had already decided to buy the manuscript. In fact, the publisher was so eager to add Peter to his list that he asked if Peter had another novel.

In fact, he had finished his second novel and was working on a third. So much for a writer who did not look like a writer.

Before Peter died, we were to do business on 24 different novels and I was to learn many of life's lessons.

Noir and Gestalt:
The Life of Peter Rabe
By George Tuttle

Gold Medal Books discovered many talented novelists who could write hardboiled fiction, but in 1955, the editors felt that they had found its biggest discovery, Peter Rabe. On the cover of Peter's second novel *Benny Muscles In* (1955), their opinion is expressed: "Not since Dashiell Hammett and Raymond Chandler, who—-under the guidance of that great editor, Joe Shaw-—established the school of hard-boiled fiction, has a writer and a style come to the front with such brilliance and power as Peter Rabe. The editors of Gold Medal can remember nothing like it in the last quarter of a century."

Gold Medal Editor-in-Chief Richard Carroll believed that Peter could be a new giant in the mystery field, a status eventually obtained by fellow Gold Medal writer John D. MacDonald. But unlike MacDonald, Peter never reached that exalted level. Though he had a successful career throughout the 1950's and received high praise from the likes of New York Times critic Anthony Boucher, his success did not carry on into the 1960's. This article will try to explain what happened to Peter Rabe; why one of the most promising writers of the 1950's fell short of fame.

Peter Rabe died on May 20, 1990, of lung cancer, fifteen years after his last novel. In 1967, he felt forced to walk away from professional writing to become an Associate Professor at California Polytechnic State University at San Luis Obispo. Five years later, while still a professor, he returned to Gold Medal with *War of the Dons* (1972), and then after one more book under his own name and two under a pseudonym, he stopped writing crime fiction for publication. Peter loved writing and continued to write for his own amusement, but he quit attempting to sell his fiction.

The novels of Peter Rabe will give you little insight into the man. Unlike some writers whose stories are filled with personal feelings and experiences, Peter always keeps a certain distance from the characters he created, and the stories he told. His thrillers are almost all written in the third person and are not attempts to live vicariously. Instead, these novels are truly the theater of his imagination, and though Peter directs the action, he is not a participant.

An example of the distance that he maintained is revealed in the settings he used. He rarely set his novels in places where he lived, at the time, but instead, he preferred to use settings from his past and often used places that he had only known briefly. In *A Shroud for Jesso* (1955) and *A House in Naples* (1956), there is the Europe experienced as a child, updated to contemporary times. In *Stop this Man!* (1955) and *It's My Funeral* (1957), there are scenes from L.A., where he lived for a short time, during the early 1950's, while attempting to establish a career as a practicing psychologist.

Peter's early novels (probably just his first two) were written while living in Maine. Later, Peter lived in Cleveland and in the scenic town of Provincetown, Massachusetts. By the late 1950's, Peter had moved to Europe. *Bring Me Another Corpse* (1959) was set in Cleveland, but by the time it was written, Peter was probably in Germany receiving treatment for a misdiagnosed terminal illness.

Peter grew up in the Germany of the 1920's and 1930's. His father Michael Rabinovich (Rabinowitsch, the German spelling) was a Russian Jew, who had immigrated into Germany so that he could study medicine. After attending the University of Strasburgh and being interned as an enemy alien during World War I, Michael moved to Halle where he enrolled in the Martin Luther University. There he met a secretary who worked in one of the departments, Elisabeth Margarete Beer. They were married in Halle in January of 1921. Peter was born November 3, 1921. A few months later, they moved to Hanover, in Northern Germany, where Michael set up a practice as a physician and surgeon. Two more sons, Valentin and Andreas, would follow about a decade later.

As a child, Peter learned to live with intolerance, even though he was only Jewish on his father's side (his mother's family was Lutheran.) One memory he shared, years later, with his daughter Jennifer was an outing in which he participated with a group of boys. At one point, during their hike through the countryside, they had to ask a local property owner for permission to cross his field. In response to their request, the man looked at the crowd of boys, pointed his finger at Peter, and said, "All of you can cross but him. Not the Jew."

As the Nazi movement grew, it became apparent to Peter's father, Michael, that it was no longer safe for his family to stay in Germany. One day, he was ordered to appear at the Gestapo office and was confronted with a huge file of transcripts of conversations he had had in his office with patients on politics. It wasn't long after this that, in October 1938, Michael and Peter, who was nearly the age for military service (or possible internment) immigrated to the United States, first settling in Detroit. Michael's brother, Robert Rubin, sponsored them. Peter and Michael stayed with the Rubin family while Michael took a course in obstetrics in Chicago and got his license to practice medicine. He later located a village named New Bremen that was settled by Germans and needed a doctor to replace a retiring one. Michael bought his office and telegraphed Peter's mother to come to America. Peter's uncle, Robert Rubin, who had changed his family name, recommended to Michael that he do the same. The family name was changed from Rabinovich to Rabe ("RA" from Rabinowitsch and "BE" from Margarete's maiden name); hence Peter Rabinowitsch became Peter Rabe.

Peter, who could speak English before he came to the United States, adjusted quickly and soon enrolled into Ohio State University and received his bachelor's degree. After a stint in the Army, he attended Western Reserve in Cleveland, where he got his Masters and Ph.D. in psychology and worked as an instructor. It was while he was at Western Reserve that he met and fell in love with Claire Frederickson. She was five years younger than Peter, but like him, she was also a psychology major and she and her family had fled Europe to escape the Nazis.

An important fact about Claire is that she had a passionate interest in literature. She would sit in on the meetings that the graduate English majors held in the University's cafeteria. It was during these sessions that Claire became friends with Max Gartenberg. Claire introduced Peter to Max, a man who would later become a fundamental part of Peter's writing career.

Peter and Claire's relationship led to marriage, and after they'd finished their studies at Western Reserve, the couple moved to Bar Harbor, Maine, where Peter had received a post graduate grant from the National Institute of Mental Health and worked for Claire's brother, Emil Frederickson, at the Jackson Memorial Laboratory. Peter admired Emil and felt that Claire's brother was brilliant.

Despite his respect for Emil, he grew to dislike the work, which consisted of psychological experiments on animals. These experiments went against Peter's love of nature and respect for animal life. The research resulted in two papers: "Experimental Demonstration of the Cumulative Frustration Effect in C3H Mice" (The Journal of Genetic Psychology, 1951, 79, p163-172) and "The Cumulative Frustration Effect in the Audio-Genic Seizure Syndrome of DBA Mice" (The Journal of Genetic Psychology, 1952, 81, p3-17).

When the project was finished Peter and Claire traveled to Los Angeles where Peter set up a practice as a therapist. He quickly discovered that the market for a therapist in Los Angeles was sewed up by those receiving referrals from established psychiatrists. By August 1952, the Rabes returned to Cleveland, Ohio, where Peter eventually found work at a factory, but was soon elevated from a blue-collar job to writing copy, doing layouts and illustrating for ads. Around this time, Claire became pregnant. She gave birth to their first child, Jonathan, on April 5, 1953. This experience was the basis of Peter's first book, a book totally unlike the novels to come. This work was a humorous narrative, illustrated by Peter, about the trials and tribulations of childbirth.

Peter submitted the manuscript to an agent, who tried unsuccessfully to sell it, telling Peter it was not marketable. Peter was still unwilling to give up on the story, and since the agent had tried only book publishers, Peter decided to submit it to McCall's magazine. After waiting two months, he called McCall's and was told that they were enchanted with the story and planned to publish it.

The story appeared under the title "Who's Having This Baby?" in the September 1954 issue. After its appearance, Peter was contacted by Vanguard Press, who wanted to publish it as a book. To work out the contract, Vanguard recommended that he get an agent. So he contacted the agent he had used previously, the one who couldn't sell it, originally. The story was finally published in book form by Vanguard, in 1955, under the new title *From Here to Maternity*.

As all of this is happening, Peter happened to have a completed novel called *The Ticker*. It is the story of Tony Catell who steals a radioactive ingot of gold and is unaware of the deadly nature of his actions. Tony travels to sell the ingot and starts a cross-country manhunt. Of all of Peter's books, this one is more of a traditional thriller, rather than noir. The story has a hero, Jack Herron, and a clear, distinct resolution. It isn't an anti-hero story like many of his later works.

He showed the manuscript to his agent, who told him that she didn't handle those types of books, what the publishing trade called "blood 'n' guts" stories. So once again, Peter was on his own. He submitted the book to Gold Medal.

Meanwhile, Claire had heard that her old friend Max Gartenberg had formed his own literary agency. Since Peter would eventually need representation, she went to New York to see Max and ask him if he'd be interested in checking on the status of *The Ticker* and handling Peter's next book, *The Hook*. Max said, "Yes."

Max happened to have a friend at Gold Medal, an editor named Hal Cantor. He contacted Hal and was informed that Gold Medal was delighted with *The Ticker* and wanted to do more books by Peter. So Max offered them *The Hook*. Peter's career was off with a bang.

Gold Medal's excitement over Peter's work led Gold Medal's Editor-in-Chief Richard Carroll to look for a way to give this new author a big send-off. Carroll decided on getting an endorsement from Erskine Caldwell, one of the biggest selling authors in the history of publishing, and sent the galleys, with an endorsement fee to Caldwell's agent. But since Caldwell didn't have time to read the book and the agent didn't want to turn down the fee, his agent endorsed the book for Caldwell, with the words' "I couldn't put this book down!"

The Ticker was released August 1955, under the title *Stop this Man!* When Peter visited the offices of Fawcett after the publication, he asked

Carroll if he could have Caldwell's address so he could thank the famed author. In response, Carroll said, after a long pause, "Peter, do you know why Erskine Caldwell said,'I couldn't put this book down?' It's because he never picked it up."

The humor of the situation wasn't lost on Peter, who took the incident in stride. Endorsements were all part of how paperback originals were marketed. Peter accepted this and didn't resent Gold Medal for doing what it felt necessary to promote a book. Likewise, he took it in stride when Gold Medal changed the titles of his novels – when *The Ticker* became *Stop This Man!,* and when his next novel *The Hook* became *Benny Muscles In.*

Title changes were a standard operating procedure for Gold Medal. They saw a book's cover as the chief means of advertising a paperback and reserved in the contract the right to change the title to something more marketable. All of Peter's early novels had their titles changed. The only exceptions were *A House in Naples* and *The Box* (1962), though in the case of *A House in Naples*, the title was actually suggested by Max Gartenberg, Peter's agent.

Even though he didn't care much for the titles chosen (most were too crass for his tastes), he didn't let this color the fact that he liked writing for Gold Medal. He was intrigued with the type of situations dealt with in crime fiction. He liked the directness in which the characters reacted to one another and how the situations unfolded. These stories came easily to him and were well received by Editor-in-Chief Richard Carroll, who was very enthusiastic about Peter's work.

To write a novel, Peter would start with an outline. Using a clipboard and unlined yellow paper, he would write down the basic events that made up the plot. Once the outline was finished, he would work at the typewriter with the clipboard next to him, creating the story as he typed. He typed quickly and would only occasionally pause to light a cigarette, take a drag, and place it in the ashtray where it was usually allowed to burn out. He composed his novels directly on the typewriter, typing quickly and rarely rereading what he wrote.

During the mid-1950's, Peter's life changed for the better. His writing career took off, and he bought a summer cottage on Commercial Street in Provincetown, Massachusetts, a scenic town on the tip of Cape Cod. His family grew. A second child, Julia, was born on March 6, 1955, and later, another daughter, Jennifer(November 22, 1957).

In 1958, the success in publishing continued, but a complication developed. Peter started having health problems due to a stomach tumor. By July 1958, he received a report from a specialist in Boston recommending a gastric resection. After the procedure, a suspicious spot was biopsied and diagnosed as cancerous, and he was told that his condition was terminal.

As a result of the surgery, Peter lost weight and looked close to death.

Peter's father made arrangements with the Ringberg Clinic, which specialized in alternative treatments for cancer. The clinic sits along Lake Tegernsee in Bavaria, Germany, and was run by Dr. Josef Issels. Peter moved his family to Taormina, Sicily, while he relocated to Germany. (Claire had no desire to revisit memories of Nazi Germany.) So Peter and Claire separated. While his family stayed in Sicily, Peter received treatment in Germany, hoping for the best, but preparing himself for the worst.

Soon after this happened, a second event occurred that would severely damage the writing career. Richard Carroll stepped down as Editor-in-Chief at Gold Medal Books, due to his own health problems. He eventually died on March 11, 1959. Carroll was one of Rabe's biggest fans. He thought Rabe could become a major writer of hardboiled thrillers, and Rabe might have if Carroll had lived. It's rare that a writer can find an editor who is truly willing to work with him. Carroll was that type of editor. He would let Peter know precisely how he felt about a novel. If a story had a weakness, Carroll would let Peter know where it fell short. In a 1991 interview (published Paperback Parade, issue 25) Peter described Carroll as "a very incisive and swift person, but he was open to dialogue. There was nothing particularly dictatorial about him. He was very explicit about what he didn't like, so, I liked working with him."

Peter's health had no immediate effect on his writing. Carroll's departure did. Knox Burger, who had been in charge of Dell's First Edition line, eventually replaced Carroll at Gold Medal. Since Knox had no previous ties to Gold Medal, he tended to favor writers he knew while working at Dell, authors like Donald Hamilton and James Atlee Phillips. This made things tougher for most of the old regulars, Peter included. Though Rabe sold several novels to Gold Medal while Burger was in charge, he didn't have the close relationship with Burger that he had with Carroll. Burger did think highly of Peter. Peter was one of the few writers from the Carroll era that Burger respected. He later describes Rabe, in a 1992 interview for Mystery Scene (appearing in issue 34) as one of "two or three very good writers I thought had been sort of mishandled by the previous regime." Burger seemed to think that all the writers under the previous regime were either hacks or mishandled. Burger's attitude did not mellow, over the years, particularly when paperback collectors and fans would ask him questions about David Goodis, Wade Miller, Lionel White, Bruno Fischer, and other writers associated with the Carroll years and would neglect to ask questions about Burger's pet writers.

Meanwhile in Europe, Peter's health improved. The reason for the improvement was uncovered when his father Michael double-checked Peter's test results and found a major blunder. The results of Peter's biopsy had been switched with that of another patient. Peter's biopsy was cancer free. Michael telegraphed Peter the news. Soon after receiving the telegram, Peter left Germany, in July 1959, and returned to Sicily.

The separation and the emotional strain of this whole episode had severely damaged Peter and Claire's marriage. The whole series of events that brought them to Europe were not easy for either to handle. The fact that much that had happened was needless didn't help the situation.

In an attempt to salvage the marriage, Peter and Claire left Sicily and moved the family to Torremolinos, Spain, in the hope that the change in environment would help. It didn't. After about six months, Peter left for the United States, while Claire and the children stayed in Spain. Some time later, after attempts at reconciliation failed, they divorced.

Peter returned to America a different man. Many things had happened to change his outlook on life. First there was the illness that had been diagnosed as fatal, then the discovery that it was all a mistake, and finally, the split in his marriage and separation from his family. The man who returned to America in the early 1960's was not the same man who left, and it showed in his writing. In the sixties, Peter's style became less direct and more ambiguous. His sentences no longer had the crisp, simple clarity of his early writing. Peter explained the change in the 1991 Paperback Parade interview, stating that he had gone through "some very deep disturbances. Out of those disturbances emerged a man who no longer felt like writing that sort of thing."

As his writing style changed, so did the book publishing market, and unfortunately, it didn't change in his direction. The bottom dropped out of the paperback original market and a number of companies died or cut back on originals. Though Gold Medal stayed prosperous with a number of successful series like Shell Scott, Matt Helm, and Travis McGee, it found itself less interested in noir fiction. From 1961 to 1964, Gold Medal published only one new Peter Rabe novel unlike the previous four years when it published ten.

That one novel, *The Box* (1962) is a story about a man who crosses a crime boss and is punished by being packed alive in a box and shipped around the world. Max Gartenberg, who had heard of a similar incident from his cousin, a lawyer, gave the idea to Peter. It was one of his finest novels, clear evidence that his talent had not died.

In an attempt to weather this lean period, Peter started selling to Beacon, a paperback house that specialized in sexually suggestive literature. Beacon's trademark was a lighthouse and probably the greatest example of the use of a sexually subliminal image to market a product. Many paperback original writers who fell on tough times during the sixties, sold to Beacon, Harry Whittington, Ovid Demaris, Michael Avallone, and Robert Turner to name some. It wasn't a high paying market like Gold Medal, but it was a paying market. At the time, Peter needed money.

The first book Peter wrote for Beacon was *His Neighbor's Wife* (1962). It's a good work of noir in the tradition of some of his best Gold Medal work, but it is unlikely that Beacon was completely happy with it. The problem with the book from Beacon's point of view is that it's centered on a criminal conflict, not a sexual conflict. Since they specialized in sexual-oriented fiction, it's doubtful they would have been happy with this novel. The book focuses on a hit-and-run accident and the psychological effects of the accident on the driver Martin Trevor and the passengers, his wife and another couple. Though the book has its share of sex, the sex is only a subplot, and hardly transforms the novel into the wife-swapping romp that the cover blurb promises. *His Neighbor's Wife* is a good book, but it's wasted on a publisher not interested in a psychological crime thriller.

Peter's next two novels for Beacon were more tailored to their need. *Her High-School Lover* (1963) and *New Man in the House* (1963) are the type of erotic thrillers Beacon is associated with, but not the type of book that Peter had interest in writing. Though not a prude, he had no desire to write novels based solely on sex. Peter was not proud of these efforts, and published them under the penname Marco Malaponte.

As Peter was trying to get his writing career back in order, he also tried to piece together his personal life. He met and fell in love with a blond Scandinavian beauty named Kristen, nicknamed Kiki, and they married. But the marriage lasted about as long as Peter's relationship with Beacon. They lived awhile in Spain, where Peter could be close to his children, and then moved to California where Peter and Kiki divorced. Little came of the brief relationship, though while Peter was in Spain, he developed a friendship with writer Lorenzo Semple, Jr., who would later join Peter in California, where they both tried to find work writing for television.

Television seemed to be the logical next step, since the paperback original market was suffering due to television. And though there was initial optimism, the optimism was quickly crushed. By June 1962, Peter writes in a letter from L.A. that out of ten TV script outlines he's sent out, only one has been rejected. The rest were all still under consideration including one for Hitchcock they'd asked he write based on one of his books. He also had a script accepted by the producer of the "Alcoa Hour." But later, both, the Hitchcock and Alcoa projects, were rejected by the sponsors. Interest followed by rejection characterizes Peter's career in television.

Around this time, Claire Rabe wrote a book called *Sicily Enough* (1963). The book was published in Paris, by Olympia Press. This short novel was later anthologized in The Best of Olympia (1966) and became a minor classic, receiving praise from authors Henry Miller and Thomas Sanchez. It was later reprinted with a collection of short stories by Claire, under the title *Sicily Enough and More* (1989). Claire is a totally different type of writer from Peter. While Peter preferred to maintain a distance from his creations, Claire's fiction has an autobiographical quality. The feelings and experience of the protagonists are intertwined with the author's, to the point that it's difficult to separate them. *Sicily Enough*, which is about a woman stranded in Taormina, Sicily, with her three children, mirrors many of Claire's experiences during her time in Taormina. It is interesting how Peter and Claire, who were so close, wrote fiction that is so radically different.

Throughout the Sixties, Peter continued to struggle. He roomed together for a short period with Lorenzo Semple, Jr. It was Semple who got the first big break when he landed the job of head writer on the *Batman* TV series. As a result of this break, Semple was able to send work in Peter's direction and Peter penned the episodes: "The Joker's Last Laugh" and "The Joker's Epitaph." Peter did other writing for *Batman*, but it was not used because of a format change in the series, the addition of Batgirl to the cast. Though Peter did other television work, the *Batman* episodes were the extent of his screen credits.

Peter moved regularly during this time, living in Anaheim, Hollywood, and Laguna Beach. He would occasionally take trips away from the West Coast. One trip was to Provincetown, and showed in an ironic way, that his readers had not been forgotten him. Peter's old home had sold, and he had come east to remove his things, and transport the bigger items, temporarily, to a friend's home, outside New York City. Unbeknownst to Peter, there had been a string of robberies of summer places on the Cape, and the police had a description of the car, a model that resembled Peter's. Peter finished what he had to do late on a weekend night, packed the back seat full of paintings, lamps, and other furnishings, and started out for New York. On the way, he was pulled over by a small town cop, who spotted the suspicious car full of what looked like loot, and Peter ended up in jail. Peter tried to reason with the officer, but the cop, who was also the jailer, kept stating that nothing could be done until the Justice appeared Monday morning. Eventually, the cop realized that he had read several of Peter's books and asked him to autograph one of them – but still the law was the law, and the officer had to keep Peter in the tank until Monday.

While Peter was trying to break into television, he continued to write novels. He created the Manny deWitt series for Gold Medal and wrote a novelization for the movie "Tobruk." To make ends meet, he also delivered newspapers, drove a taxi and did other odd jobs.

In 1967, Peter married Barbara Renard, whom he had known back at Western Reserve University and had met again while in Hollywood. As a result of Barbara's insistence and the need for a steady income, he quit professional writing and reluctantly returned to the field of psychology. He obtained a teaching job at California Polytechnic State University at San Luis Obispo. They eventually bought a home in nearby Atascadero, California. Had it not been for Barbara, Peter might have stayed in writing and maybe roughed it out through the Sixties. As it was, teaching gave him financial security and a chance to be a father to his three children.

In the late 1960's, a little remembered actor/director, Peter Savage, bought the rights to *A House in Naples* and with producer Joe Justman, made a movie. The movie "A House in Naples" starred Pete Savage and his friend, boxer Jake LaMotta and was filmed in Italy. It had a limited release in 1969. Peter's agent Max Gartenberg, who saw the movie at a special screening, described it as awful, and said, "The negative is probably in somebody's warehouse, rotting away, which is the fate it deserves." At the time, the movie must have seemed like a disappointing final note to a once promising career.

Peter grew to love his work as a teacher. He renewed his interest in psychology and established a reputation as a respected Gestalt psychotherapist. But then his marriage with Barbara fell apart, and he gave writing another shot. The opportunity to be published presented itself when Knox Burger left Gold Medal and Walter Fultz took over. Walter provided a friendlier atmosphere for the old Gold Medal regulars of the 1950's and published Lionel White, Robert Colby, and others who had been frozen out when Burger took the helm. The result of this effort was entitled *War of the Dons* (1972) and became one of Peter's biggest sellers. It capitalized on the interest created by Mario Puzo's *The Godfather*. Rabe followed with another organized crime novel, *Black Mafia* (1974), a book in the tradition of his early gangster novels, like *Benny Muscles In*. In *Black Mafia*, an individual operator, a black man named Cutter, attempts to challenge the authority of the crime bosses. It's very much like the noir novels that first established Peter's reputation and was a fitting end to his relationship with Gold Medal, an end that was foreshadowed by the death of Walter Fultz and the hiring of a new editor.

Peter's last mass-market project was for the paperback house Belmont Tower. He wrote two novelizations based on scripts from the TV series *Mannix*. Both were published in 1975, under the penname J.T. MacCargo. Then Peter left professional writing, this time willingly. Things had changed in twenty years. There was still no one to replace Gold Medal's Richard Carroll, a man whose enthusiasm was an added incentive to stay in the business. Also, teaching was a much more stable profession than writing and a job where there were no concerns about changing markets or adapting to the individual taste of a particular editor, nor writing novelizations while waiting for markets to open up. Though he still wrote fiction throughout the Seventies and Eighties, he just no longer concerned himself with publication. He wrote for his own amusement.

As Peter made the transition from noir to gestalt, his life became more settled. As a professor of psychology, he had a greater control over his destiny. In 1971, he met Chris Neilson, a psychology student. Once again he fell in love, but this time he didn't jinx the relationship with marriage. Chris moved into his Atascadero home where they lived together until his death.

Still noir didn't abandon him. The dark images of Tom Fell (*Kill the Boss Good-By*), Daniel Port (*Dig My Grave Deep*), Jack St. Louis (*Murder Me for Nickels*) and anti-heroes of the earlier Rabe returned. During the late Seventies and throughout the Eighties, a following grew in both Europe and America for the old Gold Medal crime fiction and for Peter Rabe. In 1988, Black Lizard Books started reprinting Peter's books. He was surprised and flattered by this interest and deeply touched that he hadn't been forgotten as a novelist.

Peter career in noir was short. It started in 1955, soaring, only to crash and burn in the Sixties and then briefly resurrect itself in the early Seventies. When asked in the 1991 Paperback Parade interview, "Do you think if Carroll had lived longer that you would have stayed in the writing profession?"

Rabe answered: "I feel very sure that I would have become a better writer, a more consequential storyteller and may well have stayed in longer."

Possibly, if Carroll had lived into the next decade, Rabe would have made the transition from noir to a fiction style more marketable during the 1960's. Maybe, Daniel Port wouldn't have retired in Mexico or Rabe might have developed a series based on *Blood on the Desert* instead of creating the character of Manny deWitt. As it was, Peter Rabe did have a good life with Chris Neilson in Atascadero.

My Lovely Executioner

By Peter Rabe

CHAPTER 1

I always became nervous just before five because that was quitting time. The big hand on the clock started to creep, the boiler in the back of the laundry made twice the racket. The big drum with the squeak in one bearing cut into my ear as if I were hearing the sound for the first time.

We had quitting time just like regular humans, even though nothing much came after that. No good meal and no nice evening.

But at five o'clock the nerves always showed in all of us, including the kind like Smitty who had served most of his time with maybe ten years, fifteen at the outside, to go. He was that old.

He yanked the clutch lever of the big drum too late, and the brake too, so when I opened the lid to pull out the wet sheets I had to reach up too high and the water ran into my sleeves.

"Let her down some," I said. "How long you got to practice to get a trick like stopping the drum at the right place?"

"The way it's been going," he said, "maybe 'til I get out of the bucket. No more."

That was a nasty thing for a lifer to say, especially about himself, and it really showed how jumpy he was because he was old and mild actually, even dull. I rather think dull. The same thing, after less time than Smitty's, was happening to me.

I could get up at five in the morning, with the squeal horn waking me, with no effort or anger any more. I could file down my corridor and peel off at the right cell as if moving on rails. Even that dismal sound meant less and less, when the grilled doors slid across and went *snap* in the lock, one after the other, the whole length of the block. That would be that for the long hours before falling asleep, the three hours with lights on, and the rest, I don't know how many, in the dark.

I pulled a crate over from the side of the drum, turned it over and stood on it. Smitty said nothing and when a screw came by and saw me haul the wet sheets from the drum into the cart, he didn't say anything either. He kept walking.

"Friend of yours?" said Smitty. That was an insult.

"The Christmas spirit." I kept hauling sheets.

It was awkward work, a strain on the back, and I took it out on that instead of saying something else to Smitty. He said nothing either for a while and looked out the near window. It was steamy and had wire mesh in the glass but I could see the snow coming down into the yard and the big wall in back, cutting off the rest.

When I stopped a second, to catch my breath, Smitty tried smiling at me, to show he hadn't meant it before. Then he nodded out at the window.

"Look at the Christmas spirit come down all over," he said.

The snow was coming down thick and steady and when I squinted my eyes at it, I could hardly see the big wall. But on the ground, in the yard, all the Christmas spirit was turning black.

Then I got the draft in the back. Somebody had pushed the sliding door open, letting all the cold from the yard come in. They were dragging the new boiler through the door, on two dollies. There were maybe five men pushing and hauling, and Rand telling them which way. And two screws, naturally, but they were just standing.

I felt touchy enough; I almost yelled something at the crew, but the screws there reminded me. I couldn't yell, only take it out in some other way. Or let it lie, hoping it would go away.

With the steam torn I could see the stone walls of the laundry very clearly, how they peeled and how really wet they were. I only remember because of what followed.

The new boiler bounced me from behind, bounced the crate out from under me, and skinned the small of my back. I fell on the hard, wet floor, right between the boiler and the drum, and I could see Smitty stand by his levers. For a second I thought he was going to start up and thought of the open lid coming down, smacking me on the way around.

But he wasn't looking at me or at his levers.

On the other side of the boiler was commotion. The cursing alone was bad—nobody in his right mind, no matter what time it was, talked loud or cursed—but that wasn't all. I could tell by the way feet shuffled, making quick sounds which stopped in the middle, and by the sharp, gritty scrapes on the floor. Other sounds too.

Before the screws started whistling I had the picture.

A fight on the outside is one thing. You join, you watch, or you run. A fight on the inside is something else, because you pay so much more. The screws get you, if you join; the screws get you, if you watch; the screws get you, if you run. Or the cons get you.

I sat on the concrete for a moment, but the time seemed very long. The noise came all over me, and then, very suddenly, I came apart. It feels that way. It's something I'd never known before I came to prison. My insides start to float, especially in my belly, and the skin and muscles get harder and harder so I keep my shape. Then, hard as glass. I tighten up to get smaller than dust because if I should move, something might break. And meantime my insides keep floating and spinning faster, like an internal fire, roaring.

The others were milling around and making a lot of noise. I was sure there were more than five men now and of course more than two screws. A screw slammed his stick down and hit the new boiler with a sound like a big, holy bell.

All of a sudden it was over. Rand was yelling, the screws were whistling, and an alarm went off someplace. We got a million alarms—warning bell, hurry-up bell, break bell, riot bell—but I didn't know which one was going off. I heard Rand yelling, because when Rand opens his mouth it's important.

The screws loved him, because of how he handled the men, and the men loved him, because Rand is that way; what I would call right.

He was yelling to stop and everybody stopped.

The curious thing about him was his looks. He wasn't big and he had no special features. He had light colored hair which always looked as if it had just been washed, and the way he kept his hands in his pockets made him seem very straight.

He was putting his hands back into his pockets and everybody stopped. The fight had lasted maybe three minutes.

Three minutes or three hours is all the same though, because a brawl is a brawl. There were plenty of screws now, including some on the gallery holding their riot guns, and we got herded together and marched out to the yard. It was fifteen minutes before shut down, but the worst part would come later.

Everybody was thinking of that. There was a hook inside everybody; the fight had been over too soon.

Nobody talked, nobody made a false move. There were guns looking down from the big wall and from the inner wall, the one where we had to go through the gate to get back into the compound.

We walked through the slush in the empty yard with the screws making nervous circles a little distance away. The line of men looked like a black, silent snake. The thick snow came down all the time so that the big wall was hard to see. The snow fell on heads and on shoulders but nobody made any kind of a move to get rid of it.

I had Smitty in front of me and Rand in the rear.

"Tell him," Smitty said without turning, "that something stinks."

"Him" was Rand, of course. I don't know how I knew, but Smitty meant Rand.

Then I heard Rand's "stir" voice close behind me, the sound we learned to make without using our lips.

"I can hear you clear," he said. "And so can the screws, maybe."

"Too scared to come close," said Smitty.

"And the Christmas spirit," I said.

"I seen five riots, the time I spent here," said Smitty, "and this one stinks."

"I didn't think it was any good either," said Rand.

The snake-line bent again and we were kept close to the wall. There were screws all along the top of the wall, black humps in the falling snow.

"Maybe if it were colder," I said, "one of them might drop a gun."

The head of the line walked a little more slowly now and the snake seemed to bulge. The line always slowed here because we came to the second wall gate.

At that moment a new alarm went off.

I thought it was fire. It could have been warning bell, hurry bell, break bell, or Christmas bell. Our gate opened up, as usual, but the head of the line didn't move. When the head of the line refused to go the rest of the line kept bulging up from behind because nobody had said stop or blown the right whistle. There was a murmur from the front, which only made the rear more eager. Then we saw the fire, past the gate in the furniture shop.

The line wasn't moving and the screws with the sticks started running and yelling, because nothing made them nervous as something without a plan. This line was planless now. It had bunched up so they couldn't see single men any more. It was a mass which was too closely packed and which wouldn't move. Trouble started when one of the screws made the mistake of swinging his stick into somebody. There weren't enough screws for that kind of play and once they mingled with the cons, the screws on the walls didn't know where to shoot.

"I'll kill ya, you bastard," yelled somebody, and "Move, move in there!" And then Rand behind me, very loud. "Not the fire! Can't walk us into that fire, you crazy screws!"

The fire wasn't that close, but the words threw everyone into a panic. The snake had come apart and was turning into a beast with too many heads. The cons screamed and milled and a guard got trampled. The beast now broke up into a flying mass of little splinters, because the guards on the wall had started to fire.

"Break!" somebody yelled, and with the wild bullets from the wall forcing everyone away from the gate, the frightened men kept screaming, "Break—Break!"

The snow came thick and fast, breaking the field of vision into small, nervous flickers. Bullets twanged into the yard and soon there wasn't a mob any more, just frightened men running.

Then the splinters all got pulled together, the way metal scraps react to a magnet.

"*Big Wall!*"

Suddenly the beast had a head again, because Rand had screamed "big wall."

"*Everybody!*" he bellowed again, "*Big Wall!*"

Nobody ever got out that way unless he wore a civilian suit—prison made—with a cardboard satchel in one hand and the little white release slip in the other.

Not everybody ran to the big wall but a lot of insane fools with no thoughts but the mob yell in their heads ran that way. The bullets from the inner wall kept chasing us away from the gate in back, the snow beat through the air, keeping the big wall a faint, unreal goal in the distance, but Rand kept yelling the word and nobody thought for a moment that he would run us into a closed door.

The only ones who didn't feel the bite and the challenge of escape were the ones like Smitty.

It takes a long time to get used to the idea of serving a life sentence, but once into that zombie world, and it's hard to come out of it.

I ran into Smitty because he suddenly stopped in the yard.

"What am I doing?" he said, "What am I doing?"

I gibbered something at him, out of pure excitement, and dragged on his arm.

"I can't," he kept saying and his voice had a crack in it.

"Big Wall!"

"I can't walk through that way, I can't get—I didn't bring my—Please!" and he was staring into my face, "Please leave me be!"

But I didn't want to let go of his arm. I got stubborn because Smitty was frightened.

Rand came chasing by, yelling, and when he saw us frozen there he suddenly stopped. His breath was pumping hard. His hair came out wet from under his cap and there was wet on his lashes so that they stuck together. His eyes looked naked and big. I had never seen him excited.

"—make it," it pumped out of him, "We'll make it!"

I could suddenly feel the snow soak through to my back and I shivered.

"For godsake move!" he screamed at me. "Leave Smitty, leave go his arm!"

"I can't go this way," Smitty was chattering. "I got to get my—what was it, I got to get my—"

"He's rocky, he's forty years' worth of rocky!" and Rand grabbed my arm hard.

"They can't see from the walls," he yelled into my ear, "we'll make it! Now!"

A bullet twanged into the ground next to us, from the back wall. Nobody walks out of the big wall except with the suit and the little white slip. That's what Smitty was meaning to say, that he had to go get his blue suit and the slip. He was right, and I was right because this wasn't my break, just a sudden wild thing in the laundry, a break I knew nothing about, a break I didn't need, didn't want.

"—forty years rocky!" Rand yelled into my ear. "—and he stays. They can't do anything worse to a lifer. But *you!* You know what they're gonna do to you!"

A new siren went off. This one came on faint and got louder because it was on a truck. I could see it come from the inner yard with riot guns sticking out on all sides where the screws were leaning out as if craving a breath of fresh air, or better, craving to bite the way a dog does when he's locked in a car and somebody knocks at the closed window.

"I gotta sit," Smitty said, and it was the silliest thing I had ever heard. Smitty sat down in the snow like an idiot watching a buzz saw come his way.

I ran. A pure, lung-tearing run.

They were firing from the big wall now but only from the top. There was no guard down below, at the gate, because too many of us came running. Five garbage trucks were still lined up because when the riot had started, back by the inner wall, officials had kept the outside gate shut 'til they knew what was going on.

They knew what was going on now, and if it hadn't been for the snow cutting their view all to pieces and the trucks standing there to give cover, more of the cons would have been dead. I didn't think about this or anything reasonable at all, because there was just mindless panic riding me from behind and a mindless magnetic pull from the front where the gate showed, black in the blizzard air.

There was a con ahead of me, trying to duck under a truck, and when he started to duck I kicked him from behind so his head rammed into the tailgate, and when I ran past him I hit at the back of his neck. I didn't know why. The gate loomed bigger than ever before. Then it was gone.

I stopped between two of the trucks, sliding in the mush on the ground. Rand was next to me and he fell.

There was nothing but thick whiteness in front where the gate should have been, and then we could smell it.

They had tossed tear gas. It boiled up under the arch of the gate and the cons who had made it that far came running back. There were shots now. The screws had come down from the wall to lay a cross fire the width of the gate.

"Low," said Rand. "We can make it low while they can't see through the gas."

I could see the cons running back. The white fog stung and it blew with bullets.

"Look at it, look at it, the gate—" and Rand shoved from behind.

"Rand—I've had it—I think—"

"Don't think, you sonofabitch, don't *think!*"

We were between the trucks and he was pushing from behind, clawing from behind like a man clawing air, foam, and water just before he drowns.

"It's open," I heard him next to my ear. "It's open, so help me—so help me—" and there was a raw crack in his voice, close to a break.

He was insane and so was I.

We hit the gate. Eyes shut, breath held, and straight into the gas.

There was less gas there than before and as suddenly as the gate had disappeared there it was again, big and hard and the steel wet from the snow. I cracked into it, running, and I thought the impact, that hardness against my hands and my face, would break me.

There were shots behind and the siren kept chasing around in the yard. I couldn't see it any more, but I could see in my mind how the truck would be howling back and forth with men running and dropping dead where the truck went by. And I was glued up against the steel gate and I thought how when they found me I'd be dead and spread flat into the seams and around the rivets

I opened my eyes then. I no longer cared about the gas or how it might sting, because in a moment I wouldn't be able to hold my breath and they would start shooting a little bit better.

There wasn't any gas this close to the gate. There was a strong, cold draft on my face, watering my eyes, freezing me under the wet jacket, and next to my hand, my right hand on the steel, the gate ended.

The wing of the gate ended. Then there was a big crack between that and the other wing and that crack was a cold draft and a clear view of the outside.

There was a long, flat-bed truck outside the gate, loaded with I beams. They were very big and painted red. The truck had jackknifed on the street and two of the I beams stuck far out in back. So far back, I could touch them.

The prison gate had tried to jaw shut on the girders but had made it just so far. There was a cold draft and a clear view

"Gallivan!" Rand screamed. "Jump, Gallivan!"

There was a florist's delivery truck on the street. It drove up near the gate and then it stopped.

"You insane son of a bitch!" Rand tore into me from behind. *"Move!"*

I heard the sirens and then I said, "No."

"You insane s—"

I had never been so sane in my life. I said, "No."

I stepped aside, but he pushed me the wrong way, back against the girders, and they cut into my spine.

I couldn't see the street now, only Rand. He seemed very cool suddenly. Then he slugged me. I felt my breath knot up under the ribs and then felt my face come apart. I passed out, angry—

CHAPTER 2

The floor kept bucking into me and I thought I was having a nightmare, but then I realized I was inside the truck, a wet heap against the back door. How that place smelled of flowers.

It was the time to go to pieces or to get very calm. It turned out calm, like a flower. Phony and calm like a funeral flower.

I breathed in and out, in and out, feeling very little besides the cold air with the incongruous flower scent. I was too tired to do anything but huddle and breathe.

Maybe I blacked out. Somebody said, "What kept you?" and then Rand answered with something filthy, but he wasn't breathing hard any more. He had talked the way he usually did, very dry, and above all, without showing effort. Then he said, "Lend me your comb, Jack."

There was the man Jack, who sat in back with us and gave Rand a comb, then a driver, and next to that one a man who was holding a flowerbox. He passed back the flower box in a while and when the man with the comb put it down on the floor the box made a heavy thump.

Rand gave the comb back and asked for a cigarette. When he got it he gave it to me and took a second one for himself. He and I smoked while the car rocked back and forth.

"I was worried it was going to freeze," the driver said.

"That would have been bad," said Rand.

Nothing else was said for a while and the silence, in contrast to the remarks, showed the tension.

"Maybe two minutes," said the driver.

Rand nodded and looked at me. "Two minutes," he said, "and we jump again."

I nodded as he had. I smoked faster, the way Rand did. If he had lain down and had gone to sleep, I think I would have done the same thing.

The man in back with us opened the flower box and took out a burp gun. He said, "Excuse me," when he crawled over my legs, and then he sat by the back door. The car slowed, and as the motor became quiet we could hear the sirens in back.

"Which kind is that?" asked the driver, "chow line?"

"That," said the man with the burp gun, "is a patrol car."

"I didn't think it sounded like prison," and Rand crawled to the back and looked out of the small window.

"We're going to ditch at the underpass," said the driver, "so don't get nervous 'til then. Everybody know the move from there on?"

If Rand had said yes, I would have said yes, but Rand looked at me and put his cigarette out.

"We're leaving now. Take your jacket off."

"Do what?"

"Jacket," he said, and unbuttoned his.

He was wearing an undershirt but I was naked under the jacket, because of the heat in the laundry.

"So we won't show so much in the snow," said Rand.

He took his off and I mine. The truck stopped; the back door swung open.

"Jump, Gallivan," said the one with the burp gun.

I was sure that Rand hadn't told him my name. I jumped and the truck took off.

On one side of the street was a railroad embankment and on the other was a big field. The snow was coming and the light was going fast but the field was like a bright, clean sheet. On the other side, in the distance, I could see town again. There were lights from a street front and moving lights, where cars drove along. I could also hear the sirens, more than one now.

Then we ran. Rand went first and I followed, because I couldn't do anything else. Jump. Gallivan—

At first I could feel the snow touch my bare back and the melting cold where it ran down my skin, but in a while I didn't feel that any more. I lost one shoe in a mud hole, but that made no difference either. We ran. There were plenty of sirens now and once a red blinker came along the street up ahead. In the low light I could just see the red light, which seemed to be gliding.

"The trees," Rand called back. He could hardly talk, because of the running.

There were some thin trees to one side, and unkempt bushes. They looked fluffy and fat with snow and when we ran through there it felt like cold hands slapping my skin. On the other side of the bushes, a few yards away, was the street.

"From here we walk," said Rand.

We walked slowly, the way one does in wind and snow.

There was a man coming along the sidewalk, bent over to keep the snow out of his face, but coming our way.

"If he looks up, or makes a wrong move, hit him," Rand said.

It was almost dark now and the man coming was just a black shape.

Rand was cursing, but in a calm voice. "About time," he said, and then, "Gallivan! Come on, get in, Gallivan!"

I turned to the curb and there was a long, low car pulling up. The back door on the near side was open and when it came close, Rand jumped in.

The hood was just passing me and the fat tires made a squishing sound in the gutter.

This was no junky truck, like before. This was a big, maybe ten grand limousine, and Rand and I had the back seat to ourselves.

There was a pile of clothes on the seat next to me and Rand was putting a white shirt on. Then he humped himself up to be able to get the prison pants past his rear, and when he had them off, and his shoes and socks too, he got dressed with fresh clothes from the inside out. I noticed he was now wearing a dark blue suit and a silk tie which was almost as light as the shirt. His blondish hair was combed again and he looked very presentable.

I got dressed—mine was tweed, and a blue shirt—and when I put on the knit tie I looked down at the ends of my sleeves. They were long enough. But sleeves were never long enough and I wondered vaguely why the clothes fitted so well.

"You haven't got any shoes on yet," Rand said.

"I'm not sure they'll fit, Rand."

"I'm not either, but put them on."

"I'm beginning to think they'll fit, Rand. Sight unseen, I'm getting the feeling they're going to fit."

There wasn't any question that Rand knew what I was talking about, what I was asking him, but he ignored it.

"All you have to do, Gallivan, is follow along, not look behind you, and act sort of bored. It's the best way to cover the shakes, looking tired or bored. Besides, it'll fit the place."

"Are you having the shakes, Rand?"

"Here we are. You just follow. Put your hands in your pockets and look bored. It'll go with the tweeds."

I hadn't noticed that we had stopped but I saw Rand get out of the car. A man in uniform was giving him a hand.

I got out and saw where we were. I didn't dare have a reaction but just followed Rand into the hotel.

There were black and white marble columns holding the ceiling high over the lobby. There wasn't one desk, but two, with the sign saying Reservations over one, and Overnight by the other. I think I counted five different uniforms on the personnel in the lobby.

We had a reservation, or Rand did, at any rate. He talked a while at the desk and then we took the elevator to the fifth floor, which was perhaps half way up, and went to our room. Two big windows with view, two big beds with expensive covers, two easy chairs, one couch, one liquor cabinet.

"Tip the boy," said Rand.

I reached into my pocket and found money there. When the boy was gone I locked the door. I went up to Rand, who was by the liquor thing, and didn't know how to start talking.

Rand said, "We stay here two days. Safer than trying to beat out of town or trying to hide in a hole."

I went to one of the windows and looked at the night city view.

"I can see the prison from here," I said.

"Have a drink, seeing you're out of it."

He came over with it and I took the glass. I sat down with it, in one of the chairs, because I couldn't look at the view any more and my legs were giving out. Everything, suddenly, was giving out.

"It's a switch, coming out," he kept talking. "Every con knows it. Look at Smitty. Such a switch for him, he crapped out even before he got out."

"He stayed in," I said.

"Drink your drink."

"I should have stayed in."

"Gallivan, you talk like a dummy."

"I feel like one. Stuffed with straw."

"You look it."

"I am."

"You're out, you dumb bastard. Think of that."

And that tore it. I threw the highball glass at the place where Rand was standing.

"I am thinking of that! All the time! Three weeks from now damn you to hell and I was going to be done!"

CHAPTER 3

I got drunk, but that took care of only half of the night. It kept me from thinking anything through and it kept me away from Rand, because when I drink like that I'm not sociable. But, as I said, this just lasted half the night.

Rand was sitting under a lamp, his hands folded across his middle, and there was a stare on his face like a print in two colors. Gray and off-gray. I had a liquor cloud in each eyeball.

The light in the bulb looked gray, too, but the big window, when I looked at it, was glassy black, like something without a bottom. I could walk right through there and nothing would stop me, like free fall. There were no bars. And the door was a door, and not bars.

My hand shook and the brown liquor in the glass made small, nervous lights, until I tipped the glass up and drank it clean.

That killed the shakes for the moment. It left me stark naked, alone with the reason for which I had been drinking. I put the glass down on the floor and got up, sober now. Fake-sober, maybe, but sober.

"Don't go out there," said Rand.

I let go of the door handle, but only to turn around and see him better.

"I don't know your plans," I said, "but I know mine."

"You're drunk. Don't go out there."

"I got three weeks to go and then I'm done with my seven lean years. And not before. No liquor and no big, black view from a clear glass window is making that any different."

"You walk back to the hole," he said, "and it won't be for any three weeks."

"This way it'll never be over," I said.

I tried the door and it was locked.

When I turned back to the room Rand wasn't sitting any more. He had his hands in his pockets and was coming across, calm enough. It made me feel very excited.

"You going to tell me not to worry?"

"You're out and shouldn't worry."

"Who's paying for the liquor bill, Rand?"

"You're my guest. Cigarette?"

"No. How come I'm your guest, Rand? I stand here and think about being your guest but I don't get the proper feeling of gratefulness."

He was fairly close now, leaning against the wall.

"I told you before, Gallivan. The break cost me a lot of money and a long time to plan. A little thing like a helpless nut, like you, Gallivan, isn't going to spoil all that for me by walking around loose out there."

"You sound like a screw. And I thought I was out."

"It's cheaper to keep you close," he said.

"For two days?"

"Yes."

He lit a cigarette and we both watched it. He, because the smoke seemed to interest him, and I, because I was trying to concentrate.

"And then you take off?"

"Yes."

"Where to?"

"I won't tell you," he said to the cigarette. "I'd have to keep you around."

It struck me that I had no idea what to do after the two days in the hotel, that I had no idea what one does after a prison break, that Rand was, in a manner of speaking, all I had in this world. I had no buddies who came to jam the big gate open with I beams, who brought burp guns in flower boxes, who supplied shuttle service in a ten grand limousine.

"And this gratefulness I feel for you, Rand, this cold dish of tripe and stiff grease, did you figure on that when we walked, hand in hand, out of the big gate and into freedom?"

"What?"

I had a little trouble with my focusing and my imagery but I knew very well what I had in mind. I was getting riled that he didn't know it.

"This trouble you're going to have, Rand..."

"What trouble?"

I almost lost my temper. I got confused and began stuttering, but Rand was a patient man, patient with a drunk, though I wasn't so drunk that I'd lose hold of my point.

"At the gate," I told him, "I didn't want out. Three weeks, Rand, and why should I ruin that? Three weeks and you had to clip me on the jaw. Why?"

I suddenly had him by the lapels, wishing he would say the right thing, something that would cause me to choke him.

"I wanted out," he said. "And you were in the way."

Then I grabbed him by the throat.

"And that's why I woke up in that ice-cold truck with a smell in it so that every time I see flowers from now on I'll have to throw up?"

I had had just so much clear-headedness left, and it was gone. I back-handed him over the mouth, then swung the other way, then back again before I let go and he stumbled into the wall.

"Answer me!"

I didn't feel done though, and because my reach is good and he was still rocking, I slammed him again so his head made a sound on the wall.

After that it got less one-sided.

The difference between me and Rand was, he had a pretty clear and a sensibly circumscribed aim; to keep me off and hold his own. Me? I'm not sure what I was beating down. The big joke, the wrong luck, the crazy laugh, the useless scream that kept balling up in my gullet—

I had him down on the floor and I felt his foot in my stomach but he wasn't using it yet.

"Why? Why, Rand?"

"Gimme my wind," he said, his face red and his neck swelling big under my fingers.

"How, Rand? Was it piggyback? Did you and me gallop out of there piggyback, onwards toward freedom and a truck full of posies?"

He kicked me in the stomach and I flew off. But when he jumped up he didn't come after me. I grabbed his leg and he fell on top of me.

"Because freedom shared is such double bliss, you flower-stinking hood?" I yelled, and I got him on the side of the ear with my elbow so that he jerked over with a dizzy look on his face.

"Because anyone would have done for the job," he said, quietly. He spat, and it was a little bit pink. "Because if I was going to get hit I was going to be cushioned on the way in by whatever I could haul, drag, or tote on my back for the distance it took from the gate to the truck. Your meat was as good as any, and your meat was the handiest!"

I sat there and was tired suddenly.

"You got any more questions, about why you should be grateful?"

I felt tired. I looked at the blood which made one of his nostrils look big and I shook my head.

"No. I've said mine. About how grateful I am."

"Done?"

"Done, Rand."

"And the business part, that's clear too?"

"You need me and I need you."

"That's all."

"I stay on your back and you carry me."

But he was getting tired of this. He wiped his nose and looked at his shirt. I felt sure he was dying to change it.

"Go back for your three weeks," he said, "and they'll give you three hundred. Walk back in there, Gallivan, and I might as well be back there too. Which is not what I'm planning."

He walked to the bed and took off his jacket. Then he unbuttoned his shirt and looked at the spots on the front.

I got the idea what a reasonable man my boy was. I got the idea what would happen to me if I tried to walk out. If I didn't get it from him, I'd get it from the powers that be in the bucket.

I was confused, but I wasn't an idiot.

"To liberty," and I walked over there to the bottle.

Rand shrugged and took off his shirt.

The bottle took care of the rest of the night.

In the morning, I saw the blue sky and the sharp sun outside. It had turned colder and there was a lot of snow on the city. I stood at the big window and saw everything clear and neat, like a high-gloss photograph. The prison was in the distance, like a castle with towers, and as meaningless.

I was very hungry and ordered a great feast of a meal, and when it came I managed a little hit of coffee. Then I slept. I woke up in the late afternoon, stiff, my joints creaky like wagonwheels. One night and a day to go without problems.

Once Rand left, that would be another matter. But before this could worry me I sat down with a bottle again. It took care of the second night.

On the second day, I had one bun and some toast. Then Rand and I smoked.

"This night," I said, "wasn't as blind as the other one."

"You drank more."

"But I never fell into the pit. I kept balancing on the edge all the time, the most godawful edge, afraid to fall and afraid to stay. And dizzy. You know, when I'm dizzy while drinking, then I know the liquor isn't taking a hold."

"She must have interfered with your routine," Rand said.

"Ah—. I was afraid to ask," I said.

He didn't answer anything and I stubbed my cigarette out. I worked at it 'til the paper split open and the tobacco fell out.

"There was a woman last night?"

"Yes."

"Did I sleep with her?"

"You slept. Yeah."

I suddenly felt very irritable. "What I asked you," I said, "was, have I got carnal knowledge of this woman?"

"No."

"Do you?"

"No."

"Why not, damn it to hell?"

"You mean, what happened that you didn't lay her, don't you?"

I got up and went to the bathroom. I kept my eyes away from the mirror but bent down over the sink and washed with cold water. When I came back I felt much more detached.

"You know, Rand, I could tell you a harem story about sex, after you get

out of the bucket. That first night out of the bucket is a thing like the Arabian nights. I figured out all the details, on long evenings in the cell."
"You were talking about it."
"Yeah, that's something, huh? I was talking about it."
"You seem to have a thing about skin. You kept admiring that."
"Jaysis—"
"You were quite a talker."
"What else?"
"About Tooley. You kept talking about him."
"That sonofabitch," I said.
"Why that tone?" said Rand. "Tooley is dead, isn't he?"
"He was a filthy old bastard," I said, "and the fact that I spent three of my seven years in the same cell with him makes it more so, and the fact that he took the walk to the chair three weeks past doesn't make it any less so."
"Speak kindly of the dead, Gallivan."
"Why?"
Rand stayed on the topic of Tooley. He wanted to know how well I knew Tooley, because he, Rand, hadn't liked Tooley either. He said all this interested him, because he rarely disliked anybody, especially someone like Tooley, whom he hardly knew, except for time during yard work. That kind of thing.
"He got the chair for murder, didn't he?" Rand asked me.
"Yes, and that used to kill him—I mean—used to give him a charge. He used to say, 'One lousy murder, and an accident yet, and they give me the works. But the one hundred times I pulled it off at the trade—' Big time dope racket."
"I know."
"For all those times, he said, they didn't have one single thing on him."
"Professional pride."
"I think," I said, with a lot of vinegar in the tone, "that it made his death kind of a triumph for him."
"How come you don't like him?"
"I told you. He was a filthy old bastard."
This was a fact and there was no other reason for my feelings about Tooley. He had been one of those aging men with the leer of an ape, the emotions of a kid during puberty, and we had been cell mates for almost three years. For that matter, three years in the same cell with Saint Francis would have done the same thing to me.
"When Tooley..."
"I just as soon talk about something else," I said. "Not about the jug."
Rand didn't insist. He said I could talk about anything I pleased.
"About that woman last night, Rand, I would sure like to know more about that. After all, my first time out, and so forth."
"Sentimental, ain't you?"

"I collect firsts. I would just like to know..."

"You want to see her?"

"You mean now?"

"She's in the next room," and when he saw my face he said, "Honest. You want her?"

I didn't know if I wanted her. It was a little bit too much like the Arabian Nights.

I got myself another drink and sat down again. I said, "This is all so easy. Walking out of prison, taking a car, a fine room in a fine hotel, a, no doubt, fine female. It's all so damn—" I took a long drink and put the glass down. Outside the sun was sharp and brittle. "It's ominous," I said.

"That's because you don't know a damn thing about how much went into all this," said Rand and got up. "I'm going out," he said.

He put on his overcoat, a scarf, and a hat. Then he nodded at me and left the room.

Ominous had been the wrong word. I sat on the couch with my empty glass and made the ice cube slide back and forth. Ominous was the wrong word because there was no real weight to any of this. The day, instead, was frighteningly casual.

I listened to the radio for a while—music and disc jockey chatter, and once the news. The prison break was two days old in the news. Three prisoners were still at large, capture imminent, though. This was interesting. Also, five prisoners who had participated in the riot were dead, shot while escaping. They even had the names, this being factual news. One of the cons shot to death was Smitty.

After that I drank one fast, to keep the film on my brains. Then I got up and went to the bathroom where I stood and looked in the mirror. I pulled up my tie, combed my hair, and said, I'll be damned if I shave for that whore. Then I went out in the hall.

There wasn't a real hallway outside, but a small foyer opposite the door, with some easy chairs, a low table, and a fireplace full of green plants. Two hallways went off the foyer.

There was a man in one of the easy chairs and when I closed the door behind me he lowered his paper. He smiled at me and said, "Hi, Gallivan."

I said, "Hi," and leaned against the wall.

He kept standing there, smiling.

"What you got on your mind, Gallivan? Nothing foolish I hope."

"I didn't have anything on my mind."

"You're all likkered up."

"Just a little. To get the edge off."

"I know. Where was you going, Gallivan?" he wanted to know. He was still smiling but I didn't believe his smile.

"There was this—this girl here last night. I was..."

"Oh, Jessie," he said. He laughed. There was nothing cagey about it, though I didn't know what he meant by that laugh. "That door," he said. "But I don't think she's up."

I didn't give a damn about whether she was up or not, because if I had cared about that I would have to care about a great number of other things, even more important. I went to the door, I even knocked, but then I went in without waiting.

The room looked exactly like ours, except there was a woman in the bed. I saw the shape of her hips, one bare arm, the head with short, cropped hair. It was brown, with light streaks in it, and a little bit curly.

I looked at that pretty sight for a moment. It was very much better than my Arabian Nights, and quite different. Then I almost left the room again. But when I made a sound with the door she gave a small start and turned around.

"Who are you?" Not very friendly.

I didn't know how to explain it and wished I hadn't drunk so much.

"Oh," she said. "Last night."

She sat up in bed, knees to her chest, and put her arms over her legs. She rubbed her head and kept looking at me. "You coming or going?"

I left the door and walked towards the bed.

"You drunk?" she asked.

I nodded. I felt like an ass.

"Why don't you tell Micky out there in the hall to get us some coffee, huh?"

After I had done that I came back to the bed and asked her to give me a cigarette from her pack. She nodded at it and I got one for myself.

What are you staring at?" she said.

"Your face."

"You don't remember it, do you?"

"No."

She actually had very large eyes but they were built in a long shape, just short of slitted, and if she were to laugh her eyes would probably close, almost.

"You can stop looking," she said.

I said, "Why not? Just why in hell not?"

"I don't like to get stripped that way." She blew out a drag and watched it. "I strip," she said, "but not with that kind of a look on me."

Micky came into the room, bringing coffee. He put it on the night table next to the girl, winked at her, and went out. She winked back at him, but it didn't change the expression of her face at all.

I decided that she was a hard little bitch and I didn't get rocked by those eyes. I reached over, took the cigarette out of her hand, and lit one of my own.

"Where were we?" I said. "What did we do last night?"

"You were too drunk. May I have my cigarette back?"

I gave it to her and she kept it in her mouth—something that always looks tougher than hell to me, when a woman does it. She tucked the sheet up under her arms. Her arms were quite slim, like a young girl's, and the skin was of shiny smoothness.

She took the cigarette out of her mouth and held it over the edge of the bed. She put her other hand behind her head and looked at me with no special expression. She could have been looking at a street sign, but as if she knew the street perfectly and no signs needed.

"Do you often run into failures like this?"

"You seem to think I'm a whore," she said.

"Naw. Not you." I put my hand on the sheet where it ran over her belly and smoothed out some folds. Then I put my hand on the edge of the bed again and looked at my fingers.

"Why did you ask, does it worry you?"

"No," she said. "What you think doesn't worry me."

I thought that was just fine with me, this mutual feeling. The end of the blanket was next to my hand so I pushed my hand under it. I was looking down and didn't know what she was thinking, nor did I care.

It was warm under the blanket and my hand felt like wood.

"Get me the ashtray," she said. "You moved it too far."

I pushed the ashtray over, so she could get at it, but I didn't move anything else. Then I touched her side. I thought her skin was very warm. She was slim, because I could feel the slight dent of her ribs, but not thin.

"Why did you move?" I said.

"Your hand is cold."

She hadn't moved much, just slightly, and then I saw her put out the cigarette. After that she put both hands behind her head and looked at me. The skin was warm and firm, but I felt mostly the firmness now, because that was closer to the way she impressed me. Hard. Or I only read that into her, because actually she was just silent.

"You came to see Rand, didn't you?" I asked her.

"Yes. Is that what you came in to ask?"

"That's right. To find out what goes. Wouldn't want to cross up Rand," I said, "good friend like Rand."

I felt the waist under my hand and where the hip curved out. She wasn't wearing anything on top but had on pajama bottoms.

She said, "You act it."

"You don't." I ran my hand up her back and left it there.

"I didn't come to sleep with him," she said.

The way she and I had been going, it struck me that this was the first time that she had bothered to explain anything. Either to tell me something, or to make clear that this, my being here on the bed, was all right with her.

I said, "You haven't had your coffee."

She looked at the cup on the night table and said, "It's cold now." She moved down in the bed, to lie flat. She had small, round breasts.

I moved again because I wanted to hear what she had to say. I asked her what she meant by saying she had come to see Rand, that it sounded as if she had come on business.

But she didn't answer. She turned a little, leaning into my hand. It might have been just indifference, I don't know, but I thought she had done it in order not to answer my question. I tried it another way.

"We got off the subject before," I said, "about last night. You were going to tell me why you came and what you did."

"I?" she said. "I didn't do anything."

"Last time around you said that I didn't do anything."

"You just talked."

"About what?"

"Like a drunk," she said. "You talked about yourself."

"You mean that took all night?"

"Just about. You brought in all kinds of subjects."

"What?"

"Tooley. You brought him up a few times."

I took my hand away but then, from pure spite, put it back on her.

"Nothing about you at all?" I asked her.

"What would you like to know?"

"Why you're here."

"You seem to have made up your mind what I'm here for."

"You never answer, do you?"

"Why don't you take your hand off me," she said.

I didn't, but I said, "That's right. You're here on business with Rand. Girl secretary to Rand, the kindly industrialist."

This time she moved away. She sat up so that the blanket came down but she put her knees up, for more distance. There was expression in her face now.

"You mean crook, don't you? Not kindly industrialist. You mean sly, big-time crook. Not like you. Oh no. You're no crook or con at all, are you? In your case it was all a mistake and the fault of somebody else. And a mistake. You kept hitting that, when you were drunker. How you missed and got sent up for missing: that you wished you had shot him dead instead, and her too. But you," she finished off, "aren't a crook. Because you didn't have the conviction!"

Chapter 4

She wasn't completely right. For seven years behind the big wall I had been a mouse and for the two days I had been out of it, like a mouse's shadow. But I hadn't always been that way, though the time seems long gone.

Junior executive is just a big word for a small beginning. In one sense it didn't fit me at all because I only spent eight hours a day at it, lacking that extra push which makes the successful ones look like maniacs in a slow moving breadline.

I felt I got enough bread in an eight hour day, but nothing else. In a while, I got the regulation matchbox house with lawn, the lawnmower in the garage, the car in the driveway, the week end in the country. We rented a cabin out there. We, because around that time I got married.

I had met her during working hours, which was strange enough, because she didn't look like a working girl. And after half an hour in the same conference room with her, I didn't think she acted like a working girl either. There was a contract up for renewal, which took a lot of conniving and talking. She was with the other team. She was supposed to take notes for the other team.

I think I gave her the eye first, because of the way she was built, and then she took it up as if she had invented the game. She played it with an impatient haste, without rules, without manners, while the conference continued about costs, materials, methods, and maybe profits. Past closing time though, and her getting impatient. So was I.

She and I left together. All this is no reason to marry somebody, but I did. Maybe I married her because she played a mean game of chess, or liked swimming because of the sunbath afterwards, or felt good while dancing, or because an eight hour day meant as little to her as it did to me. The other eight hours were her time, and my time; and then, in addition, also somebody else's.

I bought the matchbox with lawn. I bought the lawnmower, I cut the damn lawn and talked about it as if I felt it was important. I got more and more edgy because we looked so solid but there really was nothing.

Of course, she was much more honest about it.

That week end we were to meet at the cabin, but I didn't go straight out there from work. I went home, and the car—she had the car—was still in the drive. And she and the other one were still in bed.

If I hadn't been edgy, with nothing more solid left than my pride, maybe

I could have walked out, because there was nothing there for me. No. Not me, with eight hours of juniorexecutive work under my belt, with house and lawn, with lawnmower in the garage and new car in the driveway

Even the bedroom scene looks like an act now, and I remember distinctly that it felt like it then.

Not to them, though. They were a petrified, captive audience. I went to the closet, opened it, took down a box, took out the gun.

I was actually shaking with rage and I'm sure they both thought it was something like wronged-husband-in-righteous-rage, though I felt confused and the anger was about that.

He jumped out of bed and ran.

If he hadn't been bare-assed, maybe I wouldn't have done a thing even then, but with that sight on top of everything else—to keep from going hysterical and bursting out laughing—I took a quick draw stance and shot him.

He fell down and screamed a lot, but he didn't die. I don't know what she did. She and I had been through for a long time.

"Is that why you act this way?" said the girl.

I looked at her and saw that she had lain down again.

"How?"

"The way you treat me," she said.

I took the pack off the night table and offered it to her.

She took a cigarette, I had one, and we smoked.

"All I know is," I said to the wall, "I'm scared."

"You don't think the break is going to work? Maybe you don't know Rand."

"I shot a man, for nothing. I paid for it in a way which I didn't even know existed. And in a few weeks, in just twenty-one days, I was going to be done with the punishment too." I shrugged and watched the ashes, how they whitened when the red ring moved back. "And now?"

"Twenty-one days from now," she said, "what would you have done?"

"Something new. Something I had never done before."

"And now?"

"That's what I asked."

I looked at her as if she must have the answers. When she didn't say anything I looked out of the window where the sky was turning milky. Perhaps there would he more snow.

"And now," I said, "the difference is that I'm not through with anything. Whatever I do, I'm not through with the past."

She said that would be asking a lot, any time. She put her cigarette out and said it again, another way.

"I don't know where you get the hope, Gallivan, but I've never seen anything that has happened disappear. It can become less important, but that's all. Only junkies think they can make things disappear."

Then she got up. She didn't care that she was half naked and I didn't. She went to a chair and put on a robe which was lying there. Then she came back to the bed where I was sitting.

"Now you can ask me more but I can't tell you anything else, Gallivan."

"No," I said. "I don't think there is any more."

"I don't either."

She was close enough so I could touch her and I gave her leg a small slap. That was instead of saying thank you. Then I got up.

"You leaving?" she asked.

"Yes. To wait for Rand."

"What for?"

"I'm no pro, Jessie. I need help to get out of town."

"Ask him," she said. "Rand is reasonable."

I knew he was reasonable. Why else would I be here?

"I'll talk to him," I said.

And then she said, "If you want, I'll ask him too."

I left the room and went back to my own. These people without any emotions, what simple and helpful lives they led.

CHAPTER 5

We left that same night, which took a great deal of pressure away. It had started with the break in the yard, where Rand had come by screaming at me to leave Smitty behind; then his play at the gate, dragging me out; then the man with the burp gun, in the flower wagon, and how he had known my name; next, the clothes in the limousine; and the guard in the hall outside my door; and the girl Jessie, who was there and available.

There had been a rational explanation for everything, but taken together it didn't make sense. It was as if Rand wanted me to come along. This was not reasonable. Which is why I kept thinking about it.

When we left, I got an overcoat of my own and a hat, to be worn low on the forehead. Rand also had a driver's license for me, for identification, with a new name and address which I should remember just long enough to get out of town.

"You mean I'll have to show it to somebody?" I asked him.

He was putting on gloves and a hat so his blond hair didn't show.

"I hope not," he said. "But nobody's likely to ask you once we're fifty miles out."

"How hard are they looking?"

"Plenty hard. But the roadblocks are off. They got a lead on us down in Nashville, Tennessee."

"Oh. A good lead?"

"A very good lead." Then he looked around the room and the look said he was through talking. "We go in two cars, and you and me don't go together."

"The man at the desk saw us come in together."

"Meanwhile, he's had time to think. You're a little too tall and I'm a little too short. Any other time we'd just be a comedy team, except this time. Wait ten minutes," he said, and left with the girl.

I stayed with the man who had been out in the hall. We sat for ten minutes.

He chewed gum. He fiddled his tie up and down, he pulled one shoe on and off again, looking for a nail, and he had a miserable habit of humming a tune and breaking it off in the middle. Every time we happened to look at each other he made a quick grin.

"Don't be nervous," he said. "I'm the best wheelman."

I didn't know what a wheelman was but it sounded professional and therefore well planned.

Planned for me or for Rand?

Then we left. The wheelman stopped grinning and walked as if he didn't know me. We didn't meet anyone in the hall, in the elevator, in the mezzanine. Two stairways curved down from the mezzanine into the main lobby and the wheelman took one and I the other. He was taking no chances. I wished I had been a foot shorter and less conspicuous.

Only one person really looked at me, and that was the doorman. He was as tall as I and he asked me which car I was taking. I stalled him off until the wheelman drove up.

We stayed in city traffic for an hour and at every red light the whole town seemed to look into the car.

"What's your name?" I asked the wheelman.

"Tim. But I'm not Irish." He grinned and cracked his gum at me. "And I'm called Micky."

I could have taken that up, for light conversation, but nothing came to me. He didn't look like a Tim because he didn't look Irish and he didn't look like a Micky, either. He looked loose in the face and had a sloppy collar. The only thing I could do with his name was to use it in addressing him and I had nothing to say. I looked around instead and watched traffic.

"Why don't you swing over," I told him, "and go faster in the other lane."

"I'm doing thirty-five. That's legal."

"Then go slower than legal."

"Listen. It won't make it more legal by going less than legal. Uh—you follow my meaning? What I mean..."

"Just take the other lane for a while, will you please?"

"But that's the passing lane, Gallivan, and I'm not passing anyone."

"There's been a car in that lane for the past fifteen minutes that isn't passing anyone either. What I want to..."

"You got your wish," said Tim. "We're slowing."

He didn't get into the left lane but stayed where he was, slowing down. The whole lane was slowing in front of us.

"Always reminds me of a snake," said Micky. "These lines, when they slow down. You notice that?"

I didn't notice that. The comparison gave me a start, but I was watching the other lane which had plenty of room.

Nobody had to slow down, but the car further back did.

When Micky drove faster again, so did the other car.

I took my hat off and wiped my face. The wheelman noticed the gesture and stopped cracking gum long enough to tell me not to be nervous.

I asked him if he had a gun.

"Gun? Naw. In case we get stopped and..."

"There's a car following us. Fifteen minutes now."

"Us? Where?"

"The one in back, in the other lane."

"Ah!" he said. "Ah, yeah, yeah, yeah. That's Rand and the dish in that car. They been there half an hour."

I relaxed because I didn't have the strength left to do anything else. I slid back in the seat and put my head against the cold window and with my foot I kicked open the little door on the heater so that the hot air went up the legs of my pants. I felt deeply tired and didn't care about anything.

When I woke up we were out of traffic. Except for the light beam in front of the hood it was black outside and the snowflakes shot through the beams like tiny tracer bullets. The wheelman was still going slowly.

"How long did I sleep?"

"Sleep? Did you sleep?"

"Just tell me how far out of town we are."

"This has been going on maybe half an hour," he said. "Honestly, Gallivan, I wish we was back in town instead of this. Soon as the houses stop and nothing but landscape comes up, it gets colder. Everything iced. You wouldn't believe it, looking at this nice looking highway here, what a slick..."

"I believe it. Where's Rand?"

"We lost him, out back. He don't drive as good as I do. He's no wheelman."

I got a cigarette from him and smoked. I noticed that he wasn't chewing gum any more, that he had moved the heater lever some, and that he was wearing only one glove. My eyes kept pecking at details like that, inside the car, outside the car, and I was getting a headache. When I was done with one cigarette I started another.

Fifty miles out of town, Rand had said, and the worst would be over.

Fifty miles out of town we came to a bend in the road and when we straightened out again there were lights on the road further ahead and two of them were red. They swung around and around, blinking.

"Now you just sit tight," said the wheelman. Suddenly, he wasn't grinning. "You sit still and let me handle this. It may be nothing at all," he said. "Most likely somebody skidded off the road, is all."

"Maybe Rand?"

"He's behind us, not in front."

"And if it isn't an accident up there?"

"Just you sit tight, Gallivan. Rand wouldn't leave you behind."

The remark was both a comfort and a threat.

They were state highway patrol and a local sheriff's car and the only thing they were concerned about was that traffic should pass them by slowly and without stopping. The other two cars in the scene were in a ditch, one to the right, one to the left.

"What did I tell ya?" said the wheelman.

He grinned his grin and started chomping the gum again. When he came close to the cop, who was waving his red torch so that we should pass, my wheelman slowed and started cranking down his window.

"What in hell are you trying..." but I couldn't say any more because he had the window all the way down and had stopped the car. The patrolman was right next to us now.

"What?" he said into the window. He looked at both of us.

"What happened, is all," said my wheelman. "Just wondering what happened."

The patrolman looked cold and miserable out there and I think he didn't like the sound of somebody cracking gum. He said, "Just keep going and keep it slow, buddy, or the same might happen to you." He glared at Micky and he glared at me, and then he straightened up and said, "Git."

His red torch waved past the left window and I had never seen such a good sight.

Micky laughed to himself and said something about coppers and that they all belonged out in the cold. He put the car into gear and rolled.

"Hey!"

The wheelman slowed enough to keep walking speed. He looked out of the back window and said, "Hey what?"

"Hold it," said the patrolman.

Tim stopped and the cop came to the window. He leaned on the door and looked in at Micky, at me.

"Where you from?"

"Town," said Tim. "Wanna see my driver's license?"

"And you?" the cop nodded at me.

"Town."

"Is that right?" said my wheelman and smiled at me. "Gee. I hadn't known you and me was from the same town." Then he turned to the cop and said, "Hitchhiker. I picked him up a ways back."

"You know whom you picked up there?" asked the cop, but he only looked at me.

"Jimmy, he says was his name."

"All right, Jimmy—" and the cop moved back just enough to get his revolver into view, in case he had need of it.

There was a lot of chatter from the wheelman. Curiously enough, I paid more attention to that than to the gun looking in and the cop behind it. The wheelman said he never heard such a thing, he'd been picking up hitchhikers right and left for these many years now and nobody ever had told him not to and nobody was going to start now. If he, Timothy Louis, felt like picking up freezing hitchhikers—

"I don't want you," said the cop, "I want him there."

That was that. I felt I was already back in prison and that the time between now and then had been a dream, a very bad dream. I felt as if I had never left the bucket, and the heavy-lidded dullness I had learned for seven years was back on me as always.

"If this is a mistake," the cop was saying, "I'll apologize. But in the meantime you look an awful lot like somebody else."

We stood by the side of the road with the snow blowing and the sweeplight coming across regularly, like a red whip.

"Like who?" asked the wheelman.

"You hear of that break the other day? Jailbreak?"

"Gee—" said the wheelman.

"Fellow named Gallivan got away. Stupid too. Had less than a month to go."

We stood around in the night snow near the spots of light from the cars and waited for the cruiser the patrolman had sent for. When the siren came closer it woke me up for a moment and the wheelman must have noticed something because he shook his head very slightly. Perhaps I imagined it and should have tried for a dash or for a clip at the cop who was holding the gun much too low now, but I didn't.

When the siren came closer it was the ambulance for the accident people.

"Why don't I go back with the meat wagon," said Micky, "so I can be checked out that much faster. I gotta get up North, you know. Like I told you."

"I know how it is," said the cop, and with the gun close at my back he watched the ambulance people move a bloody cripple out of the ditch and then somebody else who could walk.

"You got a policeman going with the ambulance anyways," said Tim, "and I can be checked out soon as..."

"You got this car here," said the cop.

"He can ride in the car with me, following the ambulance back to the next town. Like I told you, officer, I gotta get..."

"All right. Lemme think already!"

Micky drove off in his car with a local cop from the next town riding guard. Whatever the wheelman had in mind, I hoped it would work, because I myself wasn't good for anything.

One more thing happened. Rand drove by.

Chapter 6

When the car came for me it was an old Chevrolet with an old deputy driving. But his age made no difference to me. By then I was handcuffed. The patrolman apologized again by saying, "Can't take any chances, and if I'm wrong, buddy, I'll apologize," and then he sent us off with a word to the deputy not to take this too lightly and to wait at the station until State sent someone down to check me over.

We drove three miles, mostly on a side road, and I kept thinking how a handcuffed man can knock out his guard with the bracelets just as good as if they were brass knuckles, but it was just thinking. I was locked to the handle of the door. I turned the topic around and around, more awake now, but each time I tried the smallest move, trying to squeeze the chain links through the space of the door and the handle, the old deputy looked at me. He held a gun in his lap.

But I didn't feel dull any more. Perhaps the depression from before had been like a sleep which I had needed. There's just so much shock that'll sink in. The rest is irritation.

When we rolled into the small town I could see the station at the end of the block. There was a big light in front. And if my old deputy was going to unlock me all by himself, that would be that. He had only two hands, which meant no gun, and I wasn't going back to jail.

It was too late to go back. It struck me with a shock that not very long ago there had been the thought: "Go back, apologize, explain how it happened. Ask them to please let you sit out your three weeks in peace."

But that had been before the patrolman had spotted me. He had spotted me, and by his lights was just doing a job, even though I might have been an innocent citizen.

And that had been before Rand drove by. He hadn't looked right or left, and what could I do to him now that he was in open country? Tell the cops that the other con had gone North? That wouldn't be good enough to catch Rand. So I was rid of him.

And Jessie had happened in the meantime. Not that I gave a damn for the girl, but only for what she had said: "You don't make over what happened. You only do something new—"

I only knew I wasn't going back to jail.

There were two other cars in front of the station and they both were covered with little humps of snow. On the door to the station hung an evergreen wreath and there was snow on that too.

Christmas spirit. We had talked about Christmas spirit back in the laundry.

Smitty was dead and I was alive, that's what I felt now.

"You just sit tight for a minute," said the old man, "and I'll have you loose in a jiffy."

How true. He walked around the car and opened my door carefully so as not to drag me off the seat. Then he tucked his gun under one arm, got the keys out, and said, "If you'll just hold still for a moment, Mister Thorpe—"

That almost threw me. If he had said Gallivan and no doubts about it—

But it didn't throw me. I breathed that out with the next exhale I took, a big, white flag of breath which got lost in the snow coming down, the same way my hesitation disappeared.

A fine, quiet country town. Big trees with snow hoods and frilly porches around the old houses. The windows looked yellow in the dark. The only modern touch was the telephone booth. It stood all alone at a corner and made a white, unfriendly light.

He got me unhooked from the door handle and then he stood there with the key.

Then I saw the wheelman.

This was the second time he shook his head. He came out of the station door with a suddenness, as if he had been waiting for this and when he saw me he shook his head.

I didn't want to stop. I stepped back, because there wasn't the right kind of swinging room between me and the old man and the old man looked up from his key, not certain yet, but hoping to read my face.

If he stayed this way I'd break his jaw with a swing from below. If he moved farther away, for some reason, his skull was going to get it.

"Heytheremisterthorpe!"

I didn't get my arms up or down because the old man bumped into me. When the wheelman had yelled from the top of the stairs the old man got disorganized with surprise or suspicion and, on the turn, had knocked into me.

"You almost made a slip there, Mister Thorpe," Micky called from the stairs. "On that ice."

He was grinning the way he had done when he had been so nervous, but he didn't seem nervous now. Dumb, stupid talking, and who knows what else I didn't like about him, but he looked swift now, all oiled with a purpose, and I held still.

"My," said the old man. "You gimme a start there a minute ago."

He looked at the wheelman and he looked at me while he said that, and it was hard to tell whom he meant. He also had his gun in his hand again and was jiggling the barrel up and down, as if undecided.

"That's my old hitchhiking buddy there," said the wheelman and slapped me on the back. "My!" and he tore his eyes open at the cuffs on my wrists, "I never seen that type thing before."

"They're handcuffs," I said. "They mean business and no more fooling around."

"Naw, Mister Thorpe, now don't you take it like that. He shouldn't take it like that, should he now, dad?" And this time he slapped the deputy on the back.

"Well. I don't know," said the deputy. "I'm just..."

"...doing your duty," I finished for him. "And me, I've been as patient as I'm going to be," I was going to say when the wheelman interrupted again.

"I can sense his feelings. Can't you sense his feelings, dad? And patient! Why you got to tote him with cuffs and gun, dad, I don't know. You know what shows his innocence, deputy?"

"No. What?" said the old man.

"Him standing there peacefully and with you pointing that gun at your toes."

The gun, of course, came up immediately. And I hadn't been holding still out of innocence, but because I hadn't heard Micky talk that much before. I felt that he might have something to say.

"And what are you doing here?" the deputy asked the wheelman. "You got checked out while I was still here."

"I know. The truth is, I got interested in your station. All about it. How it looks, how it works, never having been in one before."

"Oh." said the old man. "We do run a fine station." Then he sighed and nodded at me. "No use waiting around in the snow—"

"That's right, dad. You got maybe two hours before the State man can show up, least that's what he told your buddy inside on the phone."

"Well," said the old man. "Might as well—" and he nodded at me again.

"And me," said the wheelman, "I got to get North before then. I'm late as it is. Good-by, Mister Thorpe, and sit tight."

"Couldn't you wait for me?" I asked him. "When I get out I won't have any transportation."

"Naw, sorry. And nothing against you, Mister Thorpe, but plain business. Good business buddy of mine has been waiting for me further North, you know him, the one we was talking about. He'll wait where he said, but I got to make time."

"Yuh. Make time," I said.

"I will, and be seeing you." He grinned, winked, and went to his car.

The grin didn't mean a thing to me. I had seen him put that on and off in a hundred situations, and all different. But I put a lot of stock in that wink.

No new move with the law for two hours, he had said. And I should wait that length of time and not pull anything crude. He was getting Rand now, he had said, not very far up the line where it had been arranged for the two cars to meet. And Rand would wait there.

The car took off in a cloud of snow.

And I would be hooked with Rand again.

"Whaddaya say, Mister Thorpe. We go in, huh?"

But the new thing was, I would rather be hooked with Rand, still an unknown factor, than with the law, about which I was certain. I could bust out of this situation—an old man and a country station—but what did I know about slipping a dragnet? But Rand knew how.

CHAPTER 7

There was another cop in the station but he had a bum foot and was turnkey. He looked up from his table where he was shuffling cards and when we shook the snow off just inside the door he looked unfriendly. Besides turnkey, I figured, he was janitor.

"Where?" said the deputy.

"George is drunk in the back one," said the turnkey, "and there's that bum in the first."

"What smells?" said the deputy.

"George. He been throwing up in the slop pail."

"I'll stay with the bum," I said.

The deputy felt that all this reflected badly on his station and told the turnkey to get a move on and change slop buckets right this minute and he told me I shouldn't mind the two hours with a bum in the cell, because that was the nicer one, actually, where a body could see more than the opposite wall.

"You can see the desk and the windows behind the desk," he explained, "and let me tell you something, Mister Thorpe, that makes a difference."

We stood by the first cell while the turnkey put his cards down and came over.

"The reason I say that, Mister Thorpe, one time last year I was painting that cell here I'm talking about and paying no mind to nothing else, when the door swung shut on me."

"You want me to change that slop bucket afore morning," said the turnkey, "that means I'll be tramping in and out. . ."

"Just open this cell here," said the old man, and then, "I was saying. Me painting that cell here and the door swinging shut—notice them locks, Mister Thorpe? New. They close automatic."

"Yes."

"And me in there all alone for two hours. Uh, would you mind stepping in there, Mister Thorpe?"

"Two hours," I said and went in.

"Like I said, two hours. The key on the desk there and me all alone in the station."

"Felt like a common criminal, huh?"

"Mister Thorpe, it felt bad. Would you mind, just a little—thank you," and he slammed the door shut.

"George says—" the turnkey called from the other cell.

"Just do that slop bucket!" Then the old man closed his eyes on the other side of the cell and said, "Where was I?"

"You felt rotten."

"Yes. And you know what it was helped me, those two hours? Looking out at that window there. Looking out at the little bit you can see through that window there."

"Yes. I can understand that."

"So that's why I said maybe you'd like this cell better."

He smiled at me from the other side of the bars, waiting for me to say thank you. I said, "Thank you." Then he turned, to walk away.

"You forgot to take off the cuffs," I told him.

He turned back, thought about it a moment, and then he decided it would be all right. He took the cuffs off, reaching through the bars.

The bum in the cell with me was like an animal, like a cat, and all to his advantage. He lay curled on the sixteen-inch plank and woke up just by opening his eyes when I came into the cell. He looked at the deputy and then at the far window and when he saw that it was still night he closed his eyes again and was asleep. There was no room on the bench for me so I stood by the bars.

An hour later I crouched down on the floor, next to the bars. Five minutes after that I stretched out my legs because I was too nervous to crouch and right after that I got up again.

"Time drags, don't it?" said the deputy.

It wasn't just dragging. It was killing me.

"I don't want to make you sore, Mister Thorpe, but I hardly think that State man is going to make it come two hours. You been watching that snow come down?"

"I can't see it from here."

"Haven't you been looking out that window? You remember I told you about..."

"It doesn't work at night," I told him. "The glass just shows black."

"Well, there's been a lot of snow. Colder too. You want me to call up once and ask them to..."

"No. Never mind that."

On second thought I felt maybe he should, but I didn't have the courage to face it. What if they said the man was gone from there maybe two hours and should be here any minute? Maybe they would say, instead, he wouldn't come at all that night, on account of the weather, and then I could relax, with more time to spare for waiting, for stewing, or for figuring something. But I didn't want to face it, if the message was different.

Figuring chances can make a gutless chance calculator out of a man.

The old man was putting a pot on the stove.

I said, "Are you making coffee?"

"Yes. This time of night, when I'm on nights, I always..."

"That's nice. You know, it's the cozyness of it, isn't it? Snow coming down outside, blowing cold, but here, in this nice room you fixed up—and I bet you were the one who hung that wreath up outside, huh?"

"Yes, for the Christmas spirit, you know?"

"I know what you mean. I love the Christmas spirit."

"Would you like a cup of coffee, Mister Thorpe?"

"I wouldn't dare ask, but if there's enough— How are you making that coffee?"

"How? I brew it, I guess."

"Ah, just as I thought."

"You got different ways, Mister Thorpe?"

I asked him if he ever used a pinch of salt and he said, no, he used sugar himself. I explained that one didn't have anything to do with the other, but once the time came that all this mess was straightened out again I'd be proud to have him over to my house and show him how we did it, using salt. Yes, he said, he too hoped all this would be over soon. Such an embarrassment, all of this.

"None of this is your fault," I said, and when he looked at me I started to smile. "No hard feelings."

"Why, of course not," he said.

"I tell you what!" It stopped him for a moment, on the way to the stove. "I'll show you that trick with the coffee, the one I was talking about. I don't often show this to anyone, but..."

Then I stopped. I let it sink in just how much I had forgotten myself, talking as if I could now step out of this cell and show him how to do that trick with the salt.

"Maybe," I said, "you could lock the door? The outside door?"

He looked doubtful, but now I was the one who seemed hurt. And such a nice gentleman, that Mister Thorpe, and patient all the time.

He cleared his throat, he frowned at the turnkey and smiled at me. Then he went to the front door and locked it with the key which was in the door. He put the key in his pocket after that, but that didn't worry me. Next, the cell. He was going to open it. After that—

He came towards the cell and I didn't even watch him.

I looked at the outside door with the two long windows in it which were partly frosted and had old-fashioned designs etched into the glass. On the other side hung the Christmas wreath.

At that point the wreath gave a jump.

There was the sound, too, but that didn't register as much as the movement. The door rattled and the wreath jumped around.

The old man stopped without having opened the cell and grinned at me to make clear we should now both be happy. "There he is! And in less than two hours!"

Easy, I kept saying to myself, easy now. Don't jump, Gallivan.

He didn't come any closer. He didn't open the cell but went to the door. "It'll look better," he said, "when he comes in."

I grabbed the bars and wanted to shake them. The deputy got the front door open and stepped back. Then I heard a man's voice saying. "Glad to see you're this careful." He was a State highway patrolman.

CHAPTER 8

He had a parka on over his uniform and looked wide as a barn. He opened his parka which showed his black belt, and all the cop equipment hanging there. His neck was thick and red.

"Where is he?"

The deputy pointed at me and held the door.

"Fine," said the patrolman.

Then he stepped aside and called down to the steps, "He's still here, Misses Thorpe."

Then she came in, running. She looked small and pretty next to the cop and there was a bright, happy expression on her face.

"Jimmy!" she called, "Oh, Jimmy, you're here!"

She came to the cell and put her hands on mine. I was holding the bars very hard. She moved her fingers over my knuckles.

"Easy, Gallivan," I heard her say.

"The man he was hitchhiking with called her," said the patrolman. The old man closed the door.

As soon as the door was closed and the cold air didn't blow in any more it seemed very static and quiet in the room. The deputy stood by his desk, the patrolman stood by the stove, and Jessie was beaming at me. I don't remember what she said, it was all for the others, but the wide-eyed smile with hope and adoration was looking at me. I had never seen her except still-faced or cold. It was a fine act.

"...haven't called in yet?" the patrolman was asking, and after the deputy said, "No, not since we've been back," the patrolman said something else at the stove while the deputy was pouring him coffee.

"But not now," Jessie was saying. It was very low, and buried between the loud things, the fake nonsense she was gabbling.

The gun was a flat, small automatic.

"Only if nothing else works," I heard.

It wouldn't be an easy gun for a target across the room, but plenty good from close up.

When I put it in my pocket I looked back at the bum. He looked at me, then turned over.

"I don't rightly see how I can do a thing on her say-so," the deputy was explaining.

Jessie stepped away from the cell, so that I could listen.

"Of course not," said the patrolman. "I didn't say that."

"I thought you said, seeing that Misses Thorpe is here..."

"I said seeing there *is* a Misses Thorpe makes the whole thing a little different, is what I said."

"How different?" the deputy wanted to know.

"Just— Well, like a man who's got a wife is not the same type of thing like a man who's single, is what I mean."

"You mean he's got more of a chance being Mister Thorpe now than before."

What they were trying to say came out all junk, and furthermore, the point about Jessie being here and helping my chances for getting out was junk, too. The deputy had no intention of letting me out now and the patrolman didn't want any such thing either, both of them getting more and more legal as they kept talking along.

Only the gun would make a difference.

"I could call them up," said the deputy.

"That's a fine idea," said the patrolman. "That way, Misses Thorpe won't have to wait so long, maybe."

The sonofabitch gave Jessie a look which made me feel like a husband. About my having to wait, in the cell, he said nothing.

"That's awfully sweet," said Jessie. "I am grateful to you for wanting to get my husband out of this horrible spot."

She was out of her mind—she was going to soft talk them into the worst mistake that could happen. They would make that call and would hear: "Hold him under heavy guard; our man is on his way and should be there now; checking your description there is no doubt the man in your cell is James Gallivan; shackle the bastard to the bars because he's insane; he made a break three weeks before release and does not think rationally; also, he hasn't got a wife—not anymore."

"You know the number?" asked the deputy.

"That's awfully sweet of you," Jessie said again.

She stood with her back to the cell, but I could tell by her voice and by the tilt of her head that she was smiling at the patrolman.

I said, "Darling," with my voice very steady.

"You know the number?" asked the deputy again.

The patrolman put his coffee cup on the stove and looked at the ceiling.

"Let me think," he said.

"Darling. Jessie."

She looked back at me and smiled. Then she looked the other way again.

The patrolman had spilled his cup a little and it hissed on the stove.

"No," he said. "But I can ask at the station."

"I know the number," said Jessie.

"Darling. Come here a minute. Please?"

"One moment," she said to the men, turned my way, and came to the cell.

Of course, the others were quiet now, watching us. There was just the hiss on the stove.

"Yes, Jimmy?" she said, and put her hands on mine again.

"If you're going to ask them—if you're going to ask those gentlemen to make that call, darling, I think it best if they also get in touch with my lawyer."

"Lawyer?"

"Micky. I think he should know. . ."

"No need for that," said the patrolman from the stove.

"Naw," said the old man. "No need of that."

"I don't think so either, darling." She gave a pat to my hand, turned away. "Now let me think what that number was," she said to the others.

I could almost reach her, through the bars, but they were so close together that my upper arm got caught in the space.

What could I have done, pull her back? Scream at her she was roping me in?

"He said when I spoke to him on the phone that there shouldn't be any delay in clearing this up," she was saying, "and I remember all that and what he said about driving right down but I can't remember the number."

"Your lawyer said that?" asked the deputy.

"Yes. Just for the formality, he'd come down."

"And in this weather, too—" The deputy shook his head. He felt admiration.

She was railroading me! The plan was to get me stuck here while the rest blew. But why the gun in my pocket?

I felt in my pocket and ran my finger along the base of the stock. There was a clip, anyway. Empty? It had to be empty or her whole performance made no sense. I had the gun in my pocket so I'd keep still, feeling safe with it, while she pulled her spiel! And once I lost my temper and pulled it, full or empty, no matter, that would fix me good!

"What was that number now—" she was saying.

"Darling—"

I have no idea how my voice sounded. It felt like steam under pressure and the lid still on.

"Why don't you look in the book," she said. "Under State Penal Commission, I think."

"That's a good idea," said the patrolman, and he and the old man went to the desk to work with the telephone book.

"Jessie. Come here a moment."

She did, backwards, and it was a good time. The others were shuffling pages and talking.

She backed the two steps towards the cell and leaned against the bars without turning. She started to say something low when it choked off.

I had her by the collar and it must have cut into her in the front. More important, I had the gun in the small of her back.

"They'll see—" she managed.

"They'll be able to see right through you, through a little hole, Jessie."

"Please—"

"Tell them to lay off that phone."

"You don't understand."

"I'm going to kill you, Jessie—"

"Here it is!" said the deputy. "Right here in the book!"

I let go of her collar some, so she could talk normally. With the gun I spiked her hard. I could feel her tremble.

"What is the number?" she asked.

The deputy read it off and the patrolman said yes, that was it, exactly.

"No," said Jessie. "That's not the one I was talking to."

"You got to do better than that," I said, close to her.

The others were arguing about what office to call.

"Better, Jessie. Make it much better."

"How about Information?" said the deputy. "They should know."

"Kill that whole tack for them, Jessie, or I kill you now."

"Maybe—maybe he'll call here!" she said to them. One simple sentence from her could have done it, something like, "Don't make that call because I remember he said nobody would be in the office once he left to come here." That's all. But she was pussyfooting, instead.

I clicked the safety and she heard it. She went limp.

"Now," I said. "You've got one second."

Then the phone rang.

The way those things happen is all in one motion which a smooth sentence, a long sentence, any kind of thing, can't convey afterwards.

The gun wasn't a revolver so I let go of the girl, hit down my hand, and slapped back the slide. It went click-clack nicely and the shell was in. Fast, all of it, and in one motion, because as soon as I let go of her collar she would make her dash.

She did nothing like it. She spun fast but stayed where she was. She turned at the bars, held on with her hands, and looked up at me, pressed close, with her face terribly white.

"Please," she said, "God— Wait!"

She was so close, so frightened—I would have had to shoot her while she was looking at me—

"Yeah?" said the deputy into the phone, and "yeah, yeah?"

I looked away from her. I put the gun into my pocket while she hung there at the bars. She was shielding the view. I poked and poked at my pocket and finally got the gun in.

Where her hands were holding on I could see her sharp knuckles and her nails turning dark.

"The State man!" the deputy called over to me. Then he listened into the phone again.

The girl had her head down and looked as if she were going to sleep. Only her hands told a different story.

"Yes, Sir," said the deputy. "Yes, Sir, right away," and he gave the phone to the State highway patrolman.

I almost touched her hand, to make it relax. Then I didn't. The patrolman was saying, "Very well, Sir. Yes. We got him."

She let go of the bars and walked away. I don't know how it looked to the others but I thought she might fall.

The patrolman said, "Good night, Sir," hung up, hitched his parka back so that it draped over his shoulders like a field marshal's mantle. He walked towards me, halfway towards me, then waited for the old man. The old man came with the key. He opened the cell, stepped back for the patrolman, and when I didn't move the patrolman stepped in. He put one hand around my arm and let the other one hang by his side.

"That was the State man. We got Jimmy Gallivan, he says. No hard feelings, Mister Thorpe."

Then he used his free hand to shake mine.

I signed something or other. The girl stood by the door and put her arm into mine when we walked out of the door. The wreath jumped around when I closed the door and there was a great deal of snow on the steps.

She had a car outside and got behind the wheel. She backed into the street well enough and went along under the big trees and past all the old-fashioned houses. We passed the telephone booth at the corner. There was a man in it and I could tell by the way he stood, one hand in his pocket, straight with no effort. Rand had made that call.

CHAPTER 9

She had a piece of paper with a small drawing on it and she used that for a map, getting us back to the highway. We went north but didn't pass the place with the accident again, unless I didn't recognize it because the snow had changed everything. There were drifts reaching into the road now. It had stopped snowing. The landscape showed white in the light and the sky was black.

She drove well and we both looked straight ahead, not talking. I thought she was very efficient. Later she slowed the car and then stopped on the bare highway. She kept both hands on the wheel and put her head down. Then she had an attack of dry, violent crying. I sat like wood. After that she drove again.

At one point she got stuck in a drift but not bad enough to keep us long. I got out and shoveled snow with a hub cap. I pushed while she rocked the car and the exercise, which felt violent to me, shook me loose so that I felt like I was breathing for the first time.

She drove again and I said something about her skill, something about her strength in all of this—I forget the words—but she only nodded her head and said, yes, or something.

In a while we came to a trucker's stop which turned out to be the rendezvous which had been arranged for the two cars. The diner looked old and steamy and in the big light in front were the pumps and a couple of trucks. The exhausts stuck up straight into the cold air and blue smoke bubbled out of them. A third trailer was pulled up by the side of the diner with the gates in back almost up to a pile of snow.

"We'll wait here," she said. "The others are late."

We didn't go into the diner but waited inside the car. We kept the heater on and smoked cigarettes.

"There are three truckers in that cab. Maybe you shouldn't park right next to it?"

"That's all right. They've been waiting for us."

By bending towards the windshield I could look up to the cab of the truck but the three truckers up there didn't look back. They talked, I could see, and one of them watched the highway. It said, *Town and Country Movers,* on the van.

When Jessie was done smoking I offered her another one but she shook her head. She took a small mirror out of her pocket and looked at her face, touching her nose a little and patting her hair. She didn't make up, she just looked.

I wanted to say something to her, about the time in the station, but I felt as if that would commit me in some way—to Rand's plan, and to her somehow.

When Rand and Micky came they pulled up next to us. I heard the ratchet sound when Micky pulled the brake. Then both men got out of the car, leaving the motor running. Rand bent to look at us, jerked his head, and went to the rear of the van. When Jessie and I were out of the car I saw two of the truckers climb out of the cab. They weren't dressed like truckers at all. They wore suits and overcoats, with scarves showing over the collars.

"I hope you left the heater going," one of them said to Jessie.

She said yes and we went to the back of the van.

Micky had the gate open and we all climbed in. The two cars we had come in took off before we were done. The third trucker, who was dressed like one, closed the gate for us from the outside.

It was cold and dark in the van and when Rand clicked his flashlight there wasn't much to see. The inside of the van seemed piled full with furniture with maybe two yards to spare to the door.

"What did he say? The easy chair?" asked Micky.

"A blue easy chair," said Rand.

They looked for the blue easy chair and found it built into the furniture wall, low to one side. Micky pulled it and there was a hole.

On the other side was more room. There was a weird, tall space, as high as it was wide, cut off behind by the wall of roped furniture and gracefully round where the van had been streamlined in front. The curve and the height of the place in the dim light reminded me of a church.

"You smell dust?" said Micky.

"Yeah," said Rand. "Nobody has lived here for a while."

There was one couch and a few blankets. Rand told Jessie to lie down on the couch and the rest of us sat on the floor. Rand left the flashlight on when he put it on the floor and when the truck began to move he put the light on a blanket so it wouldn't roll around.

I think Jessie went to sleep almost immediately. The van made little jolts now and then and the girl's shoulders moved in a loose way with each jolt. It was hard to see her in the light.

After a while the tires started singing and the jolts became sharper. There was less snow, I thought, and we were going fast.

"You're burning the blanket," said Rand.

I looked where I was touching the blanket and put the cigarette into the other hand. I said "Thank you" to Rand and he nodded back. When I dragged on the cigarette again it tasted very bad but I hardly noticed it. I got up and went over to sit next to Rand.

"And I want to thank you for the help back at that station."

"You're welcome."

"Why did you do it?"

He turned and looked at me, but his eyes always seemed to point straight ahead. He hadn't moved them at all.

"Why did I do what?"

"Get me pinched and then rescue me."

"It was an accident. Micky made a mistake; that's all."

He looked away again, and this time I could only see his profile. Everything looked smooth-black, except for a fine rim of brightness where his hair caught the light.

"Then I'll ask it this way, Rand. What about the time when leaving me behind would have speeded you up and saved you a great deal of trouble?"

"In the yard, you mean."

"Yes. You came back to drag me along. Why?"

"I've been thinking about that," he said. "You got a light?"

I gave him the light and watched how he lit up. When he blew out the smoke, there seemed more substance to the blue clouds rolling over in the light than to his face.

"You going to explain it, Rand?"

"I don't think I can."

I let it drop. He'd risked his neck getting me out during the prison break. And now he'd delayed his escape plan to get me out of a jam his wheelman had gotten me into.

"In the station," he said, "why didn't you shoot Jessie?"

He gave me a good jolt with that.

"How in hell do you know?"

"Micky saw you. He was behind the window, over the desk."

The little black window that the deputy loved so much.

"The way she stayed plastered by the bars, when she should have been near the phone, with the yokels," he said. "Micky was sure you'd drop her."

"And then what?"

"I didn't figure you'd make a play like that." He dragged on the cigarette. "Anyway, Micky had a gun, too."

"On me?"

"You? Why you?"

I thought about that for a moment but said nothing.

"You still got the gun Jessie gave you?" Rand asked.

"Yes. In my pocket."

"You can give it back now, Gallivan."

I shook my head and said, no, I wouldn't give back that gun, I would keep it.

Chapter 10

After a while we took turns on the couch because the ride was so long. We ran out of cigarettes and later the flashlight went out. When that happened it seemed to get much colder.

Once we all sat on the couch, in the dark, sitting close for warmth and long past the point of talking. I wanted to say this reminded me of a row of birds on a telegraph wire but the situation wasn't that humorous. I said nothing and the image changed to something much bleaker. Like a row of empty clothes, hanging in a draft.

Jessie sat next to me, but it was just clothes.

At one point—what point I don't know—the truck slowed, bumped a while, then stopped.

"Very quiet now," said Rand.

Later the back gate opened and we could see shafts of cold light past the furniture and feel slits of cold air.

"Stay," said Rand. "I'll get it."

Then the gate was closed again. Rand came back with a warm bag of hamburgers and a carton of paper cups which felt soft and hot. We ate hamburger and drank the coffee. After that, in the dark, we hunted for butts on the plank floor.

I tried to think and I tried not to think, because that's how the subject pushed me. I tried to get it clear that I wasn't in prison. I tried to hold on to that fact and not compare it to being out with the sentence completed. That wasn't the case and never would be. But I was out. An incomplete sentence on the book would have to be the warden's worry, and not my unfinished business. Any unfinished business I had was in the future, not the past.

Such as Rand.

They would have let me kill Jessie. They would have covered the cops from the little black window after that, to get me away. Micky's gun, Rand had said, hadn't been on me. They had watched the girl squeezed into the bars of the cell, hoping I wouldn't fire into her back, but prepared for the bargain.

Jessie dead would still have been worth it; I was that important, that damned important.

Off and on I tried to sleep.

When the truck stopped again we all sat very still, waiting. There was no sound outside except wind blowing and then the trucker's steps next to the van. He stopped and made a sound as if he were stretching, then walked again, the length of the van. He clanked the gate open in back and said, "Depot!"

Rand moved the chair out of the way and crawled through. Then the rest of us followed.

The light could have been early morning or late afternoon. The sky was thick with snow clouds and an unfriendly wind was rattling the black trees. There was a lot of white all around, and the big house where we had pulled up was white too. It stood all alone in the white park with the rattling trees, and the front of the building had tall, plantation-type columns.

"When we go in," Rand said to me, "we'll be quiet. It's a sanatorium."

I thought he had made a bad joke but I was too tired to do anything about it. Then it turned out he was serious. We went in at the side and took a big elevator. It was big enough for two or three carts, the kind they push patients around on.

Each time the little window in the door showed a floor it seemed I was looking at the same corridor. It was long and bare and there was a bulb over each door. Every so often one of them was lit. On one floor stood a roll bed, on the next a green oxygen bottle, on the third was a flowerpot next to a door, with the flowers wilted.

We got out at the top. There was no corridor here, just a little hall. There was a coatrack in the hall and one door. Rand used a key to get in.

It didn't look like a hospital any more, but still smelled like one. The corridor behind the door had a carpet, the solarium at the end had club chairs and ashtrays, and the doors had no lights over them. But a nurse passed us. She carried a tray with a sheet over it.

"Wait there," said Rand. "I'll see about rooms."

We sat in the solarium and looked out at the landscape. I think we all looked at it so we wouldn't look at each other.

Rand didn't come back. He sent a man dressed like an orderly who said, "Hi, Micky," and Micky said, "Hi, Joe." Then he showed us rooms. One for Micky, one for me, and after me he must have shown Jessie hers.

I didn't think about it, or about Rand, but only about the comfort I wanted. My room had the softest, white bed, the softest, deep chair, the softest, gray light from the winter outside. Inside, it was warm. I undressed, left my clothes on the floor, and crawled into bed. I woke up once, in the night, and found a tray with cold food on the night table. I ate the bread, cold cuts, and cheese, and drank the tea which had cooled to lukewarm. There were even cigarettes. After smoking one, slowly, I went back to sleep. It would be good to be very well rested tomorrow.

CHAPTER 11

I woke up knowing that the sun was shining and when I looked it was. The sleep had been good and the bright sight from the window was good to see. You wake up innocent as the morning sometimes, and that feeling may last for as long as a minute.

I don't think it lasted that long. It caved in very suddenly when I heard the bell. It was loud and unpleasant, and seemed to rattle off with a nervous haste. Then it stopped, but it had been enough to remind me of seven years worth of bells, signals, buzzers, which had warned, turned, or stopped every move we had made.

Not quite seven years, but three weeks short of that.

If my brain could have made a sound I think it would have been something like that bell, something sharp and nervous. The sunlight was too bright now and the morning had happened too soon.

I took a shower, found shaving stuff all laid out, then got dressed. First thing I noticed after I had put on my jacket was how light it felt. The gun was gone.

On the evidence, it would have been hard to convince anyone that I needed a gun. A friendly room, a quiet park in the morning sun—and the corridor outside my door was quiet, too. I went out and looked around but didn't see anyone. A big fly was caught in the solarium. It thudded against the glass, once here, then there, and in a while it sat down on an easy chair and seemed to be taking a rest.

I stood around for a while and listened to nothing happening. There was a swinging door in one arm of the hall and on the other side of that there was nothing except a wider hall, another elevator—small this time—and a rubber plant by the window. There were various doors again, but no sounds.

If anyone thought I was important, this was no way of showing it. I was so nervous now that I didn't know offhand which was better—yesterday's shocks or today's nothingness.

But they had taken the gun out of my jacket.

I stood there and then I heard the low voice first because it was talking more. I couldn't make out the words but when the voice stopped another one rose, which I thought was a girl's. They talked and I found the door. There were four leading off the hall, not hospital doors, but heavy, brown ones, with brass handles instead of knobs—something left over, most likely, from the time when this had not been a hospital.

I still couldn't make out the man because he seemed to be talking low, but when the girl answered I could tell that it was Jessie.

"I can't do it—"

The man, short this time.

"I'm no good at it. You know that."

"It's your neck more than mine, don't you think?" said the man. I could hear him now because he seemed to be losing his patience.

She didn't answer. Perhaps she made a gesture which showed her reaction, but I couldn't know that.

"Well?" said the man.

"All right. I'll keep trying."

"Do that. And throw it a little, huh?"

This time she didn't answer either, but if I understood the man's meaning, I could imagine that she showed some kind of reaction.

"I'm going to breakfast," she said and I got away from the door fast and just made the rubber plant when the door was opened.

She said, "Good morning," and I turned around.

"Good morning. Uh, how are you?"

She came over and asked me if I had slept well.

"And you?"

"After that truck," she said, "what do you think."

"You look well," I said.

I looked at her and it struck me that I had meant the platitude. Her face was smooth and rested and she stood up again, nice and pert.

"Did you eat?" she asked. "I'm going for breakfast."

"Where?"

"That door. Did you eat?"

"No. I'm not familiar with the place, or the routine."

"No routine." She walked away and I followed her. "You just ask for something to eat," she said, "and they bring it."

If she thought that had been an explanation, she hadn't done too well, and had she told me that this was the land of the Big Rock Candy Mountain I wouldn't have believed that either.

The room wasn't large but very pleasant. It was a dining room with long table, sideboard, place mats, and good chairs. There was even a chandelier, something spiny from Sweden.

To me, everything was much too ordinary.

"I'm going to have eggs for breakfast," she said. "You too?"

"Do we clap our hands?"

"No. I call down, with that phone."

"And with coffee, the same thing?"

"I thought you told me you had slept well," she said and then she ordered at the phone.

I sat at the table and played with the place mat. It was made out of straw and I couldn't figure out why the strands didn't come apart.

"They are glued." She sat down opposite me.

"Oh. You see, it's my background. For seven years I haven't seen anything but tablecloths."

"I forgot. You worked in a laundry."

"Yes. To this day I don't know what all those sheets were for. I never saw them, except in the laundry."

"Maybe the warden ate off them."

"The warden? Do you know what the warden probably ate off? I have a suspicion he..."

"You're awfully edgy, Gallivan."

"It's the big windows. I keep thinking I might fall out. And the empty corridors. I keep worrying who murdered the screws and where did they stuff them."

"There's a laundry in the basement. If you think you'd feel more familiar..."

"Tell me," I said, "How come you know I worked in a laundry?"

"Rand must have mentioned it."

"Yes. He is very talkative, that Rand."

"Can't you relax a little, Gallivan? We're going to eat any moment."

I ignored it and went right on. "There's that laundry, then you mentioned Tooley..."

"You mentioned Tooley."

"But you remembered it."

"What do you want, Gallivan, a scene?"

"What else do you know?"

I thought she made a great effort not to let my tone affect her. I didn't think she wanted to be with me, or to sit here and listen, but she stayed and looked pretty calm.

"Gallivan, I'll tell you everything I know about you. Then we relax, all right?"

"Tell me."

"I know why you went in..."

"I told you that myself."

"And that you only got six years, not seven, and..."

"How come you know that?"

"Micky is the talker. I think he told me about the laundry too. Micky told me you only got six years but then you got in trouble and they stretched it to seven."

"That was a blow," I said. "That was as much of a blow as getting liberated three weeks too soon."

"What trouble was it, when they gave you another year?"

"That?" I had to laugh, because I felt a little embarrassed about it, just like when it had happened. "I hadn't been in long and still had normal reactions. One day there was a con in front of me—there was a line, we were always in a line. This con didn't please a screw for some reason and the screw was riding the man. An old con."

"And?"

For some reason I had to laugh again. Then I said, "Did I tell you who that con was?"

"No."

"Tooley. He keeps popping up, doesn't he?"

"You keep mentioning him."

"Yuh. Anyway, there came the point when the screw belted him one, old man and all, and I swung at the screw."

"You did that? In prison?"

"I was nuts. What I mean is, I still had outer-world reactions."

"And the other one, was he grateful, at least?"

"I still got an extra year."

The orderly from the night before brought the breakfast, and at first sight and smell of it I felt very good. Then I started eating and the feeling went slowly.

Because of what had happened between Tooley and me, he had started to talk a lot after that. Instead of keeping his mouth shut after lights out and leaving me to myself, he talked and talked, because I was now his buddy. "Pretty stupid, but a buddy," he used to say, and he used to laugh about it and talk some more. I think he talked to me the way a lonesome man on a lonesome island would talk to a rabbit he had caught, because there was nobody else, and because it was safe.

"How long were you in the same cell with him?"

"Years."

"I thought he was going to be hanged?"

"Not then. That was still pending, or appealed, something clever like that. He was also in for plain and fancy larceny, of some kind."

"Dope."

I looked up from my plate, but before I could say anything she told me, "You said that. When you were drunk."

Very possible. I finished the eggs, glad to be done, and took coffee. Maybe with the coffee I'd start feeling better.

"Would you pour me some?" she asked.

I reached over to pour for her and knocked the sugar bowl over. After her cup was full I didn't tilt back in time and poured some more on the table. She didn't say anything and I didn't either. She wiped the table while I lit a cigarette. When she was done wiping she waited a moment before she said anything but kept looking at me. When I looked up she tried a small smile.

"It's a quiet morning," she said. "You're having breakfast with nobody looking over your shoulder, there's a nice view out of that window. Why don't you relax, Jimmy?"

"Jimmy?"

"Gallivan, if you want. But I thought it sounded friendlier."

"It did."

"But?"

"I don't believe it. I don't believe the view, the breakfast, the whole genteel set-up."

"You said genteel?"

"Like, for example that genteel trick of somebody padding into my room while I'm sleeping and lifting my gun."

When she said nothing immediately I felt I had built up to the point nicely. Then she said, "But it wasn't your gun."

Simple. It hadn't been my gun.

"That's right. It was yours," I said.

"I don't own one. I just brought it to you."

"I now feel like a thief," I said. "One who's been robbed, but a thief."

She took a tired breath.

"Why are you kicking and punching, Gallivan? You don't need a gun here. You don't need anything here. You're through."

After a moment I asked her, "What did you say?"

"You're through. You can go now."

"Go now? Go away?"

"What more do you want, Gallivan? You're out. You didn't have to lift a finger. You're eight hundred miles from the prison, you had a good night's sleep, you had breakfast. What more do you want?"

CHAPTER 12

I stared at her and after a while she put her head down and turned her cup back and forth, by the handle. This made a small sound, very faint.

I got up and went to the window where I stood looking out as if there was something to see. I had no idea if there was something to see.

"Well?" she said. The sound was like the cup on the saucer, that small.

"I don't know, Jessie."

I heard her get up and come over. It took a very long time.

"You're free, aren't you?" she said next to me.

I wished that had been funny. I would have said, yes, free like a bird. Free like a bird who knows there's a cage but he can't see it, because he's a daytime bird but it's always night now.

"You look very unhappy," she said.

I turned my head fast, ready to be angry, but when I saw her face I saw that she was only trying to be kind.

I looked out the window again and said just a fraction of what I would have liked to have said to her. "We can't get along at all, can we," I said.

I heard her light a cigarette and then, "I've never been in prison," she said. "But it must be hard."

"Yes."

"Do you need money?" she asked.

I was very glad she had said that, making the problem that simple. I nodded, almost glad to have such a real problem.

"Ask Rand," she said. "Maybe he can help."

"Rand again."

"He's the only one you know, isn't he?"

"Yes."

"He's not bad," she said.

I felt myself for cigarettes but there weren't any. She held out hers and I took a drag on it. Then I gave it back to her.

"I'd like to see him now."

"All right, Gallivan," she said.

She went to the table where she put out her cigarette and I went to the door, to wait for her there. I hadn't yet reached it when she stopped me.

"If you need—I mean, how much are you going to ask him for?"

"All I can get."

"I could give you fifty dollars," she said. "I could give you that now, and if you need more, there's a little more—"

She had talked faster and then, in the end, she had talked more and more low. If she had also said my name then, I think she would not have said "Gallivan," but my first name.

I said, "No thanks," talking just as fast as she had done in the beginning, but much louder. There was no clear thought behind my refusal at that moment, which was surprising, because in my situation I should have taken money from anyone. But that didn't strike me then.

Neither of us said anything else. She took me across the hall to the door where I had heard the voices, hers and the other one. It must have been Rand that time, who had told her to get on the ball.

"In there," she said. "And good-by."

"You leaving?"

"Oh no. I'll be around."

We couldn't get along at all—and she had just offered to help me. She turned and walked away.

The room was like a club room, or for meetings maybe, and on the other side of the big table I could see a leather couch. Rand was lying on the couch, reading a paper. He had pulled an ashtray stand up to the side and there were plenty of butts in it. I thought maybe he had smoked them. He didn't look as if he had slept much the night before. Only his suit, another blue one, seemed unaffected.

He sat up when he heard me and then he put the paper away.

"Hi, Gallivan," he said. He was rubbing his neck. "So the worst is over, huh? Sleep good?"

"Yes, thank you. Can I have one of your cigarettes?"

He watched me while I lit one.

"You look like you've come to say thank you again."

I looked up and it wasn't any easier to thank him this time, because this time I was going to ask him for something else right afterwards.

"Listen," he said. "You've lived with cons for a long time, Gallivan, but you never were one and you didn't become one. So there's a lot of things you wouldn't understand."

"Yes?" I said, waiting to hear what he was driving at.

"You don't have to make a formal thing out of a favor, because a favor's got nothing to do with Christian love and so forth."

"But?"

"I could afford it, is all. So forget it."

He looked so tired and he had talked so straight, I suddenly liked Rand very much. It wasn't a grateful feeling with the usual sense of obligation hanging on like a tail, I just liked him.

I think he saw that and made a brief smile.

"Thank you, Rand."

He got up and stretched. He was either tired and done with talking, or now came the stinger.

"So—Good luck," he said.

No stinger.

"And don't look behind you," he said. "It helps."

It was the first time he had said more than the barely necessary and I would have liked to leave then, and remember about Rand the way he had been the last few minutes.

"Before going," I said, "I wanted to ask you for one more piece of help."

"Yes?" He half sat on the window sill and I couldn't see his face because of the light.

"I'm strapped. I can't even tell you when, or how, I'll pay you back, but if you could…"

"Sorry, Gallivan. I've got nothing."

I wished I could see his face better. He must have seen that I didn't really believe him because he said, "That break cost me a fortune, Gallivan. More than I had."

"More than you had?"

I sat down in a leather chair. The shock had caught up with me, the "No," and I wanted to sit for a moment. I looked at the room with the leather and all the good, polished wood. I wondered what he meant by being strapped.

"I'm not the boss here, Gallivan. I'm a little helper. And the way it is now, broke too."

He shrugged and came back to the couch. He let himself fall into it and rubbed his face.

"You want another cigarette?" he asked.

"Thanks, yes. And thanks, anyway."

He lit his and mine and said, "What are your plans?"

"Distance," I said. "A lot of distance."

"Sure. That's good."

"Jessie might stake me. She mentioned something."

"Oh?"

"Damn white of her. After everything—"

"How much?"

"Fifty, she said."

"You want distance, Gallivan?"

I had nothing to answer.

"I might make it on fifty," he said, "but not you."

"Why not me?"

"You got no connections." Then he said, "How were you planning this?"

"Just go." Then I laughed, not for the humor, but because nothing else came to me. "After I find out where I am."

"I can help you with that. You're maybe three hundred miles south of Chicago, and..."

"I'm not going to Chicago."

"Three hundred isn't much distance, you mean."

"Without connections, it's no distance at all. I'm going to hit south. All the way south, into Mexico."

"With half a C-note."

"I can bum on less."

"You know what that'll mean, Gallivan? You'll be flopping in all the places where the bulls are going to look. You're going to ride rods where the bulls watch it, hitchhike where the bulls don't like it, you're going to look for hand-outs, day jobs, hide-outs, on the oldest circuit in the books of the bulls, the bums' route."

"Maybe," I said, "it wouldn't have been much different if I had left the pen after full time."

"You got a point," he said. "I know."

I put the cigarette out, slapped my hands down on my legs, got up.

"Well. Wish me luck."

"You want the map?"

"Yuh. I'd like the map."

"Next town is five miles from here," he said and gave me the map. "Called Florian."

"As long as it's on here."

"You're not going to be any asset to me. You know that, Gallivan?"

He was leaning against the table, looking tired as before, but frowning more. I said, "You look worried."

"I am."

"About me and fifty bucks?"

"I never thought of this before," he said, "what with everything, but they're going to nab you awful close to home plate."

"My home is..."

"My home plate. Here."

We were back to the first time I had asked the question, why he was helping me. If I kept being a liability to him much longer, I thought, maybe he'll buy me a through ticket way down to the far end of Cape Horn.

"Stay here a minute," he said and left the room.

I stayed and opened the map again. Then I folded it. I put the cigarette out because it started to taste like hot sawdust in my mouth.

I had once drifted into a slapstick crime, then through a gray, seven years, then into a movie-type escape, and now—I was going to keep drifting the way the wind blew, if I didn't remember pretty soon how a man uses his head, arms, legs, and so forth.

And how do you use head, arms, legs and so forth with but fifty bucks

to your credit and an all-state alarm to your discredit? You use connections. Of which I had only one. Rand came into the room and closed the
door.

"No good," he said.

"What?"

"I don't give money to strangers, he told me. My boss."

"You asked him for money?"

Rand nodded and then I wanted to say the normal thing, "That was
damn white of you, Rand, to go and ask that for me." Instead, I said, "Did
you tell him why? That I might haul the dragnet all over you?"

"That's why he wants to see you," said Rand, and he opened the door for
me to come with him.

I could smell it before it had happened. But what else was there to do?

Chapter 13

We walked down the corridor and at one point that sharp bell I had heard once before tore loose and right through me. I stopped and so did Rand, but only to wait for me. The bell stopped very quickly and I didn't feel like asking about it. That would have been something like asking a hangman, for instance, to be especially careful with the noose because I don't like rope-burns.

The boss' name was Mishkin and he stuck out of his leather chair the way a round mushroom grows out of the ground. Mishkin was fat and white and made no effort to get up.

"The one I told you about," said Rand.

"Sit down, Gallivan."

I sat next to his desk, and then Mishkin and I waited 'til Rand had left the room.

"You're strapped, is that right?" said Mishkin. He panted when he talked.

"Yes. You might say that, Mister Mishkin." \

"And in more than one way, huh?"

"You might say that too, Mister Mishkin."

"Stop calling me Mister Mishkin like that, Gallivan. You don't make it sound right."

"I'm sorry."

"Just Mishkin is fine."

"Fine, Mishkin." And then I wanted to know why he wanted to see me. "I don't want to take your time, but..."

"Better than something else, Gallivan. What made you think you and fifty bucks could slip a five state alarm?"

"Interest, Mister Mishkin. I'm highly interested in it."

"Stupidity, I'd call it."

"I've learned a lot, just in a few days."

"Rand was wet-nursing you."

"I know that. And I don't want that to go on, Mister Mishkin."

"If you want to get along with me, Gallivan, then stop saying..."

"I'm sorry. It's a form of respect, where I come from."

"You mean seven years ago."

"Prison too. The screws always insisted..."

He gave me a look that stopped me from going too far. I felt keyed up and had to talk this way. And besides, I thought it would show me a lot— with nothing but suspicions to go on—if I could gauge just how much he would take before throwing me out.

He said, "You remember how it was seven years ago, huh?"

"I was in business. Very polite, everything."

"What in hell do you think this is, Gallivan, if it isn't business."

"But not polite."

He took a lot, I thought. He didn't answer but was busy hunting a cigarette. When he had it in his mouth it looked very tiny in front of his fat face.

"Junior executive, isn't that right? You were on sales territories?"

"How did you know?"

"Rand told me."

"Yes. I was on territories at the time."

"The time you shot the guy out of your wife's bed, you mean?"

"That's the time I mean, Mister Mishkin."

"I never heard anything so stupid in my life," said Mishkin.

"But I would never do it again."

"I hope you learned something, in the meantime."

"Seven years of college."

"But don't talk, Gallivan, like you were still in."

"The reason why I'm trying to make distance. And the reason..."

"I don't give money to strangers."

"Yes. Rand told me. But the reason..."

"You want a job?"

Just like that.

"How come you give jobs to strangers, Mister Mishkin?"

He took it and settled back to explain. Maybe he took all of it, my tone, my intention, because he was fat and not very sensitive.

"On a job you wouldn't be such a stranger, Gallivan, because I'd be watching. On a job you also wouldn't be zigzagging across the countryside with the dicks on your tail, and me not watching. And on a job you could make yourself three C's a week. Do that for maybe two weeks, is all, and with that kind of dough I could then steer you out so nobody innocent around here gets hurt."

"A two-week job?"

"You can do it. I'm thinking of what you used to do in the past."

"That's right. Rand told you."

"Yeah."

"No, Mister Mishkin. I couldn't do that," I said.

Then I sat back. I leaned forward once to take a cigarette off his desk, but for the rest I sat back, waiting.

I should have given this kind of answer before. In the yard, in the truck, limousine, hotel, car, jail, van, all along the line. But how could I have said, "No, don't save me—"

"I can't let you walk out of here," said Mishkin. "Don't you know that, Gallivan?"

And that was, I'm sure, the answer Rand would have given me, all along the line.

"You thinking about it?" he asked me.

He had very small eyes, because of the fat, and it was hard to tell which way he was looking.

"If you're not," he said, "you're wasting time." He dragged on the cigarette, then talked with the clouds of smoke coming out. "You should be thinking about being out of prison, being out before your time was up, being green and without any connections, about not everybody every day getting a job offered to him, for three C's per week."

"What I was thinking about, Mister Mishkin, is how come I rate such a job."

"Two reasons." He was very quick. "Rand recommended you and I'm stuck."

I didn't argue it. If he was lying, he'd lie more. If he wasn't lying, I would want the job.

I would want the job anyway—I would want the first, fastest way I could find to get out from under and to learn my way. There was a herd of cons back in the bucket who would give their eye teeth for this deal. Including me.

"If I can handle the job," I said the way I had learned it in business school, "I'll be happy to take your offer."

After that he did get up out of his chair because he needed stuff from his file. One file had the bottle and glasses, another one had stacks of folders. He pulled out one and together with the whiskey and glasses he took it back to the desk. He guided himself into the chair and then he said I should pour us some whiskey.

"First job I ever been on where you drink during hours," I told him.

"You're a liar."

Then we each had a drink. I wanted another one right away but that could wait.

They wanted me badly. They wanted me badly enough to dream up a job for the purpose. And if I wanted to make it in the end, I needed money. And if I wanted to make it at all, saying no to them would be the worst thing I could do. Mishkin, in spite of double talk and a business man's caution, had made that clear. "I can't let you walk out of here, Gallivan," he had said. "Don't you know that?"

I knew that well now. The whole thing had started with breakfast, which had been the build-up for this, and the reason I felt more settled was because the doubt was now over. If I wanted to make it in the end, I'd have to fill in on two questions: Why did they want me? And why didn't they just ask?

Chapter 14

"What's the job?" I asked Mishkin.

"Distribution."

"Ah. What I used to do."

"Same problems."

"I used to worry about distributing soap."

"Not soap this time. Dope."

Even that made not too much difference right then. Maybe later, but right then it seemed natural, even preordained, that I should do the filthiest job with the coolest methods.

"I know nothing about the merchandise," I told him.

"I hope not," said Mishkin. "Besides, you'll never have to touch the poison."

"I never saw the soap either," I said.

This cheered him up. He took another finger or so out of the bottle and after he had poured it into his throat he went smack-smack with his lips.

"The problem is," he said and started fanning pages around in the folder. "The problem is money."

"I thought you couldn't lose with that merchandise," I said. "I thought the demand came from a captive audience."

"If you're gonna run something like a business, Gallivan, then don't let the fact that you're making money stop you. Understand?"

"I think so."

"Try hard. Or you'll never be anything but a junior executive."

"Do you have a man handling the territory now?"

"Just a makeshift. Al Tooley isn't much good, but whether I get somebody better or not, it's your job to dream up a better distributing system."

"I knew a Paul Tooley once." I said this very mildly.

"You did? Sounds like Al's brother. You knew him?"

"Didn't Rand tell you?"

Rand, he said, hadn't told him, but my Tooley, who was now in the electric chair heaven, did turn out to be the brother of his Tooley, who had been running some territory for distributing dope.

But Mishkin wasn't interested in talking about that, only I was. I didn't talk about it, either, but I was still interested.

"Here's the problem," Mishkin explained. "Big H has the longest chain of jobbers and middlemen in the history of merchandising. That can't be helped, because of the cops. Anyway, there they are. The thing is, with such a long line of middlemen we got an efficiency problem. Not that the stuff doesn't get to the market quick enough, but that we got too many expenses."

"You made that point, first thing."

"The point I make now is, where can we cut down the chain, but not the efficiency?"

"In this case, when you say efficiency that includes safety, I gather."

"Yeah. You gathered that fine. Safety from the law."

"Let me ask you this." I caught myself leaning back, one leg over the other, eyes up to the ceiling, with the bright, absorbed tone of voice of the old-time junior executive who, while wise and seasoned, is forever and boyishly eager to learn. "This middleman chain," I kept at it, "is that an organizational set-up which is standardized all over the nation?"

"Of course."

Now the trick with the leg down, both of the feet firmly planted, the hand on the desk, to demonstrate more firmness, and the gaze down from the ceiling and leveled straight at the boss—done with thinking and ready for action.

"Maybe that's your problem right there, Mister Mishkin. Yessir, that's it and right there!"

"What was that?"

"Let me put it this way. What's good enough for Macy's—what's the name of the other one?"

"You mean Livingstone?"

"Of course. And what's good enough for Gimbel's isn't necessarily good enough for Stanley. You follow?"

"No," said Mishkin.

"If you show me a specific territory, like Tooley's, maybe I'll find that the national pattern doesn't fit this special case too well."

"Good head," said Mishkin.

"So, if you'll show me some data, maybe something will come of this."

He showed me data. He asked me to come around to his side of the desk, he spread out the things from the folder, and we looked at the figures which told how the Big H was distributed in Tooley's territory.

It was a very masterful thing and I doubted if it could be improved upon. But in any specific case, in any set-up where a paper plan is translated into actual motions, there is always a chance to make little changes, and if worded correctly, they can be called improvements.

I knew that, and I think Mishkin knew that. It would give me a chance to look big, it would give Mishkin a chance to keep me around. He knew that.

So the job was a fake.

But it was important enough to risk showing me data which could have promoted a cop on the beat to commissioner, if he had these papers. Though they weren't entirely careless. Names of pushers and agents were given in numbers and amounts of heroin were given in some kind of standard units. Maybe I could have memorized things like that, but I wasn't a narcotics agent. Besides, why would Mishkin assume I would do such a thing. He was offering me a job. He was doing this for a con on the lam, a patsy without any connections, a confused innocent whose professionalism went no further than having committed one comic crime.

We talked a while, and it got to be like a real conference.

Then I said, "I may have to see this territory, Mishkin. At least the central town."

"I expect you to, Gallivan."

"What's the name of it?"

"Yorkdam."

I put one hand on top of the other and sat that way for a moment. "Yorkdam," I said.

"Yeah. You know the town? That would help, if you knew the town."

That was a fine, ugly quirk.

I took just a half-jigger of whiskey and sipped it slowly. I was licking it, more than anything else.

I said, "I don't think my knowing the town is going to be of much help. I know the town well enough to be known by everybody in it."

"Used to live there?"

"And got arrested there."

He grunted something and thought for a while, but then he explained there wouldn't be any disadvantage. I wouldn't be walking all over town and I would only be seeing a few people who had to do with the job. A talk here, a talk there, and all of it done very carefully. Being an ex-con, he said, should be the least of my worries.

Maybe he was more realistic than I. Or maybe it had to do with the fact that the job was a fake.

"Will I get to see Tooley?"

"You mean Al?"

"Who else. The other one is dead."

"That's right. Yes," said Mishkin. "You'll talk to him."

He picked up a ballpoint, made some marks on the papers, and then he clicked the point in and out. "May even be an advantage," he said, "You knowing the other one."

"The dead one."

"Yeah. He used to be in that area, before we reorganized."

"Working for you?"

"No. Sort of with. That was before we reorganized. Didn't he ever tell you?"

Just like that, smooth and simple.

"No," I said. "He didn't."

"I never been in prison," he said. "I don't know what cons talk about, all day."

"We work all day."

"All night then."

"Sex."

"Oh."

He dropped it and we worked for a while. For a fake job there certainly was a lot of concrete detail and it didn't take any effort to get the feel of a very real business problem. It was so easy in fact, that only the merchandise—which was never mentioned by its real name—kept the job from being commonplace but instead cast a nightmare quality over all our dry, reasonable discussion.

We took a two-hour break for lunch, which I ate with Rand and Jessie. Mishkin ate someplace else. Rand wanted to know if I'd gotten the job and Jessie managed a smile once, when she said, "That's nice."

Something was riding her. She was cold, she was hard, she showed the indifference of having been at it—at something—for a good, long time. But that didn't fit a number of things. It didn't fit a small remark she had made, wishing to help me, it didn't fit the big, naked fear she had shown at the cell in the station. And the last thing she had done—or had tried to do—had been the thing with the money. Did she want me to go?

"How long is the job going to take you?" she asked.

"I don't know yet. Mishkin thinks a week or two."

"That's good dough," said Rand.

"Yuh. I feel better already."

"The way things keep breaking for you," said Rand.

"I've got a guardian angel."

"I'd like one, sometime," said Jessie.

"I think they'd be afraid of you."

Rand left the room at that point, which gave an unnecessary emphasis to what I had said, because there was such a long pause after it. The door closed with a small snap and I wished I were sitting with someone else, Mishkin for instance.

"Jessie?"

"Yes?"

"I'm sorry I said that before."

She nodded and said, "Yes. I wish you hadn't said it."

"I'm sorry. We just don't get along."

She smiled and made a small shrug. "We don't really try, do we?"

"Too many other problems."

"I was going to say the same thing."

We looked at each other and I think we both wished the other would say something else and not stop here, but nothing happened. I was the first to cave under the silence and got up. I said that Mishkin was waiting for me and I'd better get going.

"See you around," she said, but the tough little phrase didn't fit her any more.

CHAPTER 15

Mishkin explained operations to me in a great deal of detail and he supplied some of the names which were missing from the papers on his desk. I'd be dealing with those people. Once I knew how to reorganize the set-up in the territory where Yorkdam was, I would have to explain it to the others.

"You mean convince them?"

"If you mean talking, yes."

"Why should they listen to me?"

"Because I tell 'em to," said Mishkin. "Besides, Rand will be along."

"That'll convince them," I said.

"Yeah. He's good."

Later in the afternoon I got very tired so Mishkin ordered some coffee. He stuck to whiskey. I drank the coffee and smoked too much and when I didn't think about this dope business I had a number of other things preying on my mind. Maybe that was the reason for my being so tired.

Mishkin kept drilling names into me, names of his men and what they were like, which ones he figured he could spare from the payroll and why not some others. What made me more and more irritable, as time wore on, was the fact that all this was sham. It was excellent, fully detailed, very plausible business but it all stood for something else and I was the patsy, and the more I felt like the patsy the more ominous everything became.

"You listening, Gallivan?"

"Yes. And thinking."

"You thinking how we can drop that east sector and handle that part from the rest of town?"

"No. How in hell can I? None of this stuff here," and I slapped the papers, "shows how much is pushed by whom. That jerk who's reporting on that sector doesn't know how many pushers from the other end are peddling in his territory."

"You mean Tooley."

"Whoever he is. Before I can make an intelligent move..."

"Good thinking," said Mishkin. "I wish Tooley was thinking that way."

"Maybe he didn't go to college." I took another cigarette and I noticed that it took me a while to get it lit. It didn't take much to make me jumpy.

"The other one, your buddy, he was much better."

"So hire him."

"He ran it good," said Mishkin. He didn't seem to notice my little case of nerves but was looking up at the ceiling. "Only trouble was, he kept himself awful secretive."

"Maybe that had to do with the cops," I said. "Maybe he didn't want them to know what he was doing."

"He kept himself that way all around. Did you notice that?"

"When?"

"When you knew him. You bunked with him, you told me."

I didn't get to answer that or think about the remark in detail because Rand came in.

"My, you guys keep at it. Why don't you open a window here? The smoke is something."

"Leave it, leave it," said Mishkin. "All I need is a draft."

He was getting irritable, too, but Rand laughed.

"Why don't you knock off," he said. "Give Gallivan here a chance to enjoy his freedom."

"We're almost done," said Mishkin. "Where was I?"

"How do I know," I told him. "Rand, if I could have another cup of coffee..."

"Yeah, I remember now," said Mishkin. "What a secretive bastard that Tooley was. Gallivan here was telling me."

"I was? What did I say?"

"That's right, you didn't get a chance to say. Rand came in."

I said, "Tooley only talked his head off when he had nothing to say." Which was true.

"Except when he got sentimental," said Rand. "You remember?"

"Remember?"

"In the yard once," said Rand. "You and me by the south wall when the sun was shining, half a year ago, maybe."

"They were playing baseball—" I said, trying to think.

"How sentimental Tooley got sometimes," Rand went on, while I hung on each word like hanging on a sill by the fingernails, and if I could only pull myself up and look into the window, then I'd know everything.

I had said something to Rand about Tooley. I knew something they didn't know—and something I couldn't remember!

And all this—the weird, painful escape, the weird, smoothly-planned job—all this was about something they thought I knew!

"Was hot that day," Rand said.

Cautious. But he was cautious.

"I think Block C was ahead with two runs, when we talked," he said.

So cautious, because if I should realize what he was after—

"They were always ahead. Was that the day they kept Linsky down to one hit?"

So cautious, because if they should realize that I couldn't remember—

"I don't know," said Rand. "We weren't watching too hard, anyway. You kept talking."

"About baseball?"

"Some. About home."

"I never played baseball at home. I played..."

"No, you didn't say that."

"Hell," I said, "I don't remember," but the meaning of that phrase threw me into a hot set of jitters, as if I had already told them, "Listen, Rand, listen, Mishkin, whatever you want from me, so help me, I can't remember!"

It didn't take much to throw me that day. There had been one rotten quirk after another. If Rand flipped a gun out now and hauled out for the bridge of my nose—

He laughed, which frightened me almost as much as my fantasy, and then he said, "You didn't remember then, either, so don't worry about it."

I didn't know what he meant, I didn't know what I had missed, and if this went on much longer—

"I want Gallivan to pay some attention here," Mishkin said, "and you and him can do your reminiscing some other time. You paying attention, Gallivan?"

All I needed now was somebody riding me. I looked at Mishkin and thought I had never seen anybody so sloppy fat.

"Yuh. I'm paying attention. I'm listening to Rand with my ears and to you with my intuition. Business intuition. You want to know how to squeeze a little more dough, another drop maybe, out of all the half-dead little junkies who go to high school to prepare for life, and the others who look at the river thinking how to end it. You..."

"Watch it, Gallivan," Rand said next to me.

But it wasn't a threat. He put his hand on my shoulder and said it as if he thought I'd feel better if I were calm.

"You get outa here," Mishkin snapped at Rand. "If I'm gonna get any work done on any kind of an intelligent level..."

"I think Gallivan's getting tired," said Rand.

"I think Gallivan is," I said, though I wasn't tired, only riled up and too tense.

"How are you and him going to pull out of here tonight if all you're gonna do is talk about baseball in the pen, damn it!"

"Pull out of here tonight?" said Rand.

"Gallivan's a smart boy," said Mishkin, "but not smart enough to walk out of here with half the facts in his head and the rest nowhere and him supposed to look like something in the morning."

"I can't go tonight," said Rand. "Honest, Mishkin."

"Why? You got lights out at nine or something?"

"There's a party."

"A what?"

"Jeesis, Mishkin, I just got out! Some of the others in town are making a party, and as for that Yorkdam business, I don't see how a day is going to make any difference."

"It better make a difference," said Mishkin. "Do you realize..."

"I'm going tomorrow," said Rand. "Not tonight."

"Yes," I said to Mishkin, "let's first have a party. I haven't had a party..."

"Yeah, I know, in over seven years."

"And now it's time for the seven-year itch."

Mishkin didn't like my tone and wanted to say something else when that sharp bell went off again. Mishkin looked at the door and then he started to curse, low and foul. He was done by the time he got out of his chair, but when he walked out of the door he said, "Christ, how I hate that damn thing!"

Rand and I watched the door close and then looked at each other.

"What was that?" I asked him.

"Mishkin hates to move."

"The bell, I mean."

"That's a signal for Mishkin. Well, what do you say, Gallivan? Party?"

I sat back in my chair and thought, why in hell not. I was suspicious enough now to think even the quarrel between Mishkin and Rand had been fake, to make the party less suspect to me while all along that would be the time when they'd hook me like never before. But a party was fine. Whatever was up, at least it would look like a party and since nothing looked like what it really was anyway—

"What kind of party?"

"Like the kind you think about, in the bucket."

Another illusion. I said, "That's for me, Rand." And then we left.

Five miles from the sanatorium we came to the town. It looked Christmasy when we rolled up to it, because of the snow on the roofs, the little lights in the windows, and because it was dark by then. From close up, when we drove through the streets, the town was crummy. Salt had burnt the snow off the streets and there was a mess of cinders all over.

"Whoopla," said Rand when he bumped over a clinker.

"That's a party sound," I told him.

"We won't be bumping no clinkers," he said and gave a laugh.

I didn't think the "whoopla" or the laugh fit Rand, but I wasn't going to worry about it.

"There'll be liquor, I assume."

"We'll be bumping that, and more."

"You can say it, Rand. You mean girls."

"Whoopla."

He said it as if reading it off a script. It would be a fine party.

We went up a driveway, past a house, and up to another house in a yard of junk. The clapboard was sprung on one side and the wooden porch leaned a little.

There was a wreath on the front door, with a red ribbon. When we got out of the car I saw the wreath give a jump because somebody must have bumped the door. All the windows had brown shades drawn down to the bottom. They looked almost gold with the light from the other side.

Once inside I thought I had never seen such a lousy place for a party. It was good and busy and there was a lot of blue smoke in the air, but one couch was missing a leg, one wall was missing wallpaper, the bulb at the ceiling was missing a shade. Doors there were none, just curtains.

I said, "Jeesis!"

"Something, huh?"

"Oh yes."

Everybody knew Rand. In a minute he had three cans of beer in his arm, a glass in his hand, and a red lipstick smear on the side of his nose.

The men were short, tall, with jackets, without jackets, ties on and off, but all of them noisy. Very young party, I thought. Showing a lot of effort yet. And the girls were short, tall, with dresses, with things barely called dresses, straps on or off, but all of them noisy. Very young party girls, I noticed. Showing a lot of effort yet.

"And this is my buddy, Gallivan," Rand was yelling, and then I got slapped on the back too, got a glass to hold and a can of beer and a smack of red lipstick on my jawbone.

"Hi, buddy," she said.

She was wearing an evening gown which didn't seem to start until you looked down to the waist. She was very young and I had an impulse to ask her about it but was afraid of what she might say.

"You want something, buddy?" She hung close up against me and smiled.

"Huh?"

"The way you looked," she said, "I was wondering if you wanted something."

"A drink. I want a big drink."

She took me to the kitchen. We fought through the curtain which hung in the doorway and then we fought as far as the sink. It had a wooden drainboard, stained with mold, and all the bottles on top were leaning. The sink itself, which was tin, had nothing but ice in it. Young party. Lots of ice yet.

"You want it brown or amber or yellow?"

"Huh?"

"Buddy, you keep saying 'huh' to me. What's it mean, buddy?"

"It means I love you but don't know how to say it."

"Brown, amber, or yellow?"

"Just pour, girl. As long as there's no water in it I don't care if it's green."

"You're fuh-nee," she said and gave me a highball glass all brown up to the middle.

I didn't do much talking for a while but kept smiling at the girl now and then so she wouldn't be insulted. I was still that sober. She talked about various things, about her name being Betty, about loving parties, about "Gee, did you ever see such an old fridge," at which point she walked over to it and gave it a kick. The refrigerator stopped churning on the inside and something seemed to drop, the motor maybe. She said, "Gee," and came back.

"Buddy, isn't it nicer now without the noise?"

"Betty, I love the silence. Just happy people now, all screaming."

"Fuh-nee."

"Ought to be. Betty and Buddy, like a team."

"Move your hand a little, buddy, you got such big knuckles."

I moved my hand so she could get closer and put it on her hip. She gave a squeal and a jump.

"Buh-dee, you got three hands?"

"Huh?"

"I mean, how'd you goose me just now?"

I hadn't goosed her. Somebody else had done it and she could take her pick from among a dozen.

"You said 'huh' again just a minute ago. What did you say that meant?"

"It's short for huhuhuhu! Laughter."

"Fuh-nee. My, buddy, lookit your glass!"

I looked at the glass and saw that it was almost empty.

"You always gotta drink so much beforehand?"

I didn't say 'huh' again, but "What?"

"We're gonna play, aren't we?"

She made that clear by taking my hand off her hip and putting it some-place else. Then she gave a squeal and a jump.

"I didn't do it," I said. "Somebody else goosed you."

"Such a *cold* one!" she yelled, and it turned out she wasn't talking about a goose at all but an ice cube down her back.

"Take it out," she said.

I wasn't quick enough, or not enough hands for a place such as this one, because a kid more like Betty's age got there first and found the ice cube.

"Was twice the size when I dropped it," he told her and held the cube out for her.

"Fuh-nee!" and that was the last I saw of Betty because the other one, the kid, had managed to make a much stronger impression on her.

I had more to drink.

There were herring and pickles in the refrigerator and I ate some of that at the half-way mark. Afterwards I got rid of the taste with more brown liquor and was soon well beyond the half-way mark or the point of no return. I didn't know which yet.

There was another room I hadn't seen. The furniture was pushed out of the way and a manner of dancing was going on in the middle. We had records for dancing. We had wondrous dance talent on display, unless it was the liquor responsible for the distortion. This girl really shook that dance all to pieces. She started out normal enough, except for the homburg on her head, and even that wasn't too far gone and certainly better look-ing than some party tricks I'd seen.

Except this one ended up with just the homburg in a short while, and for a strip tease it was the absolute fastest in my recollection, a rip tease, more properly.

Then a big guy came out to dance with her which meant she had to give up the hat too. Which she did. For a little while she wasn't going to dance with him or anybody else without her shoes on. She'd be damned if she did and somebody around here better cough up those shoes but right quick.

"Ain't she got spirit?" said Micky.

"Very effective, everything. I love those shoes."

"Boy," said Micky. "And you got the spirit. You talk thick."

"Don't lisp, Micky."

"Lookit what she's doing, Gallivan!"

"She's dancing."

"No, not that."

"She's taking her shoes off, that devil."

"I mean with the fat guy, the way she's turning him. He's getting dizzy, I think."

"Wouldn't you, Micky?"

"Yeah!"

"Don't be vulgar, Micky."

"Gallivan, sometimes I don't know what you're talking about."

"So. You been listening to every word, have you?"

"But weren't you talking to me?"

I felt very comfortable talking to Micky and we kept it up for a while, because here, I was certain, there were no ulterior motives.

Then he said, "Somebody been looking for you, Gallivan."

"Who, Betty?"

"No."

"Buddy."

"Who's she?"

"Fuh-nee."

"Yeah. Anyway, Jessie was."

"She's here?"

"Now where in hell would she be if she was looking for you, Gallivan?"

"Don't riddle me no riddles, feller, I've had a full day of that."

"Yeah, that Mishkin. But she's across the way."

I tried to look across the way but it was either the liquor or all the dancers—

"How many dancers now, Micky?"

"A whole floor full, Gallivan. The nekkid one's disappeared."

"Thank you, Micky."

I knocked his glass out of his hand by mistake but then I got off well enough, with all the dancers supporting me on the way. On the other side of the room I rested a moment, holding on to what turned out to be a radiator with all the fins running the wrong way. I took that in my stride until it turned out that they did run the wrong way, since the radiator wasn't connected but stood upended in the corner. I rested some more then, wishing there were some fresh air.

Then I saw Jessie. She was sitting on a table and laughing. I had never seen her laugh before and the sight gave me a shock. I couldn't see well enough to tell whether her eyes did in fact close all the way when she laughed, but I saw how her head was back, laughing hard.

I went over there and said, "Hello, Jessie."

She stopped laughing immediately.

"Jimmy, come up here and sit down."

"Before I fall?"

"Don't quarrel, Jimmy, please. Not all the time."

"I lost my drink on the way. That'll make any drunk quarrelsome."

"Get him a drink, will you?" she said to somebody and when he was gone she said to me, "You're not a drunk, Jimmy."

"I may not look like one, Jessie, but the spirit's there."

"You look like one all right. I meant it the other way around."

"Aren't you drinking?"

She said no, she wasn't, and I didn't see a glass in her hand, either.

"If you're trying to make everybody feel cheap and evil, sitting there with no drink in your hand, you have succeeded," I told her.

"Please, Jimmy."

"You wanted to see me?"

"Well, I asked for you," she said, and in my state it felt like a slap in the face. "I thought you might like it."

"Don't say 'it' like that, Jessie. At this party the word 'it' is not neuter."

"I thought since you didn't know anybody here, you might like to sit with me."

"You said sit because you think I'm drunk, don't you."

"You want to dance?"

"No. You're dressed."

"You're difficult, Gallivan."

"Complex, honey. Not a complex, though, because everything I imagine always turns out to be true."

"You're a very lucky fellow," she said.

Somebody had come back with my drink and Jessie put it into my hand.

"You should have my imagination," I said. "You wouldn't say lucky."

"Rand should have left you in jail," she said. "That's it, isn't it?"

It hadn't been nasty and she hadn't been cold about it. Besides, she was right. I took a cool swallow from my glass and nodded.

"You want to go out on the porch, for some air?" she asked.

I nodded again and we went out to the porch. There was nobody else. It was too cold.

A shiny icicle hung from the porch roof, two old fashioned fenders lay in the yard, and the wreath on the door was swinging a little. I had to think of an ice pick hanging from the roof, of two big ears lying in the dark yard, and that wreath got me.

Her dress had short sleeves and I put my hand where I could feel her skin.

"I don't want you to be cold, Jessie."

I pulled her closer and she came. The feel of her against me reminded me of the time at the hotel, when she had lain in bed. I hadn't felt a thing then, and I don't think she had either.

"Maybe," I said, "we could get along better."

"Maybe, Gallivan."

"Why don't we?"

"Why haven't we?"

"Yes."

"We never tried. I think we've tried not to."

"As if meeting at the wrong time," I said. "It's felt like that."

"I know. Or for the wrong reasons."

I said nothing to that because something nudged me, not anything physical, though it felt that way. It was a slight catch in the pit of my stomach, but my stomach was all right. It felt like the ugly quirks which had happened all day.

"Jimmy?"

"Yes."

"I just want you to look at me. You're staring away."

I looked at her, and it struck me that I had never seen her this close, and this well, and how good she looked to me. I could feel the warmth through my shirt where she leaned against me, and the bare arm under my hand, warm too. I wanted to say something to her but only the stupidest things came into my head.

"From this angle," I said, "your eyes are slitty."

"From this angle," she said, "you should see your nose. I don't know what it looks like, except large and funny."

"If I hold it right, it's not in the way at all."

She closed her eyes and said, "Show me."

I kissed her cheek first, which felt cold like an apple, and then I kissed her on the mouth. It went through and through both of us, because of the way we held on to each other and didn't let go for a long time.

Afterwards we didn't say anything. Perhaps we should have. Perhaps the tight, small knot inside would have stayed away.

"I like you, Gallivan," she said softly.

Then I said, "Is that what he meant when he said for you to throw it a little?"

I think I let go of her before she drew back because the shock hit me sooner. I had a crazy moment where it went through my head, "You didn't say it, you didn't really—she didn't hear it, she never heard it—" But that didn't last.

She had stepped back to the railing, touching it with her hands, and still looked at me. She kept looking at me while her face did the most terrible thing, it stayed tilted up, looking at me, and started to cry.

Then she put her hands up. She did it fast and stamped her foot and when she looked up again all I saw was the cold.

"You know," she said, "all I told you before was that I liked you. What sort of things do you do if somebody says, 'I love you'?"

I wasn't able to answer.

"Or don't you know? I bet you could make it a dilly, if you tried, Gallivan. I bet you could really throw it."

"Jessie, listen. When I said that..."

"Careful. You know what the word 'it' means around here, don't you?"

"Jessie..."

"Where's your drink, Gallivan? You look sober."

"Wait, it wasn't..."

"Don't say 'it', Gallivan," and then she went back inside.

The Christmas wreath jumped around and I waited for it to stop. I finished my drink and threw the glass away. Then I went to the door, ripped the wreath off and threw that into the yard, too. After that, I went inside for a new glass, with liquor.

CHAPTER 16

There wasn't any more dancing, not the kind like before, though a few couples were pushing around on the floor like at the end of a prom—slow, close, tired. It looked fairly romantic. A record was going and also a piano in the next room but that didn't bother anyone. It didn't bother me because I was for noise.

"You don't look drunk any more," said Micky.

"I had a sobering experience," I said, and took a long drink. Then I went back to the kitchen because my glass was empty.

But Micky came along because he hadn't understood what I had said.

"What did you say?"

"She said no."

"Who, Jessie? I don't believe it!"

"Ask her."

"Me? I wouldn't ask her."

"Not your type?"

"She's strange, is all. I like 'em simple."

As usual, it was more crowded in the kitchen than anywhere else and Micky reached out with his hand. He wasn't even looking where.

"More like this, maybe," he said and somebody squealed.

At first I thought it was Betty, the one from before, because this one had made the same kind of sound, but then Micky had probably done the same kind of thing. She whirled around very fast but didn't know who had done it, Micky or me, so she leaned over and gave both of us a kiss, one after the other.

"You adventurer," she said.

I thought that was better than 'fuh-nee' and took her arm to pull her closer. She pulled easily.

"It wasn't me," I told her, "because that's too backhanded for my taste."

"You adventurer."

Yessir, I thought, wrong again. At least the other one knew more than one word.

Then she said, "What's your name?" and I said, "Jimmy." She asked, "Who are you?" I said, "An adventurer."

But I didn't care how it sounded because I wasn't going to converse with this one anyway. Betty had been awfully young, built small and unfinished, where this one was much more mature. I wasn't thinking of her mind, which no longer interested me.

She said, "Why you standing at the sink, Jimmy?"

"Because I'm a drinker and got sloppy feet. After a while I might not be able to make it to the source of supply."

"Oh. Then what you want me for?"

I liked that. She had pride in her assets and no second fiddle for her.

"The drink for the cool and you for the heat."

"Adventurer."

"Listen, Baby, I wish you'd say something else."

"Like what, Jimmy?"

"Fuh-nee, for instance."

"Ooh, you've been smooching with Betty."

"*Smooching,* for chrissake—"

"I'm old-fashioned."

"Well, I wasn't. Somebody goosed her and she ran away."

"You wouldn't let that happen to me, would you, Jimmy?"

I told her no, took a big, scratchy swallow from the glass, and when I looked at her again she was beautiful. Of course, she had been sexy all along.

I had never known a blonde like her. The hair was almost white. It was short and white and, in contrast, her skin seemed to have a cast like a light, shiny tan. Her arms were bare, and her shoulders. The straps didn't count, being thin like strings. They made sexy little dents in her soft skin.

"You from Florida, Baby?"

"Yes. What you doing, Jimmy, looking for the tan-line?"

"I was."

"There isn't any," and she pulled her neckline away, so I could check.

She was good and round in front. She let go of the neckline again and leaned against me, so that I thought she was going to pop out on top.

"It's never happened yet," she said, "unless I wanted it to."

I put the glass down, turned her the right way, and we had a fearful kiss. It was so technical I could hear gears clanking and rattling.

"My," she said, "why don't we sit down?"

"That's why I did this, little Baby. Because I want to sit down with you."

We only found one seat though. We were right next to the piano where an easy chair stood by the wall and I sat down first, while she held both our drinks. I sat down and my head started going around on the inside. Then, with the soft pillows under me, I felt that I wanted to sleep.

"Jimmy!"

I could understand that tone of voice. I could do nothing about it, but I knew what she meant.

She put the two glasses on the floor and sat down in the same chair with me. It put us very close.

"You're tired, aren't you, Jimmy?"

It surprised me, because I had been sure she was going to be nasty.

"You just rest a while," she said, and put her arm around me. She kept her hand on the back of my head and we were awfully close.

"You wanna talk to me?" she said close to my ear.

"You're going to make me bawl any minute," I told her and meant every word of it.

"Go ahead," she said.

I didn't. I took a drink instead. She settled herself in a different way so that kissing wouldn't be so difficult and we sat like that.

"Comfortable?"

I was reeling, though I didn't know with what. The girl was built to do it, the bad break on the porch was built for it, and everything else. I put my hand on her and she said now I wouldn't have to answer her.

"Want me to take the glass, Jimmy?"

I gave it to her and she reached back to put it on the floor. When she did that her strap broke.

"It always does that," she said, but did nothing else about it.

The piano was pounding a rhythm into my head and stopped the reeling in there. It just pounded now, but I could see much better. I looked at the girl and she winked at me and I played with the strap which had broken. She was leaning back in the chair and I thought she had a very comfortable smile.

"You're feeling better, aren't you, Jimmy. I can tell."

She reached over and tore the other strap, because it was cutting her too much.

There were an awful lot of people milling around and I envied the girl for the simple smile she had and for not caring about anyone else in the room.

"Do that again," she said.

I didn't know what I had done.

We did what I suppose she would have called smooching though she didn't use the word again. We were hardly talking.

I could look across the room from our corner and when I did I saw Jessie there.

"What happened?" said the girl.

I don't know what I had done, but she knew right away.

"You like her?"

"Who?"

"Jessie. You're looking at Jessie, aren't you?"

Jessie was across the room, talking to somebody or other, but not laughing this time. That was the only thing I liked about the sight. She was drinking this time. But it was coffee. When she finished the cup the guy who was with her took a pot off the window sill and poured into her cup.

"Is that really coffee?" I asked.

"Sure that's coffee. She drinks that and smokes."

I had noticed how Jessie smoked. She smoked at least as much as I did, if not more.

"You don't want to play with her," said the girl. "She doesn't look playful, does she, Baby?"

"Naw. Not Jessie."

"How does a playful girl like you know a—know one like Jessie?"

"She's around. You know."

"Who is she?"

"Jessie? What do you mean, who is she?"

"I mean I don't know who she is."

"You don't want to know her, Jimmy."

"You didn't answer."

"She's in with Rand and those guys—I mean, those people."

"My. How polite."

"You know. They're big. She works with them, direct."

"Like you?"

"Naw. I just play, you know."

"Like this."

"That's right. Like this. You don't want to know her, Jimmy."

"Jealous of Jessie?"

"Of Jessie? Why, of course not, silly!" Then she leaned close to my ear and said, "Don't you know about her?"

"Tell me, Baby."

"She used to be a junky."

I stared across the room at Jessie but couldn't see her clearly any more. All I saw was cigarette smoke and black coffee, lots of black coffee, and a cold, cold face. But I was making that up. I didn't see anything across the room because of the many people.

"Reach back there and give me that glass, will you, Baby?"

"Not now, Jimmy!"

"Give it to me."

She frowned at me, but as soon as I looked at her full face she smiled. I think she really was trying to be nice. She even took a cigarette out of my pocket and sat there smoking it as if she were waiting for me.

Then somebody came up to the chair, stood a moment, and when nothing happened, he leaned a little closer and said, "Honey? Can you spare the time?"

"You mean now?"

"They want you in back. If you got the time."

She looked at me and I held the glass up to her and said, "Mud."

She shrugged and said, "I guess I got time." She wiggled around till she was free and stood up. "See you later?" she asked.

"You gotta go?"

"I'd rather stay."

"Mud."

She walked away holding the dress so it wouldn't slide all the way down to her hips. Before she went through the curtain she winked.

I didn't want to get out of the chair because I was sure somebody would grab it, so when Rand came by I asked him to go to the kitchen for me and get me a fresh glassful.

"You alone?" he wanted to know.

"Not if you bring me that blinking glassful, Rand."

"Where's Jessie?"

"Why don't you shut up, you lousy sonofabitch," I said to him, but I'm not clear whether he took that up in any way.

I know I had a glass in a while, and for another while somebody sat down in the chair with me, and then she brought me another glass, who I don't know, and after that I played the piano. I hadn't played for the usual seven years, which seemed my measure for everything, and the liquor kept slopping back and forth inside somewhere, but I kept playing. Somebody yelled in my ear, attaboy, attaboy, which made me think I was playing all right, but I don't know.

And the party wasn't over by any means, though it seemed unusually long to me. There was more of this and that, and once I ate a herring. Once I woke up freezing on the porch. The party still wasn't over. So more of this and that. I even found the backroom, not that there was a trick to it, since there were no doors anywhere. There even was something like a line, which reminded me of the usual seven years and I had a fight with somebody about it. He was drunker than I, because I was standing and he was on the floor.

I heard somebody say "fuh-nee" once and got reacquainted with Betty. There was a bed, I remember, and the girl was squealing a lot.

I don't think she and I had sex, because that was later. The girl was built differently and her round breasts lay on top of her like soft puddings. I think she was the one I had called Baby.

CHAPTER 17

Iremembered something else. I came to, clear and shivering, in the back seat of the car and the gray light outside came into focus with a snap. Rand was driving and it was very cold in the car, so we hadn't been driving long, but the cold air was full of smoke. Jessie sat next to him with her overcoat wrapped tight around her.

"You going to Yorkdam tomorrow?" she asked. She talked low, sounding tired, but her voice wasn't relaxed.

"Today, you mean."

"Yes."

"He'll be all right," said Rand.

She didn't answer. She was lighting a cigarette, one from the other. Then she threw the old butt out of the window and said, "Yes. Sure."

Rand looked at her, then watched the road again.

"But you turned out punk," he said.

"Yes. Sure."

Rand kept driving. He mumbled something, but said nothing else for the moment. I think he didn't want to talk to Jessie.

"He still out?" he asked after a while.

She looked back and said, "Yes."

"So tell me. You got nothing?"

"I'm punk, so why ask?"

"Oh for chrissake, don't take on, will ya?"

"No," she said. "I got nothing out of him. He won't give."

"Just like you, huh?"

"Rand, leave me alone, will you please?"

He looked over to her briefly and then I think he gave a pat to her thigh.

"Take it easy, honey. And just stick to coffee. All right?"

I could see her nod. I also thought that had been damn nice of Rand the way he laid off. He had done more, as a matter of fact. He had encouraged the girl.

"No," she had said. "I got nothing out of him."

But that wasn't true. I had made it very clear to her, on the porch, that I knew they were trying to pump me for something.

But she said nothing about that. She and Rand didn't talk for the rest of the trip, except once more. Jessie said, "You think he's going to be very angry—about me?"

"Well—you know what's at stake for him."

"God, he frightens me."

"Yeah. He ain't pretty," said Rand.

This meant very little to me. At first I had thought they were talking about me again, but that didn't fit, not with the emotion they showed, or held back. But they were talking about someone on top, though I felt certain they did not mean Mishkin.

I sat up after that. It didn't stop any conversation because they had stopped anyway. We drove back to the sanatorium as if we didn't know each other. The building stood big and white in the park and if it had not been cold because of the season, the sight would have made it so.

I had a few hours sleep and then Rand woke me and we left again.

It could have been a plain, bleak day, because of the thick-clouded light and because of the night before. But there was not time for the careful coasting through the hangover hours. There was no time for gently suffering through a gray day until the weather might change. Very soon now they would find out that I knew less than they, unless I suddenly managed to know—

We drove most of the afternoon. The latter part of the trip Rand went more slowly because traffic got heavier and because he didn't want to drive into town in full daylight.

"Recognize it?" he said.

I looked at him and saw that he was pointing.

"You said you used to live here," he said.

"Yuh. I recognize it."

"Nervous? You seem nervous, Gallivan."

"Rand," I said, "I was born nervous."

He laughed and said he didn't think so, he thought I was pretty steady most of the time and was just feeling the hangover. Otherwise, steady as a rock.

"Yuh. Like a rock. Like a rock bouncing down the side of a ravine. You ever notice how nervous that looks?"

"All I know is about liquor, and believe me, Gallivan, I never saw anyone put it away like you did."

"I don't remember a thing."

"It'll come back to you."

He smiled to himself and I lit a cigarette. The cigarette made me think of Jessie. Then something else stung me, and though I didn't know where it would lead, I asked him.

"Remember what, Rand?"

"What?"

"Yes. What."

"I meant the party," he said, but I thought he looked at me just a little too long and then it came back to me.

Did I remember what I had told him about Tooley in the yard, that day when the sun was shining and we looked at the cons playing baseball?

I remembered it now because of the scene outside which was all very familiar to me. I knew the roads, the skyline, where to turn off the highway to get into Yorkdam a little bit faster. That day, in the yard, I had felt sentimental, which had been the reason why I had talked to Rand. I told him about Tooley and me, reminiscing the night before in the cell.

It hadn't been reminiscing at first, but bragging. Tooley did that sometimes, as long as nobody could catch him up on it. He had said how cautious he had been all his life, why, most of the time, he had said, his buddies and even closest associates hadn't known all there was to know about him. Such as where he lived. Good precaution, he had said, when in a dangerous business.

Then he had said that he also enjoyed the privacy of it, the plain and simple privacy, with a view of a lake, a big tree in the distance, maybe, that kind of thing. I used to have a place on a lake, I told him, Bowline Lake, a little cottage for week ends.

Tooley knew Bowline Lake, it turned out, and that's how we spent the rest of the long evening, talking about that miserable lake which was nothing really, except that it was in the past and not in prison.

Once he even got carried away into details, about the kind of view he had had, the road he used to take most of the time, which was a rural route going towards a new development, and I remembered all that because I knew the lake.

And feeling sentimental, which means there was nothing good in my present life, I told all that to Rand.

In retrospect, there seemed no question that Rand had taken the subject up. Did Tooley say he used to live out there?— Sometimes. Did he say when?— I don't remember. Did he say where?— No. Not exactly. Exactly what did he say?

If Tooley had mentioned an address, I had told Rand, then I had forgotten it, but I knew the lake pretty good, I had said, and if I ever wanted to visit Tooley out at the lake—one of those weird thoughts, since he wasn't going to live very much longer—then I might very well find it.

That had been half a year before the break. It had taken them half a year to set up that break because I knew, or could find, Tooley's house.

That's why I was important.

We splashed through the town where the salt had made mud out of the snow. We passed the big building where I used to work. We passed the big building where I had stood trial. It was also the building where I had been married. But I hardly remembered about that, and I wished I could have been as finished with several other things. I was wishing again. I sat cursing under my breath because this was not a wishing game. This was no game of any sort, and I cursed that fact into myself.

There was less traffic where Rand drove us now, and fewer lights. We went into the fringe of the factory section, with small machine shops, trucking depots, and boarded-up stores. We turned into a long drive with a giant brick wall on one side and a tall wire fence on the other, and at the end of the drive was a building. The building was dark on the inside, except for one light, but I could see the sign when the headlights ran over it. *Laundry,* it said. There had to be a laundry in all this.

"To make me feel more at home?" I said to Rand.

He finished killing the motor and lights and yanking the brakes up, and then he didn't know what I was talking about. I had to explain to him about the laundry.

"I hadn't thought of that," he said. "Does it bother you?"

Obviously, it didn't bother him, and I envied him. I envied him and I admired him, and if I had to lead a life like this one I would want to be like Rand. Except there was no "if" about the life I was in. It could even be the death of me.

"You coming, Gallivan?"

It smelled moist inside and the rows of silent drums, dryers, and the white-chalked boiler in back, all that was badly familiar. The only difference here, they used something in their detergent which smelled like citronella.

Our steps made an echo, and the building looked as if it were underground because there was only one light in the back. The light was in the office, and Tooley sat there.

He looked like the dead Tooley, only younger. He had the same vapid grin on his face and gave the same impression of a lewd old man. I disliked him immediately.

He got up from behind the small desk, gave Rand a pat on the arm, and then he shook my hand as if that was the way he got his kicks.

"Gee, am I glad to meet you, Gallivan."

He would be the kind who said "gee," meaning, "to hell with you, mac."

We sat down in his beaverboard office and he pointed to a hot plate on top of a file.

"Coffee, fellers? I kept it hot just for you."

I didn't want coffee. It suddenly reminded me of Jessie.

"Gallivan here," said Rand, "has been getting the twenty-four-hour treatment from Mishkin, as you know, and ought to be able to talk business without any more briefing. Besides, he's smart," Rand added.

I took that the way it was meant, a meaningless introduction, though it might have been a message to Tooley to treat all this carefully. Then I started right in.

"The way I get it," I said to Tooley, "You deliver on a four-hundred-per cent mark-up—or profit—and Mishkin wants more. He wants more, but no price change."

I wanted to set the tone, the excuse being that I was a junior executive, the reason being, "to hell with you, Tooley."

"Gee," he said, "lemme talk to you fellers first, you know, friendly. You know, I'm happy to see you guys out. Really happy. And you and me, Gallivan, we must have a long talk about my poor brother, sometime. You must have gotten to know him good, huh, in his last hours?"

"His last hours," I said, "he spent in a special block, but I heard he ordered hot dogs for that meal they get for a fare-thee-well."

"Gee."

"Yuh. That goes to show something. Now, Mishkin explained to me—and stop me if I'm wrong—that Yorkdam lies in the center of a six-section matrix which breaks down your delivery problems. Just on the basis of desk work, and I don't hold much..."

He didn't give me a chance to go on, but this was the pitch I would have to take to do this job right, I'll have to do field work. This field work, for my purposes, would have to take me out to that lake.

And I hoped I would remember enough to triangulate the house which old Tooley had talked about. At that point I didn't even speculate on what might be there. I just had to find the house first.

But he interrupted with "gee" again, and how wonderful it was to see us fellers out, which seemed to be his chosen way of breaking the ice. Even Rand looked a little bit pained.

"I thought there'd be some more people here," I said, "your lieutenants, so to speak, because there are a few concrete things I'd like to ask about the various sectors."

"Well, yes," said Tooley, "that's what I had in mind too, at first, but then I got to thinking about you fellers just being out and I thought maybe a party..."

"We had a party," said Rand.

"And it didn't pan out," I said.

I didn't think Rand took note of that, but I would have to watch this kind of remark, I decided. This was not the time for private kicks.

"So we might as well talk some more here," said Rand. "How about you taking the ball, Tooley. You know what this is all about."

Rand, I knew, hadn't said that for kicks either, but because he didn't think there was any reason to watch his remarks in front of me. This was fine. It gave me a fine sense of safety.

"Well sir," said Tooley. "We been getting along good, of course, but if Mishkin wants better, we'll do better. Our motto, kind of. Eh, Rand?"

"Yes," said Rand.

"Now, when my brother was here," said Tooley, "the territory wasn't divided up quite this way, but he managed a four-hundred margin easy. Of course, prices were different then, but..."

"We don't want the price changed," I reminded him, and I thought the "we" sounded just fine for the touch I wanted. It was front office visiting the territories. Then I added the informed type of touch and said, "We don't feel that the suckers should be squeezed any more, because it wouldn't be worth the trouble. Just enough of them are going to crack under it and that means cop attention with all those cold turkeys running around. For that reason I don't advise raising prices."

I think even Rand looked impressed. He cleared his throat and went to get himself coffee from the hot plate on top of the file. Tooley said,

"Why, yes—of course. Uh, what I was going to say was—"

"You were talking about your brother," Rand reminded him.

"Ah, yes. Well, I mentioned him for an example. I was going to say, he had a funny system of pushers which we never quite figured out, and even if you disge—disre—even if you forget about the bigger prices then, he did get more out of just paying less in expenses."

I thought I'd cut the ground right out from under him and said, "You can account for that just by the difference in wages paid then and now. So there's nothing to figure."

"Wait a minute, wait a minute—"

He gave a very quick look in Rand's direction but I did catch how helpless it was.

"Mishkin thinks," said Rand, "there was more to it. That his brother here," and he nodded at Tooley, "might have had some kind of system. Better system than now."

That way he put Tooley on the track again, and now it was Tooley's turn. He went back to his formula.

"Gee, my poor brother," with that sickening smile of his. "It hurts me, kind of, to be talking of him just with business in mind, you know, Gallivan? What's your first name, Gallivan?"

"James."

"Jimmy. Let me call you Jimmy."

"Go ahead. About the..."

"I was the kid brother, you know? His kid brother. And he and I used to talk a lot. Used to tell me everything. He was that way. But you know that, Jimmy. You and him used to talk a lot, I bet. Huh, Jimmy?"

"No."

"No? I bet you just don't remember. I bet, being out now and all, you just don't want to think back. But you gotta think of my dead brother different, Jimmy. You gotta think how you and him, in the same lonesome cell there, how you and him made things easier for yourselves talking. What you talk about mostly?"

Rand was getting edgy. That Tooley idiot was being a little too artless.

To answer him, I said, "Sex."

Tooley giggled. Then he said, "Yessir, haha, that's important too. And what else? Did he ever tell you about the time he lived around here? He must have, seeing you and him come from the same place."

Careful. A simple "No" wouldn't do now. Rand was standing there with the cup to his mouth as if he wasn't listening, but he knew that the dead Tooley and I had talked about Bowline Lake.

"Well, we talked about fishing..."

"Fishing?" said Tooley. "My brother never went fishing."

Rand lowered the cup. He kept his eye on it, but I went stiff and shivery with the gesture. I seemed to take a hell of a long time before I came up with the simple answer.

"We talked about fishing because I like fishing," and then, being nervous, I went too far. "I used to fish Bowline Lake."

"Oh yeah?" Tooley smiled. "I bet my brother liked to talk about that."

"Well, no. As you said, fishing didn't mean anything to him." But it didn't work. We were now on the subject.

"I meant the lake. He liked that lake, you know. He ever tell you about the times he spent on that lake?"

"Fishing?"

"No. What I mean is, he lived there. Didn't he tell you?"

I was stuck with it and said, "Yes, he told me he lived near that lake."

"Where?" Tooley asked, with a lot of greed in his manner.

"Tooley," said Rand, talking slowly and with care, "you've got to remember, Tooley, that Gallivan and I don't like to talk about prison *too* much. Not so much that it sticks out, you understand me? And besides, we came here on business."

"Oh yeah, yeah. The business. Gimme a cup of that coffee, will you, Rand? Fine. That's enough," and while he fussed around with the coffee subject, trying to get his bearings, I got my own.

They want to talk about the lake? I want to talk about the lake.

"He mentioned this to me," I said, "when we had one of our talks. Now, at the time it didn't mean much to me, because I lacked background, but since my sessions with Mishkin, I feel this might be important."

Tooley's ears were getting pointed, he was listening so hard. And Rand put his cup down. But he slopped it.

"You know the Bowline development?" I asked Tooley.

"Huh?"

"There's a development out by that lake," said Rand. "For chrissakes, Tooley, do you know your territory or don't you?" I don't think he liked Tooley any better than I did.

"Yes, of course, hehe. I was just— Anyway, go on, Jimmy."

"What your brother mentioned to me didn't bear directly on our problem, which is cutting overhead. At least there was no bearing at the time."

"Wait a minute, Jimmy. You were saying..."

"Just go on, Gallivan," said Rand, "while Tooley shuts up for a while, please?"

Tooley shut up and I played it my way.

"Your brother pointed out how that end of the area wasn't covered at all. No customers at all, that he knew of. At that time they were just starting to build a big high school there," I kept improvising, "which must be finished by now and full of a hell of a lot of students."

"Was this about high school you were talking about?" Rand wanted to know.

"Let me finish. He wanted to make dough out that way, but of course he got nabbed before the development was halfway finished." And for the sake of Rand's interest I threw in, "Your brother, Tooley, knew that section well, because as you know, he lived around there."

"Where?"

"You know where he lived. He was your brother. I was saying: We want to cut overhead, we don't want to raise prices. What's one simple answer to that? Find more customers. With the same crew you got now—and I've got some details in mind which could make all this real—you just add territory to the business you got."

Tooley looked at Rand and said, "You know he's got something there?"

"I'm glad," said Rand.

I wasn't holding his interest, and I hadn't come to my point.

"But before we can go any further with this, we have to go out there, go right out there into the field, and make a head-count customer survey."

"How well do you know that neck of the woods?" Rand wanted to know.

"Like the palm of my hand. And what I don't know about the lay of the land there, such as places and such which I might have forgotten," I said for Rand's benefit, "I would remember once I stood on the site."

"Did my brother ever..."

"Tooley," said Rand. "You and Gallivan can talk about your brother some more tomorrow. When we go out to the development."

"Oh! Yeah, sure."

"That is my idea," I said to Rand. "To go out there and look the territory over."

It turned out that simple, and for one simple reason. Rand and I both wanted to go out to the lake. We both wanted to find the place where the dead Tooley had lived.

The only hitch was that I had to keep my interest from him. Rand, I knew, had the same problem.

CHAPTER 18

We broke it up at ten in the evening and Tooley drove ahead of us to show the way to the place where we would sleep. There was no school 'til morning and that was the time when we wanted to look Bowline Lake development over. It would be a daylight job, something Rand didn't like, but Rand also didn't like the way our conversation had been going. We sat next to each other without talk. We were both tired, and we were both trying to think. I had my problem, he had his.

We didn't drive far. Tooley stopped in a little street with old-fashioned, two-family houses. There were trees all along, and the street looked small-town with snow under the lamplight. There were "Room for Rent" signs every so often, and the sign on our house said, "Rooms, for Respectable Gentlemen."

Neither Rand nor I made any comment about that. Such was the mood.

There was a hall in boarding-house brown, and the usual double doors to the front room were open. This was a room of red plush and doilies with a little, old lady sitting there. But when we walked through the hall she didn't turn around.

Rand got one room and I got another. We had a connecting door and a fire escape outside our window. Tooley made a point of showing it to us.

"But you don't have to worry," he said. "Something goes sour and you'll know long ahead of time. Got a man in front, one in back, one down the block. Good night, fellers."

It reminded me that I was a convict.

I sat on the bed and after a while, because the light in the ceiling was so depressing, I flipped the switch and sat in the dark. I could hear Rand in the next room. He went out once and came back in ten minutes. It was quiet in his room after that, but he wasn't asleep. I heard the hiss of a match once, and later the soft thump when he killed the cigarette. Then the match hissed again.

I would not have much room to move in the morning. I would have to watch every question they asked, every stretch of casual conversation, and if I should try to twist it around so I could learn something from them, I would have to watch it even more. And I would have to be careful of Rand. If I looked too long at one house, hesitated a little too long— Of course, I could do all those things to throw them off, but what I really needed to do was find the dead Tooley's house. And with Rand watching me

One in back, one in front, one at the end of the block, Tooley had said.

Rand's bed squeaked.

The fire escape, I thought, would be the worst. What looks more suspicious than a man on a fire escape late at night.

Rand hadn't made a sound for a long time.

The stairs were the nicest, the quietest stairs I had ever known and the only problem would be the old lady in her room with the double doors open. But maybe she would be afraid to ask where I was going. Maybe she didn't care, or was deaf.

I think she was deaf because she didn't turn around this time either.

And if one of the men outside asked me where in hell I was going I would tell him, for a walk. Why not a walk? I was born nervous.

I only saw one of them. He sat in a car in an opposite driveway, smoking a cigarette. He didn't make a move, either for or against. Probably nobody had told him anything about a man coming *out* of the house, only the other way. Maybe he was all cued for a cop in uniform to walk up to the front door to ring the bell.

Ten minutes later I reached a main drag and found a taxi.

The cabby liked the trip to Bowline Lake because it was so far. He had been listening to the radio but he turned it off soon after I got into the back seat.

"You live out there, buddy?"

"Yes," I said.

"Where?"

"I'll tell you when we get there."

"The development?"

He was worse than Tooley.

"Yes, the development."

"What part, buddy?"

"The part near the lake."

"Buddy, maybe you ain't been home in a coupla years, but that development is too big for that kinda description."

I took a deep breath and thought that it would be easier talking to Tooley.

"Just go to the north shore highway, where it joins the one coming from town, all right?"

"You don't mind my asking you all these questions, huh?"

"I'm a little tired, is all."

"Because I live out there," the cabby went on. "Because maybe you and me's neighbors."

That would have been all I needed, I thought, but then I thought of something else.

"Is that right?" I said. "Well, well, is that right? Where do you live out there?"

"Bunny Lane. But not the new part, the old part."

"Did you say *Bunny* Lane?"

"Yeah. Why you asking?"

"It's just—I don't think I've ever heard anything quite so cute."

"We think so, too," he said. "We kept that in mind with all the streets."

Then I brought up what I was after. I said, "I'm looking for one of the rural routes."

"Did you say *rural* routes?"

"Yes. Why are you asking?"

"Because we ain't got rural routes, buddy. We got all them cute names."

"But I remember distinctly that the development..."

"You ain't been back a while, have you, buddy? We changed all that. We got all them cute names, I told you."

This was no help in trying to remember what rural route the dead Tooley had mentioned to me.

"Yessir," he told me. "We don't like numbers. There was number two-oh-seven we made..."

"That was a rural route number?"

"I don't know from rural route numbers, I'm talking about them little state highways out our way. Now, there was two-oh-seven got to be Sweetpea Street, three-three-one got to be Donald Duck Drive, eighty-four became Riding Hood Road, even though there was some of us held out for the full name, which is Little Red Riding Hood. Even..."

"Yes, I know that's the full name. I..."

"Even though there's this ordinance says a street sign can't be no longer than twenty-four inches whereas Little Red Riding Hood is a thirty incher any time."

"Hell, yes."

What it came down to, I would have to walk around out there myself and try as best as I could to remember the landmarks the dead Tooley had given me; that he could see the lake, that he could see a great, old elm tree. That wasn't much, except that the place would have to be in the old part of the development, the part which had been there before I had left the scene.

I got out where the lake made a corner, with one highway going on past the development and the other crossing over to follow the lake. After the taxi had gone it was very dark on the highway and the wind unpleasantly cold.

I could hear the lake but I couldn't see it. I could hear the wind in the big trees where the cottages followed the lake, and in the other direction I could see the neat row of lights from the one-family boxes which were lined up in the development. The jog in all that neatness was the two-story building with the Bowline Bar on the ground floor.

I used to walk over from the cottage and get beer there. Or I used to sit in the bar, Saturday afternoons, and watch the bulldozers make overtime and new streets where the new houses were going up one after the other. They were all pretty old houses now. Maybe some of them were even owned free and clear.

I started to walk because I was cold. I think I kept walking for the next half hour because I had no idea what else to do. Find Tooley's old place. Where?

I walked back and forth in the development, once this way because the other direction was too new, once the other way because there were too many cars passing an intersection and I was afraid of being seen. I assumed all that time that I would be able to see the lake if there were daylight, even though I might only see a small sparkle of it, past the corner of someone's garage, on the other side of somebody's yard. I knew where the big elm would have to be, in the direction of the cottages by the lake. There were no other trees in this neighborhood. There were none at all in the development. Had there been a big elm here before the bulldozers came, over seven years ago?

There was a sameness in the straight streets, a sameness in the size of the houses, which made my task shapeless and vast. The dead Tooley, counting white powder in grams, counting money in stacks, making black numbers in ledgers ruled with green lines, and once in a while looking out of a window where he could see the lake and a tree

I felt stupid and helpless. And if I found the house, if I said eeny, meeny, miny, mo, that's it over there, then what?

Was it something in the basement, was it something behind a wall? If it was heroin, would it have to be a big, hefty box, to make them risk a prison break, risk the play on an ignorant man who didn't know what he knew? I wasn't sure if that would be worth their while. A few years of trading would surely have made up for the loss of a box full of heroin, even a hefty one. Did the stuff keep that long?

The frozen slush on the street cracked with dry sounds while I was walking. The wind made my eyes water, because I was going back towards the lake. And I was sweating under my clothes.

Then I stopped. I stopped for a breath and to wipe my eyes, and I noticed that the sweat hadn't been just sheer nervousness. For the last stretch towards the lake I had been going uphill. The street made a gentle sweep down, in back of me, and when I saw a car pass on the highway ahead I noticed the lights going by at eye level. The lake was on the other side.

There wasn't a single place in the development where a man, sitting at a window, could have seen the lake!

I stood there and had one crazy moment of feeling successful. No more walking around, worrying how to tell one house from the other, because there was no such house and I could stop looking.

And everything for the past few days had been through the kindness of Rand, Jessie, Mishkin. And I had a three C's per week job because I was such a hot junior executive.

Something didn't fit.

Then I stood on the highway again and could see the dark mass where the old trees stood by the lake, and I could feel the wind whip at me straight over the lake.

Tooley must have sat by the window in one of three places.

There was the bar. There was a left-over farmhouse. There was a garage.

I stood away from the red and green neon light over the Bowline Bar and could see the room through one of the windows. There were booths and there must be people sitting. There was a bartender walking across with a tray.

The garage had no windows facing the lake, just the big door, which was locked now. I was afraid to walk around the dark building and look into the side windows, but if that had been the dead Tooley's place I imagined he would have to stand on a workbench next to one of the windows to look out at his view. The thought was ridiculous.

If he had lived in the farmhouse, was there a window whose view of the lake wasn't blocked by the bar? Or was there a place in back of the tap-room where a man could have sat by the window—

I put my collar up and walked. The nervousness made me short of breath.

The farmhouse, dark now, was turned to look across the fields when there had been fields. The bar cut off the view to the lake.

I crossed the parking space in front of the bar and saw a man looking out at me from the big window which had a curtain half way across. Maybe he wasn't looking at me at all, but I got hot and cold with the doubt.

I started to curse, and it got me over the hump. I started breathing again when I got to the corner and then I turned there because I had to know if there was a room in back of the bar where a man could see the lake and a big tree.

I got a safe feeling of blackness once I had turned the corner and even the sound of the ice on the ground was a friendly sound.

Then the light hit me like a fist, and if they did not see me they would see my shadow jump large across the whole brick wall and don't run, I kept chattering, don't run—

The car stopped with a lot of noise, the doors opened and there was a great deal of laughter, and before the headlights went off somebody called, "It's inside, peasant, and all automatic."

They laughed and went away. I walked like an automaton, which was the only way I could walk any more.

There were three windows. One in the kitchen, I thought, and it looked out to the development. One in the toilet, but that didn't count. The third one, to judge by the curtains, was a room where somebody might live. It looked at the back of the garage.

Then I wanted to leave again. How important was this harebrained romp by the lake, with Rand back in town—suspicious; with the man in the bar—suspicious; with an all-state alarm— Well, unless I wanted to go out of my mind while Rand and Tooley and all of them picked my brains like a flock of vultures, this little trip was very important.

I had to go into the bar, with the lights on and everyone looking. I had to talk to the bartender and hope that he didn't remember me. I did hope he would remember if there had been another building around, something which had been torn down; or if the garage had been built recently. If that were the case, then Tooley's fine view had come from the backroom window.

Why risk it? Because in the morning I would have to know something. If I turned out useless to Rand and his bosses, I didn't think they would want me alive.

CHAPTER 19

The man was still at the window and looking over the half curtain and he and I stood opposite each other for a while, he looking out, I looking in. He had a tall glass in his hand and he had trouble keeping his eyes open.

I had known the bartender pretty good, summertimes, but the one behind the counter was somebody else. I went in.

I had never been in the Bowline during the winter. An oil stove was rigged up in the middle and there was holly over the mirror behind the bar. There was no loud summer crowd in the small place, no sunburned week-enders buying cartons of beer. In the winter the place was a neighborhood bar, something settled, familiar, and not very exciting.

I sat down at the bar, with my back to the booths, and looked in the mirror. I waited for the shock of recognizing somebody even though I knew that the three couples in the booths were strangers to me. I had looked at them when I had come in. Then the bartender came around to his side of the counter and I had my shock. He was young and must have been the son of the owner because he looked a little bit like Eddy who used to sell me the beer. But he wasn't Eddy. I had seen that through the window. It had still come off with a shock. I was born nervous.

"Something?" said the kid.

"A shot. Double shot, please."

"Any special..."

"Just double."

He poured it out and asked if it was getting colder outside and I said, yes, like hell freezing over.

"Why don't you stand by the stove for a while?" he asked me.

I was dying to stand by the stove for a while, to get warm all the way through, to go straight to bed, to sleep far away—

"I'll have one more of these," I said, and swallowed the first one.

"You like that better than the stove, huh?" and he poured the second.

I didn't tell him to keep his cracks to himself, as I wanted. I would have to sit here a while and I would need conversation.

"Does it ever get warm here, this neck of the woods?"

"Woods?" He had pride in his neighborhood.

"This, uh, area," I told him.

"You should see it in the summer," he said. "We got a resort here."

"Gee. That's nice. Must be nice living here. Not having to come out for the week end."

"That's right," he said.

We weren't doing too well. I was talking more than he.

"I wish I could see that lake daytimes," I said. "Must be nice."

It was now his turn to say that you could see the lake from here, and the damnedest big elm, and that they used to have an old boarder in the backroom, watching that scene.

"You a stranger around here?" he asked me.

That was better than nothing. It was better than hearing him say, for instance, "You're no stranger around here, are you, Mister Gallivan?"

"Never been here before."

"Where you from?"

"South. All the way south."

"I thought everybody had a tan down there. Florida, I mean."

"I'm not from Florida. I'm from Texas."

"Is that right? Hey, if you wanna meet a landsman of yours, you see that redhaired feller with the pretty girl there, the last booth there? I bet he'd like..."

"No, never mind. I..."

"I bet he'd be tickled to death, you know that? Only Texan around here I know of, and always complaining nobody speaks his kinda language and so on, just in fun, you understand, but always..."

"Please. I really don't feel like it. Another shot, though. This time single."

He came back with the bottle and looked at me before tilting it.

"Come to think of it, you wouldn't be speaking his language anyways. You don't talk like a Texan anyways."

"Thank you," I said and picked up the drink.

"How come you don't talk like a Texan?"

"Because I went to college," I said.

He hadn't gone to college either, I noticed. His face pinched up a little, the same as when I had said 'neck of the woods.' I was doing everything wrong.

I bought cigarettes and offered him one. He didn't smoke. I asked him if I might buy him a drink, and he said he could get them for nothing. I laughed about that. I made it good and hearty, hoping to drag him into the spirit. He smiled a little but without paying attention to it.

"Tell me," I asked him, "you run this place all by yourself?"

"No. I'm helping my father."

"Fancy that," I said. "The way you handle this thing, I would never have thought—you know—"

This time he smiled good.

"When he's on vacation, I run it all by myself."

"Fancy that. Yessir. Is he on vacation now?"

"No. Why? You a salesman? Because I do the buying when it comes to items like chips, pretzels..."

"No, no. I wouldn't have asked for your father at all, in that case."

"Why did you?"

Why did I. To hear that I was safe from his father whose name was Eddy and from whom I used to buy beer seven years ago.

"Because of the weather. You know."

"Oh. Naw. He's sitting home."

"Ah. Watching TV. That's good."

He looked at the clock on the wall and looked doubtful.

"Almost done now," he said.

I didn't listen to that because I had finally found my in. We would now talk real estate.

"You live in that development out there?"

"No. We been here longer than that. We live in that farmhouse next door."

I got nervous for no other reason than the thought that Eddy was sitting next door.

"I noticed that nice old house. How come the development didn't swallow that up?"

"Dad wouldn't sell, is all."

"I like that. I like that kind of attitude," I told him. "But there must have been plenty of houses around here, old ones that got torn down."

"Some."

"Where?"

Maybe I had sounded too eager because he looked at me for a moment, but then it turned out to be something else. "I was just thinking, you got the time?"

I looked up at the clock on the wall, but he said, "No, I mean do *you* have the time. That one's off, lately."

The clock was fifteen minutes off.

"I better call before he blows his stack. Twelve sharp I should call him, he said."

"That's customer service," I said, because anything for a little joke now to keep the good feeling between us and so we wouldn't get interrupted. I found out in a second bow much I needed a little joke.

"Customer hell," he said. "The old man wants me to call him. He's got to do books yet."

He pointed to the books next to the register and then he went to the phone.

"Wait a minute!"

He looked at me, he waited—which was what I had asked—and I caved and could think only of running.

I drank my drink while he called his father and I sat there because I didn't want to run.

He came back and said, "He'll be right over. Another one for you?"

"No."

I don't know where the strength comes from sometimes; because it has nothing to do with thinking. I said no to the drink, got off the stool, and said, "Got to go. Too bad about all those old houses they tore down."

"I don't think so," he said. "I think the new ones are prettier. When I get married..."

"Think of the view they had. Those new, little flat ones can't even look over the rise."

"They didn't have any view. They were over that way, where the high school is now."

"Oh. Nothing torn down around here, huh?"

He shook his head and looked at the door. So did I. A man came in with a wool cap down on his forehead and he went to the stove. He nodded at everybody and warmed himself. He wasn't Eddy. When he unbuttoned his overcoat I could see the uniform jacket and the badge on one side. Village cop.

"When they don't tear 'em down they build 'em up," I heard myself say. The voice was strange and only the effort behind it was really mine. "Like when they put up that garage next to your place. Shame how that cut off your view."

"What makes you think that?" said the kid. He was tapping beer for the constable.

"It looks newer."

The kid looked at the door again and this time the man who came in was wearing a wool cap, too, but nothing else for the street, just a suit and a sweater under his jacket. He was in house shoes.

Eddy had gotten fat, but I recognized him.

"No," said the kid to me. "That garage was here before we built the bar."

I didn't listen to all of it. I was trying to count money out on the bar and I tried not to show my face.

I put the money down on the bar and when I stepped back Eddy was looking at me.

"Hi, there," he said. He had a nice, friendly smile.

"Hi, there."

He nodded and I nodded and then I went to the door. Eddy picked up his books behind the bar and I left. I didn't start to shake 'til I was out, but then it stayed with me all the way back to town.

CHAPTER 20

There never had been a house with a view, and there never had been a view from the backroom at the bar.

I told the taxi to stop, I would walk the rest of the way. I could see the boarding house in the middle of the block because the car which was parked there made it easy to spot. A white cloud of exhaust was rolling out of the tail pipe. The man was keeping warm, at any rate. Perhaps he was even asleep. There would be another one at the back of the house, and there should have been one at this end of the street.

None of that made much of an impression. I was tired, because it was two o'clock. I was tired, because I was back now without knowing a thing.

I lit a cigarette and walked to the boarding house. I looked at the car on the other side of the street and the driver was there, sleeping. There were two others in the back seat. They were sleeping too. That simple, and that tired.

I went upstairs and found my room. The light was on. Rand was in one of the chairs and he watched me come in.

"Where you been?"

I dragged on my cigarette and then I closed the door.

"For a walk."

I exhaled and Rand's eyes followed the smoke. Then he looked back at me.

"Are you out of your mind?"

"I'm tired."

He got up and went to the connecting door. Before he left he stopped there and said, "Gallivan. Don't do that again."

Then he left.

The change was clear enough the next morning. Rand watched me just by being around. He talked less than usual but he was not a blank. He was always there. He woke me up and said it was time to go. Then he left the door open between his room and mine and while I got dressed he sat in his chair, smoking. When I came back from the toilet he was out in the hall. He had a tray with some breakfast things and we had them in his room. Then we went downstairs. Tooley's car was in the drive, pulled back so it was out of sight from the street. Tooley was behind the wheel. The air was cold and the sun was coming up.

"Sleep good?" said Tooley.

Rand said nothing and I said yes, it had been a fine night.

"Rand don't look like he slept good," said Tooley.

"You sit next to Tooley," said Rand, "and I'll be in back." But when he opened the door Tooley turned around.

"I got a call for you," he said. "You should call back."

"Who?"

"Mishkin. And pretty important, he said."

"But he didn't say what?"

"To keep in touch, he said. You should call early."

"To hell with Mishkin," and Rand sat down in the back.

"But he said..."

"Did it sound important?" Rand was ill-tempered.

"Well, he didn't say anything. He just said what I said and..."

"Drive," said Rand. "Bowline Lake. And I'm going along."

It sounded like a threat to me, though that could all have been nerves. But he sat behind me—he'd never done that before, either—and I could feel his eyes on the back of my neck all the time.

When we got out to the country the sun was up and the cold air clear and brilliant. Tooley said how nice it was out here and, "Leave it to my brother—when he was alive, I mean—to pick the nicest spot."

I didn't take that up because there was nothing to say. The dead Tooley had never lived out here and if I should tell them so, that would be that. The farce of going out to that high school now, to count prospective customers for the trade, it wasn't even ghoulish any more but just plain nonsense. And if I didn't play it, I'd be dead.

"Recognize the place?" said Rand.

I couldn't see him behind me, but I could feel him. For him, there was no more nonsense now.

"Yeah," I said. "There's the lake. I recognize it."

"Good enough to find your way around?"

"Sure. It's all very familiar. Over there, in the reeds, used to be the best fishing."

It sounded smart aleck, but I didn't feel that way. I was getting depressed.

"What parts out here are new?" Rand wanted to know. Then he would know where not to look for Tooley's old place. I knew the reasoning. I'd gone through it myself the night before.

"The development's new back that way. Here, by the lake road, it's old."

"By old you mean it was here when you were around?"

When Tooley was around, he meant. He was getting pretty direct.

"Yeah. For instance, right around that bar there."

We all looked at the bar. It wasn't open yet.

"Didn't you tell me," said Rand, "that you and Tooley had sort of the same view, you from your cottage and he from his place?"

"Yes," I said. "I think so."

And I knew that it didn't make a damn bit of difference. I even wished I could tell Rand where the dead Tooley used to hole up, tell him in the same zig-zag way in which he put his questions, but plain enough to tell him what he wanted to know, and to leave me out of it. I would have been done then. They might even have let me go.

But the landmarks didn't match. I didn't know enough. We went by the bar and all I knew was that the right view would have to be out of the back window, if the garage weren't in the way. If Tooley could have looked through the garage, or over the garage, then everything might

Christ—he *could* look over the garage!

The bar had a second story. Blind windows, one broken, but all of them high enough to look at the lake, at the big elms by the lake, right across the roof of the garage, and that must have been the place, that had to be the place.

We passed and I swiveled around to look at the bar with the second story. Why in hell hadn't I thought of that before, last night, just a few hours earlier, when I had been in the bar? That had been the right time to ask the right questions.

"What you looking at, Gallivan?"

"Oh. The bar, Rand."

"You know that bar?"

"I used to buy beer there. What I mean, a good place to stay away from, now. Maybe they could recognize—"

I didn't bother to finish, because Rand wasn't listening. He turned to look out the back window. He moved his head back and forth so that I could tell what he was doing. He was looking at the windows of the second story and then he looked to see which way they faced, what a man sitting behind one of those windows might see.

"Tooley ever tell you about that bar?" he asked without turning.

"No."

"Or how you and him might have been sitting in the same place there, drinking beer, and not knowing each other?"

"I don't think so," I said. "I never heard him say that."

And that would have been the time to let it drop that, yes, Tooley knew the place, Tooley lived in the place, Tooley said he had stashed a fortune on that second story—anything like that to give them their clue and to leave me alone.

Except I suddenly couldn't do it. I'd give it away to them and they wouldn't need me any more. Once they didn't need me any more, I was finished.

The way I had thought of it when I first knew what was up, that was the only way. I would have to get there first. What kept me alive now was that they didn't think I knew what they wanted. What might keep me alive for a much longer time was to have what they wanted, whatever was up there, behind the windows.

"I got a place that way," said Tooley and nodded to the side where the cottages were. "And there."

I would have to shake them once more. Just once more, and this time knowing where I was going.

"Income property," Tooley was saying. "Them cottage grounds are a gold mine."

They were nothing. The good part of the lake was around the bend. But I was sure he had bought land closer by, just as he said, hoping to catch a whiff of his dead brother's old place.

"Drive through there once," said Rand. "Gallivan might like that, for old time's sake."

"No. I just as soon..."

"Drive through there once," said Rand. "I want to know where Gallivan used to live."

Rand was pressed for time, too. He didn't seem to give a damn any more if I got spotted.

"Turn your collar up, Gallivan."

We turned towards the lake. It was a dirt road where people in shorts walked around during the summer, where the lake showed through the bushes on one side, where cheap little cottages were all over the place.

"I got me that one," said Tooley. "And two over there. Good income."

Chickenfeed for a man peddling dope. But what he owned was all in a pattern. It was the wrong pattern, but they must have thought, buying here, that the dead Tooley might have lived in the oldest part of the summer colony. We drove by under the big elms, the ones the dead Tooley used to see from his window. There was undisturbed snow on all the closed cottages, white in the sun, and with blue shadows.

"Where was your place, Gallivan?"

I pointed that way but it didn't look promising to Rand and Tooley. It was too far away and in the wrong direction.

"I don't think my brother ever lived thataway," said Tooley.

They were getting more and more careless. Even Rand seemed to think so.

"He's sentimental about his brother," he said. "He wants to visit the shrine."

Tooley didn't like that remark and they had a few words about it, but then Rand cut that short and said we should drive back to the highway. Tooley turned and went slowly. There was more talk, with Rand guiding it, about who used to live there, in that cottage; who used to rent here, while I knew this neighborhood; also, which houses were owned. And then when we crossed into the Bowline development, which streets were already built up seven years ago and which ones were newer. We got very close to the bar again. Somebody was shoveling snow in front.

"They haven't got as nice a view from here as the people in those cottages," said Rand.

This being daytime he spotted right away that you couldn't see the lake from the development.

"Except from the garage," said Tooley.

"Or that bar. It's got a second story."

It had taken Rand no time at all. It had taken me hours.

"I'd live in a cottage," said Rand. "Like Gallivan did. What was your view, Gallivan, from the cottage?"

"Just the lake. But from the other direction."

"What do you mean, other direction?"

I was damn glad he was in back of me and not watching anything but my neck.

"I mean," I told him, "the other direction from this development here."

Then I turned a little, to catch a glimpse of Rand. He was looking at the bar.

"I think old Tooley and me must have lived pretty close, come to think of it. He must have lived on the other side of the lake," I kept prompting.

"What's built there," said Tooley, "is just five years old."

But Rand didn't answer. We rolled up towards the highway and were heading for the bar again. I was biting my lip and felt a little hysterical.

"Drive right by," said Rand. "And don't look that way."

"You mean the..."

"Just shut up and drive."

Then I saw what he meant.

There was a car pulled up next to the bar. The front door of the place had opened and Eddy was there with another man. They didn't know each other too well because they shook hands and were very polite. The other man shoved a notebook into his pocket and went to his car. Then he went out of view.

"Did you know him?" asked Rand.

I almost answered. I was sure he wanted to know if I knew Eddy and then, when had I seen him last, or something like that. But just in time Tooley answered.

"I'm not sure," said Tooley. "But he did look cop."

"Did you see his license plate?"

"Just a little. I think the letters checked though. I think he was cop."

"That's all we need," Rand mumbled. "That's all."

"It's a long chance he'd even look at us," said Tooley. "He's most likely checking out a complaint about noise or about serving to minors. You guys just outa stir are too nervous, all the time."

"I didn't say he was looking for us," said Rand. He sounded plenty sharp and ill-tempered. "I just spotted him and told you to keep driving."

"I wasn't going to stop there for a beer, for chrissake."

Rand didn't answer. I hoped the two would have a quarrel and forget about me because I couldn't think straight with Rand sitting in back of me and most likely watching the way I breathed.

Because maybe that cop in civilian clothes wasn't there to check on the liquor laws. Maybe he had come out because Eddy had called him. Eddy might have remembered me—

"Listen," said Tooley. "Let's take a look at that school, huh, Rand? We're out here anyways, and the way Gallivan talked about that school yesterday..."

"All right. Go ahead."

So appearances weren't gone altogether and Tooley wasn't going to let a good thing go by just because Rand had been sent down with some harebrained thing about his dead brother and a dumb con like me. He was a business man, after all, wanting to broaden his market.

He turned into the new part of the development and where the street widened we could see the school.

"Nice and modern," said Tooley.

Rand wasn't much interested because he said it was eight-thirty and counting students going in at this hour wouldn't give a good average anyway.

"They start at nine, wintertime," said Tooley.

He parked the car so that the low, angular building lay to one side. The school had big windows and there were paper cut-outs taped to the glass. Tree leaves, stars, candles, all different colors. Then some students crossed the street and went into the building.

"Lookit them pretty ski pants," said Tooley. "You ever see such colors?"

"They're too young," said Rand.

"Yeah."

More came. Their feet made a dry sound in the snow, and they all had red cheeks. The sun was very bright and the air like glass.

"Don't bother counting," said Rand.

"I never touch nothing less than fourteen," said Tooley. "Don't work."

"This is the grade school," said Rand.

"Big like that? Let's sit a while and maybe something older comes by. Then we count."

"There's a teacher," said Rand.

"No market."

We sat and watched the children.

In a while Tooley rolled down his window and when the next bunch of kids came by he called to them and one little girl came up to the car.

"Where's the older kids, honey?" Tooley asked her.

"We're the older ones. The kindergarten is..."

"No, no, no, honey. You ain't old enough. I mean the real old ones."

"You mean the high school?" Every time she talked her breath came out white and then disappeared. She had a sweet face with big eyes. Tooley would not look at her with any interest for another eight years, maybe, or at best six.

"Yeah. I mean the high school."

"You drive around that way and they are sort of in back of us."

"Thank you, honey."

He reached into his pocket but by the time he had come up with the quarter the girl had turned and was going across the street.

"What the hell," said Tooley. "No use spoiling 'em," and put the quarter back in his pocket.

I said, "Besides, she won't save it 'til she's fourteen, anyway," and he laughed about it as if I had made a joke.

Then he drove away slowly, because there were so many children crossing the street.

CHAPTER 21

We could see the high school right after the turn, and that looked much better to Tooley. He kept saying, yessir, yessir, all research and action now and to hell with Rand and that fluky business. There were high school students on foot and by car, and most of them the right age.

"I go a lot by the hairdos," said Tooley. "You ever notice them funny hairdos on some of the boys?"

"Don't think like the movies," said Rand from the back seat. "Since when do they need a ducktail to get themselves hooked?"

Tooley stopped the car and would have liked to argue the point but he wanted to count sheep. He had two mechanical counters and gave me one of them. I would count sheep at the near door and he would count sheep going in by the far door.

"Try to leave out the one's under fourteen, fifteen, Gallivan. There's no point in..."

"I know. You explained that."

Rand sat in back and I could feel his impatience. He said that all this was nonsense, and, for instance, the kids that came with cars went in through a back door and we couldn't count them from here. If this hadn't been so macabre, sitting quietly in the car, counting Tooley's junkies who didn't know it yet, I would have felt the same way as Rand. The sun was sharp on the snow and after a while I hardly looked any more. I could think of no way out of this sick farce. I could think of no way to get to the bar again, as long as Rand was sitting behind me.

A car tried to stop next to us, didn't make it because of the snow, and with wheels spinning came sliding back. The one who was driving was the same man who had parked in front of the house when I had come out during the night. Rand had his window down already and was waiting. When the driver had his down he first complained about how long it had taken him to find us in the neighborhood.

"Get to it," said Rand.

"You was supposed to call back. The sanatorium."

"Mishkin again?"

"No. Hell, no. The other one. The wheel."

I didn't know who the wheel was but I knew now that Mishkin, like Rand, was just one of the hands. And Rand didn't sound irritable any more, or unfriendly. He seemed a little bit worried.

"He say what he wanted?"

"Yeah. You. And why you didn't call back."

Rand thought for a moment. Then he said, "Call him back for me, will you? Tell him I got nothing yet but maybe..."

"Nix, Rand. Nix. You call him back. He wants you."

Rand got out of the car and just turned around once.

"You stay here, you and Gallivan," he said to Tooley. "Don't make a move 'til I..."

"They'll all be inside that school," Tooley said. "Another fifteen minutes or less and there won't be no point..."

"You wait here," said Rand. "That's all I'm telling you."

He got into the other car and drove off, Tooley made a sound like a Bronx cheer and forgot to count.

"He's gonna get the shaft so he takes it out on me. You notice that, Gallivan?"

"I did, Tooley. And I don't think you should take it."

"Yeah, I don't think so either." He counted a while, because there was a late bunch going up to the door, and then he said, "To hell with him," but nothing else came after that.

"We ought to drive around some more," I told Tooley. "We ought to give the whole neighborhood a good once-over, Tooley, and get an idea of the income group. Like the shopping center can give an idea, the type houses in this part of the section, the kind of people that sit in the restaurants, bars, that kind of thing."

"Hell, yes," he said. "We'll do that. Yessir, Gallivan, you got a business head on your shoulders. How many you got counted off on your clicker?"

I looked and said eighty-six.

"I got hundred and sixty. What's hundred and sixty plus eighty-six? I can't figure so good without..."

"Two-forty-six. But we ought to..."

"Just a minute, just a minute. Now let's say we make that round with the ones we didn't catch and say three hundred. More maybe, because of the ones home with a cold. We start out with reefers, let's say three to four hundred a week, after one or two months of good work—we got this down to a science, Gallivan, let me tell you—and a little junk here and there. Once in with the reefers there's no problem finding the stickers among them. I'd say, after half a year of working it easy..."

"Listen, Tooley. You can figure all that out at home, nice and comfortable. We..."

"Wait a minute, wait a minute. Just a few decks to start, two months from now. Just a few at a buck for a teaser, and after three to six months, let me figure this, after three to six months we should have, at four bucks, a fin maybe, we should have..."

"You can't figure it in your head, Tooley. You need paper and pencil.

Come on. Let's go."

"Yeah. You're right." He put the counter into his pocket and started the car. "Remember that number to start with, Gallivan. Was that three hundred round?"

"Yeah. Three hundred round. Drive, Tooley."

He drove. He kept mumbling and muttering about all his new, future customers, about how long it would take to pull in an extra thousand a week with no extra overhead, happy thoughts by the look on his face, and we kept driving around through the neighborhood. I directed him and he just went along, and in a while I could see the bar again, at the end of the street.

"We'll stop there," I said. "Good place to get an idea of the type of customer around here."

"Huh?"

"The bar, Tooley. You can borrow a napkin and a pencil in there and do your figuring. I'll have a conversation with the bartender there."

"Wait a minute. Didn't you say they might know you in there?"

"You go first. You tell me if there's a big, blond man, getting bald, and if not I can come in safely enough. Besides, it's been over seven years."

He stopped the car and said yessir, yessir, a few times, liking the way the day's work was going. I don't think he gave a damn about Rand's problem. That would help.

I let him go ahead and he looked into the bar, through the window. He didn't call me when he was through but came back.

"Only thing is," he said, "I don't like the customer in there. I'm not sure, but he looks cop."

"Crap," I said, "not twice in a day."

"Maybe just liquor trouble."

I didn't know what to do. Maybe just Gallivan trouble?

"Tooley," I said, "go on in and listen."

And if he heard them mention my name, at least I wouldn't have walked in on it. I could still explain it to Tooley then, that naturally they'd ask around in my old neighborhood, seeing I had just busted jail, that a criminal always wants to go back to the place where he's been most happy, and so forth.

He went across the street. He hesitated once when a car passed on the highway and when it let out a screech with the brakes. But it wasn't a cop car. It was two-tone. I got out and stood by the hood, watching Tooley. He went across the street and then he looked over again, to the highway.

The car came fast, and I had to think of the high school kids we had been counting, because of the hopped-up driving the car was doing. It started to slither, trying to brake, and kept bumping the curb. Rand was out of the car before it had stopped.

If he said, "I thought I told you to stay by that school—"

He said nothing. He was white in the face and when he was close enough he swung back-handed and the knuckles slammed into the side of my nose.

I fell because of the slick snow. I got my feet under me and then I was going to jump Rand and tear off his head. I'd had it. I didn't care what it meant for the moment, I just wanted to beat the insides out of Rand.

I saw him step back. Not that it would help him. He even had his hands in his pockets, as always, and I was up now and going at him.

"Get in the car," he said.

For that I'd hit him a little bit longer. I pushed away from the fender, for leverage.

"Get in the car, you sonofabitch. You've been spotted!"

That stopped me.

CHAPTER 22

I could sit in the back again, and Rand, in front, didn't even bother to look back. He told Tooley to drive like he was normal and to stay away from the town.

"To the sanatorium," he said.

"You mean just drive you there, don't you?" Tooley was back to normal. He was afraid of Rand or whomever Rand worked for.

"Just drive there," said Rand. "The conference is for Gallivan."

"Mishkin?" I asked him.

"No. Not Mishkin."

I didn't think he was in the mood to explain any more. He was tense and jumpy, and I got a picture of Rand which hadn't showed before, behind his blandness. I decided that Rand could get very ugly.

We drove awhile without talking and it was worse now than before, the not knowing, the little pawn in the big game, but now with a crisis.

And what did I have? I didn't know until I knew what they had. Except that I knew where the dead Tooley used to live. They didn't have that, yet.

"Who spotted him?" Tooley asked.

"Some jerk in town. I don't know the details."

"Was that what the phone call was all about?"

"Yuh."

"They knew at the sanatorium?"

"If nothing else works around here," said Rand, "at least the pipeline still works. Some citizen called into central and he used to know Gallivan. And he thinks he's seen Gallivan." He didn't turn around, but he said, "You listening, Gallivan?"

"Thank you for saving me at the last minute," I said. "With that nose breaker."

"Don't make jokes, Gallivan. There's no more jokes, from now on."

"I can't figure," said Tooley, "when somebody saw him."

"Funny, isn't it?" said Rand. I didn't see his face when he said it, but he sounded mean as hell.

"So whoever saw him," said Tooley, "musta seen you at the same time. Or me even!"

"I'm not worried about you, Tooley," said Rand. "You're getting to be dirt around here."

"And you? They spot you means nothing maybe?"

"Yeah. Nothing. I'm not known around here," Rand told him. "Drive slower."

"I'm driving..."

"Today," said Rand, "you drive twenty-five when it says twenty-five. Or minus three if it says minus three. All right, Tooley?"

"All right, all right—"

With caution and detours we got to the park and the big, white house by late afternoon. It was getting dark, the half light washing out everything which wasn't either white or black. The trees were black, the house like a large mausoleum.

We pulled up to the side where the big elevator let out. There were no windows on that side of the house. The patients, if they were the kind who looked out of the window, would have no idea what came and went on this side of the house. And like me, they would have no idea what went on at the top floor of their hospital.

This time there was one of those carts in the elevator, one to wheel bodies. It rolled a little when the elevator started up. Rand stopped it with one hand and kept looking up at the ceiling.

I wanted to nod at the cart and say, "Someone's expected?" and then Rand would say, "Yes. You." Silly jokes like that kept going through my head.

Upstairs was nobody, like always, except this time it felt worse. We went to the place where the corridors came together and where the chairs stood and the plant.

"Wait here," said Rand.

I sat down and kept my coat on. To take off the coat would have interrupted the waiting. I was too anxious to do anything but what I was told. Later, I knew, something would happen, something would come, and I would need all the energy I had. Don't waste it now, don't waste energy taking off coats. Sit still, save it.

Rand went through one of the doors, into the room where I had been with Mishkin. Rand came back out after a while and sat down, too.

"We just wait," he said, before I had opened my mouth. Rand took his overcoat off and smoked. He crossed his legs one way and then the other. I sat inside my overcoat like in a cocoon. In a while Rand got up again.

"You stay here," he said. "Don't go away again, huh?" Then he left.

It got darker and nobody turned on any lights. I saw one empty chair, closed doors, the plant. I particularly disliked the plant. Once I heard a door, feet, a door. I got up to look down the corridor. There was no one around.

I walked a little. Back to the elevator, and there was a man this time, smoking by the window. He looked at me 'til I left again. I went the other way, sweating now, and there was a staircase I had never seen before, a swinging door in the corridor and a staircase behind that, and a man sitting on the first step. I didn't go through the door and the man on the step didn't see me. Not that it made any difference.

I walked back and I took my overcoat off. I didn't do it because I was hot but because suddenly I couldn't stand the weight. Then I saw Jessie.

It was dark in the corridor but I saw the girl. Then she disappeared through a door.

The hall where the plant stood was empty. I left my overcoat on the chair—to let Rand know that I was still here—and then I went back to the door. It didn't occur to me to knock.

Because it was dark in the room I could only make out her shape, bent, near a chair, with the window behind her. She had one leg on the chair and that, too, was ordinary enough, this being her room, and perhaps she was straightening a stocking. But her movement was pure fright.

She whirled around. There was a sound from her throat, and then she stood very still against the light from the window.

"You—" she said.

"Jessie?"

"Get out!"

It was like a violent hiss, and if I could have seen her face I would have known if it was anger, fright, what—

"Jessie," I said and walked to her, "I just wanted—"

I was close enough then to see her face—a mask of cold rage. Then I made the wrong move. I reached for her arms, and she slapped my hand out of the way. When she made that violent movement she dropped it.

I knew what it was without being able to see. When she bent down for it I yanked her back. There was a night table next to the window and I reached for the lamp. I got it lit while she clawed at my face. When the light snapped on we both drew back from each other and looked down at the floor, at the same thing.

It wasn't a filthy eyedropper, with needle taped to the end, but a good, ten cc syringe and the needle had probably been sterile before she had dropped it to the floor.

I reached for it and she kicked at my hand. I held her leg and she hit me in the neck. Then she jerked her leg free and all the time I was straightening up she was hitting me hard on the head and the shoulder. She got in one good smack on my face and then I got her hands out of the way. I hit her face, twice I think, and she fell back on the bed, next to the window.

I went back to the syringe and stepped on it. The glass ground into the carpet and there was a wet stain.

When I went to her again, where she sat on the bed, she was somebody else.

"Jimmy," she said, "I'm sorry I hit you. Really, I'm sorry."

Her eyes looked awfully big and she took my hands. The wrong note was her voice, much too fast.

"Don't worry about that, Jessie. I'm worried about something quite different."

"I know, Jimmy. You've been reading the papers and you see some horrible thing, some gizmo apparition that's called an addict. You see that, don't you, Jimmy? And then you look at me and you say, poor, poor Jessie. And such a nice girl—"

She waited, looking at me, and then I said yes, I was thinking something like that. She smiled a warm smile and shook her head. She closed her eyes when she did that and then opened them again, big and soft.

"It isn't like that at all, Jimmy. Really."

I had to look away for a moment because the girl was getting to me. She had her voice much more under control so that it matched the look in her eyes.

"It's true, Jimmy. Look at me. Do I look like a—a junkie?"

"No," I said. "You don't, Jessie."

She took a deep breath, a relaxing sound, and then she stroked my cheek.

"But I don't know what a junkie looks like," I told her.

Her face seemed to drop off and another one jumped into place, hard, sharp like a weasel.

"You smoke, don't you, Gallivan? Did you ever try going without for a day, did you, Gallivan? You know how it feels, don't you? You can't stand it. It's not worth it, that state of craving the drag, and what's a cigarette, this one cigarette, that sort of thing, isn't it, Gallivan?"

"Yes. It's something like that. But..."

"But nothing, Jimmy." She put her hand on my shoulder and she looked entirely different again. I began to wonder who was who and which was which. "But nothing, Jimmy, because I'm not that way. Here, Jimmy, I'm not excited, worked up. Here." And she took my hand and put it under her breast. "You feel how slowly the heart beats there, Jimmy?" She smiled at me and said, "Or here," and put my other hand to her neck, so I could feel the pulse there. And she had moved her arm so that she held my other hand where it was, close by her breast.

"Jessie—" I started, but she wasn't through.

"I admit it, Jimmy. I had it bad once. Really. But do you know I shook it and there hasn't been horse, or tea, or anything like that for three whole years, Jimmy?"

I think I believed her. I was startled by her sudden use of that slang but the way she looked at me, the calm voice, how we sat together, I believed what she said.

"So you see, Jimmy, it isn't the same as with that cigarette you're trying to skip for one day. Nothing like that at all, really. I've had nothing for all this long time." Then she shrugged and looked very off-handed. "So this," and she nodded at the floor where the stain was and the broken syringe, "that's not anything, really."

"Good, Jessie. Good."

"Because I'm not hooked."

"I believe you." I took out my cigarettes and lit one for her. I put it in her mouth and then lit one for myself. "But you were hooked once?"

"Yes. Then I shook it."

"You remember how it started?"

"Started?" She dragged hard on the cigarette and let most of the smoke come out without having inhaled.

"Wasn't there that one jolt, two maybe, which didn't matter at all? The one before you got hooked?"

She took the cigarette out of her mouth and paper got stuck. She bit at her lip.

"So that you got hooked on the ones which didn't matter?"

She got up from the bed with quite a bounce.

"You sonofabitch," she said. "Get out!"

"No."

She threw her head back and laughed at the ceiling but when she looked down again her face was sharp, almost pointy.

"What are you going to do," she said, "beat me?"

"Yes, Jessie. I might do that."

That got her for a moment and before she got any further I said, "You remember so well about the ones that didn't matter, like that one there. Do you remember about the others, when you tried shaking the monkey?"

"I told you I went through all that. I said..."

"But right now you're not remembering. About the one like a cigarette you can't have. About that, only worse."

She puffed hard and went to the window. But she didn't turn away.

"I've only read about it, Jessie, but isn't there that point where it's like claws in your guts, in your brains, in every big and small muscle? And then like a big, wonderful breath that unlimbers the cramp everywhere, when you get the jolt—*only it doesn't last?*"

"You're a pretty good talker, Gallivan."

She wasn't. She used a flip sentence but it didn't come out that way. It came out with fear.

"First time I met you, Jessie, you said only a junkie thinks he can make forever. You must know about that. Is it true?"

I got up when she didn't answer and walked to her. The cigarette was down to a stump.

"You remember how it doesn't work, don't you, Jessie?"

I pulled her close and held her head against me.

"And the reason you remember it now is because you're not hooked. Like you said you weren't, Jessie. That's why that jolt on the floor there is nothing. That's why you can take a deep breath now and nothing else needed."

I felt her take a deep breath and then let it out, carefully. She talked very low.

"It's all right now. But a minute from now?"

"You did it for all those years. What happened?"

"Just let me stand like this for a while," she said.

I had my arms around her and stroked her back.

"That's what helps," she said. "Standing like this."

"I won't go away."

She made a dry sound, like the start of a laugh.

"How free are you, Gallivan?"

"Yuh. That was a funny thing for me to say."

I felt her nod, and then we said nothing for a while.

"It worked for three years, and then what happened?"

She moved away from me and then she walked the length of the room. She started talking from the other end.

"I got hooked once and was a pusher. I was a pretty important pusher because for a longer while than most I didn't really come apart. I was a smart, hooked pusher."

"And then?"

"It doesn't happen very often," she said, "but I took the cure and it worked. That impressed them."

"Them?"

"Yes, them. Like the ones on this floor. The businessmen. Because I had been such a good worker and now clean to boot, because of that I stayed on and they liked it. I know an awful lot about them. With a junkie that doesn't matter, but I was clean."

"You spent a dirty three years."

"Yes. I did, Gallivan."

"But it worked well enough to keep you clear of the needle, all that time."

"Give me a cigarette, Gallivan."

She came over and I gave her one. I sat down on the bed and she on a chair.

"It didn't work well enough," she said, "or else I wouldn't have tried that," and she nodded at the stain.

"What happened?"

"What happened?" and she shrugged at the smoke drifting off. Then, like an afterthought, "The other night happened."

"What did you say?"

"Sounds stupid, doesn't it?"

"The party? What I did on the porch?"

"Well," she said down to her lap, "not that important. It just capped it."

I got up and went over to her. It was awkward bending down to her and not knowing where to touch her, or whether to touch her, but wanting to show a lot of warmth.

"My God, Jessie, don't talk it down like that. I can't excuse what I did, I don't even want to explain it. But if how I felt afterwards is any measure of what..."

"Still, Jimmy, it just capped it. I can't live like the last three years and have nothing build up. Then it's just a question of time and you know that once a junkie..."

"No. Please, Jessie, listen to me."

"You know something?" she said and looked up. "You're talking to me now, the way I tried it with you, that day in the hotel room."

"You did well then."

"Yes," she said. "Look at us."

We smiled at each other because we didn't know what else to do. It went with her remark. It was quite mechanical. Then she said, without smiling, "They had you hooked from the start, and you never knowing a thing."

"I want to thank you for trying to stay out of it, Jessie. I don't know what happens next..."

"I know what happens next."

"Let me finish. I want to thank you for not playing it right that first day in the room, and for the time when you stood in front of the gun, hoping that I wouldn't use it, and for the time when you managed so badly when we had that breakfast here. And the party, where you didn't pan out either, but were just being Jessie, who kept wishing I was human."

"Yes," she said. "Thank you. It's too bad."

"But not so bad that you have to take that," and I showed her the stain again.

"No. Not now." Then she turned away so I couldn't see her face. "But when it gets bad and there's nobody to run to, or when it gets bad *because* there is nobody to run to—"

Then there was the shrill, hard peal of that bell.

She came around in the chair, looked at me.

"You see. Now it's over."

She meant a hell of a lot more than I had time for at the moment, but maybe we could have that later. Though I don't think I wondered about that right then. Everything got very fast and the questions very simple.

"What's that bell, Jessie? Answer me." I picked her up out of the chair and we both stood there as if saying good-by with the train already leaving.

"That bell, Jessie. If that's got to do..."

"That's Mister Simon."

"Who's that?"

"You'll see him. They brought you back to see him."

"Top man?"

"Yes. Here."

"And?"

"That's all, Jimmy. No 'and.'"

"But I don't know anything. Jessie! Why all..."

"That was the good thing so far, Jimmy. That you didn't know anything."

"I know this whole thing was engineered. I know something I should-n't. Something they want to know."

"And once they open up to you, Jimmy, if they do, then you know it's the end."

"What do they want? Do you know, Jessie?"

"Something the dead Tooley had. Something he left behind."

"What, for God's sake!"

"I don't know. I really don't know."

Then the bell rang again, like a knife cutting at us. And Rand would be looking for me. Any minute—

"Jessie. Listen to me."

She looked up, flighty and nervous.

"It isn't over, Jessie. Will you help?"

"Can I?"

"You got a car?"

"Yes. But if you..."

"Just listen. Jump in that car, drive out to the lake on the other side of Yorkdam. Bowline Lake."

"Where Tooley used to hole up and nobody knows..."

"I know. Drive out the highway to the lake and there's Bowline Bar. Go there and wait for me."

"*Wait* for you?"

"Damn it, I just might make it!"

I had yelled it at her pretty loud and maybe it was just the shock of that that did it, but she said, "Yes. I think you just might."

"And you, Jessie, you just wait for me there."

"Should I do..."

"Nothing. I just want you around."

She almost cried then and I gave her a kiss.

"All right, Jessie?"

"Sure—"

"You can call me Gallivan," I said and grinned at her.

"All right," and then she smiled. "Jump, Gallivan," she said, and held the door for me.

CHAPTER 23

Iran down the corridor and thought, if she holds out, if she doesn't need any more of the stuff for the next twenty-four hours and if she holds out—and then I could see the plant, my coat on the chair, because the light was on now, and Rand was looking at me, waiting.

"Where you been, Gallivan?"

"Don't worry about it."

"I'm not," he said. "Come on."

It was clear enough. I think I was now Simon's worry, whoever he was.

We went down a corridor, very slowly I thought, and then we stopped at a door and didn't go in. Rand looked at the bulb over the door and leaned against the wall. The bulb wasn't lit.

"Simon?" I asked him.

"Yes. Mister Simon." Then he looked at me and said, "How was she?"

This wasn't the time for the noble act and I had no intention of slugging Rand but it must have shown in my face. He kept smoking but said, "I didn't mean it that way. I meant, how she was. She's on again, isn't she?"

"How do you know?"

"He gave it to her," and Rand nodded at the door.

I had never seen Mister Simon before. I had just been afraid of him. Scared sick even, when I thought back at the spider web he had made all around me. But that had been a piddling emotion. Now I hated his guts.

"That's for you," said Rand, and the bulb over the door was on.

Rand opened the door and let me go first.

This was a hospital room. There was a bed and a lot of equipment. That was the first impression. Shiny equipment, glass and chrome, a thing which might have been a stomach pump, a long-necked stand to hold up a transfusion bottle, a heating pad wire going into the bed, a rubber tube coming out of the bed. Only after seeing all that was there time to find Mister Simon.

He was small in the bed and I had no idea how old he was. He was rolled up into a sitting position and a big, littered bed desk made him look smaller than he probably was.

He was bald. He had waxy skin on his skull and gray, papery skin on his face. He wore glasses, not too thick, but too big. Unless his face was unusually small. The false teeth made big ridges around his mouth and they tightened his skin. When he talks, I thought, maybe he'll sound like a parrot.

"If you like to sit," he said to me, "take that chair, so I won't have to turn."

The voice was bigger than the rest of the man. Or perhaps the voice was the only thing normal about him, the rest of the man sick, dried up, wrong to be living.

"You've made time even shorter than it was," he said. "I'm sorry you got spotted."

"So am I."

He didn't act as if he had heard. He seemed to be concentrating on something else. With all the sickness he showed, he conveyed a kind of strength which came through in his voice, which showed in his directness.

"When you were out in Bowline Lake development, Gallivan, did you remember where Tooley lived?"

When they get direct, Jessie had said, when they don't bother to hide their interest any more, that'll be the end.

"I never knew where he lived," I told Simon.

"You have indicated that you do. You did so when you spoke to Rand, while still in prison, and I get the impression from your behavior since you have been out, that you might know more than you have been telling."

"So far, Mister Simon, I didn't know I was supposed to tell anything."

"Where were you last night, Gallivan?"

"I took a walk."

As far as he was concerned, I hadn't said a thing. He went on, "I think you got spotted on that walk, Gallivan. The only explanation for that, at that hour, is that you went someplace where you were known."

"I used to live in Yorkdam."

"Did you go to that bar where Rand found you with Tooley today?"

I got a cigarette out, hoping to cover everything with that tired, old gesture, hoping a good, meaningless answer would come to me in the meantime.

"Please don't smoke," said Simon.

I put the cigarette away, and he talked again.

"Did you ever wonder why I went to the trouble, Gallivan, of getting you out in that expensive, that very risky way?"

"Why you engineered the break?"

"Yes. After all, I could have waited three weeks, 'til they let you out legally. What I mean is, you might think so, as you wonder about this."

"You don't make sense. Nothing does."

"I always make sense, Gallivan. Roll me down a little, Rand, will you?"

Rand did that and Simon's upper body moved downward in a short arch, a movement of an inanimate thing.

"Your accidental cell mate," he said, "this man, Tooley, he and I used to work together. Then we had a falling out."

"Anything to do with the fact that he was in under death sentence?"

"No. His own fault, that. But a vindictive man. Maybe you noticed?"

"I didn't like him."

"That has nothing to do with it. At any rate, having gone this far, Gallivan, please listen to the rest."

Once they tell you everything—

"He is dead now, but he is still endangering my life."

"You seem well enough."

"I'm half dead, Gallivan, but just half. As I was saying, he was a vindictive man. And then, I know something else. Tooley was secretive, and he was a hoarder. They go together sometimes, have you ever noticed?"

"You want to know where he lived."

"That's clear now."

"So you can get back that kilo of heroin he had hidden."

"Don't be ridiculous, please. The reason I tell you all this, is so you get a sense of the importance of my interest in you. What I'm after is something Tooley has kept in his place, not in the place where he lived in town, but the other one which we must find, something he had no time to remove, I'm sure, because he got arrested unexpectedly."

"What is this dangerous thing?"

"All I want from you, Gallivan, are answers, not questions. You still don't remember where he lived? Very well. I'll go on."

He reached under his blanket and I heard something click. Then he talked again.

"Now as to my hurry, Gallivan, my not waiting for you to sit out your three weeks. Tooley let me know, before execution, that a short while after his death he would get me. Those are his words, but I won't have to make them any clearer."

"No. He meant the half of you which is still alive."

"That deadline—" he closed his eyes and smiled at the word he had used, "that deadline is up just two days from now. He sent me the date, to give me discomfort. And that date, as you notice, falls before your release. You had a little more than two weeks to go."

"Two weeks and three days."

"Yes. That was a pity. We tried finding his place without your help, even while the break plans were being made, but no matter. Now you're here, now you know what the pressure is. Now your move, Gallivan."

"What's in his place?"

"Would that help you remember where the place is?"

"Any little thing, Mister Simon—"

"You shouldn't be flippant, Gallivan. Really not."

"If I remember, if I could help you find Tooley's house, room, whatnot, then what?"

"Then thank you and I'm through with you."

"Through with me."

"Well?"

I'd never get out alive once he knew but as long as he didn't I would stay alive. Two days, anyway.

"Please, Gallivan," he said, and it sounded bored, "I'll get it out of you. Don't you know that?"

"Buy me?"

"Since my life is involved, I can't. Don't you know that?"

"I'll die easy or I'll die hard. That it?"

I felt my voice shaking. I think he heard it.

"Are you afraid of pain or are you afraid of death? There's a difference, you know."

He waited for me to answer but I didn't, because of my dry throat. So he said, "I have nothing else to discuss with you, Gallivan, and I want you to go now. I give you the whole night. Tomorrow, please take Rand here to that place where Tooley used to live."

"And if I can't?"

"You can. You mean if you won't. Then, Gallivan, for heaven's sake use your imagination. There are innumerable ways, all terrible. Don't you know that?" he smiled and said, "You're sweating, even now."

A nurse came in with a covered tray. She put it on Simon's bed desk and told Rand and me it was time to leave.

"They know that," said Simon to the nurse. "Or do you want to tell me, before you go?" he asked me.

"I hope you die in the night," I said to him.

He blinked, and for once said nothing.

"And if you don't—what was that deadline? Two days later?"

He clicked his teeth and the nurse said that we really would have to leave now and what kind of behavior—

When we got out to the hall I had to lean against the wall. I thought about this unreal talk—it happened all over again, is what I mean—about the unreal calm of the words, about the man in his bed who was scheming for the half of his life which was left and no matter what.

"You going to faint, Gallivan?" Rand asked me.

"No."

"You going to bed or you want to eat something first?" Rand asked me.

There was a sound from the man in bed. I think he was cursing the nurse. She answered very little and then opened the door. She took the tray down the hall, past the door to the staircase, and there was a little lift in the wall and she put the tray into that. She pressed a button and then went back into the room.

"Well? What first?" asked Rand.

"First," I said, "I'm going to figure a way to kill Mister Simon. Don't you know that?"

CHAPTER 24

I even ate something. I did it for the semblance of normalcy. Then I went to my room where Rand closed the door for me.

"It's four stories up," he said, "and of course you don't get out any other way. Spend the night thinking, Gallivan," and he closed the door.

It was nine. The bar closed at twelve. Two hours driving left one hour to get out of the house. If I had told Jessie to wait for me with her car, that would have been even smarter, but the way things were now I spent no time at all thinking about that deadly boner. I felt as alive as I ever had because I would get out or die trying.

I spent ten minutes of my hour at the window, thinking, and looking out at the moon. It looked sharp and clear, and that's how I felt.

After ten minutes in the room I went out. I had no idea where Rand slept, but I had no doubt he would show up soon enough once I started walking around.

He stuck his head out of a door when I got to the potted plant. There was that blond halo around his hair again, from the light in his room, and his face was in the dark. I went back to him and put it on.

"Rand," I said, "one last favor."

"What?"

He was as reasonable as ever. I counted on that, his cold feelings. I was glad he wasn't quirked and vindictive, the way the old Tooley must have been.

"I'm going nuts in that room," I said. "Like you said, this is the night I'm going to spend thinking. But I'm going nuts in that room, Rand. Can you follow that?"

"Yes. So far. What's the favor?"

"I got to walk around. I don't want to wake anybody, I don't want to alarm anybody or get clobbered by somebody guarding the elevator, I just want to be allowed to walk back and forth. You can understand that, can't you, Rand?"

"You're a pacer, huh?"

"Since stir."

"The door to Mister Simon's room is locked. The nurse sleeps in there with him."

"I wasn't thinking of that."

"You sounded like it when you made that remark before, about killing him."

"Do I sound nuts, Rand? Do I sound nuts to you now?"

"No. Just nervous."

"I'm a pacer."

He nodded and came out into the hall. He went to the elevator where he told the man, and he went to the stairwell where he told the man. Then he came back.

"They know you're out here," he said. "So pace."

I started to go.

"That also means they're going to be twice as awake."

I walked away and he closed his door.

Problem one, finished. I could walk around.

I walked fifteen minutes, the same way mostly. Elevator hall, stairwell hall, elevator hall, stairwell hall. Twice I passed Rand's room and the second time I could hear him breathe. He slept on his back, probably.

Stairwell hall. Mister Simon, I was sure, was by nature and illness a very light sleeper and for that reason was probably heavily doped. I heard nothing from that room. When I passed the door to the stairwell I looked through the glass in the door and nodded at the man on the steps. I had done this now several times and he would nod back. Then I went as far as the service lift in the wall and pressed one of the buttons. That made the lift go from the basement to the second floor, according to the buttons. It also made the thing hum.

When the guy from the steps came into the corridor I was at the other end. He looked my way, with gun, and then looked at the lift. Now he knew what was humming.

Problem two, finished. There was a precedent for the humming.

The next time I paced the corridor I didn't nod at him, through the glass in the door. As a matter of fact, he never saw me pass, one way or the other.

When I had five minutes left of my hour the lift was on my floor and what would another hum be to a man with a gun, watching for Gallivan to come through the door.

I sneaked past the door again, doubled over, and stopped by the lift. I wasn't even worried if it would snap a cable and break my back. I was getting light-headed and thought only that if it did happen I would probably die.

Getting in was the problem. I'm very long and that was the only thing that panicked me. One knee would stick out. It would scrape going past the opening, going past the sill, but after that, 'til the next sill on the next floor, there would be room for the knee to stick out. Maybe something would break—I wasn't thinking any more.

I eased into the cubicle, sat tight like a spring, and could just reach the low button outside. The lift hummed and there was a godawful lurch downward, but then my fright got interrupted.

My knee hit the sill. The only thing which kept the scream inside me was the fact that I didn't have enough air. The way I sat I could hardly breathe. The sound seemed to be the worst thing, the way the knee scraped. Then it was warm and wet, with the afterpain just starting, but by that time the first sill was past and I was in the black shaft.

The mechanism in the top of the lift had a whine in it, a new whine, which had not been there all the other times I had run it. I held my ears-

—

There were three more sills. It was so bad, waiting to hit them, that I don't remember about it too clearly.

The lift swayed with a very soft dip, so much of a dip that I could hear the cable twang overhead. When the thing stopped I was in the basement. And I was past the opening. But not bad. Not too bad, I kept saying all that time. Not too bad.

I don't know how long it took me to get out of the thing, but when I fell to the basement floor I could see a clock on the wall which said ten past ten. I had started down from the top five before ten. That trip past three floors hadn't taken fifteen minutes.

I could walk. It was hell, but nothing like the trip down that shaft. I walked through what turned out to be the laundry, and up a few steps to a door which had a light on the outside. I could see snow there and the tracks we had made with the car.

All together there were four cars in the big port to the rear and two of them had keys. They were both doctor's cars, by the sign in the back, and I was even steady enough to think about them and to hope that they slept in the sanatorium.

Except for the knee I was fine again when I got to the bar. Fine means, I was running mechanically, without human interference. It was quarter past twelve, a quarter past closing, but there were still two cars outside the bar. One, I was hoping, would be Jessie's. The other one, maybe fat Eddy owned it. Or the cop who had been there to take down my description.

And if he was there, and if nothing else occurred to me, I'd say, yes, I'm Gallivan, and this is the story. Maybe that would have been the way out all the time.

The knee was stiff, but just from the swelling, and the pain didn't mean a damn to me now. I just wished Jessie would be there. Just to be there—

When I got into the bar and closed the door I felt how warm it was. I went to the bar and leaned on it for a moment.

Eddy turned around and said that the place was closed. He didn't have his glasses on and didn't recognize me 'til much later. He was all the way up to me then. I was hoping that Jessie was in the bar, but I couldn't see past Eddy.

He opened his eyes and his mouth and just stood there like that. I was thinking much clearer by now but never got to use it. Eddy kept standing with his eyes and mouth open. He was holding the broom out a little, but he wasn't looking at me at all. I felt the draft on my neck and didn't bother to turn. From the look on Eddy's face, the man behind me had a gun. Who would follow me in here with a gun—

"This is the place, huh?" said Rand.

I rolled myself against the bar, to have both elbows on it, and looked at Rand. There was Rand with gun. Simple.

"You couldn't have done it easier?" he said.

I kept standing the way I was because nothing had happened yet. I remember clearly that I wasn't afraid.

But fat Eddy was the stupid one. He probably thought he was full of courage but what really showed was how stupid he was. He swung the broom at Rand.

Rand let him. When the broom came down he grabbed, it, yanked, then jabbed it back. For this simple trick the gun was on me, but Eddy got the broom handle in the belly. The big man fell down, rolled on his back, tried to roll over again. Rand went over and stepped on his face.

"Is this the place?" he asked me.

"I think so."

He didn't hold the gun on me any more because there was no point to it. He walked around a little, looking at the walls, and wherever he went his one heel left a wet print. Eddy's nose was bleeding a lot.

"Where?" he asked.

"Would you believe it? I'm standing on it."

He came over and looked at the floor where I stood, but he did not come close enough.

Then he looked at me and said, "You saw what happened to the fat one?"

"You're not going to do it to me, Rand."

"Stop sparring. We can't stay here forever. Where?"

"It was here," I said, and tapped my foot, "but I gave it to Jessie."

"Jessie?"

"Yes."

"Where? I mean, where is she?"

"In the back booth."

He didn't turn. He couldn't have seen her leg anyway, from where he was standing, and when I shook my head at her, so that she should stay put, he just thought that was the oldest trick in the world.

He started to smile about it but then he dropped it. Here we stood, after all, in a lit place with a big window.

"All right," he said, and picked up the broom which was lying between us.

I looked at the booth and said, "All right, Jessie. Show him the gun."

He almost turned, but felt too clever. Jessie didn't have a gun, but then Rand thought that there was nobody at all. So when she made a scraping sound in the booth he spun like a top.

Just far enough.

I snapped away from the bar and he must have forgotten about my reach. I got his gun arm and with everything that had happened coming to a very fast head at this moment, I had a great deal of strength.

His arm went too far back, too unnaturally, and the gun flew out of his hand and Rand flew down to the floor from the leverage. He lay there with something broken and groaned.

I got the gun. I cocked it and went back to Rand.

"Jeesis—" he said. "Gallivan!"

"Close your eyes if you want."

"Gallivan—"

I shot him someplace high. I wasn't going to have him following me around any more. I had come too far.

CHAPTER 25

Jessie came out of the booth, white-faced and her hands trembling. She didn't come across but just stood there.

The first thing she said was, "I had three more bindles in the drawer, Gallivan, but I didn't take any. I left them behind. But I want one now. Badly."

In spite of everything I had to smile at her, happy, because she had made it this far and could talk about it.

"Please don't let me," she said. "Please, Jimmy."

I nodded at her and she smiled back. Just a short one, but it was real.

We found a flashlight behind the bar and took that upstairs. Walking up through that dust everything felt already over. It was like a rest. I didn't know how much I would need it.

Tooley, I think, had rented the place and then, one day, he hadn't showed up. I'm sure his name hadn't been Tooley for the matter of rental, and his name in the paper, if there was much of a spiel, wouldn't have meant a thing to Eddy downstairs. I think Eddy had just closed up the place when his roomer hadn't showed, because a lot of things were still up there; some furniture, bed stripped by now, and a trunk with some clothes.

I made dust clouds with the clothes when I ripped at the linings. Jessie sat on the bare bed.

"Gallivan."

I looked up. She was still white but not trembling any more.

"Why don't we leave and that's all—"

She saw my face and sighed.

"No," she said. "I didn't think you would."

"I'd never stop running," I said.

"Yes."

But there was more.

"I know what's here," she said.

"What Simon wants?"

"It's a baggage check. Two days from now the suitcase, or whatever, will go on the block. That happens after twenty-four months of no claim."

"I know," I said.

I felt dead. She hadn't told me, back in the room.

"Gallivan," she said, "at least you can make it. I got twelve hundred cash. I'll give it to you and at least you can make it."

"You don't want to find the suitcase, or whatever?"

"I don't want you to find it."

She wouldn't say any more. After a while she even helped look for the thing and we found the baggage check where those things usually are. Behind the paper lining of the trunk. She found it and she gave it to me.

Downstairs she even stopped to put a wet rag on Eddy's face and then she called a hospital to send down an ambulance. I hadn't thought of that. We left. Rand, I think, was breathing.

The check was from a baggage room at Greyhound in Yorkdam. It wasn't for a suitcase but a briefcase with more clothes in it. That was the stuffing. Then there was a typed folder.

I wanted to look at it right away, standing there at the baggage-room window, but suddenly the rush went out of everything. It was just that kind of a moment. Nothing to do now but look at the print, black and white. And Jessie looked pale and finished.

There was a coffee shop at the other end of the station and I took Jessie's arm.

"Come on. We'll sit down."

"Sure," she said.

There was a juke box in the place and five kids standing around it, bobbing and weaving.

"I'll give you twelve hundred," said Jessie, "which is all I have. And you can go to Mexico. Didn't you say once you would like to go to Mexico?"

"Yes."

"Is it nice there?"

"I don't know. I just said Mexico because I've never been there."

"Oh," she said, and then she looked like once before, at the baggage window. She took a cigarette and smoked.

"Read it," she said. "Aren't you going to read it?"

"Yes," I said.

"Read it," she said. "With that they'll forgive you the three weeks you missed."

I read it and I knew she was right. They'd forgive me, for bringing this to them. And they'd kill Mister Simon for the things he had done. Tooley had all of it documented. The dope import, the custom murders to tighten up the organization, the other murders which were hard to trace, because the dead ones were junkies.

And they wouldn't kill Jessie for what she had done, by this record, but she would grow old in jail.

"Is this true?"

"I pushed dope when I was on the junk, and I helped Mishkin when I was off. You know what Mishkin does."

"He sells H like beans and you were his secretary."

"Sort of like that."

"You can't pay for that."

"No."

"Locking you up pays for nothing."

She looked away, to the long window which showed the buses by the ramp. I looked, too, but there wasn't a one that said Mexico.

"If you throw those papers away," she said to the window, "and they catch you—"

There was one bus that said Bagette, or something. I knew nothing about the place, or where it was.

"Did you hear me?" she said.

"Yes. I heard you."

I put the folder back into the briefcase. I took the clothes out and dropped them on the floor and just left the folder in and closed the briefcase.

She looked at it and bit her lip.

"I don't think I can face it," she said.

"Yes. I can look as far as this table and you, Jessie, and no further."

She put her cigarette out. It made a dry sound.

"I can see further," she said.

"I turn you in, we both lose."

She shrugged.

"We run together," she said, "and we both lose."

The bus with the name on the shield made a noise on the other side of the window and then I could see it move.

"If I'm going to lose you," she said, "I don't want you."

She got up and took a deep breath and looked out at the bus. I got up too.

"Only hopheads think they can have forever," I said.

I turned her around a little, so she'd look at me, and when she did she said, "That's right."

Then we went out to the street. That bus was coming by and we watched it drive off. It had no lights on inside and I couldn't tell if there was anyone in it.

We went across the street to a hotel with a closed bar on the ground floor and two stories on top. We spent the night there.

It wasn't forever but it was she and I. Later, the morning came up, some kind of morning, and she slept next to me, so I could feel both her warmth and her distance.

Perhaps it was best. Because it wasn't a finish to anything and, God knows, it wasn't a start—

The girl woke up in the morning. She saw that there was no sun but it was very light. In a while she got dressed. She was not sure what to do next, to walk away, to sit awhile longer, because God knows, she thought, it isn't a start or a finish and without those, there is no rush. She had Gal-

livan's message, which he had left so that she wouldn't miss it. The briefcase was empty. There was a glass tray next to it, which was full of frail
ashes.

THE END

Agreement to Kill

By Peter Rabe

CHAPTER 1

It was half a street. One side had houses, a few stores, and people walking. The other side was a blank wall. Along the top of the wall and around the large gate were a few geometrical frills in stone, but it was senseless. The wall meant prison and the gate was steel. It opened without sound, the movement almost casual.

A tall man stepped through, stooping as if afraid he might hit the top of the frame, and he straightened up when the gate shut with a clank. He didn't turn at the sound. For a moment he stood on the bare side of the street and squinted in the sun's sharp, high light.

With a sudden movement he started across the street. The way he moved looked greedy. Then he stood on the sidewalk, his back to the long wall on the other side of the street, watching the stores, the people, the whole view without prison in it.

After a while, he said to himself, after a while it will feel the way it should. He would know that he stood here on the street, not imagining it. He breathed faster, but the feeling of not being here didn't leave him.

He squinted nervously, as if an insect were bothering him. Then he walked. A half-hour walk to the bus, and then a three-hour ride on the bus and he'd be home. He wouldn't even have to go all the way into Stone Bluff because the bus passed the farm and he'd get off right there. Walking, he felt the strain in his face and then the tense set of his jaw. He rubbed his face. Then he put a cigarette into his mouth so that his jaw would have to relax.

A half-hour walk to the bus— He went over it as if afraid he might forget the routine, then caught himself. No need to think about it. No doubts and no need for decisions because he had it all laid out beforehand and had decided his steps. The simplest, the straightest, the hardest way of all. Done with prison, go back to the farm, check over the damage and work. Three years' fallow might even have been for the better. That's how he was going to think about it; no other way. Any other way and there would be nothing for him to hold on to.

He didn't notice it, but his jaws were clenched tight again, as if he were holding something tight in his teeth.

The prison was at one end of town, which didn't make any difference to the rest of the city. The center was full of noise, amusements, and neon. The neons jumped and sparkled even though the sun was shining bright. When he stopped at a traffic light a hand plucked his sleeve, another came up to his eyes. It was cupped around a picture.

"Special today, feller. The whole dozen..." The voice stopped, then started to laugh. "Hell, it's Spinner. Just got out today?"

He looked down at the man and nodded. "Just now. And let go my sleeve."

"Sure, Spinner," and the man laughed again. His old back was bent and his old face was grinning. "Beat you by maybe a week," said Moss. "Good thing for you I ran into you."

Spinner crossed with the light but the old man stayed next to him. "Seeing you and me is fraternity brothers..."

"Beat it, Moss. I'm not buying."

Moss was still grinning. He almost always did. He walked along next to Spinner and stuck the pictures back into his pocket.

"Where you going? Back to that farm you got?"

Spinner ignored the slur in the old man's voice, turned the corner, and walked into the bus station.

He bought a one-way fare to Stone Bluff and folded the ticket into his pocket. He had imagined it differently. He remembered thinking that once he bought the ticket the feeling would be something like a final decision. It would be like the show of strength which meant he had guts to go back, some magic touch which meant that for once and at last everything had to go his way.

None of this happened. He had bought his ticket and when he turned Moss was there waiting for him.

"I'll buy you a cup of coffee," said Moss. "From one con to another."

"Con?"

"You been in jail, Spinner. That makes you a con."

Spinner ran one hand down the side of his face to cover the jump in his muscle. It felt as if the muscle was sticking out like a bent spring and everybody could see it.

"And lucky," Moss went on. "Hell, you ought to be happy. I seen buddies of mine got twenty years for assault, against your three."

Spinner stopped and said, "Moss, listen. I'm so happy I don't need another thing in this world. Not even you. So go away. I keep smelling jail when I look at you."

"Here's the counter," said Moss. "Two black, for my buddy and me," he called to the girl, and then he sat down without doubting that Spinner would, too.

Spinner sat down, because he suddenly felt very tired. He thought there was no point making a struggle of everything, to make an issue over a cup of black coffee and how he envied the ease in Moss, his grin, and the way he relaxed on the stool. His ease—no. That didn't fit Moss. There was a wormlike softness in the way he acted.

"I know how you feel," said Moss, and watched Spinner sit down. "Every time I get out I go through it."

"Through what?"

"The way you feel. Like you ain't out yet."

Spinner put down his coffee and crossed his arms on the counter. "I'm out."

"Sure. Like down and out. Listen, Spinner, you got to work at it."

Spinner squinted his eyes as if the sun were in his face. He hunched his big shoulders together. It helped keep the anger down. From somewhere the anger had come up inside him and he didn't know why or what to do with it.

"Now here's how you work at it, Spinner. Expose yourself to the nice things in life, get it? Give the nice things in life a chance to get at you."

"Like that filth you showed me?"

"Naw. That's just the come-hither, the teaser. Now, my real business..."

"I never knew a pimp your age, Moss."

Moss laughed. The laugh made Spinner want to spit. "Don't worry about it, Spinner. Just sit there for a minute while I make a phone call."

"Thanks for the coffee," said Spinner. "But that's all."

Moss was getting up, taking a dime out of his pocket.

"Just work at it, Spinner, while I set it up. Just sit there and work at it." He went to the phone booth.

Spinner's shoulder started to ache and he made himself loosen up. But his anger was there again, from somewhere, and it made him work the muscles inside his throat to avoid choking on it. Something had started it—what Moss had said. Work hard and you can't lose, or something like that. Must have been his father who said that. Not his mother. He remembered she had been dead by the time his father started with his homey lessons. He knew lots of homey sayings and lessons and they all had to do with work hard and you can't lose.

Then his father had lost half the farm, then his job, and in the end he had lost his life.

"All set." Moss came back from the phone and sat down. He stared into Spinner's face and seemed to be thinking. "You know, I just remembered something. You're from Stone Bluff."

"And I'm going there in about fifteen minutes."

Moss ignored it.

"Isn't that where Dixon's got his place?"

Spinner held still. He hadn't been thinking about Dixon and he had thought that the name Dixon would no longer give him a jolt. He had thought he had handled all that in his mind and with his new attitude.

"How come you know Dixon?" he said. He heard his own voice like a stranger's.

"How come? He's big, ain't he?" In that way Moss borrowed Dixon's glory.

Jake Spinner shrugged. He kept turning around to look at the clock.

"He's in with St. Louis," said Moss, making it sound like magic. "Don't you know that?"

"I know that."

Moss was not making any impression. He sucked his teeth and looked Spinner up and down.

"What's the matter," he said. "You know him so good this ain't news to you? Lemme tell you something, Spinner. He may be big in Stone Bluff, but he's just one of the men in St. Louis."

Spinner sipped coffee. He did not want to hear more about Dixon. He knew enough already—that Dixon lived in Stone Bluff, that he always had lived there, and that the townspeople liked to call him Old Dixon, which was the homey way of covering their feelings when it came to a man who owned most of the town, who had made a great deal of money before repeal, and who had his fingers in everything.

That's how Spinner's father had lost half his farm—because Dixon had wanted it. He was building a park for himself.

And that's how his father had lost his job, because when the farm was cut in half, in the depression, he had started to work for Dixon in St. Louis. They had lived in St. Louis and Spinner's father had worked for Dixon at something or other, and all the while he was trying to teach his son homey sayings: work hard and you can't lose. Maybe the old Spinner had never worked hard enough, and in the end he'd been fired. There had been an argument over losing the job, something nobody did with Dixon, and Spinner's father had got thrown out of the office. That had been the last time he had ever tried anything. He had tried walking back in and Dixon had stood there, watching two of his men throw Spinner's father back out again, after roughing him up a little.

That's when Spinner's father had given up. He went to bed with a headache and died with a hemorrhage. That's how Spinner saw it. His father had given up.

"And because he's small fry," Moss was saying, "he acts big the only way he can do it—in a burg like Stone Bluff. Hey, you listening to me?"

"Sure," said Spinner, and gave Moss a short look. He did not like looking at Moss.

"I tell you something else," said the old man. He put his hand on Spinner's arm and before Spinner could pull away Moss said, "Watch your step in Stone Bluff."

Moss was pleased with the pause it brought on. He saw Spinner sit very still and he saw the nervous squint around Spinner's eyes.

Moss grinned. He would milk this dry. "Ain't you gonna ask what I mean?"

"What?" said Spinner. It sounded curt, so that his voice wouldn't show how anxious he was.

"I get around," said Moss. He looked at the clock to check how soon Spinner's bus would leave, and then said, "I keep my eyes open. All the time."

"And your mouth," said Spinner. "But nothing comes out."

"No? Then listen to this," Moss leaned closer, his hand on Spinner's arm again. "Dixon's in trouble," said Moss.

This time the pause did not give Moss any pleasure, because he saw Spinner relax. Another moment and Spinner would lose interest altogether.

Spinner said, "I thought you said I should watch my step."

"You live in Stone Bluff, don't you? Dixon does, don't he? And when Dixon's got trouble..."

"He lives on trouble," said Spinner, and turned to look at the clock.

"Not this kind. Listen." Moss grabbed Spinner's sleeve to keep him from leaving. "He's not in trouble in St. Louis; he's been monkeying around with the county vote. You know what that means? He's been getting around St. Louis itself and back at them with this monkey business from outa the county. Here they thought he was just sitting around in that Stony Bluff burg and..."

"Let go my arm," said Spinner.

"Wait, where you going? Hey, I got it all set up, like I told you—"

"Beat it," said Spinner and Moss had to run after him. "Beat it? Listen, friend, I don't go to no trouble for nothing. You don't want it, is your business, but you owe me..."

Spinner yanked his arm free and slapped it back, making Moss tumble. He didn't see whether Moss fell or not because he ran through the gate to the ramp and caught the Stone Bluff bus at the last minute.

CHAPTER 2

At first he tried concentrating on the landscape outside, the flat land getting rounder and the fields and trees slanting up against the hillsides. He hadn't seen it in a long time and it should mean something to him. It should mean he was going home, the way he had planned it, that he was sticking it out though God knows it was harder than he had thought. That mention of Dixon hadn't been any help.

Spinner took out a cigarette and smoked for a while. It made a dry heat in his mouth, which reminded him of the farm and that he was going back to it. He was coming back at the wrong time. High summer. Dry heat. Same as the last time, when he had come back to the farm from the army. That had been the wrong time. Or the time before, after his father had died and Spinner had left St. Louis to try to put the farm back in shape. That had been high summer.

It seemed he never did anything but go back to that place, work hard, as his father's homey sayings said he should, and lose out. The first time he'd come back, after St. Louis, the place was almost a working farm when the army had gotten him. The second time, after the army, he had tried again. It would have been easier if Dixon hadn't owned the best part of the farm. It was now Dixon's park.

One day Dixon had come up to the fence on a horse. Spinner had let him talk because he was tired from work and Dixon took a long time making clear what he wanted. He always wanted something, but first there had been small talk about the old days in St. Louis. How close he, Dixon, had been to old Spinner, how one good turn deserved another, and if young Spinner would take it as a favor, then he, Dixon, would buy the rest of the farm for high cash. As a favor.

"Not for sale," said Spinner.

"Jake," said Dixon. He favored first names when he was in Stone Bluff. "You can't make a go of it. But with cash you can do anything."

"It's a better farm now than when you cut off half of it to waste on your bridle paths."

Jake Spinner didn't like Dixon and after all the hard tries and losing each time it was suddenly easy to blame Dixon for all of it.

"Jake," Dixon said, "I want that farm. Be smart like your pappy," and then he yanked on his horse and rode away.

Spinner didn't like Dixon any better for that remark, and for the threat in his voice. Work hard and you can't lose wasn't something that had proven itself, but Spinner was still trying. More so now. he discovered—now that his anger had found a direction.

"Your pappy could tell you," said Dixon the next time he came around, "you oughtn't to cross me."

Spinner got off his tractor and climbed over his fence. He walked to the place on Dixon's road where the car had parked, with Dixon in back and the chauffeur in front. By the time Spinner got there his voice was low and controlled. He said, "It's not for sale."

"Learn something, hick," and Dixon got out of his car and walked up to Spinner.

"The farm's mine, Dixon."

"You don't look right when you're mad, Spinner. You look like some-body's gonna take a fall."

"Don't worry," said Spinner. "I'm holding back."

"Meaning you," Dixon went on. "You don't stand there and look at me that way, Jake boy."

It had been just talk so far. Jake Spinner tried to keep that in mind, keep out all the rest and just think of the situation right now, of Dixon asking a stupid question. Spinner tried to keep it out of his mind how Dixon got what he wanted, how Dixon the crook always got his way, and how Dixon kept coming up like a private plague.

Then Dixon swung.

Maybe he had been thinking of Spinner's father or of other times when crude muscle had turned the trick.

But Jake hit back. He hit back out of pure rage. It jumped out of him with the sudden push of his panicky feeling that he was going to lose again, that there might be no end to his losing.

He hit just once and then had to wait till Dixon got up out of the dirt, quite a while later. Dixon's chauffeur had looked away when it happened and didn't get out of the car to help the man out of the dirt until the last moment when Dixon had started to stir. Dixon got into the back of his car and left without saying anything else.

What kept Jake Spinner from worrying too much was the thought of one thing. It had been with him a long time and had gotten sharper. That he wasn't going to lose forever. It wasn't a plan and it wasn't a formula. But it gave him intent.

But Dixon had more than just a feeling. The next time he didn't come himself but sent the sheriff, and for the time being Dixon let the farm plans go by. He would get to that later. The real-estate plan could wait for a while, and for a better price. And it needed more than a pushing around because Dixon had learned something about Spinner's intent. He wasn't like his father. Dixon would have to go to more trouble. With all the pres-sure at his command Dixon made the best of Spinner's intent. Spinner was sent to jail for assault with intent to kill.

Spinner thought how easy the homecoming would be if Dixon weren't waiting for him. But that wasn't completely true, because the homecoming was bigger than anything Dixon could mean. Spinner had tried three times and lost twice; if he lost a third time, if he still had no luck, then he might lose his intent.

His shoulder ached, for no good reason, and Spinner held it carefully.

If that should happen, he thought, if he should lose his nameless intent, he would save it by finding a name for it. He had one, ready made; an intent to kill.

CHAPTER 3

He spent the first night at the farm without having seen anyone. He got off at the farm before the bus reached Stone Bluff because he wanted some time to rest and be alone—to get ready to start, he said to himself when he went to bed in the evening. Then, lying in bed late at night without sleep, he saw he had done it this way because he was afraid.

He must have slept some of the time because he woke bathed in sweat. He got up early and spent all day on the farm. Fields to look at, the barn, the house, prime the pump—and he should go to town. The utility company should hook up his current, he should call at the lumberyard for wood for repairs, he should see the farmer down the road who had rented most of Spinner's equipment.

It was evening before he was ready to go into town. Had he been back in his cell now, he was sure he'd be able to imagine it all with so much reality, so much so that— Spinner started to curse. He should not have to imagine that he was back!

Then, from somewhere, the intent came hack to him, the thing he had saved without knowing how, and though it was nameless it rode him now like a man with a whip.

He went to the pump and washed his face, and with a careful feeling in every move, he walked down the road to town.

He remembered the signs along the way, telling that almost all of it belonged to Dixon—the filling station at the fork in the highway, the ice plant further down, the long concrete sheds where Dixon kept his construction equipment. And there was a new one. The sign said *South End Development Co., Prop. T. Dixon,* and *City Homes in the Country.*

A lot of land was torn up and leveled, including a big part of Dixon's park. It was getting dark, but a crew with equipment was still working away from the road, cats and a bucket. The cats were working toward Spinner's farm.

Spinner walked on to town. If he stopped now he would lose his momentum, he would lose his mood of careful attentiveness, and something else might come over him. He walked into town and found everything very familiar. For a moment he even felt light, felt like smiling. He went to the square in the center of town, anxious to see it, and even when the light, happy feeling started to leave him nothing worse happened to his mood. It felt mostly quiet and he would have had to pay real attention to the shades of his feelings to know that it was like two eyes in the dark, looking, looking.

He wasn't recognized right away because of the hazy evening light. He got halfway around the small square before anyone spoke to him.

"Jake! Hey, when did you get back, Jake?"

He stopped, hands in pockets, and walked back to the man on the bench.

"Just yesterday. How you been, George?"

George got up, wiped his nervous hands on his overalls. "Hey," said George. "You got a tan, even," and he laughed.

"Outdoor work. The rock piles," said Jake, but the joke felt forced.

George must have felt it too. The first impulsiveness of the greeting was wearing off, and he rubbed his hands along his thighs again, slowly this time.

"Well, guess you'll be around. Gonna work that farm again?"

"That's why I'm back. Why you asking?"

"Just wondered. You know. Well, I gotta get Ruth. She's shopping. See you around, huh, Jake?"

"Sure. You'll see me." Spinner watched George walk toward the row of stores.

That crack about working the farm had done it. Had it been a crack? A normal question, except that Spinner's answer had been too sharp. George was going into a store to pick up his wife. He had left because he was picking up his wife.

Spinner got a few nods while he walked, and a few times there was small talk. No back-slapping and pumping the hand, because these people weren't made that way. Would he have worried about their casualness if he had come back from somewhere else, for some other reason?

Nobody mentioned Dixon. Did he expect they would? Did they ever?

Then he got invited to have a beer. Should he worry why nobody else had asked him, why only Eddy? Eddy wasn't so different from all the others, except that he came to town only once in a while. He worked in St. Louis.

"If this is the first beer since you're out, Jake, I want to know about it," said Eddy. "I want to know what it's like after two years."

"Three."

"I mean three. Must be really something."

They walked into the bar and Spinner still thought about Eddy's remark. Not about the beer, but about having been gone. An easy remark, making no strain between them. Spinner smiled and was suddenly anxious to have that beer. Maybe for Eddy's sake. He would drink that beer down and sigh a big sigh, shaking his head, to show Eddy what three years without beer could mean and how good it was to be back.

The first counter was low, for eating sandwiches and soup. Turtle soup when it was in season and fried catfish sandwiches all year round. The next counter was high, for beer and hard liquor, and a few men were standing there, staring at Spinner and Eddy till they could make them out in the light over the bar. A few waved, and some nodded, and one of them shook hands with him.

"Jake here," said Eddy, "is going to give us a demonstration. He's gonna show what the first beer is like after three long dry years."

There was some laughing, because of Eddy, but mostly there was the same kind of waiting that Spinner felt. He took out a cigarette and lit it. And when ash had formed he would let it drop on the floor, the way all of them did it, because this was the bar in Stone Bluff, not the mess hall with lysol smell or the cell with the concrete. He looked at the oiled boards on the floor, dull and uneven. That sight was as good to him then as the open door out to the square or the windows with nothing but glass in them and an old cactus for decoration.

"Tell you what," said Eddy, "if the first one don't carry a message, you got to buy the second yourself. Here, try not to drop it."

Spinner grinned at the glass on the bar, feeling self-conscious. He said, "Maybe I lost the taste for it, Eddy. Maybe you're wasting a beer."

Eddy stared, because the thought hadn't occurred to him. Then he saw Spinner's face and they both laughed.

Spinner picked up the glass seeing cool yellow and the soft foam on top and winking at Eddy.

"There's just a chance," he said, "mind you, just a chance, and this beer's going to bring back my taste for it."

"In detail, Jake! When it's down you got to tell me in detail!"

Spinner held up the glass and held it for a moment. "Tell you what, Eddy. You lay off for three years or so and I won't have to tell you about it."

"Come on, man. Drink it!"

Spinner drank the cold beer down to the bottom, and it was the best he had ever had. He put down the glass, gave a deep sigh, and started to shake his head. He stopped in the middle of it.

"Not wasting any time, huh, Spinner?"

It was the tone of voice more than the words. Spinner turned to see who it was, very slowly, because he had suddenly realized that this was the kind of thing he had really expected—cold dislike and an edge in the voice to needle him.

"Hi, Sloan," said Eddy, and some of the others said hello to him too.

Sloan wore his khakis rolled up so the work boots showed at his ankles and he stamped his feet a few times, making the dry mud break off in small pieces.

"I thought you jailbirds wasn't allowed no liquor once you got out." Sloan made a big laugh. "So us peaceful citizens shouldn't have to worry," he said.

He scratched his chest, laughing again, and when he passed Spinner he gave him a hard slap on the back, like a taunt, but too casual to make anything of it.

"I'll take another beer," said Spinner.

Sloan may not have heard it. He walked to the other end of the bar with three of his buddies following behind.

"You been working late," said Eddy. "I never knew road gangs worked late. Or at all," he added.

There was laughing again, which stopped abruptly so that Sloan could give his answer, but Sloan kept laughing and didn't bother. He walked to the pinball machine and put in a coin.

"When you work for Old Dixon," he said, "you keep jumping. Right, Spinner?" Sloan let the plunger slam home.

The pins made short buzzes and the scoreboard clacked with electric sounds.

"I wouldn't know," said Spinner.

"And if you don't work for Old Dixon, then you really jump. Right, Spinner?" Sloan laughed again, then shot the next ball.

"Is Dixon gonna break ground soon?" said Eddy. "On his South End development?"

"That's why we're pushing the road," said Sloan. "We just tore up the cut-off to the turnpike on the south end."

For a moment it seemed as if Sloan was through. He watched the tallies flash on the board and shot the rest of the balls.

Eddy turned back to Spinner and said, "How's your farm look, Jake? Could you tell it was there, under the weeds?"

"It's there. It'll take some doing."

"I mean to tell you!" Sloan was back at the bar. He leaned forward so that Spinner could see the grin. "Now I don't know farming from nothing," he said, "but I know it don't go with excavating." Then he waited.

Spinner was tapping his empty glass. He noticed how the slight move made his shoulder hurt.

"We figure on tearing it up starting next month. Part of the South End Development."

"Like hell," said Spinner.

"Like hell?" Sloan walked the length of the bar. He made his face look surprised. "You ain't selling to Dixon?"

"He knows it," said Spinner.

"He knows it? Now I'd say that's strange. How come he don't tell me those things? How come Dixon tells me a different story, huh, Jake? You think maybe he was lying to me?"

"Why should he lie to you, Sloan?" Spinner held the glass in his hands, rolling it back and forth in his palms. The glass felt warm. "Dixon lies only when it's something important."

It took Sloan a moment to get it all and when he did he took a low breath.

"You calling my boss a liar or you telling me I ain't important?"

"Forget it," said Eddy. "You gotta remember..."

"You shut up, Eddy, unless you want the same thing Spinner is getting any minute now."

Spinner felt his hands trembling, but he knew he wasn't afraid. He wasn't afraid till he noticed the rage pushing up inside him, with heat on his skin and the sense of his muscles swelling.

"I'm waiting," said Sloan. "I'm dumb and you better explain it again."

"I'm not supposed to get into trouble," said Spinner. It hurt his throat, saying it. "So forget it."

Sloan's grin spread out slowly and it showed how much he was starting to like everything.

"Well," he said, "well, well, well." He leaned on the bar next to Spinner, very close. "You mean you wanna apologize? Go ahead. Lemme hear it."

Spinner swallowed and moved his neck. His shoulder was aching. "Leave me alone," he said. "Will you?"

"Say please."

"Please. Just forget it."

Sloan grinned more. He stood back and put his hands on his hips.

"Hey," he said. "You're sweating! How come you're sweating?"

Spinner didn't answer.

"It makes you look yellow all over, Jakey. How come?"

Spinner pushed away from the bar and turned to the door.

"Let me through," he said and looked down at Sloan's foot.

"Say please again."

He couldn't talk, so he stepped back and looked past Sloan, at the door. He couldn't see the door clearly, but it gave him a point of attention, to try and see the door clearly.

"All choked up, Jakey?"

Maybe Sloan would lose interest. If Sloan would hear please again, perhaps that would be the end. Spinner coughed.

"What you say, Jakey?" Sloan had a greedy look on his face.

"Please," said Spinner.

Nobody made any sound and Sloan stood there, gaping. His arms were hanging down. Then he started a slow, unbelieving laugh.

"What? What you say, Jakey?"

Spinner's voice didn't feel like his own, it was quiet and even.

"You can either get out of the way, Sloan, or you can try staying right there," he heard himself say. "And if you stay, I'll break your back."

This time, at the end of the pause, Sloan said nothing. He moved his mouth, stopped. Then he moved his foot with a slow scrape, and then jumped—not at Spinner, at the bar. He grabbed up the empty glass and in one motion smashed the wide rim and swung for the strike.

The door banged. There was a yell, "Hold it!" Sloan couldn't stop, but he swung wild. His hand hit air and Spinner set his back for the spring.

"Hold it! Damn you to hell!"

Spinner was sure it was the badge that stopped him. He saw the sheriff, the gun at his belt, his hands up by his hips, and how he stood wide-legged, ready to move. But the badge stopped Spinner.

"Drop that glass, Sloan, or I'll draw on you!"

Sloan let it drop and watched it roll.

"And you there, Spinner!"

Spinner stood still and looked at the sheriff. The man's hair had gone all white since Spinner had seen him three years ago. The red face made a contrast next to the hair.

"All right," he said. "What is this?" His breath was coming fast and gave hoarseness to his voice.

Sloan started talking, but the sheriff cut him off angrily, and Spinner didn't say a word. Eddy explained it and the barman said the same thing and the others nodded. The sheriff told Sloan to get out, and said that the next time he wouldn't care whom Sloan was working for, he'd run him out of town.

"You won't see the day," said Sloan and went to the door, his buddies following.

"Just git," said the sheriff.

Sloan stopped at the door. "I got better rights than that jailbird," he shouted. "And see if Old Dixon don't hold with me."

"He's got nothing to do with this," said the sheriff. He jerked his head at Sloan to get out, but Sloan came back in.

"It don't? That's what the whole thing is about! First day out of jail and he comes in here insulting Old Dixon. I got my loyalties. No jailbird threatens my boss and gets away with it!"

The sheriff looked at Spinner and said, "This true, Jake?"

Spinner shook his head but the sheriff didn't see it.

"Ask the rest of them," Sloan was shouting. "Did he call Dixon a liar?"

The men at the bar looked away. One of them went to the door in the back and walked out to the alley.

"You better get one thing straight, Sheriff!" Sloan had pulled himself together.

But the sheriff didn't want to listen. He said, "Out, Sloan, I don't need you for this."

He stood waiting, and Sloan backed down. He walked out of the bar and one of his men slammed the door after them.

Jake Spinner rubbed his hands over his face and the sheriff said, "I'll want to talk to you." Then he left.

CHAPTER 4

W hen Jake Spinner came out of the bar it was dark on the square and the small crowd which had looked in at the windows had walked away again. A dullness came over him, obscuring his mood, and he let it be that way. He gave a brief glance at the square. The center was indistinct, and he turned away, not wanting to know who might be there. To the left the North Highway came in and Jake stood looking away from the square. Only details registered for him. It was too painful to think about Sloan or the sheriff.

The trees stood very still and the blinker light where the highway entered the town made impersonal winks. He watched the headlights of a car dip up, then spread closer. The car slowed before reaching the square and turned into a side street. Concentrating on details because he didn't dare think of the other things, Jake saw that the car moved without hesitation, knowing the way, and that the plate was from a different district, St. Louis, most likely. Jake crossed the street and walked along the far side of the square. Now the trees had started to rustle.

"Jake," said the sheriff.

Spinner slowed to let the sheriff catch up with him.

"On your way to the station?" asked the sheriff.

He hadn't been. He kept walking and said, "You wanted to tell me something."

"Jake," said the sheriff, "maybe it isn't your fault, what happened, but it will be if it gets worse."

Spinner took a breath and kept walking.

"Just lay low," said the sheriff, "because I don't want trouble around here."

"You?" and Spinner heard himself laugh.

"Don't get chippy. Just do like I say."

"Do what?"

The sheriff sucked his teeth. Then he looked the other way. "You deciding to sell your farm?"

"You don't sound like you're asking," said Spinner. He wanted to say more but kept it down.

"Best thing, to my way of thinking," said the sheriff.

"I do my own thinking."

"Don't get chippy, Jake. I seen you grow up, and all I..."

Spinner stopped and turned on the sheriff without caring who would hear him.

"You fronting for Dixon, like that Sloan bastard? I don't thank you for it, just so you know. And I don't scare." Spinner bared his teeth with the strain in his face and went on. "A lot of things scare me, believe me, and half of them I don't even know. But this thing I know, and it doesn't scare me one bit. I keep what I've got. I want my place!" If Spinner's voice hadn't been so loud the sheriff might have thought Spinner sounded puzzled. "Hell!" Spinner shouted, "Hell. Why should I have to want something I already got!"

He walked off abruptly and for a moment the sheriff stood still. He had forgotten what he had wanted to say before Spinner had started to talk. He grunted and went after Spinner. He'd just tell him the same thing again.

"Wait up, Jake."

Spinner waited. They were off the square now, on a street dark with trees, and the sheriff couldn't make out Spinner's expression.

"Just this, Jake. Keep to yourself and don't set a bad example. I'm warning you. We got edgy days in this town right now. Dixon's been edgy lately."

"I got my own troubles."

"But when Dixon's got them he makes them everybody's. And I don't need to tell you he don't like you in particular."

"Don't tell me his troubles."

"I'm telling you yours. Sell out and get out, while Dixon's still buying."

"I'm not worried he'll drop his offer."

"He's got troubles, I tell you. Out-of-town troubles, and he's nasty enough to make all of us feel it. So I'm telling you, Jake. You just came back home and you don't know. That's why I'm telling you."

Spinner felt his mood swing and he almost said thanks, but there was too much of a backlog of other things. He said, "I'll look out for my own. I've learned that."

"And how good have you been at it? Tell me, how good?"

Spinner didn't want to think about that. He killed the sick feeling that started to rise in him. A flat smile was on his face.

"Maybe Dixon will die," he said. "I got to have luck some time."

There was a short silence.

"One wrong move," said the sheriff, so low that Spinner could hardly hear. "One wrong move and I'll be right behind you."

Spinner hadn't meant his remark that way, but there was no time to correct it. The sheriff walked off toward the square and Spinner turned the other way. He walked with his hands in his pockets and stared in front of him without really seeing. Once he spat. He walked to the end of town and then angled back along the south end, meaning to walk till he was worn enough to lie down and to sleep without thought.

He had not imagined it would be this bad, the fine edge between rage and despair. He walked with the fear riding his back that some small thing might break the balance....

Half an hour after Spinner had watched the car turn off near the square, he watched it pass him again on the street. He was walking in the south end of town now and a few minutes later Spinner saw Dixon's house. It sat back from the street, though plainly visible, and the lighted French windows downstairs gave everything on the veranda the sharp lines of a silhouette.

Dixon stepped into the light, stood for a moment, and was shot dead.

Not very much later the sheriff was close after his man. Jake Spinner was running down the street, and the sheriff chased after him in his car. He had to sap Spinner unconscious, which was the only way he could take him in.

CHAPTER 5

He sat up to get the glare of the bulb out of his eyes. It hung over his head, in the ceiling, and when he sat up he swayed a little. He saw the black bars, the bare station room beyond, and the screen door to the outside. It took a while before he could focus beyond that. They stood on the other side of the door, and what Spinner saw mostly were foreheads, white where they pressed into the screen. The eyes were in shadow and Spinner could only feel them. There was no meaning in the faces. It made the silence unbearable.

"He's up." The faces behind the door moved. "He's sitting up."

Spinner heard a chair scrape and boots coming closer. The deputy opened the cell and said, "Come on out."

"You're in deep," said the sheriff. "He's dead."

Spinner knew that. Dixon was dead, but nothing had changed for Spinner. Everything was as before. He did not even feel it was worse.

"And resisting arrest," added the deputy, as if it mattered.

"Where's the gun, Jake?"

"How come you shot him?"

"Where'd you get the gun, Jake?"

"How come you went to see him?"

Let them talk. Let them talk and don't listen and get back the strength to keep them away, even the sick strength of hate.

"I've known you all my life, Jake. You can't get any worse now."

The old bastard with the voice like a father. The old bastard with the gun and the sap and the baleful eye, as if he were worried.

"Why'd you do it, Jake?"

"Listen to me," said Spinner. It was his own voice and he was begging them.

"Sure. Go ahead."

But the deputy was licking a cigarette and the sheriff looked at the door.

"Listen!" Spinner shouted.

They didn't. The screen door opened and Sloan stuck his head in.

"We're right out here, Sheriff, so if you need any help, any kind of help—"

"Get out," said the sheriff. "Slam that door shut, Teddy."

The deputy slammed the door and the sheriff took Spinner's arm to lead him into the back room. There was a table and chairs, a small window, and behind the glass a white face, then two, then more.

The sheriff yanked the shade over the window and sat down. Outside there was a slow murmuring.

"Jake," said the sheriff, "I can tie this thing up without your saying a word. You understand?"

That's what Spinner had needed. It shut his face, put steel over his insides, and gave him back his intent. "You listening?" he said.

"Jake, before you…"

"I didn't kill that bastard. I'm glad somebody did, but I didn't kill that bastard."

The sheriff didn't want to hear. He wanted to say more, before Spinner got worse. "I can tie this up, I told you." The sheriff stopped. There was a slow swell of voices outside and when it sank again it did not leave altogether.

"Jake, listen to me."

Spinner had clamped his hands into each other, so they wouldn't shake.

The sheriff said, "Dixon's dead. One thing, Jake. That means you'll have a clean trial. It means nobody's trying to tie you up any more. This town, Jake, without Dixon—"

He stopped again and the three men in the room looked at the covered window, as if they could see it there, the new garble of voices, the sudden swell and sinking of sound. But it stayed stronger now than in the beginning.

The sheriff saw Spinner sweat.

"Jake, you listening to me?"

Even the sheriff's low voice seemed frantic to Spinner. The covered window seemed alive with a terrible motion.

"I'm trying to tell you, Jake, so you wouldn't be scared—"

The old fatherly bastard pouring oil on the waters. The old fatherly bastard trying the old fatherly trick of bribing.

Spinner was breathing hard, as if he had been running. The voices outside were chasing him, they were brewing his insides with acid.

"Scared?" said the deputy.

Spinner had an ache in his throat and he turned it into a laugh, a queer, hesitant laugh.

"Listen to 'em," he said. The words were chasing out of him. "Listen to how happy they are about all of this! They're so crazy happy about Dixon being dead they don't want to stop there. They don't…"

"All right, Jake. All right now."

"Listen to the stupid…"

"Don't listen. Listen to me. Dixon made them stupid, but not forever, Jake!" The sheriff slapped his hand on the table and watched Spinner react. It made Spinner turn and look at the sheriff. The sheriff saw the face set, and the eyes come back into focus.

And at the same time the murmur outside seemed to die, the shaded window making the room a separate thing again.

"Tell me what happened," said the sheriff.

Yes, tell him. For a moment Spinner felt a great gush of feeling inside, a feeling that opened him up and wanted to make him lean close to the man on the other side of the table.

"How come you shot him?" said the deputy.

Like the clank of a door or a whip at his heels. Spinner stiffened.

"Just tell it, Jake. Unless we know—"

What he knew could save his life! Unless they knew, soon, now, it might be too late to save his life, and Spinner forgot the deputy, didn't hear the voices outside, didn't wonder about the sheriff, but talked, fast and eager.

"I didn't kill Dixon, but somebody did! Find him. This car came down the street twice. The same car I saw turn off by the square. That was the first time I saw it. He knew where he was going and he had out-of-town plates, same plates on the car on Dixon's street, and right after I heard the Garand..."

"How come you know it was a Garand?"

"Shut up one minute!" The voices outside grew big again and Spinner started to shout. "The car drove on down the street, going south! I can show you. Maybe there's time. Sloan, back in the bar, he was telling they just tore up the cutoff on the south end and somebody who didn't know was driving out that way to get on the turnpike..."

"How come you know it was a Garand, Jake?" The sheriff talked as if he hadn't heard a thing.

"Why shouldn't I know? I shot one for more years than..."

"Shut up," said the sheriff. He leaned forward, listening.

They heard the front door open and feet on the wooden floor. Not many, but hard and aggressive.

The sheriff cursed and jumped out of his chair. He ran into the station room but before he could say anything Sloan was talking.

"Sheriff," he said, "I offered once and I'm offering again. Me and the boys..."

"When I need help I call the state troopers. Any more crap out of you and your riff-raff and I'll call the troopers right now. You open your mouth again, and I..."

"You talking to me like that? You think you can pull that stuff like in the bar twice?"

"Get out!" The sheriff yanked at his holster. "Either you..."

"Pull that gun on me, huh? You know who's out there, waiting for me? Citizens, you dried-up old coot. You got a notion now Old Dixon is dead..."

"Out, you son of a bitch!"

Sloan's feet clattered when the sheriff pushed him, but Sloan kept on shouting.

"I'm here to talk Dixon's cause! I'm here—"

The door banged, the lock made two clicks, and the sheriff came back.

"Bolt the back," he said to the deputy, "and break out two rifles."

Then he stood in the doorway, one hand on his gun, looking up at the wall. The crowd outside the building was suddenly silent except for one voice. The words weren't clear, but the pitch of it lashed back and forth like a whip.

Spinner started to sweat. The doubt pulled at him with an equal strength—that he must lose, and that he must not give up. In the stalemate he found the worst pain of all, that all this needn't have happened, that if only they would believe him—

Glass crashed and a stone beat through the window shade which flapped wildly, and tore.

"Put him in the cell." The sheriff ran past the deputy, who came up with two guns. The sheriff picked up the phone, a wild pounding shook the front door, and the sheriff yelled again, "Lock him in the cell."

It broke the stalemate for Spinner. He got up before the deputy was back in the room, stood next to him when the front door splintered. The deputy's head snapped around at the crash and then he ran into the front room. Behind him the door slammed.

Spinner flicked the lock, snapped off the light, and pushed the table under the window. The commotion was in front. The crowd would clog at the sight of the guns, they would stop at the door with the back pushing up to see the performance and the front men trying to gauge the danger. Maybe shots even—Spinner wasn't waiting to hear. He knocked out the rest of the glass with a chair and lunged out of the window headfirst.

The fall didn't stop him. He raced across the back lot and headed back to the street where it had all started. He ran automatically because there was nothing else to decide.

He didn't go all the way back to the Dixon house, but turned to the end of the street that ran out into the country. He had gotten this far once before, running after the out-of-town car until the sheriff had caught up with him and the chase was over. The street became a gravelly road and Spinner continued running. The chase wasn't over for him, and this time he was the hunter.

There had been a shot—a Garand, Spinner was sure—and before the fact had sunk in he had seen Dixon against the light on his porch, spinning suddenly, then falling with a thud. Spinner had stopped and without any transition he had felt the panic. Nothing worse could happen to him than Dixon's being killed. He hadn't thought about this but the panic had said it for him. And then the car. With the feeling of disorganized speed inside him Spinner had thought the car was going too slowly. It shifted with normal sound and headed out to the south end, but never going too fast or hunting for the best way out of town. It found its way steadily, which Spinner could see because the car lights had been on.

The gravel made dry rattles under his feet and he swerved to the side of the road to let the grass absorb the fast thud of his feet. His breathing was painful now. This is the way the car went. As if the driver had been a native, knowing the short cuts out of town, avoiding the center, knowing the lanes that went through the fields and where the highway would be. If it was the same car he had seen near the square, if the driver wasn't a native, if he had just come in, if if if— The effort of running kept Spinner from thinking too much, so the doubt never grew big. And what else could he have done? He would run just the same way to keep from dying of doubt. It had to be this way.

Sloan had said they were cutting a road for the South End Development, worked until dark to cut it through there. Across from the highway? He must have meant that or else there was no sense in tearing through the south end land with road equipment, no sense tearing this lane in two in order to make an inroad from the highway for Dixon's equipment.

And no one driving a car into town from the north late in the evening— no matter how well he might know the country—could have known that Sloan and his crew had that evening torn up the lane on the south.

He would find the marks in the fresh ground. Later, perhaps, they could find the same soil dragged onto the highway by the car's tires, to show which way the car went, how much it weighed, or even fantastic things like the make and the color and the registration and the place of sale and the name of the owner and the reason for all that had happened.

It wasn't fantastic to Spinner. It was his life, and all he was running for.

Slow now. If it is true, any part of it, it had to be true now.

He smelled the loam.

Spinner slowed and stopped. Sit down for a moment? It was sure now, he could smell the loam, he could stop and imagine that all the rest was just as true as the ground broken up on the other side of the rise. He could even lie down and go to sleep and imagine— He started to curse at himself and moved. But the new, faint smell stopped him rigid.

The blood roared in his ears and his breath was the loudest of all. The smell was burnt rubber.

There should be a sound, he should hear something, if his blood and his breath weren't roaring in his ears.

He crouched on the rise, squeezed low, and felt himself tremble at wheels spinning free and a motor making a useless whine.

Spinner lay on his belly and when the trembling went away it slipped off smoothly and he took a deep breath. He almost laughed.

The car had come down the short incline, and at the bottom, where the road was supposed to continue, had slid through the fresh loam and buck-led into the ruts running sideways. The speed from the incline had pushed him there. The car had plowed through a pile of dirt that ran the length of the road bed. Even if he hadn't been stuck in the ruts he couldn't have made it back.

Spinner grinned to himself and took his time. He crawled down very carefully, keeping out of the skyline, but it was more like a sport now. The car was headed the other way, and whoever was at the wheel kept gun-ning and idling the motor, on and off, on and off. Some time the man in the car would have to come out. He would open the door, walk to the back, and bend down to check how badly the wheels were digging in.

Spinner sat crouched next to the car and tried thinking it out before it happened. He was a few feet away from his man, next to the spinning wheel and the burnt rubber stink strong in his face and the car trembling now and then. Just a few feet, he kept thinking, just a few feet— He tried forcing patience but it made things worse. Wait—a few feet—wait—a few feet—kept buzzing at him and the wheel at his right buzzed and spat dirt and the door a few feet ahead of him never opened. Spinner stared at it, and felt the muscles along his back swelling, arching him like a bow. The wheel whined and the car made lazy nods, not half trying. He found the door handle. Spinner jumped.

The car confined his movements, but Spinner didn't need much room. His concentrated violence had only one dimension—from himself to the man behind the wheel. A gun dropped to the floor, the clawing of the mark behind the wheel grew aimless, then both men staggered out into the open as if grown together, and Spinner never stopped. When Spinner swung and swung, the sharp pull in his neck was pleasure and when the other man struck back it was like a tonic.

Spinner didn't realize it, but very soon after his man had lost the gun there wasn't really any fight. Then Spinner noticed an odd passivity, a yielding as if nothing Spinner did could matter. The man stumbled and fell into the ditch, and Spinner stopped because there wasn't any more resist-ance. He walked up to the ditch and wondered if the man were still alive. He was. He was breathing slowly.

Spinner bent down and picked him up. The man was small and frail. A hiss of pain came out of his mouth, but he said nothing. Spinner let him down to the ground, again aware of the man's frailness. It made Spinner think that there ought to be something warm, a blanket maybe, or some-thing soft to put under the head.

Spinner stepped back to the ditch and lifted the man's feet to the level ground. One leg, then the other. He held the leg and then—with a hasty shake of the hand—he dropped it. He had touched a clubfoot.

Chapter 6

The man wasn't marked up very much. It made no sense to Spinner but there was hardly a mark. The man's face was long and white. Spinner stepped back and said, "Get up, killer."

The man rose on one elbow and then no further.

"Get up!" Spinner was angry, impatient, and kicked at the man, hitting his leg.

The killer didn't get up. He laid down slowly with a constrained breath in his throat. He raised his hands and put them over his mouth. Spinner saw he was wearing black gloves of tight leather, the fingers tensed into the white face like hooks. When the man relaxed again he said, "I can't. My foot. The good one."

There was a swelling over the ankle. It had pushed over the shoe and tightened the laces. When Spinner touched the foot the man gasped.

"Lie back while I do this," said Spinner, "and bite on this." He picked a piece of wood off the ground and held it out to the man.

"Just go ahead," said the killer.

"I'm taking the shoe off. Bite."

The man lifted his head and tapped his teeth.

"They are false. They would break," he said and lay back again.

Spinner took the shoe off and felt the heat under the sock. It might he broken, he thought, but he didn't know. He thought of wrapping the foot when he suddenly stood and listened.

"Sirens," said the killer.

"Christ, yes—" Spinner shouted, and then, with a shock that was stronger than the high grating sound, he stopped.

"They are not coming for me," said the killer. It was dark where he lay. He was just a voice.

"Shut up," said Spinner, and the siren grew in his head and images spun and flailed at him; blank walls, men with saps, blank faces, walled cells, Dixon dead, run, police, run, police—

"Are you turning me in?"

A question. A question of taking on a new role, to go to the police of his own free will and to let them decide for him.

"They won't believe you," said the killer.

His voice was flat. There was no doubt or emotion of any kind. The killer was sure and Spinner was not. The killer had planned and Spinner had nothing. He had a hope that they would decide in his favor.

"What makes you think they'll believe you?"

Spinner started to breathe fast and shallow, with the sirens beating at him and the voice sifting at him, bland and impersonal, from the ground.

"I will tell them I saw you on the street. I will add that to the rest of my alibi. I have..."

He could run away. He could run and be without past and— The sirens were reaching closer.

"Are you taking me to the police?"

Same question. It meant, "Are you going to let them decide? For you?"

"They scare you," said the voice from the ground. "You must know them."

A frail cripple lay on the ground, a killer who could not move any more, but was not scared.

"Have you decided?"

Spinner was going to let the men with the saps decide for him—that's why he was scared. That's why he was more crippled than the man on the ground, all his life crippled from one loss to the next and then the last loss because he had never broken the rules, only suffered from them.

"Are you going back?"

"Like hell!" Spinner suddenly felt the difference. He felt free as a man's thoughts in delirium, and he lifted the killer off the ground, put him into the car and slammed the door. The sirens were shrieking in town and Spinner felt the sound like a goad. The more they screamed the clearer his new intent. He was going to make his last try, and a new one.

"Hold on!"

The car lurched and bucked and Spinner never had any doubt he would make it. The Garand was on the floor. He threw it out, for more room.

"Now! You and me, killer, we're going to make this a break!" and Spinner shot free.

CHAPTER 7

The killer sat in his corner and didn't talk except to give directions. He knew the terrain well. Spinner took country lanes, crossed fields, and followed highways for short stretches and then turned off into the country again. There were no more sirens now and the fields under the moon looked as if nothing had ever happened there.

"Stop after the turn," said the killer.

Spinner stopped to one side of the lane, where the bushes reached toward the road. They scraped the car and made black patterns against the windshield.

"Do you know where you are?" said the killer.

"To the north of town," said Spinner. "I'm not sure how far."

"About ten miles. To the south."

Spinner looked at the man without saying anything because the remark had lacked something. There had been no flavor in it; no reprimand, no bragging, not even a real wish to correct.

"You cross this field," it went on, "and follow the lane on the other side till we get to the woods. Park there; it's about five minutes on foot back to the place where you found me."

Spinner stared at the man, who had stopped and was concentrating on shifting his leg.

"You left my shoe there," said the man. "Bring it back here."

"Your—your shoe?"

"It's custom made. They might trace it."

At first Spinner didn't know what to do with his voice. It had taken Spinner a lifetime of pressure to make his decision that night, and the killer was already taking the step for granted.

"Go back?" said Spinner. "Go back there to get you a shoe?" Then the anger broke out. "Your lousy lousy custom-made clubfoot is on the other leg, you ugly creep!"

"They are both custom made." No change in voice, no change in manner, only more information.

Spinner had to do something, so he hit the man.

The killer had tears in his eyes from the blow. They looked like water. The man blinked once, to clear his eyes, but otherwise made no move. He was oddly passive and his lack of resistance defeated Spinner, as if the killer were constantly out of reach.

The man said, "You don't understand—" but then he stopped, seeing

Spinner's face.

"Understand!" Spinner roared. "You understand why I'm here? Why a hick like me jumps in the car with you and drives..."

"I don't," said the killer. "But you said you would drive me. So if you're..."

"Shut up! I ran after you because you killed Dixon. You killed Dixon and I got the blame for it. I've been getting the blame for everything I never did till it looks to me there must be a better way. I'm trying it now! I'm sticking to you and I'm not going back! That clear in your mind?"

"Yes. You're afraid to go back."

"You're damn right, killer." It seemed to make no impression. "And you need a driver, right? So the hell with your shoe." Spinner threw the car into gear.

"Better go back first. You left the Garand there."

"Garand? So what? That's your gun."

"That gun can't be traced, or the forty-five, either. But they have your prints on them."

He turned his head to watch how Spinner would take it, but he didn't wait for an answer. Spinner had set his teeth so the shock wouldn't touch him, and stubbornness showed in the set of his head. The killer looked ahead again while Spinner shifted, because there was no point arguing with a man who acted by hate.

"Don't cross the field," said the killer. "Follow the road."

They drove without talking and after an hour or so, when Spinner recognized the north highway at a point beyond Stone Bluff, he began to relax. But there was no change in the man next to him. Spinner thought he was like stone. Spinner tensed up again, unable to form a meaningful picture. They were driving straight and fast now, with no need for directions, so the killer sat silently and sometimes didn't even seem to be there.

"What's your name, killer?"

"Loma," said the man.

On a turn they touched briefly. Was that Loma? He was like skin, with a ghost inside. Any other man with a name like Loma would explain more. Is Loma the first name or the last name? What kind of name is it?

"Loma?" he said aloud. "What kind of name is that?"

"Just a name."

"Where'd you get it?"

It seemed to surprise Loma, unless he hesitated because he didn't think an answer would be important. Then he said, "What's the difference? I'm using it now."

They had talked and Spinner knew nothing. Skin with a ghost inside called Loma.

"How's the foot?" asked Spinner.

"Bad. Keep driving. We have to make time."

He answered but it always turned into an answer about something else.

"All right," said Spinner. He kept his voice even, trying to get used to the way Loma acted, but controlling himself only made Spinner more edgy. "All right. I want to know a few things."

There was no immediate answer, since Loma was waiting to hear the rest, but Spinner was silent. He was still listening to the sound of his voice which had come out flat, empty, reminding him of Loma's voice.

"You want to know what?" said Loma.

Spinner coughed.

"Why'd you kill him? Dixon, I mean."

"I don't know."

"What?"

"I don't know why. I was hired."

Spinner cursed under his breath, then kept still. If Loma had heard it he didn't show it. The highway rolled up and down without curving and the end of the headlights sealed off Spinner's vision at a fixed distance.

"Who hired you?" Spinner asked.

"St. Louis."

Spinner remembered what Moss had said, that Dixon had tried getting too big.

"Who in St. Louis?"

"A St. Louis contact hired me."

Did Loma think Spinner knew how it was done? St. Louis hired me; I don't know why he was killed. A death had never seemed so mechanical to Spinner, not even at the worst times on the Islands when there were more corpses than living things and killing had become a day's work. But never like this: a final act for no final reason, a business decision, not a matter of life or death. Dixon had been killed because he no longer fitted into somebody's enterprises.

It was the wrong way of thinking. Now, having switched, either think of death, the way Loma did, or don't think of it at all, the way Loma did.

"I didn't know," said Spinner, "that Dixon was in that deep."

"Neither did he," said the killer.

Done with it. Pushed out of the way like a small stone pushed out of the way with the foot.

Loma was back with himself, or wherever he went when he said nothing. He was leaning into the seat but he wasn't sleeping. His eyes were open. Once Spinner jerked the wheel to avoid a raccoon crossing the road and Loma turned his head. Then he looked front again. No, thought Spinner. He faced front but didn't look. There was nothing to see. His eyes were open the way a box is open. That's how he had looked at Spinner. There was nothing to see.

Suddenly Spinner said, "I'm Spinner, Jake Spinner."

"I see."

A lie. The bastard saw nothing he didn't care to see.

Spinner was behind the wheel, a part of the car, and the car was running. So why bother with Spinner.

"Understand this, Loma. You listening to me?"

"Yes."

"So you got it clear what goes on here. I'm driving you and I'm not going back. You need me and I need you and that's our bargain."

"What bargain?"

"My driving you! How far do you think you can get with those feet you got?"

"That's why you're driving me."

Spinner frowned. He wanted to back away from his confusion but then had to stop. Where would he back to? It was clear that he could not go back. He had gone through all that. But the rest was clear to Loma, that Spinner was driving him because Loma himself couldn't drive.

"Anything else?" Loma said.

Spinner hadn't wanted to see it yet, but it had been clear all the time. He could not go and find work, because he had no past. If he had a past, if he told it, there was his record, and worse, the new crime hanging over him. Whether it was an indictment for murder or as an accessory after the fact, it hung over him and would ruin him. It would ruin him, if he tried living again by the rules. There was no other way out.

And with a gentle switch, which Spinner noticed just barely, he made up his mind. It did not feel like a decision but like something he had known a very long time, ever since his father had lived wrong, in spite of his homey savings, ever since Dixon had been in his life, living high, wide and wrong, and ever since prison.

There was no other way out.

"Loma," said Spinner. "You're my in." And after a pause. "I'm switching sides."

It happened that simply.

"I can't be of much help," said Loma, but Spinner did not seem to hear. If he heard, he was not ready to answer. The full weight of his decision kept him silent and he was absorbing the weight so that he would never have to feel it again.

"I can't be of much help," Loma said again.

"Why? You got friends and contacts."

"My contacts wouldn't do you much good."

"Bull. You're going to show me how."

"I have only two kinds of contacts," said Loma. "The ones that pay me and the ones I get paid for."

Spinner started to curse when Loma interrupted again.

"I don't give advice much, but…"

"So don't."

Loma turned his head slightly and Spinner could see the goat eyes looking at him. There was a moment's recognition, a brief impatience with an object, and then the eyes went blank again.

"Because it can save me trouble later." said Loma. "You want to become a—what would you call it—a hood? Don't do it."

"Leave that to me. You just…"

"How can I? You asked me to give you an in."

"And that's all I asked. Not advice."

"You're not fit," said Loma.

"Loma, my old man was in with St. Louis and if he could do it, I can…"

"Where is he now?"

"He's dead. But…"

"Uh," said Loma and whether he meant it or not, it sounded like a conclusion to Spinner. "You're still alive."

Loma turned his head, but Spinner didn't see Loma look at him. Then Loma looked away, saying nothing.

"Understand this," said Spinner. He was not straining about it, he was just telling Loma. "I set this up like a bargain." He lit a cigarette and then said, "You don't do what I say and I make you regret it."

Spinner left the thought vague, but Loma answered it to the point.

"They are looking for you, not me. You keep forgetting that."

Nothing got to him. Loma stayed untouched and Spinner's skin prickled with irritation. Kick his foot. That'll make him take notice. Kick him hard and watch if he's human. Spinner let the thought warm him but left it there. Then he said, "I don't care who they're after. There's one man can set them after you."

Now Loma would have to take notice. He would have to deal with Jake Spinner.

"You?" said Loma.

"Yeah, me!"

"Don't try it," said Loma.

"More advice? I couldn't do it, you think?" and Spinner heard the rasp in his voice and felt revolted. He hadn't meant it to take this turn. "What about that shoe you left behind. Doesn't that make you anxious?"

"No. A very long chance they can trace it. That's why I let it go by."

"To hell with tracing, killer. I mean me fitting the shoe on the foot, me telling them whose special-made shoe it is."

"My clubfoot is on the right," said Loma. "The shoe I lost could fit anybody. Even you."

"I'm twice your size, Loma." Spinner thought this would be the place to laugh, loud and hard. But he didn't feel like laughing.

"I use my left foot more than the club foot," said Loma. "My left foot is big."

It had started to sound like a conversation to Spinner, a casual, empty conversation between two people who meant nothing to each other. Everything that touched Loma seemed to turn into nothing. Spinner distracted himself by gunning the motor. He raced and let go, raced again, let it go. He would keep his temper, the way Loma did, and make his point again.

"Like I said." He sounded as casual as he had imagined, and felt as empty. "You and me got a bargain."

Loma said nothing.

"What, Loma? You got another solution?"

Nothing from Loma. He was holding his breath while shifting his foot.

"Shoot me dead, maybe, once I got you out of this?"

Spinner didn't see it, but Loma was closing his eyes. It could have been from the pain, or—this being the first time he had closed his eyes—it could have been his kind of sign which showed emotion.

"Thinking about it, huh, Loma?"

"No. I wasn't," said Loma. He stroked his hand over his hair slowly, and said, "I've never shot anyone for personal reasons."

Chapter 8

Spinner didn't want to talk any more. He drove on, and started to smoke. He let the smoke idle back out of his mouth, making it burn in his throat. But he ignored it. Or, like Loma, he was not there to feel it. The night air became colder and the inside of the car had a chill. Spinner thought of turning the heater on, but he didn't. Feeling cold would keep him awake, he reasoned. It would make him feel alive. He was on the point of asking Loma if he were cold, but he didn't really want to hear the answer. Spinner imagined something weird would come out, something about cold means feeling alive and that's why corpses felt cold. Spinner shook his head sharply, and imagined that it was the strain and no sleep that was making him think this way.

He looked at the dashboard, to see something small and concrete. "We need gas," he said.

It broke the spell, and Spinner was even hoping that Loma would say something in return. But Loma just nodded.

"This looks like the stretch before Landon," said Spinner. "There's a station on Main Street that's open for twenty-four hours."

"Take the black top to the right, just before town," said Loma.

"I said we need gas!" Spinner's foot went down on the pedal and he kept it there.

"I know. I have gas."

But Spinner didn't hear it. He felt that Loma was not only ignoring his person but also his words, his judgment, and his decisions.

"There's a twenty-four hour garage…"

"Why do you forget, Spinner," said Loma, "that they are looking for you?"

It was the first time Loma had used Spinner's name and it gave his words a surprising weight. Spinner turned, but Loma looked as before. It was a disappointment.

"What did you say?" asked Spinner. "You have gas?"

"Turn right at the black top," Loma repeated. "I'll tell you where to stop."

He told Spinner to stop past a small bridge over a creek and to walk down to the leg of the bridge where he would find a five-gallon can of gas.

"You got this planned as if you knew I was going to be along."

"No. I have it planned so I don't have to be seen this side of Landon. It's too close to Stone Bluff."

Spinner made no comment, and after he had found the can and poured the gas into the tank he threw the can into the ditch and came back to the car.

"Pick it up," said Loma. "Put it in the car."

Spinner stopped. He couldn't see Loma's face in the dark and without seeing it he couldn't make out the man's tone of voice. But the face wouldn't tell him and the voice was always without inflection. Loma had told him to do something the way he would move a lever or press a button. He was using Spinner.

"Put it in the car," said Loma. "It's safer."

Of course. The goat-eyed bastard was right. Spinner went to the ditch and picked up the can. The grass there was wet with night dew and a bush dropped wet against Spinner's neck. He almost swung at the bush.

Spinner threw the can into the back seat and drove off. Where to? Where Loma said they should drive. Stop where? Where Loma said they should stop. It wasn't the way Spinner had imagined his break. There was going to be free action, free anger, and to hell with everything else. Instead he was like a button on a machine and Loma giving a press now and then.

That wasn't going to be it. Between now and the time they got to St. Louis, Spinner was going to make his impression. Not easy, maybe, not with a ghost like Loma, but Spinner was going to make his impression because that was going to be the new life.

They drove in a long silence and Spinner almost didn't see his chance. Once he said, "How's your foot, Loma?" and when Loma didn't answer Spinner cursed himself for having said the wrong thing. A personal question, asking about pain. Loma couldn't know about pain and being personal with him was like hugging a rock.

"Damn it!" Spinner yelled. "Answer me!"

Loma said something in a voice that slurred everything but the pain he was feeling. He sat low in the seat, rigid with effort, holding his leg as if it were an object that didn't belong to him.

"Jesus," said Spinner, and slowed the car to a stop. "Bad, huh?" He leaned over the man.

Loma was gritting words. It sounded like, "Drive—don't stop—drive—" but Spinner didn't listen to him.

"You got any bandages, rags or something? How about aspirin?"

Loma shook his head slowly, not to make too much movement, but he didn't say anything. His eyes were shut tight and except for the pain giving him presence he was hardly there.

"So we'll get some," said Spinner and started to drive again.

Loma breathed more like a human being after a while.

"Just keep driving," he said with effort. "Till after Fort Timber. Let me know, after Fort Timber."

"What happened?" said Spinner. "With the foot?"

"I hit it. On the turn."

"We're going to take care of that," said Spinner.

"Keep driving," said Loma. "Just keep…"

"Just shut up," said Spinner.

The beam in front of the car didn't seem to cut him off any more, but sucked him forward, and when the next cross road came with a sign that said *Spoondale, 3 miles,* Spinner slowed to a stop, backed up, and took the turn.

"Spinner," said Loma, "this is wrong. Wrong turn—"

"Leave it to me."

Loma tried to sit up.

"I told you…"

"I'm driving."

Loma didn't say any more. He briefly thought of stopping Spinner, of making him do it his way, but gave up the idea. It wasn't important enough and would mean effort without any good reason. This road, in the long run, would come out as well as the other….

They got to Spoondale at three in the morning, which meant the small town was dark. A red light burned over the gate of the fire station, but it always burned and meant nothing. With everything dark and the tree-lined streets deserted Loma didn't pay much attention when Spinner slowed down. Spinner slowed, then stopped, and cut the headlights.

When he got out of the car and walked halfway into an alley Loma still didn't pay much attention. But then, forgetting the pain of his foot, he sat up and watched closely, because he didn't understand Spinner's behavior. As long as Spinner served his function, and drove, Loma didn't care whether he understood Spinner or not. People were an effort to Loma, the kind of effort that irritated him. Spinner especially; he was confused, with a disorganized push behind all he did.

The car was parked near the dark front of a store and Spinner was now in the alley, trying a window. Loma made out the sign over the store, *Drugs, Prescriptions,* it said. Spinner was forcing the window.

A stupid act of bravado, a thing Loma himself would never do. But it was hard to stop Spinner now, and not really worth it. He would watch and see how Spinner made out—ten minutes, unless something went wrong.

Loma did not have a chance to wait for ten minutes, because a short time after Spinner disappeared through the window there was the noise of a car taking off fast and a few moments later a light went on in the back of the store.

Spinner heard the same noise and saw the same light, but unlike Loma, he had no plan for that kind of switch. Unlike Loma, he went only by stubborn intent and by the push of excitement.

He crouched next to the big rack in the middle of the store and watched the door with the light under it. The door opened, throwing a bright shaft into the store, just missing the side of Spinner's leg. And then the shadow.

"That you, Dad?" it said.

"No. But stand still," said Spinner.

He stood up and walked toward the door with a brazen grin on his face.

She was much younger than Spinner had judged by her silhouette. A high-school girl with long hair, with make-up she didn't need, and her clothes the national norm of low shoes, thick socks, long skirt, loose sweater. Her small breasts were trained into high cones and there was a small pin on one of them.

"You—you aren't—" she started.

Spinner pushed her into the room and closed the door.

"You got lipstick all over," said Spinner.

She couldn't help putting her hand to her face, but kept staring at Spinner with an unsettled look, part curious and part waiting for the fear to take over.

"Was that your boy friend taking off with the car?"

After a moment she said, "You—are you a—a criminal?"

Somehow Spinner didn't feel brazen any more. He gave a short laugh and looked over the room.

"Where's everybody?" he said.

"They'll be…"

"I know. They'll be right hack." He took her arm and pulled her into the store. "Show me the bandages.. And a splint, if there is one."

When she pulled her arm away Spinner didn't grab for her because it hadn't felt like that kind of a move. She stayed right next to him.

"Listen here," she said, "who you pushing around?" Spinner was sure she had her hands on her hips.

"Just show me the shelf, girl, and you and me won't argue."

He hadn't taken up the tack she had wanted, so she tried again, doing it differently.

"You got shot? Or a buddy of yours got shot?"

It sounded so tough and in-the-know Spinner wasn't sure whether to laugh or to feel embarrassed.

"Moll," he said, trying to live up to her expectations, "don't waste my time."

He reached out to take her arm again but it was dark and he missed, and next she was close up against him, with her arms tight around his back.

"Go ahead," she whispered. "Go ahead."

Spinner was sure she meant he should kiss her, but even if he had been in the mood her stage whisper made it too ridiculous.

"Go ahead," she said again. "I'm not afraid."

He had the sudden idea to disillusion her, to say that he never had been in a stickup, that he didn't sell dope, fix races, run rackets, that even prison had been only a spiteful mistake—when it hit him that with Loma as an in, he'd soon be exactly what she had taken him for. The thought confused him. The confusion didn't stay with him long because anger took over. He remembered what he had left behind in Stone Bluff.

"Stop horsing around," he said and pushed her away. "Show me the shelf."

He had hurt her, and she let go immediately.

"All right, over here," she said and led him around the rack in the middle of the store and behind a counter.

"Tape, elastic bandage, anything like that," he said.

She found both and held the packages out to him.

"Where are the pills, heavy drugs?"

She turned immediately and walked to the back where the pharmacy was sectioned off. Spinner followed close behind. He could hear her breathing.

"They're locked up," she said. "In here."

It was an ordinary wood cupboard but with a big lock. Spinner put one fist into the other hand and rammed his elbow into the door. The panel splintered and he reached inside.

"Light a match and hold it," he said, and gave her a match book.

She did as he told her and while he sorted through the small boxes and bottles she watched with eyes wide and mouth open, and when she lit one match from the other she did it with fast, eager motions.

"You—" She swallowed, then started again. "What drug are you on?" she said quickly.

"Saltpeter," he said, but didn't watch to see if she got it. He felt tense and on edge.

He took out the big bottles last, which meant he didn't find the codeine till he had gone through all the small stuff. He shook a handful of the pills into his pocket and then took the matches out of her hand.

"All right. Get back to your room."

He pushed her ahead of him and then through the door into the light. He stayed in the dark.

"Now listen to me, girl. You stay in this room and don't move. When Daddy comes back..."

"He won't be back till the morning, don't you see? That's why Jimmy and I..."

"I know how it is. Now just shut up and don't move. You know better than to make a commotion, right?"

She meant to protest, to explain that it wouldn't enter her head to make a commotion and that she wasn't afraid, but Spinner slammed the door in her face and headed back to the dark window where he had come in.

"Do you need any money?" She stood in the open door looking at him.

He came back to the room with long, fast steps. He wasn't sure whether he should yell at her, paddle her rear, or lock her into a closet somewhere. She stepped back when she saw Spinner coming, so that he didn't reach her until he was well into the room. Of all the emotions that Spinner was able to read into her face, fear wasn't one of them.

But suddenly she turned stiff.

Spinner came around fast, to see what made her stare. There was a door to the outside which swung open slowly and the darkness outside gave the movement a ghostly appearance. And there was nobody standing there.

Loma was on the floor, the pale face a mask of control, with the strain to move showing only in the stretched neck, and he was holding a gun.

The gun didn't show very long. Perhaps only Spinner had seen it. Loma had judged the situation with mechanical speed, and when Spinner lifted Loma and put him into a seat the room looked casual enough; Loma sitting back and guarding his ankle, Spinner with tape and bandages under his arm, and the girl looking eager and curious.

"That's your buddy, isn't it?" she said and walked up to Loma. "Where's the wound?" she asked him. "Is it bad?"

Loma seemed to shrink like a dead leaf. He turned to Spinner and said, "You must be out of your mind. Carry me back."

It was the first time Spinner had heard the killer speak sharply. The tone of voice stung him, like a reprimand to a wayward child, and Loma's having followed him to watch that Spinner made no mistakes was the worst part of it. And Loma had come with a gun. That pale creep had been carrying an extra gun all the time.

"You been carrying that all the time?" Spinner nodded at Loma's belt.

Loma answered with a cold look.

"How come I didn't know?"

"Why should you?"

"And how come you didn't use it before?" Spinner stepped slowly closer. "There've been a couple of times..."

"There hasn't been any good reason," said Loma.

An unclear, sudden anger made Spinner move fast. "You son of a bitch," he said through his teeth. He yanked the gun out of Loma's pocket and stuck it into his belt. "You son of a bitch—"

Loma did nothing about it. It would not have worked right then.

"A glass of water," said Spinner, and while the girl drew water from the sink in back Spinner took out three pills.

"Take me out of here," Loma said. "You hear me?"

It meant exactly the thing that Spinner wanted to change. It meant Loma stopped him and Loma told him what next.

"Take them."

Loma said, "No."

But there was more to it. A swift look of life had come over his face, too fast for Spinner to judge it, and then Loma had shut his mouth.

"Come on. Open up."

Loma wouldn't. But it meant more to Spinner now than just the pills, and Loma saw it. He saw Spinner step closer and he saw how Spinner's manner turned very quiet.

"Take them, Loma."

Loma pushed back into the chair as much as he could.

"What are they?" he said. "I can't..."

"Take them!"

"Listen to me! I can't take them. I can't—"

"Why is it," said Spinner, close to Loma's face now, "why is it you always want the opposite, Loma?"

Loma closed his eyes to shut everything out. He felt pain eat into his foot and leg, feeling it more now because Spinner was making the pain an issue. Take the pills, or Spinner would make an issue. He was not easily predictable. How to handle Spinner—take the pills. They would wear off in a while. Perhaps they were very strong and the best that could happen, if he could not be wide awake, was to pass out completely.

Loma opened his mouth and Spinner put in the pills.

"Now give him the water," he said to the girl.

She held the glass to Loma's mouth and watched him drink. Even when his peculiar eyes looked up at her she did not look away. She was fascinated.

Loma looked back at her with a blank expression. It guarded the shrinking feeling inside him, the sense that she was some unnatural, insane specimen and that everything around him was unreal.

CHAPTER 9

Loma closed his eyes and waited for it to happen. The pain would go away and there would be nothing. It would mean that the drug had taken over his body, his thinking and his feeling, and none of it would be his own. A thin sweat covered his skin and Loma clenched his hands into tight, bony fists because the waiting was terrible.

"When the pain starts easing up let me know. I'll put on the bandage."

God, thought Loma, God— And if I open my eyes, I will see the ceiling, he said to himself. It will be spinning on an off-center axis. Something brushed his arm.

"Gee," said the girl. "Did I hurt you? The way you jumped—"

She didn't say any more. She didn't know what to say to a face with eyes like a goat and the thin features drawn with disgust.

She stepped away from the chair. She said, "Gee," again, to Spinner this time, and "What's the matter with him? All I did was..."

"Never mind him."

Loma could hear that Spinner was no longer close to the chair, but somewhere in back.

"Come here," Spinner said to the girl.

Then Loma couldn't make out the words, just something indistinct. But they were there, to the side. He could open his eyes and see.

"All right—" Loma heard, and then he heard movement.

Loma did not open his eyes.

And then, "Here," said the girl, but Loma opened his eyes abruptly to stare at the ceiling as if that could shut out all sound.

It didn't spin, not yet, but a bulge was moving from one end of the surface across to the other. Now! It was spinning, slow and ponderous, but Loma already knew it would soon get faster.

Why didn't they make a sound? The silence was like no air and nothing to breathe. A sound, any sound, even the traveling bulge on the ceiling might make a sound. There would be a dry, inhuman sound to distract from Loma's listening. Loma tensed, hearing Spinner. It was a deep-throated breath from Spinner.

The drug spinning his blood, and the room—

Then Loma screamed. "No!"

They turned at the sound and saw Loma staring up with neck rearing back and his hands in the chair like two clamps.

Spinner had been drinking water and was going to hand the glass back to the girl when Loma screamed.

"Loma, you all right?" Spinner was by the chair, anxious. "You got pain? Didn't the pills work?" and Spinner touched Loma's arm.

Loma relaxed at the touch and when he turned his face toward Spinner it was hard to believe that he had screamed. He said, "It doesn't hurt. I'm fine now."

He sat very still now, the way he usually sat, except that his eyes moved a lot. He looked at everything in the room, at Spinner, at the girl by the sink.

"Bring me some scissors," said Spinner.

She brought them and stayed close to Spinner, watching him cut off the sock.

"Little girl," said Loma. "Do you have any milk?"

They both looked at him, startled. There had almost been banter in Loma's voice.

"The pills," he said. "My stomach. Some milk would calm my stomach," he said.

The girl looked at Spinner and Spinner was watching Loma's face. Then he said, "Go get him some milk."

The girl went to the icebox and got a bottle of milk. Spinner was frowning.

"Little girl," said Loma. He took the bottle from her. "Are you going to ask me whether I've had enough?"

There was an obscene taunt in his voice. Loma had made no move except to reach for the bottle, but the girl drew back. She stood close to Spinner and was afraid to look at the man in the chair.

"Gee—" The word didn't sound right even to her. "Is he—is he safe?"

Loma suddenly laughed—like a goat, thought Spinner, only louder.

"Safe? You say safe?" Loma leaned forward then and when he turned his ankle too much his face gave a start. He changed it into a grin. "You couldn't be safer, little girl," and there was no laugh in his voice any more. His eyes started to wander, but they kept coming back to the girl and the look was vicious.

"All right," said Spinner. "Just hold still now."

He started to cut strips of tape and put them up along Loma's ankle to make a Gibson boot. He did it fast. He was nervous. Loma was holding still but he kept blinking his eyes. They had a fever glitter. And Loma was still smiling.

"Little girl," he said, "would you give me that milk again?" It was next to his chair, where he had put it. "You couldn't be safer, little girl. All I want is some milk."

Spinner was almost finished. One more strip. He was rushing.

"Loma," he said, "you're losing your grip." He stood up, ready to take Loma out of the chair.

Loma turned his face toward Spinner and there was a soft smile on the face. The whole movement was soft.

"My grip," said Loma, "is the last thing that goes. Show me your hand." He held out his own, and his smile gentle as ever. "You see?" he went on, and suddenly Spinner's wrist was caught in a surprising vise which shot excruciating pain up Spinner's arm. And all the while Loma was smiling.

Spinner tried to yank free, but it made no difference, and then Loma was talking again, "Little girl, I want you to ask me—"

"You crazy dog!" Spinner started and hauled out to slam Loma's face when he saw the face change and for an instant it held him as if charmed by the eye of a snake.

Then everything broke.

The clubfoot jammed hard into Spinner's middle, everything gagged, everything froze, and the last thing Spinner knew was a sense of bursting with pain and of having no breath. Even his rage didn't help him move. It just kept him awake so that he could hear.

She made a scream, very short and cut off, and then nothing. A strong buzzing in Spinner's ears kept him apart and far away and the rest of the room was far away because Spinner saw only gray and white shapes that kept coming apart.

He heard the girl gasp, and then she started to whimper. She did this forever, while no other sound mattered. Perhaps Loma was talking, whispering— Spinner heard, ". . you couldn't be safer, little girl. The scissors—"

Then Spinner felt sick.

He was without any strength, but the room was much clearer now, and very static. Loma was in his chair with his legs out on the footstool. The girl was standing next to the chair, and she wasn't moving, but she was rigid. Spinner could not make out clearly how it was done but Loma had her in some kind of grip and it kept her still. She was whimpering.

The static look of the scene was an illusion. It had to do with the rigid cramp which lay like a giant knot inside Spinner and with the pain that kept him from moving. It made a nightmare out of the thing he saw, a nightmare that trembled with force.

Loma was talking all the time, a fast and monotonous sound which gained its intensity from the low key he forced into his voice. And the fast and monotonous sound seemed even more charged when Loma moved. His leg with the black chunk of his deformed foot came around slowly, coiled slowly around the girl so that she couldn't move.

He let go of her with his hands; he had the scissors in one hand and with the other hand he wasn't doing anything yet.

"Little girl," said Loma, fast and monotonous, "look, you couldn't be safer. Look, you're standing up and I'm sitting here. Look, you couldn't be safer—"

Her hands were over her mouth and she was too afraid to make any sound. Her sweater had been moved up at the waist, showing white nylon. Loma watched it. It was slippery and breathing. "I won't touch it," Loma said, "I won't touch it—" and his free hand waved around aimlessly, ready to settle somewhere but still without aim.

Loma mumbled to himself and every so often gave her a smile. And he said, "Little girl," over and over. "Little girl. For a little girl your shape is all wrong, like a bad joke—" Then he hesitated and looked at her sideways. "Is it real?" he said and his hand stopped waving around. His hand came down on the little cone of her breast and sat there like a bug with five legs.

Then Loma started to laugh. It was a high, anxious sound and only the rhythm reminded Spinner of laughter. His hand twisted, he had the scissors, and when the girl screamed it sounded like Loma's laughter.

There was now a round hole in the sweater, open over the tip of the cone, and the nylon showed shiny and white.

"Shut up," said Loma. His hand slapped the girl hard over the mouth. "White," he said. "I don't remember it white—" And when the girl gagged on his slap Loma did it again. He cut a hole and then dropped the scissors.

Spinner had started to crawl with an effort that made him faint. Loma is out of his mind, he was thinking, Loma is out— Spinner, on hands and knees, fell on his face and fought to keep the black out of his eyes.

"White," said Loma, "I remember it darker—" He sounded more urgent now, but Spinner didn't hear the words. Spinner thought he himself might go insane, straining and fighting to see.

The girl was pressed down on her knees and nearly unconscious with fright. Her head hung back and Loma's grip on her waist made her arch. It looked as if Loma were clinging to her and Spinner could hear him again, his voice like a terrible wail. "Please, please, little girl—please ask me. Please—"

By the time Spinner was up and close enough to them Loma had dropped the girl to the floor. She looked boneless there, and when Spinner pulled her up and hoisted her on the couch she still was like that. Then she opened her eyes and saw Spinner. Her face screwed up and she started to cry. A little girl now. Spinner thought he should give her a blanket. But there wasn't any. He turned away to find Loma, because now he had to decide about him. Kill him, maybe, for the weird and threatening thing he had done, for what he might want to do next.

Loma was in his chair. He was not even looking at Spinner. He wasn't looking at anything, but had the bottle of milk in both hands, drinking from it with long, even pulls. Milk ran over his face.

He dropped the bottle when Spinner came up, and lay back. Loma's face was exhausted: He barely looked at Spinner and gave a faint smile.

"Don't," he said. "I'm only pretending." Then he fainted.

CHAPTER 10

When Spinner carried Loma back to the car it had started to rain. Spinner walked quickly, in spite of the ache in his middle, walking bent, as a man does in the rain. Loma was limp and light in his arms. He put him into the back of the car, bending him so he fit on the seat and his injured leg would lie steady. He had an impulse to loosen the collar around Loma's neck, but when he touched the skin there he changed his mind. He got into the front seat and drove away. He watched the windshield wipers wave back and forth, a smear and a click and a smear and a click. The rain made no sound; he heard only the wipers clicking and the car making a whine. Spinner rubbed the side of his face and then his shoulder. The air was damp and his shoulder ached.

Spinner took out a cigarette and smoked. He kept moving it from one part of his mouth to the other. It didn't seem to fit anywhere. He held the cigarette in his hand but it interfered with his driving. He threw it out and tried to feel as he had before, pretending it was a commonplace trip, from here to there.

How long would Loma sleep? Spinner slowed down a little, because of the rain, and wondered. Then he slowed even more.

Without Loma, Spinner did not know where to go.

The gray morning came. Spinner's throat was raw from smoking, and no matter how he had turned himself under the wheel he had felt stiff and uncomfortable. He had pulled off the road under some bushes which made wet sounds on the side of the car. Sometimes, with a gust of wind, a thick splatter hit the top of the hood. The drops scurried and then flattened out into broad puddles. Spinner turned to the back seat, but nothing had changed there. Loma slept in a small heap, his small hands folded and the face very quiet. There was sweat on the forehead, a moist sheen which Spinner kept looking for as if it were the only sign of life in the man. Spinner no longer knew how he felt about Loma, a small man with small limbs and the clubfoot like a gross thickening which didn't belong. What belonged was the tired mouth and the moisture on Loma's forehead.

Spinner fingered the limp pack in his hand and wondered whether to smoke his last cigarette.

"Why did you stop?"

There was no change in the voice and Spinner was startled.

"How long have you been here?"

"A few hours," said Spinner.

He turned around and saw Loma sit up. Loma took a white handkerchief out of his pocket, wiped his face and his forehead, and then his hands. There was nothing left of what Spinner had seen a short while ago.

"You want to sit in front?"

Loma nodded and Spinner helped him out of the car and into the front seat. Loma seemed less concerned with his ankle but he breathed deeply for a few moments. It had hurt when he had moved to the front. They both sat and looked out. There were no hills now and the fields spread wide in the misty light, a gray, loveless sight. Spinner took out the cigarette he had left.

"What road is this?" Loma asked.

"I went to the cutoff before Fort Timber. This lane goes back to it that way." Spinner dragged on his cigarette, exhaled slowly. He looked out the window and added, "This is east. The white streak on the sky."

Loma nodded and said nothing.

"How's your foot?" Spinner asked.

They both looked down at the bandaged ankle. The skin bulged where the tape ended.

"It's too tight," said Spinner. "I'll have to change it."

He lifted the foot up on the seat and loosened one side of the Gibson boot. He stopped when Loma gasped.

"Bad?"

"Yes, it hurts," said Loma.

"We can wait. Take another pill and we wait for fifteen minutes."

"No," said Loma.

No comment, no gesture that went beyond the simple remark.

"Look," said Spinner. "You take it here in the car and you can pass out all you want."

"No," said Loma.

The lack of contact was between them again and Spinner felt irritated.

"No little girls here." He sounded vicious. "Take the pill, and. . ."

"I can't," said Loma.

"You've said that."

"You think it makes a difference whether I'm alone or in company?"

It must be very bad, Spinner thought. Loma never put any feeling into his words, nor did the restraint seem an effort. But this· time his voice had been uneven and he had tried to cover it by grating his throat.

The swelling was shiny and dark, with pressure lines where the tape had ended, and while Spinner was retaping the support Loma sat very still and did not breathe.

When it was done Spinner opened the window, because it felt very hot in the car.

Loma sat back and closed his eyes. He said, "I'd like one of your cigarettes."

Spinner turned his head to look at Loma, but the man's face was immediately closed.

"I didn't know you smoked," said Spinner.

"Do you have one?"

"None left," said Spinner. "But the next..."

Loma looked at Spinner with a quick turn of the head. "The next town, you mean? Stop and buy cigarettes?" Spinner didn't have time to say anything because Loma went on, unusually sharp. "You didn't have enough? Last night was par for the course?"

"You blaming me for that? Those pills knock you out so hard you don't remember?"

"I don't care about blame. But I want you to keep in mind..."

"And the whole point of that thing last night? To get you some help for that busted foot, that you don't remember?"

"It feels much better. What I want you to keep in mind..."

"That's all? That's all you can say about it?" Spinner asked.

Loma didn't answer immediately. He looked at Spinner as if he were trying to decide what Spinner might want. Then he said, "Are you thinking that last night, whatever you had in mind, was all right and worth it because of this?" He nodded at his foot on the floorboard. "That's not good enough. You did it for no good reason."

"No good reason—"

"You don't think that girl's going to keep still?"

Spinner recovered himself and said, "Listen, you bastard. I knock myself out..."

"I didn't ask you. And from now on remember they're not just looking for us; they also know where to look!"

"That kid was no trouble until you lost your head."

"It won't happen again, but she's trouble now."

Maybe she wasn't, thought Spinner, but he didn't say any more about it, and followed Loma's directions.

They stayed on country roads most of the time and they no longer headed for St. Louis. They were still going north, but toward one side of the city where no towns showed on the map. Loma didn't explain the place but said it was a hide-out. Spinner didn't ask any questions, because as long as it meant sticking with Loma he would go along. He never questioned that part of his moves, because by now, and without quite knowing it, that part was the only thing in which he still had a choice.

CHAPTER 11

They drove, they ate, and then Spinner needed to sleep. He drove by Loma's directions, he bought food in a town and then walked back to the car which he had parked near the outskirts, and at noon his head swam so much he pulled the car into the parking lot of a busy restaurant on the highway. Loma gave no argument and Spinner slept sitting behind the wheel.

Then Spinner drove again, feeling as dull as the day. "Stop the car," said Loma. "We'd better change plates."

"What?"

"We have to take the main drag for a while, so we'll change plates."

Spinner slowed the car. Loma told him where to find the set of plates, under the mat in the trunk. After Spinner had exchanged them Loma told him to throw the old ones away.

They drove again and nothing changed. The light was the same gray as in the morning, rain threatened, and they didn't talk. A car overtook them and Spinner, almost automatically, pressed down the gas not to fall behind.

"Stay at sixty," said Loma.

Spinner said nothing, because it would have meant an argument. He did not want to talk, so he slowed back to sixty and watched the car disappear into a dip in the distance. He felt as dull as the day....

A little while later they passed the car where a highway cop had stopped it to the side of the pavement. Loma said nothing about it and that too made Spinner feel irritated. He started to whistle and drove.

"Slow down more," said Loma.

Then Spinner saw Loma sit up.

"You see it?" said Loma.

Spinner had seen it, but it hadn't meant anything. He had sat wrapped securely in the dull task of driving, forgetting why he was driving and who he was, too tried to act his new role.

"Easy now," said Loma. His hands were on the dashboard. "A roadblock."

It was far away, but one of the cruisers had the red light on top revolving, and of the two cars stopped for inspection one had the trunk lid open.

Spinner cursed. It had nothing to do with having sat at the wheel half asleep, because now he was thinking of nothing except what to do now. He wanted to do something violent, something to keep him from racing the car or cross the ditch or jolt the car into the fields.

There was nowhere else to go. Fields, a farm, or a straight, slick road up to the roadblock. The red light on top of the cruiser got brighter.

"Turn back," said Loma. He was sitting as before, his back straight, but leaning forward.

"They'll see it. How about that farm?"

"Turn back at their drive, but slow, now."

"It's too damn close to that bunch up there, Loma."

Loma held out his hand but kept looking straight. "Give me the gun."

Spinner gave it to him without any question.

The car moved fast and in the only direction that was open, straight toward the roadblock. It looked unconcerned from a distance, like all mechanical motion, and when the car slowed, turned into the drive, it rolled toward the farmhouse like any car going home. The car stood there for a moment while nothing moved, just the fast, red wink from the light shooting through breaks in the hedge.

There were rain-heavy trees, the damp farmhouse, and a dark barn further on. The farmer stood in the hall of his house and looked through the glass in the door.

"Loma, you stay in the car and I go in alone."

"Do it right," said Loma. "That's all."

Spinner didn't answer. He reached into the back and pulled up Loma's overcoat.

"Around your legs, like a blanket. And then take a shirt or something, a towel—" Spinner pulled Loma's small canvas bag out of the back—"and fix that arm. A bad leg or the clubfoot will give you away that much sooner, but a bad arm…"

"Go in," said Loma. "I'll be ready."

Spinner got out of the car and went up to the house, where the farmer was standing behind the door. Spinner saw him. Then the door opened.

"You want something?" said the farmer.

He stood in front of his door and watched Spinner come up to the porch.

"I'm sorry to bother you," Spinner started, and he tried to smile. "My friend and I…"

"What?"

He could have used any other word. He had only said something to show his dislike. He was dark and thin, his patched overalls much too large for him.

Spinner came closer and said, "My friend's in the car there and I've got to get to a doctor. Can I use your phone? He's in a bad way—" Spinner felt himself smile. He felt his smile begging the man to help.

"What's he got?"

Spinner's smile stayed, growing stiff, covering the hate he felt for the man. "He broke his arm and the pain is getting bad."

Spinner thought the farmer was thinking and said nothing for a while.

The eaves dripped slowly and something turned in the dark barn.

"I got wood in back," said the farmer. "You can pick a right piece and make him a splint."

The red light from the highway kept flashing behind the hedge and each time the flash came it looked like small sparks through the leaves, small pin sparks that stung into Spinner.

"Next to the barn," said the farmer and stepped back, closing the door.

Spinner did not think any more. He was through the door, and stood close to the farmer, holding him tight by the front. He heard his own voice like a dry scrape in his throat. "I need help, man, I need help bad, so don't stop me. You hear? Don't stop me—"

The other man's face had changed from sudden shock to growing wonder. He wasn't scared yet, but puzzled, with the fear growing slowly.

"Where's your phone? Come on!" Spinner gave him a shove.

The sudden movement and the change to an understandable sentence broke the spell for the farmer. The phone. He understood that. "This way," he said, and walked down the dark hall. Spinner was walking behind him, out of sight, and the farmer said, "I want pay for that call. It's fifteen cents if you're calling the next town."

The kitchen was as dank as the rest of the house. A can was open on top of the stove and two dirty pots stood there. Spinner went to the phone and when he had the operator he asked for a doctor, any doctor. It took long enough for Spinner to feel the shock coming over him, remembering how he could have ruined the whole delicate plan, everything, because he disliked this man and was not going to take it—couldn't take it! Spinner stared out the window at the barn and the fields beyond that. And then he heard a new sound. Sirens. The sound grew and Spinner had to clench his teeth. It was a sound and a waiting just like the first time he had listened this way, back in the mud where he had found the cripple, and when he made the switch.

The switch was over. There was no wish to run, but a growing coldness now that kept him immune. He was learning what Loma did, learning it step by step without knowing it....

"...Yes, are you the doctor?"

"Doctor Calvin," said the instrument.

"Doctor Calvin, I'm in a bad fix with a friend. His arm's broken, bad, and I'd like you to come right away. I'm..."

"Broken arm? He can walk, can't he?"

"Listen, I want you to come get him. I'm out— What's the name here?" he asked the farmer. "Come on, hurry it!"

"Ransom."

"The Ransom place," Spinner said to the phone. "You know where?"

"Bring him in, please. I can't leave my office and in a case like..."

"You refusing the case?"

"Is it compound? Does the bone protrude?" Spinner heard, but his impatience made the conversation lose all meaning and his mind was skipping around madly, thinking of other ways.

"No. We'll be over," he said and hung up. Then he called the operator and asked for an ambulance service, fast. It would have been good to ride through that roadblock with a physician, but the ambulance might even be more impressive....

"...will he there right quick," said the mortician who ran the ambulance service, and Spinner hung up. He reached into his pocket and found a half-dollar coin.

"I owe you thirty cents." He held out the coin.

"I got no change." The farmer took the coin and stuck it into his pocket.

Spinner left without saying a word. The farmer was no longer a sour man who revolted him, but only something he had finished with. Next, the shortest way from the house to Loma.

He could see Loma in the car—his arm wrapped in a towel, his shirt made into a sling, and his cautious posture favoring one side. Spinner walked up and then gaped. The man with the sling wasn't Loma, but with a face so terribly old that the smooth, black hair looked wrong and out of place. The face showed tired sagging and a worn look of pain.

"Loma—"

"I took out my teeth." His voice hissed, like some old mechanical gadget. And then: "What did you arrange? Hurry up, the farmer is coming."

Spinner turned, saw the tall man stand on the porch, watching them.

"I couldn't get a doctor but an ambulance is coming. Maybe five minutes. He's rushing it." Spinner looked at the porch, saw the farmer come closer. "Loma, listen to me. Once in town we're going to play it all the way through. You're going to see that doctor."

Loma's eyes were closed. He nodded. He did it carefully and in obvious pain. "We're splitting up."

"Once we get—" Spinner stopped, put his hands on the door, hard. "What did you say?"

"Shut up. He's close."

"You son of a bitch, listen to me," Spinner's voice was a whisper. "We don't split! Before I let you get away—" He trailed off, watching the farmer. The farmer had gone to the hedge and stopped there. "And how in hell you expect to drive? Look at you sweat. You're trembling. The pain's killing you—"

"I'm seeing the doctor. You can join me there. Better not to cross the roadblock together."

"Like hell. I'm not letting you out of my sight!"

"Ambulance coming," said the farmer, and walked up to the car.

Spinner felt like hitting the farmer, bashing him hard into that miserable, glum face.

"Can you drive a car?" Loma was asking. He was looking at the farmer.

A long, black hearse swung into the lane. It moved silently, and the red light on the front did not blink.

"Sure," the farmer answered. He walked to the ambulance.

"What was that for? Why'd you ask him?" Spinner was frantic, time pushing him.

"In case you don't get through," Loma said. "I'll need the car." He shivered with pain, but none of that reached his clear, inhuman thinking.

"Loma, I'll kill you first. I'm sticking. I'll spill all I know. Those cops are two minutes from here. You son of a bitch, I can—"

"Why should you?" said Loma. "Your way, you're in for murder. You have a chance my way."

The man from the ambulance had opened the doors in back and was coming over, smiling. Spinner ripped open the door of the car and picked Loma up. Loma was light as a ghost, and could disappear like a ghost. Spinner wouldn't allow himself to think about that. There was only one thing to hold to. Stick with Loma.

He hoisted Loma into the back of the ambulance while the mortician was pattering. "Yes sir, that's the way, let me give you— Ah, you got it. Yes sir, in no time at all you'll be right as rain. Are you going to come along too? Ah, I see you are," he said when Spinner got into the back. Then the mortician started closing the doors.

"Leave them open," said Loma.

Spinner started to climb into the back of the ambulance when Loma said, "I left my grip in the car. Go get it for me."

Simple enough. Simple way to get Spinner out.

Then Loma whispered, "The gun. It's under the seat."

They needed the gun, but the farmer stood near the car, watching. Spinner jumped from the ambulance and ran to the car. He heard Loma call to the farmer to get him away from the car—and then Spinner found the gun under the seat. There were no more tricks left in Loma, because he needed the gun and Spinner had it in his pocket. He also picked up the grip and went back to the ambulance, to ride with Loma.

"Start driving," he said to the mortician and jumped into the back of the hearse. The farmer was walking away, folding some bills into his pocket. Spinner paid no attention. He looked at Loma once and then turned away. He held himself by the hinges of the open door because the hearse would start moving now.

"What—"

"Quiet," said Loma.

"What in hell—"

"I told you. I might need the car," said Loma.

The ambulance started rolling. Spinner held on, swaying, then got his balance and let go his hold. Then a touch, just a touch between his shoulders without any force or speed but right enough, decisive enough to make Spinner lose balance and fall through the open doors of the ambulance and hit the lane.

He rolled for a moment, stopped, reared up to shout. But he couldn't. The ambulance was in the turn and to shout and run after it would mean they would look up at the roadblock and want to know why he was calling after a hearse.

His way, it could mean murder. Loma's way, he had a chance.

Spinner walked down the lane, brushing the dirt off his pants.

CHAPTER 12

He had hitched a ride at the end of the lane and he had driven through the roadblock with no trouble at all. At the roadblock they had a minute description of the man they wanted. He was fifteen, blond, and wanted for hit-and-run driving.

All the way into town Spinner sat in his seat with arms folded, clamping his hands under his arms. He had the shakes. All the tension and straining for nothing—except to show once again that Loma came out on top.

When Spinner got off at the doctor's he was not shaking any more. He did not look like the man in the lane any more. If Loma was gone, he would find him and tear out his brains. If Loma was here, that would be even better.

Spinner saw the car then. It stood in the lot next to the doctor's office, half hidden by a garage. Loma must have told the farmer to do that. Loma, half dead with pain, had taken one of his little precautions.

The waiting room was the glassed-in porch of the house. There was nobody there. Spinner walked to the door where a sign hung saying *Doctor In.* He heard nothing. He knocked. When he knocked a second time the door jerked open and a pale young man in a white coat stared out at him.

"What? What do you want?"

That was Doctor Calvin. Spinner remembered the same tone from the telephone.

"Your patient there." Spinner saw Loma sitting on a couch. "He's a friend of mine. I'd like to come in."

"I'll be through shortly. When I'm done you can..."

"Let him in," said Loma,

Doctor Calvin frowned. Then Loma said it again, exactly like the first time, and Calvin still didn't know how to take it. Spinner saw that Loma had the same effect on other people.

Calvin let Spinner pass, closed the door, and came into the room with hard little steps.

"Are you the one who phoned and told me this man had a broken arm?"

"That's right."

"There is no damaged arm. There is a damaged ankle."

"Well—"

"Precisely. And you thought I'd come out to that farm on your diagnosis."

"It turns out," said Spinner, "the patient is worse than I said over the phone. Maybe you should have come." He stared at Loma, hating the man, not knowing what he could do with his hate.

Doctor Calvin walked up to Loma, and they seemed to be continuing something that started before Spinner came in.

"You are in no position to argue the point. If you think such heroics will help you to imagine that the damage is less severe than is actually the case—"

"Just go ahead, as I said."

Loma sounded different without the teeth in his mouth but the coldness was there as always, and the impersonal tone which made the listener into no more than an ear. It made Doctor Calvin shout at Spinner.

"You talk to him. The leg needs a cast and he refuses an anesthetic!"

Spinner looked at Loma and then away again, quickly. He shrugged and said, "He's your patient, Doctor Calvin."

Doctor Calvin pursed his mouth but said nothing. He sat down at his desk and tapped a spatula into his palm. It made fat little smacks.

"I'm not in the habit of arguing with laymen on matters like this." He spoke quietly and with an air meant to convey his detachment. It made him look mean. "As a professional—as your physician," he said, "I refuse to assume responsibility for results limited by your lay—"

"Just put on the cast, will you, Doctor Calvin?"

"I was speaking to the patient."

"All right, but I heard you too."

Doctor Calvin got up and went back to the couch.

"Perhaps this will clear it up for you. I don't have adequate restraints on that table for anyone who's going to get your kind of pain. Does that make more sense to you?"

Loma sighed and looked at his hands. His new features kept the meaning of the sigh unclear. He said, "I'll pass out, probably. That should help you."

Neither Spinner nor Calvin knew what to say next. Calvin turned on his heel and went to the far end of the room. He started preparing the plaster.

"Put him on the table," he said without turning.

Spinner did that. Loma seemed now a very small man, frail built, with eyes that wouldn't tell what was behind them. Spinner put him down on the narrow steel table and wondered why the pad on top was so thin. Because nobody lies here and is conscious, he thought, so the hardness doesn't matter. He said, "Loma, you know what happened?" He mumbled it. "The roadblock is off. They got their man."

For a moment it looked as if Loma would spring off the table. Then he closed his eyes and lay still. His eyelids had a small tremble.

"They were looking for a hit-and-run driver. A fifteen-year-old kid."

Loma didn't blink, didn't move. If Spinner had hoped for some sign of anger from Loma, anger over the wasted effort, none came.

Loma said, "Good." Nothing else.

Doctor Calvin put down his dish with the plaster and laid out bandage and instruments. Spinner kept looking at that and wondered what kind of a pain it would have to be before Loma's cold mind would boil over. Or what kind of a poison the doctor would give him and what impossible stresses would show in Loma's face.

Spinner stood behind Loma's head so that if Loma should start to squirm Spinner could hold him down on the table.

Doctor Calvin cleaned the leg and the foot with a wet swab and then he laid out the leg the way he wanted it. Spinner wasn't looking at Loma but he felt the table make a small move.

"No anesthetic?" said Doctor Calvin.

Loma shook his head.

Then Calvin started the bandage. It meant he had to position the foot.

How Loma kept still is hard to know, but a short while later his eyelids fluttered. With a long sound of air from his throat he seemed to flatten out on the table.

Doctor Calvin let go of the foot. Loma knew it and Loma could hear. There was the faint clink of glass, and Doctor Calvin became busy with something.

Spinner watched the syringe suck up the clear liquid. He heard Loma's breathing, a thin sound which could almost talk. The thin sweat was on Loma's face, on the white forehead. Loma did not move, did not blink, but his eyes were suddenly open and staring up into Spinner's face. The eyes were no longer blank but open in a way which Spinner had never seen. Anything Loma would say after this wouldn't mean much.

Then it was gone because Loma did not have the strength to keep his eyes open. But he could still hear, through a sick fog.

"What's in that hypo?" Spinner's voice came from directly above him.

And from the end of the table, where his foot was screaming with pain, came Doctor Calvin's voice like a thin bark.

"No more interference. I will not be responsible unless this patient, like any other case, receives adequate preparation."

Loma heard, but he was past action. The pain and the fear left him immobile, with all his remaining strength glued to the voices, all of him drained except for the strength he might gain if he sucked in the sound of the voices.

"I asked you, Doctor."

"Stay at your end, please."

"He can't stand it. Drugs do terrible things to him."

"When I need your advice..."

There was movement, movement, and then a thin sound of glass break-ing on the floor.

"Now get to work on that foot." Spinner's voice was harsh.

Doctor Calvin had not yet touched the foot again when Loma let go and passed out.

It was warm inside the cast. The soreness warmed it. Loma moved his foot on the floorboard, just to feel again that the pain was so much less than before. Then he looked at Spinner behind the wheel, then at the night outside the car.

They hadn't talked at all since they started driving again. Loma hunched over, arms folded, and looked out at the night. Without turning he noticed how Spinner drove. Loma wondered why Spinner didn't seem tired. He noticed that Spinner looked at him once and then front again. Loma noticed even the least important of Spinner's motions; he rubbed his nose, he swallowed a few times. Spinner said nothing, looked blank, but Loma knew he was present. It has to do with the pain, he thought, the relief.

"How is it?" said Spinner.

Loma was surprised. "Fine. Much better."

A while later Spinner said, "Why don't you put your teeth back in?"

"Oh, yes," said Loma. He took them out of his pocket and put them in. Then he said, "You have time to buy cigarettes, Spinner?"

Spinner gave him one. After holding it for a while Loma opened the window a crack and threw the cigarette out. He rarely felt like smoking, but this time he had thought he had wanted to smoke. But the unsettled feeling had to do with the foot, it had to be that because it was the only thing different. Perhaps exchange a few words, for distraction.

"We can make it by morning," said Loma. "Can you drive through?"

"Fine with me," said Spinner.

"Uh—Spinner."

"Yes?"

"At the office—why did you do it?"

"What you talking about?" said Spinner.

"I'm talking about the drug. I heard you and the doctor."

"Oh, that."

Spinner might have said more, but Loma didn't think he had made himself clear and had to say more. It was nonsense, but for the moment, to be talking was important.

"What I mean is, there was no good reason for you—"

"I don't know what you heard there," said Spinner. "But Calvin was going to give you a shot. I told him not to."

"Yes. Yes, I know that part." Loma looked out past the beam from the headlights. "But you did it for no good reason—"

Loma let it go: it was nonsense anyway. Also, he no longer wanted to hear whatever Spinner might answer.

CHAPTER 13

When morning came they had both come back to their old ways with each other. They hadn't talked any more, and in the silence Spinner had become glum again. He was gnawing the inside of his cheek and his eyes squinted as if there were something to see where there was nothing. And Loma, as most of the time when he didn't talk, was hardly a presence at all.

They had made a wide swing around St. Louis and gone into the hills. The sun came up clear, hurting Spinner's eyes.

"Take the road that goes into those woods," said Loma.

"How much longer, wherever you're going?"

"An hour, perhaps."

"What is it, what kind of a place?"

"A resort," said Loma.

"We're going to hide out in a resort?" But Spinner should have known better than to ask. Loma didn't answer, and Spinner was too tired to bother with any more questions.

The road through the woods was new and well kept, but if there were a resort nearby it was not advertised at all. No signs, no traffic, only the road through the woods. Once the car passed a small lake and a rowboat was pulled up where the water came close to the road, but there was no sign of a human.

"This resort," said Spinner. "Does anybody go there?"

"Yes."

"Where's the traffic?"

"There are several roads going up to it," Loma said. "Quite a number."

And at the end of those roads, none of which showed anywhere, was a deserted farmhouse, or a house looking deserted with blinds drawn and a closed garage which had doors going both ways. Something like that, thought Spinner. And for good measure an old mountaineer on the front stoop. He would be chewing a blade of grass, maybe spit tobacco at a fly that kept pestering him, and across his lap he would have a shotgun. The image had become set in Spinner's mind when the next turn in the road showed the cabin on the side of a hill, a squat little building with a chinked chimney and bushes growing up to the windows. But the road never turned that way. It swung off again and the cabin disappeared from view.

"Hour is almost up," said Spinner.

"I know."

Spinner was dead tired. He felt he was awake only where his palms touched the wheel, where the sole of his foot pressed the pedal, and where the road and the trees moved past his eyes.

"You're passing it," he heard.

Loma had said it twice. The cutoff was as good as the main road, but it climbed more. Spinner had to back up, swing hard to the left, and once on the road he could see nothing from the car but tall woods and a curve ahead. Each successive curve turned the other way, and then came the last one. The road seemed to splay as it dipped into the plateau and for a moment Spinner kept driving as if he hadn't seen the change; the tennis courts to the left, the lawn with the benches to the right, and the golf course which leaned up the side of a shorn hill in the distance.

"Not there," said Loma. "The big house. The one with the porch."

The big house with the porch was a small hotel.

"Pull up to the stairs," said Loma.

Spinner pulled up and looked. There were a few guests on the porch, mostly men. They wore colored shirts, and were reading papers or talking over drinks. Then a younger one came out with a tennis racket and the man with him explained about foot position for a good backhand. They walked past the car. A sign tacked to the porch railing read *Movie Tonight: Lonely Love.*

Loma rolled down his window and watched the man come down the stairs. A bellhop was following him, but without that signature the man still would have looked like the host. He was dressed in a business suit with a carnation in the lapel and in his hand he carried a pencil. He came down the stairs smiling his happiness, and his free hand made eager little pats across the thin hair.

"Gentlemen!" he began and then he saw Loma. His face became more reserved and he said, "Oh."

"You have room?" said Loma.

The host looked from Loma to Spinner and back.

"He's with me," said Loma.

"Oh."

"Well?"

"Uh—of course. If you say so. It's just that I didn't know..."

"I'm working for St. Louis."

"I know, I heard that. But I didn't know you were coming here. What I heard..."

"Right now I need a place, Betman."

"Uh—how hot are..."

"I don't know if I am. That's why I need a place."

"All right," said Betman, not wanting to hear any more. He tapped the pencil against his front teeth and looked into space. Then he said, "Number Seven. You can have Number Seven." Then he stepped back, waiting for Loma to come out.

"Show me the place. If it's what we need—"

"Very well." Betman walked ahead of the car.

Spinner followed slowly, past a croquet game on a lawn and down a small road with cottages visible in the woods. Loma was known, apparently. They hadn't expected him, they weren't happy to see him, but Loma seemed to command a certain respect.

Number Seven was the last cabin at the end of a clearing. Several roads left the clearing, Betman held the door of the car while Spinner carried Loma into the small house. There were two rooms, a bathroom, and a carport with a door into the cabin.

"Is there a phone?" asked Loma.

There was a phone. There wasn't the right kind of chair for Loma, and Betman promised to get one immediately. Loma paid a large sum in advance and sent Betman away.

There wasn't much for Spinner to carry in from the car, and then he sat on the bed, rubbing his face. Loma stood by the window on one leg.

"I'm going to sleep," said Spinner.

"Before you do, see if that phone will reach here."

Spinner brought the phone to the window and went back to the bed. He wasn't even interested in what Loma was going to do next. Loma couldn't walk, and he couldn't drive. That's all Spinner thought about for the moment—and sleep. He stretched out on the bed and thought about sleep. The trip was over, the strangeness was wearing off. Loma stood by the window on one leg and that too seemed commonplace. Spinner was no longer in touch with anything but the slow pleasure of sleep growing in his body. Loma was talking now, a talking bird on one leg by the window.

"...not alone," he was saying. "I'm staying here for the moment."

To whom would he tell this? Betman again?

"Send me your contact," Loma was saying. "I can't come in to St. Louis."

Long distance, perhaps. His employer.

"No... As short a time as I can... Yes." He hung up.

At the hide-out, for as short a time as possible, and he wouldn't go to St. Louis, at least not until they sent him another man!

Spinner sat up with a sudden shock, trying to focus.

"What!" he said. "What was that?"

"I was on the phone," said Loma. He had moved so that he half sat on the windowsill.

"I wasn't out," Spinner said. "If you think you're going..."

"What did you hear?"

Spinner got off the bed and walked to where Loma was. The tiredness stayed with him but the anger gave him a look of aliveness.

"You don't skip out," he said, close to Loma's face. "You and me stick till you're no good to me any more. No other way, do you hear?"

"Go to sleep," said Loma.

Spinner shouted, hoping to wake himself. "Do you hear?"

Loma didn't blink, but he moved his head a little.

"I told you right from the start, killer, just the way..."

"You want to know my plans?" said Loma.

Spinner nodded. He was surprised and could only nod.

"My job didn't run the way I had planned it. I don't know how bad it turned out, or whether I'm covered."

"How about me?"

"I don't know about you. I'm telling you my plans, since you asked."

Spinner kept still, waiting.

"I'm staying here to see what develops. Until I know if they're looking for me, or just for you, I'm staying here."

"You son of a bitch." Spinner said it low and with heat, but, as he could have expected, he got no reaction from Loma. Spinner said, "But that phone call. I heard..."

"You know my job was for St. Louis. I called them so they would know where I was. And the contact," he added, "is the man who brings me my money."

Spinner tried to think about Loma's answers, but things were slow in his head. He said, "Are you lying, Loma?" Spinner was hoping that was all he had to say to get an answer and no more doubt. He was very tired.

"I don't lie," said Loma.

Spinner believed him. He went back to the bed and sat down.

"No. Maybe not. And as soon as I fall asleep you just as soon put a bullet through my head as give me the time of day."

He saw Loma reach into his belt and then, with the soft movements he had, Loma tossed the gun on the bed.

"There wouldn't be any good reason," he said. "Go to sleep."

Spinner fell asleep without having touched the gun.

Chapter 14

He woke in a sweat and when he opened his eyes the sunlight slammed at him, making him curl over and away from the light. He lay that way for a moment. Then he jumped up.

The gun wasn't there, and Loma was gone.

Spinner didn't bother to look in the other room or to check the door to the carport, but ran to the front, where the sun beat down on the clearing. Two men on the opposite side looked up from their checkerboard when Spinner came out the door, making it crash against the side of the cabin.

He saw the tail end of the car stick out of the port but that didn't mean a thing. Not after the phone call Loma had made, even asking Spinner to get off the bed so he could reach him the telephone; bothering to explain himself—something Loma never did; performing the gesture with the gun tossed across the room, like a melodrama; and he, Spinner, too drugged with sleep or too stupid with trust to watch that man, to watch that machine of a man whose insides were so unknown to Spinner—

"Over here."

Loma sat under a tree where the shadow seemed black. He was in a wheelchair. He was shaved, wore a fresh shirt, and his black hair, as always, was combed back smoothly. The empty goat eyes left Spinner to read his own meaning into the look.

"What time is it?" shouted Spinner.

It was stupid, both the question and the way he had shouted, but it helped a little.

Loma said, "I don't know."

Spinner walked to the tree and stooped when he got into the shadow.

"What did you say?"

"I said I don't know."

Spinner pulled a bench closer and sat down, feeling angry. He got out a cigarette, but the thought of smoke in his mouth made him throw it away. Maybe he should kick Loma's cast, crack it maybe. It would mean something violent done and Loma might scream. Hell, he wouldn't scream, not Loma. Loma would pass out, slip away, smooth and soundless. The way that ghost could make silence

"Well?" said Spinner. "What next?"

"When?" said Loma.

Spinner took a deep breath and crossed his arms. He concentrated on dipping his foot up and down over one knee and then he noticed how

Loma moved his wheelchair away a little. Spinner stopped swinging his foot.

"I was too worn out to ask the right questions before," said Spinner. "Tell me again. What happens next?"

"I told you. I'm staying here for a while."

"Yes. I know. But how about me? Why keep me around?" Before Loma could answer Spinner said, "And don't tell me I can go where I please or some wash like that."

"I wasn't going to."

Spinner had nothing to answer and Loma went on.

"I'm here to see what develops. I told you that. And when I know I can plan how to move next. As for you—" he swung his chair around with a push on the wheels—"I don't know how you are going to act. That's why I want you in sight."

"You—you want me in sight?"

"Why are you surprised? You know more than you should."

It hadn't occurred to Spinner that Loma might think this way; as if normal cautions weren't the kind that Loma needed to worry about.

"Tell me, Loma. And if I go to the cops..."

"I didn't say that."

"You didn't have to. When you said I know more than I should..."

"Perhaps you think I've forgotten, Spinner, but I'm keeping in mind why you came along, and how you did it. You came along to get in and that, most of the time, was behind everything you've been doing. But..."

"Most of the time? What in hell do you think I've been doing the rest of the time?"

"I don't know," said Loma. He looked away, but then turned back and talked as before. "It doesn't matter. It matters to me, though, that you must have forgotten what I told you. I can't give you an in. I don't know anybody."

"You're working," said Spinner, sounding vicious.

"I work alone."

"When you called St. Louis before..."

"I'll tell you again. I can't help you. And you don't understand, believe me. That's why I need to know what you are doing, because you're not listening to me and I can't predict you."

Spinner sat back and had the feeling of having been watched without knowing it. For a moment it gave him a strange feeling of pleasure, that Loma had taken account of him, that he, Spinner, had all this time not been a blank to Loma. But the satisfaction didn't last very long, because what Loma had said was that Spinner was on his own, as in the beginning, as if Spinner had never met Loma at all. As if all this and what had gone before had been nothing.

"That's your side," said Spinner. He got up abruptly and stepped close to Loma's chair. "You called somebody in St. Louis."

"Yes."

"When is he coming?"

"Some time today."

"I'm going to meet him. You want me out of your hair, Loma, here's your chance."

"You can meet him."

"Who is he?"

"I don't know. Just somebody they're going to send."

"It'll do. Anybody of flesh and blood will do, Loma." Spinner walked back to the cabin.

He used Loma's razor and then he took a shower. He didn't feel like getting back into his dirty clothes but he didn't have any others. Then he sat in the front room. From there he could see Loma under his tree. He didn't have to talk to him and he didn't have to suffer his silences. If there had been some money in Spinner's pocket he would have liked to buy himself something to eat. But it would have meant leaving his watching post. The last one maybe, because once Loma's contact showed up Spinner would make his pitch. He felt for a cigarette but forgot to light it. He had no pitch. All he had was intentions, but that wasn't going to stand in his way. Anybody with reasons like his behind him didn't need a pitch. Spinner didn't puzzle about where he had gotten his confidence, but he kept feeling that way as he watched Loma.

Nobody stopped where Loma sat. A few times someone would walk past the tree and a few times someone nodded at Loma without waiting to see if he nodded back. A man with a blonde came by Spinner's cabin and he heard the blonde say, "You mean you know him, over there?"

"I'd just as soon not," the man said, and they talked about something else.

A warm pine odor blew into the cabin. Spinner leaned back in his chair and put his hands in back of his neck. But he couldn't see Loma that way. He leaned forward again and then he stood up.

The Cadillac looked out of place coming through the trees. Passing from light into shadow, the big body flashed on and off and then the car stopped under Loma's tree. A brown-haired girl was behind the wheel and a man with a glittering thread in his sports shirt got out of the car. He walked up to Loma, nodded, sat down. They didn't shake hands.

Spinner got up and licked his lips. He wished his shirt were clean. He walked to the tree with long steps and when he looked down at the two men he said, "That him, Loma?"

The man in the glittery shirt turned around and looked up at Spinner, his mouth open. His eyes showed a lot of white, and he had thick, black hair.

"You don't know much, do you?" he said, and when he started to laugh it was just a loud sound without mirth.

"Loma and me..." Spinner started, and the man stopped laughing.

"Is that the guy?" he said to Loma.

"Yes."

"Come back in five minutes, okay, boy?"

"Why?" said Spinner.

"Give us a moment," Loma said.

"Yeah. Say hello to precious over there," said the man. "She deserves the best."

Spinner ignored it and walked away.

"But watch out," the man called after him. "She's in a biting mood." Then he laughed again.

Her brown hair was curly and came down over her forehead. It made her eyes look very big. She watched Spinner with no special interest, but kept turning her head as he came around the car. The way she sat in the big car Spinner couldn't see much of her, except that she wore a white blouse, and that her arm was brown from the sun.

"Who is he?" said Spinner and nodded his head at the man with Loma.

"Some bum."

He didn't have patience for her troubles and her answer made him feel hard, just the way she had sounded.

"So what are you doing with him?"

"He pays high," she said. When she saw Spinner squint at that she started to laugh, a laugh with no interest in it.

They didn't talk any more and Spinner leaned against one front fender and smoked. He watched a buzzard making a turn over one of the hills.

"Who are you?" the girl said.

He didn't turn. He didn't want to hear her voice. It had a slight hoarseness in it, making him listen to it against his will. She got out of the car, walked over in front of him.

"Who are you?" she asked him again.

"I haven't got a cent," he answered.

"Now that you told me you can be crude, do you feel any better?"

He looked at her full length the first time. She was very attractive. What spoiled it was what he had said, and what she had said, and he might as well stop looking.

"I bet you'd like to say you're sorry," she said.

If she laughs now, he thought, if she laughs now— She didn't laugh, though. She leaned against the fender, the way he was doing it, and looked at the buzzard too. After a while the buzzard wheeled out of view and the girl moved away from the car.

"Now that we lost that conversation piece, let me ask you something else."

Spinner said, "How come you act that way? Had a fight with him?"

"That's right."

"Don't take it out on me."

"There's nobody else," she said. "Besides, you don't look too sensitive. Are you?"

"Like you," he said.

She gave a short laugh for an answer and turned away. She walked back and forth a few times, kicked at a stone, then came back to the car.

"Can I have a glass of water?" she asked.

Spinner nodded and led the way to the cabin. Halfway there he regretted having said yes, because it meant leaving Loma and the man with the shirt out of sight. But that was foolish. He regretted going because he didn't like the girl. That was the reason. It wasn't her needling that bothered him, it showed her spirit. But the hard part, her coldness, that made him dislike her. Cold, like Loma, he thought, except that it didn't jar when he thought of the coldness in Loma. With her it did, as if no woman had any business being cold.

He gave her a quick look and then coughed. They went into the cabin.

"How can you stand the heat in here," she said.

"The bathroom's this way." Spinner walked ahead of her to look for a clean glass.

She stood in the room and fluffed her blouse.

"You live here with that Loma?"

"You want this water or don't you?"

She came into the bathroom and took the glass from him. She drank and ignored his remark. Spinner watched her chin and her long neck curving back. The skin was whiter there, where the sun hadn't reached, and if she hadn't been such a cold bitch, Spinner thought, he would tell her what a fine neck she had. Then she put the glass down with a satisfied sound and licked her wet lip. Spinner looked away, at the glass.

"You want more?"

"No, thanks. Leave the bathroom a minute, will you?"

She turned on the tap before he got out and he heard the splashing while he stood at the front window.

"Don't you have any towels?" she called.

He didn't know where to look for one. If she didn't like the ones in the bathroom let her shake her hands for a while and they'd be dry in this heat soon enough.

"Every towel in here is wet," she called. "You got any more?"

"All right. Just a minute."

He started to bang drawers open and shut. The girl in the bathroom started to whistle and Spinner felt himself getting on edge, without knowing why. The waiting, it must be the waiting. Throughout the trip with

Loma he waited, now with the man from St. Louis he waited, and on top of that, as if nothing else mattered, she whistled in there, looking at herself in the bathroom mirror, most likely, to see how she looked while whistling. Probably turning and posing in front of the bathroom mirror, to see how good she looked and taking the sight for granted, the whistling for granted, and Spinner hunting around for a towel for her, for granted, too.

He found a drawer with towels and yanked out the one on top.

"Can't you find one?" he heard.

Spinner pushed the door open and held out the towel but then he let it drop down again. She was watching herself in the mirror and with arms up was fluffing the short brown hair. Spinner could see the skin white on the inside of her arms, where the sun hadn't reached. The rest was brown and shiny with water. She had kept on the skirt and her bra but the rest of her glistened; face, neck, shoulders, and the roundness over the bra.

"Give it to me," she said and held out one hand. Aside from that she ignored him. "You wouldn't have a comb, would you?"

The bra was white and next to it was the brown of her tan and Spinner thought he could smell the warm skin. A cold bitch like her—

"In the cabinet," he said.

She opened the cabinet which made Spinner's mirror image swing into view. It stared at him with fine lines at the ends of his eyes and the brows drawn together. And he didn't like the look of the mouth, or the chin, or anything showing. He looked away, feeling rotten without knowing why and there was the girl again. The bathroom was very small.

"Watch my elbow," she said, "when I comb my hair."

Maybe he expected too much. Maybe Loma wasn't a cold bastard with a feel like metal and the girl, maybe she was just like any of them or all of them and he, Spinner, with the heat of anger inside, just expected too much.

"Step back some," she said.

It wasn't too much to expect that she didn't really feel like a stone, and he put out his hand. Her arm felt warm.

She stopped combing and said, "Forget it, will you?"

She felt warm, but she wasn't, and with sudden anger he grabbed the soft arm and yanked.

She looked up at him and he didn't like the slant she put on her mouth.

"You can't rape me, you know," and she pulled her arm out of his hand, quite slowly, as if it didn't matter.

"You always talk tough like that?" he said.

"With your kind, it helps." She suddenly jerked away. Or almost, because he held on again, feeling the muscles move under her skin.

She relaxed suddenly and it almost stopped Spinner—but then she laughed. It was like a kick. His arm clamped around her back, more like a hit than anything else, and he heard the sound when it squeezed the breath out of her. She didn't tense again and she didn't struggle, and Spinner might not have gone ahead had he known how she felt—feeling nothing.

Chapter 15

She sat up on the bed, shook out her hair, and got up. She smoothed down her skirt and adjusted the brassiere. Then she went to the bathroom and Spinner heard the faucet again, as before. When he got up he walked around the end of the bed and saw Loma with the man in the glittery shirt. They hadn't moved, though Spinner didn't pay any real attention. There was a pack of cigarettes in his pocket, and the Cellophane made a crackling sound. He took the pack out, dropped it on top of the dresser. He pushed the pack to the edge and watched it drop into the wastepaper basket that stood there. Spinner wished he knew how he felt.

In a moment she'll turn off the water, he thought, and then what. But the water kept running and Spinner couldn't continue to stand at the dresser because the edge cut into the back of his thighs, hurting him. And he wanted to see her.

When he came in she took her hands away from her face and shook off the water. Her face was wet, and the rest of her, too, as before.

They looked at each other and he said, "Here. I brought you a towel."

She didn't take the towel right away because she was still looking at his face, but then, whatever her expression was going to be, she let it go and reached for the towel.

"Thank you," she said.

Spinner leaned against the door frame and watched her rub herself dry, and for a brief moment it felt as if he knew her and something felt good. But that happened only for a brief moment when everything else came back to him, except without the anger.

"I don't know your name," he said.

It would have been the time for her to make a crack, some very seasoned kind of remark, and he even got ready for it, ready to ignore it, but she only said, "Ann." She wasn't looking at him. "And yours?"

"Jake. Jake Spinner."

She nodded at that. "I forgot where I put the comb. Do you have one of your own?"

He gave her the comb from his pocket and she started going through the back of her hair.

Spinner didn't know how to say it but then it came all by itself.

"We were lousy."

Then there was nothing else to say. She put on her blouse while Spinner walked back into the room in front where the windows looked out on the clearing. After a while she came in and opened the door.

"I'm going back," she said.

"Yes. Let's go back," and they walked together toward the car.

Chapter 16

The sun had moved just enough to reach the bottom of Loma's chair, and touched the cast, which lay white and hard. It gave the impression of not belonging to anything. Loma looked down at it, but didn't move.

"I can't use him. Perhaps you can."

"He's your problem." The man picked up a twig and stuck it into his mouth. "If you can't take care of him, who can?"

"We'll see," said Loma, and then looked up.

They both watched Spinner and the girl come back from the cabin. The girl walked toward the car and Spinner came to the tree. But the man wasn't watching Spinner. His face spread with a wide grin and he called, "Ann, doll," and when she looked at him from the car he said, "how was it, Ann, doll?"

Spinner said nothing, but he hoped that the girl would have an answer. She said, "Is that how you get your kicks?"

She watched from the car, waiting for more, but the man only laughed. When he looked up at Spinner the laugh petered out and he spat the twig on the ground. "Loma says you drove him back."

"This is Keel," said Loma to Spinner. "From St. Louis."

Spinner sat down on the bench next to Keel and looked the man over. He might not like Keel, but this was what Spinner was after. This was the whole point of having come this far.

"I drove Loma for an introduction. My name's Spinner."

Keel leaned back and grinned.

"Changing jobs, or something?"

"More than that. But I'm looking for a job."

"Well," said Keel, "jobs like driving Loma here, and busting his ankle, don't come along every day." He laughed.

Neither Loma nor Spinner showed any reaction and Keel stopped laughing.

"You're in hot water," said Keel. "I don't call that a recommendation."

"Me? No more than Loma."

"You ain't Loma, uh—what was that name?"

"Spinner. Jake Spinner."

Keel worked his tongue around the inside of his cheek and started to frown.

"Spinner? Where you from?"

"Stone Bluff. The same place…"

"Yeah. Dixon. You got a name rings a bell, Spinner, but I can't place it."

"My father worked for Dixon some years back."

"Is that so?" said Keel.

For a moment Spinner had thought that his father, in a queer, tangled way, would suddenly be of some help, but the tone of Keel's voice didn't let it happen.

"Dixon used to pick up all kinds," said Keel. "I think I heard the name." And after a pause, "What did he do? Your old man, I mean."

Spinner didn't answer right away. He looked at the green on the side of the hill and then up the hill where the trees looked darker. He wished there were nothing else to do but look at those and sit in the shade here.

"I don't think he ever did a damn thing," Spinner heard himself say. "He fell down the stairs and died from that. Why you asking?"

"Just questions. I thought maybe he was big with Dixon or something. Seeing I remember the name."

"He wasn't. What's that got to do with anything?"

Keel shrugged. "You're looking for a job, aren't you? So I'm asking. Qualifications and so forth."

"Then ask what's important! I don't waste time…"

"I don't like lip, Spinner."

"Loma—" Spinner looked over at him—"is this guy the best you can do?"

"He's the one that come," said Loma, showing no interest.

Keel looked from one to the other, as if he didn't believe his ears.

"Hey!" he said. "Who says I got to listen…"

"You tell this when you get back to St. Louis," said Loma. "Tell them he saw the whole thing from the beginning. That he has made no wrong move, so far, for only one reason. He told you what that was." Loma paused, to see if Keel was listening. Then he said, "And you can't kill him. He and I have been together ever since Dixon. If they're looking for me and he turns up dead, it would be bad. If they're looking for him and he turns up dead, it would be the same because they'll be after me."

Keel went more by the tone of voice than the content and he didn't say any more. Spinner had followed the reasoning and he didn't say anything either. The shock was Loma's inhuman bookkeeping. Not that this was anything new; but it hadn't happened so clearly before, with Spinner the cipher that had to be balanced.

And it made sense. Spinner felt cold, but said nothing. It made sense, and this was all part of his switch and he mustn't forget it.

"I don't get paid to argue," said Keel, and got up. "I'll tell 'em."

"Let me know tomorrow," said Loma.

Spinner said nothing. The machine was set in motion and this was all part of the plan. He mustn't forget it.

When Keel got to the car Spinner got up from the bench and walked into the sunlight. He didn't want to sit under the tree with Loma. He looked at Ann, who was standing next to the car and who dropped her cigarette when Keel came closer. She made a short laugh when she saw his face.

"What you been doing? Tried arguing with somebody?" she asked.

Keel frowned at her, then looked down at his sleeve, brushing it. When he looked up he was grinning. He felt best when he could manage a grin.

"There's us with beautiful bodies and then your kind, with the brains."

"Either way you turn it," she said, "I come out on top."

Spinner heard how they were talking and he walked up closer. Keel was saying, "Either way, I can buy you." His grin made it sound worse.

"For cold cash, what temperature do you think you'll be getting?"

Spinner put his hands on the end of the hood and held the ornament. He could feel it bite into his fingers.

"Hell, you talk like I want something from you. Hey, Spinner—" he cocked his head, looking at him like a buddy—"what makes these dames think they got it all? Tell her."

Spinner saw Ann look away and he wondered about her expression.

"Maybe, just to show her," Keel went on, "I'll go back by myself. Hey, Ann."

She turned back and for a moment Spinner thought she was going to look at him, but then she didn't. Keel grinned at her.

"Annie, you ever been dumped?"

She didn't answer, and any moment Keel was going to laugh.

"She's staying here," said Spinner.

Keel's mouth came open but Spinner was looking at Ann. He could see nothing in her face.

"What did you say? What did he say, Ann?" he heard Keel ask.

She nodded her head slightly and said, "I'm staying here."

The best Keel could do at that moment was laugh. He roared himself up and down the scale a few times and got into his car as if he didn't care one way or the other. The girl stepped back and Keel kicked the starter, while his laugh slowed to a wheeze.

"Back to the farm," he said; "back to the farm." And then he added, "Anyway, Annie. I'll be up tomorrow. I'll see you tomorrow."

"I'll see you," she said, and watched him drive off.

The girl and Spinner stood with the space between them where the car had been, and neither of them said anything.

CHAPTER 17

He squinted at the hill behind her and then looked down, without having seen anything.

"Spinner," a voice said from behind him, where Loma was under the tree.

Spinner didn't turn. He took his hands out of his pockets and walked toward the girl.

"Spinner," Loma said again.

"In a minute," he said. He stopped in front of the girl. "I don't know you, Ann. But I didn't like—I didn't like what Keel was doing. I thought it was too rough," he finished quickly.

"It was," she said. "Thank you."

He looked at her and gave her a short smile.

"You don't have anything with you. Clothes, or anything?"

"That's all right. He'll be back tomorrow."

"Yes." He coughed once and said, "You understand, this doesn't mean a thing, about tonight. If you want to go back to town," and he waved at the car sticking out next to the cabin.

"Yes, I know. It's all right, though. I think I know some people up here."

"Oh?"

"Spinner," Loma called.

"Sure. Don't you know this place?" she went on.

"My first time here."

"Most of the guests," she said, "are from St. Louis. Like Keel."

"Oh."

"He wants you, I think." She nodded in Loma's direction.

"Yes. Come along."

Loma had moved his chair but wasn't able to get any further. A root was caught in one wheel. Spinner untangled it and when the wheelchair was free Loma pushed at the wheels with both hands to get away.

The girl said, "Which way are you going?" and put her hands on the back of the chair.

Loma looked up at her but kept turning the wheels. "I'm not going far. I can manage."

"The cabin?" she said.

"Yes." Loma looked straight.

At the door Spinner had to lift the chair over the sill, and then Loma wheeled himself to the phone.

"I'm going to order something to eat," he said. "Do you want anything?"

He was looking at Spinner.

"Why don't we go to the main house," said Ann. "It's cooler there."

When Loma looked at her Spinner noticed that she didn't react to the stare in any way, as if his eyes and his manner—as if Loma himself were nothing different.

"You've been here before," he said.

"Sure."

"Then you understand why some of the guests, like Spinner and I, don't mingle."

"I know what this place is. That's why you don't have to stay out of sight. Look across there." She pointed out the window. "You know who's playing checkers there, in front of that cabin?"

"I'm not interested," said Loma, and reached for the phone.

"Suit yourself," she said. "And I was going to push your chair all the way to the main house."

Loma, of course, didn't react to the joke. He held the phone to his ear and said to Spinner, "There's a menu on the dresser. Order something."

"I'm going to the main house."

"Just a moment," said Loma into the phone. He covered the speaker with his hand and looked at Spinner. "You seem to forget," he started but Spinner cut him short.

"We're not running any more. We made it here."

Loma didn't answer. He didn't understand Spinner's remark, and when he realized that Spinner was one of those who thought that you run for a while and then rest, and then run for a while and then it is over, he dropped the argument because it wouldn't do any good.

Loma turned away and talked into the telephone.

Spinner took Ann's arm and led her out of the cabin.

They had their food at a corner table in the big dining room, next to a window where a pine branch kept scraping against the screen. The sun was going behind the hill and it got dark suddenly. The pine branch started to get on Spinner's nerves but he said nothing about it. He looked out the window, then at his food, and out the window again.

"You notice how it gets dark here?" she said.

"Yeah. You've noticed it before?"

"Yes. I've been here before."

"That's right. You said that."

When they stopped talking he heard the pine branch again and he tried to think of something to say.

"See anybody you know?"

She stretched her neck and said, "I haven't looked. No. I don't think so."

"Maybe you don't recognize them."

"Who?"

"I don't know who you know," he said, and when he shrugged his shoulder he felt it ache.

They ate for a while and then she said, "This man you're with, who is he?"

"His name's Loma."

"I know. Keel mentioned it. Are you with Loma?"

"With Loma? How do you mean?"

"You know. Work together."

"I just met him. I don't think he really works with anybody."

She took a sip of water and then she licked her wet lip. Spinner had seen her do it before; it must be a habit, he thought.

"You know," she said, "I had the same kind of feeling. He doesn't even look as if he is in a racket."

"He's got to be," said Spinner, trying to end the topic. "Why else would he be here?"

"What I mean is," she went on, "whatever he does he doesn't look as if he works it like a racket. You know what I mean?"

"Yes. He doesn't."

Ann didn't say anything else because with some people she knew it wasn't good to ask certain things, but she thought from Spinner's answer that he knew Loma better than he had said.

"You want more coffee?" Spinner asked, but the remark didn't do what he had meant it to do; a casual thing to say, to make him feel casual. It must be because they had talked about Loma, as if Loma still bothered him. Why should he? He had set it up for Spinner the way Spinner had wanted it, and even tomorrow, perhaps, they would be through with each other. And Spinner would have his wish and maybe go to St. Louis.

"Why did you talk to him the way you did?" he suddenly asked. "You expect a cold bastard like that to go for an ordinary kind of joke?"

"Talk how? I don't remember…"

"Why'd you push his chair, for instance. You think he liked it?"

A waiter came up to take the dishes away and when they had been cleared she put her elbows on the table.

"Why not? He's a cripple."

Spinner laughed, a hard sound. He leaned over the table and said, "You know what kind of a cripple he is?" and then he frowned, trying to think of a way to express it.

"I don't know what kind," she said. "Should that make a difference?"

Spinner made a sound that could mean anything, and leaned back in his chair. He didn't want to think about Loma. He shook a cigarette out of his pack and offered it to the girl.

"Here. You smoke?"

"Sure." She took one.

"I don't know if you smoke, I don't know anything. What else do you do?"

She blew out smoke and smiled. The topic meant nothing to her and she would go through it with practice.

"I used to be a model. Sometimes I model."

"Is that so?"

She laughed when she saw his face, because he was stuck. She had a number of remarks for that situation.

"I'm a whore, because it pays better," she said, and then she saw that it hadn't been the right choice. He didn't take up her tone.

"I don't know," he said. "It's got to do more for you to stick with it." He looked at her. "Doesn't it?"

"What makes you think I'm going to stick with it?" she said, and this time she had lost her easy way of looking at him and started to rub her eye as if smoke had gotten into it. She rubbed hard and the exaggerated motion made her feel angry. "How would you know?" It came out mean. Then she controlled herself and tried to make it more superficial. "Perhaps you've known a lot of them," she said, but she didn't feel light about it. "Intimately," she added.

"No," he said, and then, "Intimately?" He covered himself by making a laugh and asked, "Can you?"

"How do I know? I don't remember the subject ever having come up before."

It struck Spinner that this was like the time with Keel, when Keel dug at her and she had talked back at him sharp enough, but all of it surface. He felt again that he didn't like this to happen to her.

"I didn't mean to pry at you," he said and tried to smile so the whole thing would sound easy, "about why you—why you do this work."

"Money," she said.

"I know."

"I don't know why we're even talking about it," she said.

He said nothing for a while but she saw he was thinking about it. She hadn't said the right thing again and it made her feel uneasy.

He looked up at her and said, "I know why. Just a while back, you know, we went to bed together."

"That's right." She reached for another cigarette and lit it herself. "And this is the rehash."

"I don't know. Anyway, that wasn't money. You knew that ahead of time."

"I make mistakes."

"Yeah. And it never got anywhere."

She had no wish to talk any more and tried to think of something else, almost anything else, even looked across the room to see someone she knew, perhaps, when she heard herself saying it anyway.

"Maybe that's why I keep trying," she said.

She wished he would say something now to distract them, but he didn't and she kept her head down while she stubbed out her cigarette because that way she wouldn't see how he looked or what he was doing.

After a moment she heard him shift in his chair.

"Someone to see you, I think," Spinner said.

She looked up and saw someone she hardly remembered which was the best, she thought, because it was more familiar.

CHAPTER 18

One was called Joe and the other was Phil and they had a girl with them whom they all called Dickie. The one Ann knew from before was Phil, who didn't look much different from his buddy Joe, both feeling on top of the world and much younger than they acted. They invited Ann and Spinner to have a drink at the bar and later, maybe, they'd think of doing something else though who the hell cared what happened later. They couldn't talk to each too well sitting side by side at the bar so they went up to Phil's room on the second floor of the main house. The girl Dickie took off her shoes first thing and Ann took hers off too while the men dropped their jackets. Spinner kept his on because his shirt was so dirty.

"Come on," said Dickie, "let's make a racket. I can't stand those damn crickets outside and they get louder when it gets dark."

"How's this?" said Joe and started to sing a loud, dirty song. Dickie knew the refrain and made harmony while Ann laughed a lot and held her glass out for Phil to fill.

"You're the one never says 'when,' ain't you, Annie?" and Phil gave the bottle an upside down tilt, spilling whisky over the glass and over Ann's arm. They all laughed like crazy and Ann kept shouting it tickled when Phil grabbed her hand with the glass and started to lick up her bare arm.

"That Phil!" said Dickie, "just like in the song. You got more verses, Joe, any more?"

"The rest I'm too young for," said Joe, and slapped Dickie's rear.

"What about me?" said Dickie. "I'm younger than any of you."

That meant more laughter and Joe slapping her rear and yelling, "You can't prove it by me. Lookit that. You can't prove it by me!"

Spinner drank faster than any of them and tried to get into the spirit of things. Like a nasty pup a voice kept yapping and yapping at him that this was the way when you switch and this was the new life which had its good sides to it, like now.

"Jake," said Ann and stood close to him. "Let's you and me dance while they sing," because Dickie had started one of her own and the two men were chiming in at the right places.

"The hell with that," said Spinner. "I'm getting drunk."

"Here, Jake," yelled Joe, "take it." He waved the bottle at Spinner.

"You trying to make that boy pass out on the floor?" said Dickie.

"The faster the better," said Joe. He laughed loud when he said it and gave Ann's arm a loud slap. "Huh, Annie?"

Spinner thought that he'd get used to the tempo after a while and even gave Ann a slap too.

"And another thing," Joe was saying, "when it comes to. . ."

"It won't come to that," said, Dickie, but neither of them knew what they were talking about so they took a long pull from the other bottle and then Joe started saying the same thing all over again. "When it comes to that, and even that—"

Spinner felt the pressure behind his eyes and gave his bottle to Phil.

"You take it," he said. "You pass out."

"No," said Phil, "please. Be my guest. I'll join you later."

"Join what?" Dickie called from the bed. "You talking about your double-joint jaw again? Jake, let Phil show you his double-joint jaw."

Phil put his hands into his mouth and then, without any noise, his jaw ended up at a crazy, undershot angle which shortened his face and seemed to make his nose very flat.

Dickie squealed at the sight and said, "I can't stand it. Hang it together again."

"I can't," said Phil, without moving the jaw back into place. "I gotta pass out. It don't work any other way."

Dickie jumped up from the bed and ran over to Phil. She hugged him around the middle and kissed the side of his neck.

"You're not even warm," said Phil, in that peculiar murmur the jaw gave him. "Do it again."

Spinner shook his head a few times and worried about not having fun like the others. And here was a game that was going to include everything. Part of this game ought to be slugging each other, he thought, and started to look at Phil's jaw with interest. Ann was looking too and started to rub the sides of her face. Then she turned away and sat on the bed with Joe. They made room for Dickie, who flung herself on her back, and started to moan, "Why do I keep asking him that. I can't stand it—"

This time the thing did make a snap, giving Spinner a start, and Phil looked all right again.

"It starts hurting after a while," he said to Spinner. "So I always put it back in. What happened to Annie?"

"On the bed," said Spinner.

"You bring her up?" asked Phil. "She's with you?"

Spinner knew what he was going to answer but he didn't answer immediately.

Ann said from the bed, "No. He's with Loma."

Joe and Phil looked at each other and nobody talked.

Then Phil, to be doing something, picked up his glass from the dresser and looked at the ice cube.

"Gee," he said. "You know Loma?"

"Sure."

"You mean—you mean you're working with him?"

"Christ," said Phil. "He even takes on apprentices?"

"No," said Spinner. "I just met him."

"Who's Loma?" Dickie wanted to know.

"You mean you never heard of Loma?" Phil made it sound big. "He's a trigger man."

"Yeah. For who?"

"Whom," said Joe.

"Nobody. He's like calling in a consultant."

"So why you acting all scared?" said Dickie. "No consultant would be looking for you. For you they'd hire themselves some kind of broken-down pug who—"

"Will you stop talking like that?"

"I'm sorry, sweet. I didn't mean."

Phil shrugged and grinned at Dickie. Then he looked at everybody in the room with an expectant smile, but the mood had gone away. Phil shrugged again.

"We're not scared, you understand," said Joe. "It's just, you know—you talk about Loma and you talk about something different. You just hear about Loma. You don't know him."

"That's right," said Spinner.

He put his glass down and looked over at Ann. She didn't see him. She was fixing a button on the front of her blouse.

"All right," he said. "I'll see you guys around."

There was no more party and he went to the door. He didn't even look back. When he was through the door and tried pulling it shut, the knob came out of his hand and he turned. He stood in the hall and Ann was closing the door, half leaning against it and holding both hands on the knob behind her.

"I want to go with you," she said. "Didn't you ask me?"

CHAPTER 19

They walked side by side at first but after a while Spinner took Ann's arm and they walked closer together. It was dark under the trees and they kept their bearings by looking up at the sky where the trees stood apart over the road.

"I wanted to ask you," said Spinner, "back at the brawl, but I know you so little."

"That's right," she said and laughed. Spinner couldn't see her face.

"This way," he said. "You're walking into the woods."

It seemed a long walk back to the cabin and the quiet made the girl stay close to his side.

"If you want, Jake," and her voice sounded too bright, "we can go back to the party."

"I don't want to."

"Loma will be in the cabin," she said.

"I don't care. I wish you wouldn't."

She didn't say anything then, but Spinner knew she was trying to. She tried laughing instead but the sound got nowhere.

"Stop thinking so hard," he said.

"Jake?"

He waited.

"You know, we can just go to bed. I'm so tired."

They stopped at the clearing and Spinner wished they could see each other more clearly, but she thought he was smiling at her and he stroked her arm.

"Sure," he said. "You'll sleep well."

They started to cross the clearing when the moon fused through the clouds, making a cold light in the air and on the ground. Next to the door, a small shape, sat Loma.

"Oh," said the girl, and then, "you shouldn't be out here this late."

Spinner couldn't see Loma's face in the shadow but he knew the expression, and he knew how the eyes looked, and he knew how Loma would sound, like the cold light.

"I couldn't get in," said Loma, "because of the step."

Spinner let go of the girl and cursed under his breath. He walked up to Loma's chair and started to reach for it.

"Leave me here," said Loma. "I'll stay out here for a while."

It didn't hit Spinner immediately but when it did his scalp prickled with heat and he couldn't find enough breath with the anger squeezing him. Everything Loma touched, everything—

"You shouldn't stay..." the girl started, but the violence of Spinner's movement made her stop. He yanked the chair up to the house, pulled the screen door open and kicked it back with his foot, and then he pushed Loma's chair through the first room, making the wheels turn with a fast whisper.

"You can get into bed yourself?" he asked Loma.

"Yes."

"Fine," said Spinner, not daring to say more. He came back to the front room and slammed Loma's door.

The girl stood by the window and he could see her unbutton her blouse. He watched her. Something in the way she undressed made him relax, and when he walked up to her she smiled at him and then turned back to what she was doing. Spinner was no longer upset. She waited for him while he took off his clothes. She stood by the window, holding her arms, rubbing them slowly as if she were cold.

When they lay down her head was next to his face and he put his chin into her hair. He held her with one arm down her side and one hand near her throat. He could feel a small pulse there and after a while it seemed to slow and grow softer. She stretched out her legs and turned her head toward him.

"Does the light bother you?" said Spinner.

"No. I don't even see it."

They lay like that for a while, with Ann so quiet that Spinner was sure she was asleep.

"Do you hear something?" she said.

"No. What was it?"

"It's so quiet," she said. "I'm not used to it. I keep listening for something to spoil it."

"You can hear small noises outside," he said. "But they don't spoil it."

She nodded. He felt it on his chest.

"What did Keel mean," he said, "when he said back to the farm?"

"Keel? I don't remember he said that—"

"I thought perhaps he meant that's where you came from."

She laughed and said, "No. Keel just said that to be in line, I guess. Something like country girl comes to the big city and gets good and bad, or whichever."

"Oh. I see."

"Why do you ask? I look like a farm girl?"

"Oh no. Not at all. I'm from a farm."

"I've been on one, but that's all. Fact is, I'm from a bigger city than St. Louis."

"How'd that happen?"

She laughed again, to herself this time.

"New York wasn't big enough for me and my family. It was either their way or no way."

Spinner shifted a little but didn't let go of her.

"I can see that," he said. "Running around with the likes of Keel, I can see why they..."

"There weren't any Keels. Just nice, approved bastards my family liked. The real filth. So I picked my own friends." She paused. "At least they weren't filthy."

"So how come," Spinner asked, "you ended up with the Keels?"

She moved her head away and looked out the window.

"I just—I lost my bearings somewhere along the way."

Spinner lay still and stroked her side. He felt her grow stiff under his hand, or perhaps he imagined it. "Anyway, it's okay if you like it in St. Louis."

"Sure," she said. "What happened to your farm? You didn't like it?"

He stopped moving his hand, and put both his hands up behind his head.

"Oh. I liked it all right."

"Did you lose it?"

He laughed at the thought, remembering that he still owned it, but what did that get him?

"No. It's still there."

"But you can't go hack?"

"Sort of like you," he said. "Why don't you go back?"

She turned on her side, to curl herself up, and then said, "Sort of like you and so forth."

Her tone gave them an out and they pushed the whole thing aside, laughing about it, but then had nothing else to say. They didn't want to talk or to think any more and when she turned the next time, his way, that was the distraction. He pulled her closer and she didn't say no or try to lie the way she had done before. It was more familiar this way, even to the kiss, which was mechanical. Then she was going to laugh and say something about it always ending this way when Spinner held still and listened into the dark. She heard Spinner curse.

"Doesn't that bastard ever sleep?" he demanded.

"Who?" She sat up too.

"Loma. Don't you hear him?"

Then she heard the sound of somebody breathing. It was in the next room.

"He never breathes like that," said Spinner. "I've never heard that before."

Spinner let himself drop back and stared at the ceiling.

She leaned down on one elbow, and said, "Why does he bother you? He never does anything and he always seems to bother you."

Spinner didn't know what to answer, but hearing the breathing in the next room he couldn't keep silent.

"Because he's all wrong!" And when it didn't feel like enough, "He's everything opposite!"

The girl lay down next to him, and Spinner saw her nod. Then she turned to put her hand on Spinner's face.

"Why are you with him?" she said.

"Yeah. It's a question."

She kept her hand on his face and he turned her way, and then she moved closer.

"I don t hear him any more." She kissed him, small and warm.

"Stay close."

"Jake," she said. "I'm glad he interrupted, before." She knew that he felt so too when suddenly Spinner pulled back their sheet.

"Come on," he said, "get up."

"Now? You mean—"

"Come on. Let's get out of here. You and me."

She started to laugh and held his arm when they ran out of the cabin because of the way he was dragging the blanket along. She took one end of it and he the other and they went a short distance into the woods.

Chapter 20

Loma—it turned out in the morning—could walk. Spinner was tying his shoes, and Ann stood smoking and watching him when they heard the hard sounds, as if something had fallen. Loma opened his door.

"Christ," said Spinner.

Loma was holding himself with both hands in the frame of the door. His small body was bent to balance himself and the foot with the white cast was swinging slightly, tapping to find its place.

"Here," said Ann, "let me help you," and she went up to Loma to take his arm.

"No. You needn't."

"Doesn't it hurt?" she asked.

"No."

He let go of the door frame and walked with a grotesque stumble till he got to the bed.

Spinner finished tying his shoe and sat up. "Loma, how come you always say no? She asks you if it hurts when you can barely crawl; but you got to..."

"The pain is minor," said Loma. "I have trouble walking because I'm used to favoring my other side." He looked down at his clubfoot. "As it is, I have to learn it the other way."

Spinner looked at Ann and said, "You see? He's got a reason. Always no, but he makes a reason." He shrugged and got up. He hadn't been aware of it but his tone when he talked about Loma had been something new, as if either Loma were human or Spinner didn't care one way or the other.

"We were going to breakfast," said Ann. "Sit in your chair and I'll wheel you down."

"He's going to say no," Spinner said and watched Loma.

Loma sat down on the bed, near the phone, and moved his leg with the cast so it would be more comfortable.

"Keel is coming this morning," he said. "Or is it no longer important to you?"

It was. That and the fact that Loma could walk, if he wanted to, meant a great deal. Loma no longer needed him and St. Louis was sending word whether they wanted Spinner or not. It should feel like a turning point, but Spinner could not force a feeling beyond that of a strange, very vivid dream. It meant that he might wake up, had he thought of it, and then he would not know what to do.

"That's right," said Spinner. "We'll stay here, so I don't miss him."

"He's also coming for you?" said Loma and looked at the girl.

Spinner had turned away so that the girl saw only the back of his head.

"Sure," she said. "For the ride."

They had breakfast brought to the cabin and then they waited for Keel, hoping he would come soon.

Keel had left St. Louis early, as he had been instructed, but no part of his errand was very important. A message for Loma, instructions about Spinner, and to pick up Annie—if she were free. None of it seemed too important to Keel so he stopped on the way for breakfast, stopped again where he saw a big sign on a barn which read *Auction,* and when he came to a railroad crossing where a freight train was coming through he sat counting the cars with interest.

Driving into the resort he made a bet with himself that Loma would be under that tree again, and another bet—with odds much lower—that Annie was still in bed, and that it wouldn't be with Spinner. Keel knew Annie from way back; they were all alike, they didn't faze him one way or the other, and this time when he took her back, no more monkey business. If there was anything he despised, Keel said to himself, it was a dame acting up.

He roared up to the clearing, made an impressive stop, and saw he had won one bet and lost two. Loma was under the tree; so was Spinner, and Ann was sitting next to him. Keel started laughing, first thing, because he thought the three of them looked very funny, and it also kept him from tallying up how much he owed himself for the lost bets.

"Hey, back to the farm, huh?" he yelled and walked over to the tree.

They all nodded hello at him and Keel stood looking from one to the other.

"Boy," he said, "lemme tell you it's getting hot in the city. Even early this morning."

"When did you leave?" asked Loma.

"Eight in the morning. I had to be in the office before eight, and got chased out to here right from there. And the heat   ..."

"How come you didn't get here till now," said Loma, "if you left that early?"

"Hell. I don't know. The road, I guess. How you been, Annie, had a good night?"

"Yes. Thank you."

"Thank you?" and Keel started laughing again. "Hell, I had nothing to do with it. I wasn't even here!"

But Spinner, just sitting there, dampened Keel's fun. Keel sucked his teeth and looked at Loma.

"Well, I haven't got much. Little early to tell."

Loma looked at the girl and said, "Would you leave for a moment?" He followed Ann with his eyes when she got up and walked to the cabin, and then turned back to Keel.

"Let's hear it."

"Well, there's nothing on you, right now. You either got through clean or they're playing it cagey."

"What about the trip?"

"Looks like the little girl in the burg you stopped in and that doctor in that other burg you stopped in didn't report a thing. And that farmer outside that one burg don't know from nothing either. He thinks you're a fine little gentleman, he says."

"You talked to him?"

"Me? Hell, no. We got a man there doing legwork."

"I don't quite understand about the girl," said Loma. He treated the whole thing as if he hadn't been in it. "After all, the store got robbed, and so on."

"Oh. She said that was robbers. She got scared and hid in the closet, she said, and didn't see who it was."

Spinner looked at Loma's face, wondering if there would be relief, or perhaps doubt, any emotion about that part of the trip. There was nothing, and Loma went on.

"What about Stone Bluff?"

"Oh, that. Dixon's dead, all right. You knew that," he added, smiling.

"Go on."

"And nobody's looking for you there, that's for sure. They're sure as hell looking for him, though," and Keel nodded at Spinner.

It was nothing new to Spinner, and should have meant nothing to him. He looked away. His face felt tight and he squinted at the hill in the distance.

"They figure they got him dead to rights, with evidence and everything."

"What evidence?" Spinner asked.

"We didn't get that part. That sheriff and prosecutor aren't easy to get by." Keel scratched his ear. "Because Dixon's dead, that's why, I guess."

"Anything else?" said Loma.

"No, I think that's it, so far."

"There's got to be more," said Spinner. "Aren't there any details, anything else about what happened in Stone Bluff?"

"How come you're so anxious?" said Keel. "Hell, you got out from under. All they're doing is looking for you."

"All? If I'm going to stay healthy..."

"Hell, you should worry. You should know what they got against me!" He started to laugh again. "Or Loma here, huh, Loma?"

Keel was just about to slap Loma's back when he suddenly stopped laughing and changed his swing with the arm into something else. He slapped his leg and coughed hard, thinking how terrible it would have been to slap a man on the back who was wearing a cast, or sat in a wheelchair, or had a clubfoot—anyway, a man like Loma.

"Well?" said Loma. "What else?"

"What about—did they find the place where I met Loma? Where the car was?"

"I don't know," said Keel. "So what?"

"If that's all," said Loma, "you can go back to town. Tell them I'm staying a few days longer, to be sure nothing else develops. Tell them I want more information tomorrow."

"Okay, Loma. I'll do that."

Keel turned to Spinner. He put his hands in his pockets and started to grin.

"Now I bet you're anxious as hell about what's with you, huh?"

"Let's have it, Keel."

"I'm taking you back with me, to St. Louis. They want to see you. Happy?"

Spinner hadn't heard the last part. They wanted to see him and he was going with Keel, that's what he had heard. He inhaled deeply, held it, and let the breath come out slowly. He clenched and unclenched his hands which he held between his knees, and repeated the words in his mind to make them sink in. He should feel something terrific right now, because this was it. The way he had planned it, the way he had imagined it, and now it was true. There should be a big sense of another step taken and a big scene of strength about everything but maybe this caution was better. The way Loma would feel about something like this: hold it a little bit longer, until it was sure, until it was over, and then—like with Loma—it would be over without any feeling at all!

"Come on," said Spinner. "Come on, let's go, this is big!"

He had talked so loud that Ann stepped out of the cabin to see what went on. Spinner kept pushing himself.

"You got something else to say, tell me about it on the way down. The way I've been waiting for this, Keel, this is no time to..."

"I want you to bring him back afterward," said Loma, ignoring everything, and before Spinner had time to react to it Keel answered the same way.

"Sure. He's supposed to, anyway."

"Why? Why in hell..."

"Jesus, stop yelling," said Keel. "This is just for a talk. After that you hang around some and wait. And that's what this place is for. Come on over, Annie." Keel waved to her.

The girl came back to the tree and nobody except Spinner felt there was any more to say. Loma wheeled himself back to the cabin, Keel started asking the girl again what kind of a night she'd had, and Spinner was left with what he had heard. It still wasn't over, maybe it never would be, and maybe this was part of the switch too, waiting for somebody's word and someone else's decision. It was maybe not much of a switch from anything else.

CHAPTER 21

The ride back was a pain in the neck to Keel, because Spinner started out acting sour and when Keel tried to make light conversation Spinner got mean. They sure knew how to pick them, thought Keel, first Loma and now Spinner.

Then Keel tried it with Ann but she didn't even start out easy, the way Spinner had done it, but got rough right from the start. She said she was sick and tired of listening to the same tired old line and that he, Keel, couldn't do a thing for her. Talked as if she had to be convinced, like some square with a job someplace or a boy friend waiting for her somewhere out of town.

It saved the day for Keel when he told himself he could take 'em or leave 'em, they were all alike. He drove fast and steady and paid no attention even when Ann suddenly climbed into the back, never mind top down and wind blowing, and sat in the back with Spinner. It didn't mean a thing, Keel could tell, because they hardly talked and just sat there. He couldn't hear what they said, the few words now and then.

"Let me off at my place," she said when they came in on St. Charles Rock Road.

"Your place? What do you mean—"

"You know where I live."

She cut him short so hard Keel was glad to get rid of her. She didn't live much out of the way.

When he stopped at her apartment house he let her push the front seat out of the way herself and the same with the door. When she slammed it shut again he knew she wasn't going to say good-by but he hadn't expected she'd talk to Spinner either.

"You'll come by?" she said.

"As soon as I'm through."

"I'll be ready," she said and Keel wondered whether she was going to kiss Spinner. He started to make a bet with himself but was too slow. Ann smiled at Spinner and gave a small wave with her hand. Then she walked away.

"Come on, Keel. Let's go."

That jerk in the back seat again, as if looking at somebody walking up to an apartment was against the code.

"Come on, sit in front," said Keel. "You're no big shot yet."

Spinner did. He couldn't even he insulted, like his buddy, that Loma bastard, except Loma never got mean but kept still, as if he was nothing.

When Keel parked in a downtown lot he was wishing that Spinner would try his stuff on Mercado. That's when Spinner would learn a thing or two, once he was with Mercado. Except nobody ever acted up with Mercado, and also he wouldn't be in on the conference. But Keel thought about it.

"You watch your onions once we get in here," said Keel. "This is a legitimate business."

He opened the frosted door with the name St. Louis Distributors on it and walked right through the front office, where a girl sat at a switchboard and another one was filing her nails. Spinner followed close behind and then through a door marked Number 2.

"Wait here." Keel made a general wave with his hand.

There was a conference table and charts on the wall. Keel knocked on the next door. He went in when a voice said to.

Keel never had time to shut the door. He stayed very close to it so that Spinner could see his back, and did nothing to interrupt when the voice started yelling at him.

"You stupid cluck, come in through the front door? With that Spinner? Don't you know he's hot from here to hell, you stupid jackass? And how'd you drive into town, with the top down on that bus you got? Never mind! Just get the hell out of my sight!"

Keel left fast, with just enough time to tell Spinner, "He's ready for you."

Mercado was a man who wore green tinted glasses at all times. The color did not disguise his eyes and there were no fancy rims for the sake of appearance. He wore these glasses for one reason only, the fact that light irritated him. He sat at a desk with his back to the windows, he gave Spinner the briefest of looks, and while Spinner sat down Mercado picked through the mess on his desk, his movements hasty and sharp.

It was like a job interview starting bad; the applicant silent and the boss distracted and showing no interest, except that Spinner didn't think of it that way. It was bigger than that. It was the last and the necessary suspense before everything else became final.

"I hear your old man used to work for Dixon. Is that right?" It was very sudden, and Mercado had hardly looked up.

"Yes. Some time ago. The reason I'm here..."

"What did he do, you know?"

"What did he do?" Spinner didn't know and wasn't interested. He was interested in now, and that had nothing to do with his father.

"You don't look like you know," Mercado went on.

"I was a kid. And besides..."

"He went around and saw voters. Sometimes he worked an adding machine."

And all the time Mercado acted as if all this annoyed him because it was an interruption, and if he got snide enough maybe Spinner would go away.

"Look," said Spinner. "I don't care if he ran an elevator someplace. What I..."

"Honest man, though, the way those things go. Are you?"

"What?" Spinner might have said more, but Mercado didn't wait.

"You were in jail for three years, right?"

Spinner moved in his chair, leaning forward and twisting his head, because the light from the windows kept him from seeing Mercado's face clearly enough. Perhaps that's what made this whole thing so abrupt and disconnected. He and Mercado weren't seeing each other and weren't talking about the same things.

"Meet anybody there from St. Louis?"

"Where? You mean in jail?"

"What about you and Dixon? You ever do jobs for him?"

"About jail," said Spinner, trying to get his bearings; "the way I got into jail..."

"I got a record on you."

"Let me finish for once! How can I get anything straight if you keep..."

"What are you trying to say, you went to jail as a fall guy?" For once Mercado looked straight at Spinner and there was no doubt that Mercado was annoyed. "That doesn't cut any ice, Spinner. We're all fall guys, when you look at it right."

And then, as if he were sorry that he had bothered, Mercado looked down and piled some papers together.

This was all part of the big switch, this was all part of the small details after a big decision, and don't lose the long view or nothing made sense. Spinner wiped the palms of his hands together but stopped it when Mercado looked up at the sound. Mercado looked elsewhere immediately but Spinner felt more watched than before, and the worst was the confusion about it. Watched for what? Was it an interview, was it a brushoff, was it anything that showed anyone's interest?

"I'm going to start from the beginning," said Spinner. He didn't look at Mercado because Spinner was going to say this without interruption and get back the sense of importance about all this. He was going to get through because the push inside him was bigger than Mercado and his petty annoyances.

"I'm here because I'm through trying anything else. I want a job and what I have to recommend me is no commitment to anything else. If that doesn't sound like much, here's what it means. Anything you got, I'll take. If I like it I stick with it. If I don't like it, I'll do it so good you got to give me something better. You don't know me and I don't know a soul here, but what I got for a recommendation..."

"Never mind."

"Never mind?" Spinner got out of his chair and Mercado had to sit up to see Spinner's face. "You call me in here to do me a favor? You don't owe me a thing. I'm here to show you what I can offer and if you don't need anything, say so. Either that or pay some attention!"

"You think I got the time for some kind of a confession or something, then let me..."

"I wasn't finished!" Spinner was standing and Mercado had gotten up too, glaring, but Spinner didn't care about that. He didn't care about what had gone wrong or what had been lost but only that he shouldn't lose more.

"Why in hell you ask me up here, to see if I can keep my temper? I can't! I've kept my temper for..."

"Next question," said Mercado with a fine edge in his voice.

"Next? I'll give you..."

"Shut up, the next one is mine. The next one is what can you do, Spinner?"

"Qualifications? What qualifications has that boob out there, this Keel with the gorgeous shirts?"

"How about yours? It's so dirty I can smell it from here."

"I make a better hood with a clean collar on?"

"All right, next question. Can you figure odds? Do you know why it's good business paying the Water Commissioner more than the Chief of Police? Do you know why a half per cent return on the pinballs is all we need? Have you got..."

"Did you when you started? To hell with it!" Spinner turned on his heel and walked to the door.

It felt good, and he even knew how to explain the whole thing to himself later, when the heat had worn off. There hadn't been enough difference between this and what he used to know in the past. Not half enough of a difference and that, in the end, was what mattered.

"Spinner!"

Spinner stopped with the door half open and turned.

"What? Some parting advice?"

"You got a job."

After a moment Spinner closed the door, then gave it a small tug to see if the latch had caught. He came back to the desk and put his hands in his pockets.

"Why?" he said.

"On the level. You'll get..."

"I said why."

"Not because you blew your stack, if that's what you're thinking." Mercado was as irritated as he had been before. "I got you all down here, in the record. That's why." He sat down again, not looking at Spinner. "Keel is going to take you back to the resort. I don't want you hanging around town till you're needed."

"When?"

"Tomorrow! The day after! Wait your turn. You go back with Keel, you wait a few days, and then you'll get your instructions. Here." Mercado reached into his pocket. "Buy yourself a clean shirt."

The bill was for a hundred dollars. Mercado told Spinner to beat it.

CHAPTER 22

Keel had the top up when they got into the car and he watched Spinner as if he expected a comment. Spinner made none. He sat in the front, arms folded, and stared out the window without seeing a thing. Once he felt his pocket and heard the bill make a crackling sound. There was the bill. The whole thing was real. It had happened but Spinner sat feeling as if it were just going to start. Then he thought it all through again and came to the part where Mercado said, "You got a job." And that had happened too. What had not happened yet was a feeling, how Spinner felt about it, how he might safely allow himself to feel about all of this— because all of it hadn't happened yet.

Spinner gave his head a sharp shake. Drifting off the way he was doing, guessing and checking and hedging, he might even forget what had happened. The real thing was better than planned, faster and easier and as sure as the hundred bucks in his pocket. Spinner pulled out the bill and started to grin. He waved it at Keel and said, "I'm in!"

"In what?"

But Spinner wasn't listening. He put the bill back, stretched in the seat and grinned to himself. Why feel surprised? He couldn't lose. The big part had been over a long time ago, the time he beat Loma into the dirt and then made Loma show him the way. Ever since then, Spinner felt now, he hadn't been able to lose.

"Hey! You're halfway out of town, Keel!"

"I'm a good driver. You know, when I set my mind..."

"Turn around, damn it, I'm picking up that girl!"

"Oh, Annie? I forgot about Annie."

"Turn around and..."

"Couldn't do that, what with all the things I got to do after dropping you off."

"Keel, listen to me. I told Ann..."

"I know, I was there." Keel took off after his stop at a light and swung the car up the ramp to the freeway going out of town. "You shoulda reminded me. I clean forgot."

That's all it was. Spinner was sure Keel hadn't meant anything by going straight out of town, because Keel really didn't care one way or the other or he would have acted different about Spinner and Ann long ago. Keel took a cigarette out of his pocket and licked the end. "Got a match, Spinner? My lighter don't work. The car cost me six thousand plus and the lighter don't work."

"At the next ramp, Keel, I want you to turn back."

Keel looked up from his driving and said, "You really mean that? Hell, Annie's a nice kid, here and there, but hell, I don't see…"

"Just do what I say."

"Listen, Spinner—what's your first name, Jake? Listen, Jake, don't take it hard or anything. She's been stood up before, she don't give a damn."

Spinner kept still, watching for the next ramp.

"You know, she and another kid like her. Paula, from New York, they used to have an arrangement where one…"

"Just shut up, Keel, will you?"

Keel frowned and licked his unlit cigarette.

"I don't get you. How about that match, Jake? I'm still waiting."

"There's the ramp. Slow down."

This time Keel didn't answer. He laughed most of the time, or talked most of the time, but that was only half of him. One reason he drove the car he did and paid the prices for the shirts he wore was because he made money like dirt. He was paid well because he followed orders and was a hard man to stop. He was dumb, but very valuable. Spinner reached for the wheel. Keel gave him a hard slap in the teeth.

"Don't do that again, Jake."

Spinner hadn't expected it, but the next thing was automatic. He saw the cutoff fly by, lunged for the ignition and when he had the key in his hand he drew back to wait for the car to slow. The next thing after that was even surer; he'd beat Keel's ears off and then argue.

Keel let the car roll and watched Spinner out of the side of his eye.

"Feel my pocket, Jake."

"Just get that car on the grass safely and then I'll give you something to feel."

"Here, just touch it," said Keel. He wasn't laughing and he wasn't angry; this was just business, so when Spinner made no move to do what Keel had said, Keel reached into his pocket and his hand came out with brass knuckles over his fingers. They were big and shiny. "You interfere once more, Jake, and I'll peel your face."

Keel put the hand with the brass knuckles back on the wheel and let the car roll to a stop. There was no doubt in Spinner's mind that Keel would do what he said.

"Put them away and I'll show you a trick or two," Spinner said.

"You nuts or something? What you think I got it for?"

"Is this a habit or did you just think this up, pulling a stunt like this for nothing?"

"I don't go around hitting for nothing at all. Hell, what you take me for?" Keel braked the car to a stop on the shoulder and held out his free hand.

"Gimme the keys."

Spinner gave them to Keel. He didn't get any of this and sat there puzzled.

"What do you call nothing at all?" he said finally.

Keel didn't put the keys in right away because he was watching Spinner to see if he had changed his mind.

"You don't think," he said, "I can let you just go and walk all over me, do you? I'm taking you back, and I got things to do, that's all."

"That's all?" Spinner still didn't get it.

"What else?" said Keel and looked puzzled.

This time Spinner gave up because Keel had him convinced. This was something to learn, Spinner thought. Keel seemed to have no troubles to speak of, but drove a big car, liked all the chores he was doing, or, at any rate, didn't have any feeling about them, like an ape. This was something to learn.

"All right, Keel. You can put it away."

"You gonna be good?"

"I'm going to be real good, Keel. Let's get going."

It took Spinner longer than Keel to forget about what had happened, but after a while he did. He worked at it, thinking of Keel and of Loma. They both had it down pat, this thing to be like an ape or a machine. Spinner thought about Ann now and then, but he pushed it away, working on it.

When they got to the cabin Spinner got out and Keel drove off immediately. Spinner walked into the cabin.

"You're back sooner than I expected," said Loma. He sat up and swung his legs off the bed. He had been lying on Spinner's bed.

"Yeah. Anyone phone here?" said Spinner.

"No. Who would?"

Who would call. Spinner took off his jacket and tossed it on a chair. Ann would, he was thinking, but the hell with that kind of thinking at a time like this. Loma got into his chair and wheeled himself out of the room. And to hell with telling Loma the news. And if Loma had asked about St. Louis, that would have been the real pleasure, telling him to mind his own business and to hell with all of it. I'm going to sleep.

"I'm going to sleep," said Spinner, but Loma was already out of the room and couldn't have heard.

Spinner slept for a long time. He tossed and a few times made sounds in his throat, but kept sleeping until the sun was almost down. He woke very suddenly and sat up, but then lay back feeling exhausted. There was no good reason to feel that way, and the thought irritated him. Everything he looked at and the small, meaningless sounds he could hear from outside, everything irritated him. He twisted to look at the phone and the squat, black shape which did not move or make a sound. He got up, took off his clothes, and went into the shower, but the pleasure of that got killed by the thought of the clothes he was going to put on afterwards. He still only had his dirty shirt. He had a hundred bucks, a future, and a dirty shirt to irritate him.

When he got dressed he looked into Loma's open door and saw that Loma was gone. He saw him under the tree, in his wheelchair. Loma was learning to get around by himself. He got the wheelchair out of the door and sat where he wanted to sit without any help. Then why still use the wheelchair? Spinner could hear what Loma would say. He would say, "There is no good reason why I shouldn't."

Spinner put on his tie so that the dirty collar of his shirt wouldn't show. He raked his fingers through his moist hair and stood by the door for a moment. Now what? Till morning or the day after there was nothing. Go eat, and talk to Loma. Or talk to anybody, maybe Dickie.

He tried not to think about Ann.

Then he suddenly cursed under his breath and walked out the door.

"You haven't told me," said Loma when Spinner got to the tree. "What happened in St. Louis?"

Spinner sat down on the bench and crossed his legs.

"Everything else being equal," said Loma, "if you made your contact in St. Louis, that means I can be rid of you."

"What makes you think that, killer? What makes you think I want to be rid of you?"

"I didn't say that."

"But that's how I'm putting it. I fall, you fall. Remember that."

Loma looked at his hands and then said, "You keep thinking I want to do you some kind of dirt. Why should I?"

"You said you want me around, remember? You said..."

"Once it looks like I'm in the clear and they aren't looking for me, then you don't mean a thing."

"The gadget wears out, throw it away." Spinner got up from the bench and suddenly talked with a hard rasp in his throat. "You got another guess coming, killer. This gadget's got life in it! You'll never know what I'm going to do next!"

"I don't know what you mean," said Loma. He leaned back a little, because Spinner was bending close, but aside from that he didn't change.

"I mean you get on my nerves and all of a sudden it comes into my mind to finger you to the cops. You can't figure that out on your adding machine, can you, killer?" Spinner straightened up and started to laugh. He sat down and was still laughing when he said, "I forgot. I keep calling you killer and I forgot what your answer is going to be. Shoot my head off, right? That's what you'd do."

Loma took a deep breath and let it out with his mouth stretched so the lips disappeared. It made lines in his face, but didn't change his eyes one way or the other.

"I told you once before, Spinner. I don't do that..."

"...for no good reason," Spinner said for him. "Or for no pay, is that right? Tell me, what else can you do?"

"I can stop you in a hundred ways, if I have to."

It was the closest Loma had ever come to sounding ominous, with threat in his voice. He felt annoyed with Spinner, and with himself, and wished that Spinner would take his mean streak out on something else.

"Like what?" Spinner kept on. "Maybe you finger me?"

"It's one way," said Loma.

"Boy!" Spinner laughed, forcing it out. "That's brains. That's real, high speed, electronic brains! You think that's going to shut me up?"

"It'll keep you out of my way."

"Until I've sung my song to the dicks and chase them after you. Man," said Spinner. It sounded hearty and confident. "You and I don't understand each other at all."

"You wouldn't talk," said Loma.

"I wouldn't what?"

Loma moved his cast leg into the vertical and put some weight on it, testing. When he was through he said, "You're the one that isn't thinking this through. You have the brains, probably, but you're not thinking this through. If you get arrested, Spinner, it'll be for murder."

"Yes. Your murder, the one you did. And you know, don't you, Loma, I wouldn't sit on that secret."

"You may not, but so what?"

Spinner grinned with an evil line down the side of his face, and started counting off on his fingers. "One, your gun."

"Could be anyone's."

"Two, your shoe and the place where you got stuck with the car."

Loma just shrugged.

"And to prove you were around, there's a few upstanding witnesses who saw us together. There's the little girl with the torn sweater, the farmer with the big connections, the doctor who hasn't had a patient since he came from up north, except for you."

Loma shook his head while he kept looking at Spinner. "Why should you bring that up?" he said. "All those people who saw you and me together think of us as being together. You helping me, you calling me buddy, you seeing to it we made out all right. If you try making a stink about me killing Dixon, and if you use those witnesses to show I was in the neighborhood, then you come out an accomplice. Don't you see that, Spinner?"

Spinner did. But before it made him feel caught, before anything else happened, he remembered that none of this need concern him. He was in, which made him safe. He had made his switch, and what Loma was talking about could never happen. He sat quietly for a moment and then said, "You trying to scare me, Loma? What makes you think that you got to try?"

"Nothing. You brought it up."

Loma was right, as always, right from beginning to end. Even that didn't bother Spinner any more, because Spinner was in and could feel the dry crackle of the bill in his pocket to prove it. He laughed and looked over Loma's head, watching a squirrel on a tree back in the woods.

"You asked me what happened in St. Louis."

"Yes."

"I'm in." He smiled the proper smile for a time like this.

"Whom did you see?"

"Mercado. Some kind of wheel down there."

"I know Mercado. He's no wheel."

"Anyway, Loma, he gave me the message. I'm in."

"That was very fast," said Loma.

Spinner sat back and looked up at the foliage over their heads, a big, moving, green roof. He smiled again, and though he had meant to be no more than a murmur it was loud enough for Loma to hear: "I can't lose," he said. "Not after everything—"

"Too fast, almost," Loma was saying.

Spinner sat up and a sharp line cut down the side of his face. He was gnawing the inside of his lip and the sharp line came and went.

"Why? You hate seeing me go?"

Loma didn't bother to answer.

"Then what? You don't see why they should take me? Or maybe you got an idea..."

"What can you do?"

"Mercado asked me the same thing, Loma. And then he hired me."

"I believe you. But do you know why they took you?"

"Because they can use me. No other reason."

"Of course," said Loma. "Of course they can use you."

"So don't sit there like a dried-up lemon and make out that none of this makes any sense. I'm in. That's what I came for, and that's what I got."

Loma shrugged but then he started up again, which surprised Spinner. "But you don't know what for."

"All right, Loma. I don't know what for. I didn't ask because I figured one thing at a time wasn't bad for a starter, seeing I just got what I wanted and not being worried whether I can do any damn thing they want done. What else do you want?" He added, "And why this sudden keen interest? Something wrong with you, all of a sudden?"

"Maybe there's something wrong with your job," said Loma. "They don't often hire that way."

"Oh. How did they hire you? With a trial period and a long look at your pedigree?"

"By reputation," said Loma.

"And me, because of my good looks and because I needed a clean shirt! And if you don't believe that, then you tell me why."

"All right," said Loma, "I will."

Spinner wondered about the sharpness in Loma's voice—a rare thing—and sat very still while Loma explained it.

"You've got nothing. You don't have the background and you don't have the training. What you think you got? A sharp interest in making a change in your life—and that they don't count. That's your interest, not theirs. But you've got one thing they can use. You got a hard push behind you and it's got nothing to do with your wishes. It's got to do with the fact that the cops are after you! They're after you so hard, once you figure it the way St. Louis does, that you'll bend over backwards to jump when Mercado says to. Because you think they're giving you a good deal." Loma paused to lick his lips. "And they've got you double, Spinner; it's got to be that way, because what if you get caught? Did you think of that? If you get caught they've got to be in a position to wash their hands of you. It's got to be that way, don't you see?"

"Say it, Loma. What's on your mind?"

"I can't tell what the job is, but I can tell that it's got to be dirty. The way they took you, to give you one reason, it's got to be real dirt. The only other thing I'm sure of is that once you've done the job it won't matter to them if you're caught."

"Why, you lousy—"

"You asked me. You have no value except for the thing they have in mind and you're going to do it. After that they don't care. It's got to be that way, because you're nothing to them."

Spinner suddenly felt exhausted. Loma's hard talk, his hard argument, there was nothing to answer.

"You're the brain, Loma. What's the job?"

"It fits murder," said Loma.

CHAPTER 23

Keel drove Spinner almost all the way back to town, and then cut off on a road that went down to the river. A few times, with the turns of the road, the Mississippi showed flat and shiny, but after a while the view got dark where a deep stand of old trees grew down to the river. It smelled moist under the trees, and nothing was moving. Then they came to the estate, with lawns in the sun like big clearings and the old trees making a frame. When the car stopped at the house they could see the river again. It lay in back, and, like the lawns, was there to give the big house a setting. White paint made the house look new, except for two-story stone columns on which green stains showed in streaks.

"Come on," said Keel. "I don't like to keep Talbot waiting."

Spinner got out of the car and hitched his jacket so that less of the shirt would show. The night before he had washed the shirt, and stretching it in the right way the wrinkles didn't show very much, except at the collar. The tips curled up and the white cloth had wavy shadows. But the shirt was clean. He hadn't rinsed it enough and every time he moved Spinner smelled soap.

They stood at the front door and Keel pressed a button that seemed to make no sound anywhere, but a few moments later a butler opened the door, unless the uniform meant something else. Except for his clothes and manner, the man had nothing to remember him by.

"This way, Mr. Keel," he said, but Keel was already ahead of him.

Spinner came last. He studied the ballroom staircase, the big vase with wisteria, and smelled the wax that seemed to be on the woodwork everywhere.

"Come on, Spinner. I hate to keep Talbot waiting."

The setting distracted him and Spinner walked slowly, to keep his bearings and to remember what this place was like.

"Jesus," Keel hissed at him. "You trying to louse yourself up? They're waiting. Make an impression!"

The door was open and in the back of the long room, against curtains that looked like tapestry, stood a short man.

"Come on in. Close that door."

"Sure, sure." After closing the door Keel led the way across the long room.

Spinner saw that the man's tie was pulled down, that the shoulders of his suit hung back without finding support, and that his thick hands weren't clean. The man sucked his teeth once and when Spinner stopped, he said, "Let's go into the next room."

They all went into the next room because the long one didn't have any chairs. The next room had chairs, a table, and a portable bar. Mercado was there, putting down a drink.

They sat down, except for the short man, who put his foot on a chair. Now it was real. Now, Spinner thought, in spite of the queer meeting with Mercado the day before, and in spite of Loma and all he had said, this was real. Spinner plucked at the collar of his shirt, then put his hands under the table. They were all looking at him and Spinner felt a twinge in his shoulder. Waiting for him—he was through waiting.

"Where's Talbot?" he said.

"I'm Talbot," the short man answered.

"All right. What's the job?"

"A hit," said Talbot. Talbot sat down, looked at his nails for a moment, and then said, "You're the man for it, Spinner. Glad to meet you."

"A hit. Who gets murdered?"

"You're the man for it because for you it's a setup." Talbot got up again, put his foot on the chair, and picked at his nails.

"Who?" said Spinner.

"Loma."

Spinner felt very hot but when he wiped his hand over his face it came away dry. He looked at Keel and Mercado and Talbot and then he looked to the back, at the bar.

"Give him a drink," said Talbot, and Mercado got there first. He came back with the drink and said, "What's the matter, you got an attachment to Loma?"

Spinner swallowed the drink. The whisky was good, but Spinner wished it weren't so smooth.

"No," he said.

He held his lip in his teeth, not knowing what next. Keel was looking at him, not understanding what all the hesitating was for. Mercado pushed at his glasses impatiently, and Talbot leaned on his knee.

"What are you staring at?"

Spinner felt like something for sale. It stiffened his back and his eyes got narrow.

"I don't see this thing yet. I'm confused because I don't do this kind of thing every day."

"We know that," said Mercado. "We got your record."

Talbot shifted his legs and made a grin.

"Sure, Spinner. Just take it easy. Give him another," he said to Mercado.

"I don't want another. I want to know why."

"You get paid five thousand," said Mercado.

"Are you in?" asked Talbot.

They were rushing him. They wanted to buy because Loma had figured it right. He, Spinner, had the qualifications. Spinner felt the hate rise inside him because of the pushing around they were giving him. He didn't like it. He got up from the table and walked to the windows that looked over a lawn running down to the river. Who looked out of this window, he thought, and enjoyed that sight? He turned back to the room and the three men at the table tried to see his face against the light from outside. When he came closer they saw how hard it had gotten. That could mean he was good for the job or maybe he was going to be trouble.

"Why me?" said Spinner. "How come Keel doesn't get this? I bet Keel could…"

"There's no setup for Keel, don't you get it? You know Loma, you live with Loma, you and him might even be buddies. Christ, Spinner, all your work should be a setup like that."

"Setup. You know damn well Loma's ready to blow. All that's holding him…"

"We're holding him. He's waiting to hear if he's clean. He's clean all right, but he won't hear about it." Talbot sat down at the table and suddenly slapped his hand down. "All right, Spinner, you want this five G's or don't you?"

That hadn't been the right way either, because it rushed Spinner and he wasn't through thinking, The whole thing was a shock, so strange and foreign that it had taken till now to really reach him. But that mustn't happen, that wasn't the way you talk about business no matter what the merchandise was, so Spinner cut it all up into small details and questions. He had many questions: He might have to ask them all before he was sure of his grip and knew how to hang on. That's how he had to do it.

"Why Loma?" he said. "I don't get…"

"You don't have to get nothing," said Talbot. "You just…"

"I don't like a job, I don't do it. Not any more. You open up and tell me about this or I might kill the wrong guy, I'm that dumb."

"Not that dumb," said Mercado and his ill temper made him sound as if he had another appointment somewhere, something important. "You're not so dumb that you think we can't make you…"

"Shut up," said Talbot. He said it off-hand and it wasn't clear if his tone had done it or the look he gave Mercado. But when he turned back to Spinner, Talbot looked almost friendly. Impatient, but friendly. "It's Loma because he fouled us up. We don't go for that. Simple."

"Fouled up what? I don't get it. He made his mark; I saw him do it!"

"Look, you're new," said Talbot. "But you're here to do a big job for the outfit so I'll lay the whole thing out for you. A professional like Loma gets paid for a clean job. If it ain't clean the dirt comes off on the employer, get it? If…"

"Don't gimme that double talk," said Spinner. "He made his mark and got away."

"He run into you, didn't he?" said Talbot.

"And how come he didn't drop you and get away clean?" said Mercado. "We pay for a clean job. We expect..."

"Shut up," said Talbot and then, with his patient look, he turned back to Spinner. "The thing is, fellow, Loma knows a hell of a lot; maybe you know that." Talbot watched Spinner until Spinner realized he was supposed to answer.

"He's a clam. I don't know what he knows."

Talbot nodded and went on.

"He knows why he had to do the job, he does the job, and he remembers who paid his bill. Then he gets maybe picked up and they twist him a little..."

"You son of a bitch," said Spinner and the low voice, very intense, made all of them sit up and listen. "You just said a mouthful. And when I get done with Loma, who's gonna do it to me?"

"What are you talking about, Spinner? This ain't no mountain feud, damn it."

"You just said..."

"I said he knows stuff. You don't know nothing!"

"You can walk out of this when you're done," Keel put in, "and you don't even have to stick around here. You can blow. Nobody cares. You can talk, but what can you say?"

"Or I can get shot to make sure," said Spinner.

"Hell, why?" There was real puzzlement in Talbot's voice. He rubbed his nose and then he said, "Damn it all, I've never gone through anything like this before. Maybe you don't know business, but in business you don't do more than you have to. With you we don't have to, with Loma we do. And for an easy mark and five whole G's I can't figure why..."

"Because I'm eager. I'm so eager for that five G's I want to be sure I can collect. So all these questions keep bothering me. Here you say Loma got away clean, then you say Loma's got to go because he messed it all up. Come on, straighten me out."

"He got away clean," said Talbot, "means for right now. But he's been seen."

"Yeah. By me."

"You don't count. You're in it yourself, and you open your mouth and it's curtains." Loma had said that too. "But there's three civilians that seen him..."

"Where do I stand?" said Spinner.

They frowned at him and Talbot said, "You're in, aren't you?"

Spinner closed his eyes because he hadn't heard them say it before. He was in now.

"That's why I asked," he said but he still wasn't sure.

"All right. So in a while they catch up with Loma—you know he's in this business full-time—and they can tie him up with the job he done here. Don't you get it, Spinner? It's simple!"

"Maybe so is Spinner," said Keel. "Hell, it's all in how important the mark is. Take you, you ain't important. Loma is."

"And after Loma, I am."

"How can you be?" yelled Talbot and banged his hand on the table.

"Maybe he likes Loma. You like Loma?" asked Mercado.

"How can you?" said Keel. "Don't you know about Loma? He don't belong! So how..."

"All right! Lemme think!"

They looked at each other and then back at Spinner. He was as crazy as Loma, Keel thought, and wrinkled his nose. And Mercado kept telling himself that it was worth the trouble because Spinner was made for this job. Talbot sat back, sucked his teeth twice. Better push a little, before the thinking got much too heavy.

"Spinner," he said. "You don't want the job?"

This was a new tone. No more wheedling him, no more doing it his way, no more going along with him because Spinner was dumb.

"You want in, or you want out?"

"Out?"

"Out to where they're looking for you!" yelled Mercado.

"In or out, Spinner?"

If you did it like an ape or a machine it was simple. Spinner breathed and the air felt heavy inside his lungs. If you did it the other way, the old way, then you were out, and outside they were waiting to kill you. Spinner's skin felt cold.

"If you kill you live, if you don't you die," somebody said. Could have been anyone of the three saying it. Could have been Loma. Is that why Loma lived?

But already the question was hardly a thought because thinking that way was no way to live. The choice now was already a technical one—to do it, like an ape or a machine. He didn't like Keel, but he hated Loma. Like a machine then. Spinner said, "I need a gun."

Chapter 24

The early evening made a strange, colorless light, turning greens to grays and washing out contrasts, but to Spinner it would have looked the same in any other light. The change had already gone far. He sat very calmly, watching Keel drive. Keel moved the wheel this way and that, turned his head and his eyes as required, but the drive meant nothing to him any more. He hardly thought, because all the thinking had already been done; there was nothing more to decide, because all the decisions were over. Spinner was in.

The car pulled up to the clearing and when Keel stopped the car bounced. Keel liked to brake that way.

"Hey," he said, "there he is."

Loma was at the side of the cabin, leaning there with one hand and testing his foot. The wheelchair stood behind him.

"I'll say hello," said Keel, and got out of the car.

Spinner got out of the car too and watched Keel cross to the cabin. He heard Keel say, "Well, lookit you. Looks like you'll be up on your feet pretty soon now, huh?" Spinner didn't hear any more but they talked for a while. Loma probably was asking what the picture was, if the police were looking for him, and Keel was probably answering they didn't get a clear picture yet, but they'd have one tomorrow for sure.

Then Keel came back. He looked at Spinner and said, "See you tomorrow." Then he grinned and slapped Spinner's shoulder. "All yours," he said. Then he drove off.

There had been a low, gnawing ache in his shoulder, the way it happened to him off and on. But now the ache started burning painfully.

Loma started to walk along the wall of the cabin, carefully, holding himself, watching his feet. The sight was like nothing Spinner had ever seen before, but when he looked away it wasn't because of any feeling. He looked away to see if anyone else was on the clearing. Nobody was there. Not that it mattered. Then Spinner walked toward Loma. His shoulder seemed like a pain that didn't belong to him and his walk was normal, because things were working all by themselves.

"You want your chair?" said Spinner.

Loma was at one end of the cabin and the chair at the other. Spinner stood with his hands in his pockets and watched how Loma's feet moved. The feet stopped their struggle and Loma said, "No. Not yet." Loma turned around slowly, holding the wall, and Spinner watched the two crippled feet make their short, sudden movements. "Was I right?"

"Right? Oh. The job."

The feet stopped and Loma leaned by the wall, breathing hard.

"Yes," said Spinner. "You were right."

"Are you going to do it?"

"What else?" said Spinner and looked at the feet again. They weren't resting. They made small shifts and anxious plays for balance.

"When?" said Loma.

Spinner looked up and thought Loma's face and Loma's feet were not part of the same man. The struggle and pain in one, and shut blankness in the other, except for a thin line of sweat down the side of Loma's cheek.

"When?" he said again.

"Pretty soon," said Spinner.

Loma wiped the side of his face and took a deep breath. He looked at Spinner and said, "Can I have my chair now?"

Spinner brought it and wheeled Loma under the tree. It was darker there, with even less contrast than the rest of the evening. Spinner took out his cigarettes and sat on the bench.

"Want one?" he said mechanically and held the pack toward Loma.

"Yes."

That's when Spinner remembered that Loma didn't smoke, only sometimes. He lit both cigarettes and leaned back to exhale, as if tired.

"I'm sorry you're going to do it," said Loma.

Spinner felt himself tense. He sat up straight because his shoulder had touched the backrest. The sharp ache was like a drill in the point. But he, himself, seemed to be somewhere else and that's how he could talk very evenly.

"You say you're sorry? I've never heard you talk like that, Loma."

"I rarely talk," said Loma.

They sat in the silence for a while. The evening spread down, big and quiet. Spinner turned his head along the dim clearing and all the cabins were dark. They had said they would see to that. It was all ready.

"I don't think you should do it," said Loma. "I don't think you can."

"No? You can. I'm no different from you."

"But you are," said Loma.

Spinner shrugged. It made him wince with the pain in his shoulder. Then he thought about how he was sitting here talking to Loma and Loma was going to be dead in a short time. Loma was now talking for the last time, but there seemed nothing final about it to Spinner.

"What's there to it?" he said.

"Did you ever hear me say that?"

"No. You don't talk." Spinner crossed his legs and rubbed one sole into the earth. "But now that you're—now that you're talking, wouldn't you say so?"

"Yes, I might. But you can't."

"Yeah, I know. You're better than most, in everything."

"It's not that way."

Loma stopped and Spinner saw the red glow of Loma's cigarette brighten twice, very hot. Then he spoke and the smoke had made him hoarse.

"I can't do many things." He stopped to let the cigarette fall, not watching it. "Many things. And you can."

Spinner got up and stretched. He walked out from under the tree and stretched again.

"I'm going in," he said, and started walking across the dark clearing. "You coming?"

Spinner didn't hear whether Loma answered. A sudden weird waving of light hit the tops of the trees and when Spinner turned, the white eyes of the car dipped over the rise. They nodded toward him and then stopped.

"Jake? Oh Jake!" Ann came out of the car and ran toward him.

Against the light he saw her fine legs, then the rest of her, she was waving at him with her face dark and in shadow. He didn't see what was there and didn't look for it because the shock of the change in everything pounded at him. There was noise, there was light, the dark clearing was gone, and Spinner was no longer alone with Loma.

"Jake," she said, "what's the matter?"

"I didn't expect you. I—"

She was up to him now, and hesitated. Then she stopped. She started to smile but then stopped that too.

"I just thought, the way we missed each other in town—"

"I couldn't help it. I'm sorry." He tried to look past the light and see Loma. She turned that way and then she smiled, like changing a topic.

"Is he there? Your friend? I've got something for him," and she ran back to the car.

Loma was wheeling himself into the light, and watched when the girl came back.

"Here," she said to Loma. "Nice? I thought you could use it.'" She held out the cane she had brought.

Loma stretched out his hand and took the cane.

"Thank you. That was very nice of you."

Spinner had moved back where the light wasn't strong, and nobody saw how his face had grown stiff and his hands were shaking. Ann pushed Loma's chair to the cabin and when she stopped Loma got out and entered the cabin using the cane. The light went on inside, first one room, then the other.

"Jake?" Ann called. "Will you turn off the car lights? I forgot."

He turned off the car lights and saw her small bag on the front seat. Then he went to the cabin.

"How long are you staying?" she was asking Loma. "Till your foot is better?"

"That would be too long," Loma answered, and when Spinner came into the room Loma looked up. "You can close the door," he said, "I'm going to sleep."

Ann said good night. She walked out of the room while Spinner held the door for her without looking up. Then he closed the door and he and the girl were alone. She had sat down on the bed, but when Spinner had closed the door she got up.

"I—I don't want to bother you," she said. "I just thought, the way we missed each other, I thought you might still—" she stopped and bit her lip. Spinner thought she looked angry. "Anyway," she said with a different voice, "anyway, I wanted to see you."

To keep himself the way he had become Spinner looked at a detail, the lobe of her ear, and tried to think of nothing else. He saw where the lobe had been pierced, which he didn't think was done any more. Then he felt her hand on his arm.

"What's wrong, Jake?"

He stepped back, making her drop her hand. "Nothing, Ann. I didn't expect you, that's all."

"And you don't want me to stay?"

"I— No. I don't want you to stay. I'm leaving myself."

"Oh? Business?"

"That's right. That's why."

It would have been time for her to leave then, with nothing to say and with her hopes dropping away because she'd been wrong again. But she stood for a while longer unable to find the right way, the old way for handling this kind of thing. It wasn't a new situation. What was new was that she allowed it to happen this time.

"Okay," she said. "If you're in St. Louis sometimes you know where I live."

"Yeah. I know," and he took her arm to lead her out of the door.

Perhaps the push did it, or the fact that Spinner didn't seem himself and she hadn't really been talking to him. She stopped in the doorway. They stood very close. "Jake, I just want to tell you..."

"What?"

He said it fast, very sharp, because he did not think he could hold out much longer. Not at this time, when everything had been decided and the girl and many other things had been left out. Later, perhaps, when the job was done and his new ways were a little bit better established.

"Listen to me," she said, and looked at his face. "I'm going to say this now because I don't think I can again."

"Not in here. Outside." He pushed her out the door. The interruption, he thought, that's what would do it. Either she would go away or be like the first time, clever and hard to reach.

But she kept hold of his arm, walking quickly, not wanting the feeling to go away. Once outside she stopped. She pulled him to the wall of the cabin and talked fast so that he could not interrupt her.

"I don't know you at all, Jake, like anyone else I can call by name. Except there's a difference. Jake, are you listening?"

He was listening, wishing he didn't hear.

"With a difference, Jake: I want to know you."

Let her finish, he thought, and when she's through it'll be over.

"I don't know why, Jake, I don't know that any more than I know why you suddenly changed. But I do know! It's happened to me when I suddenly can't go on any more. But I know I must because there's nothing else to do. I can go on because I've learned how to turn myself off. You know how to do that, don't you, Jake? You can go on because you feel nothing. You can do a million things feeling nothing, Jake; a million. I know!" She held his arms hard, and he reached out to her.

"Don't touch me!"

He winced, pulling back, but the wall behind him didn't let him go any further. His shoulder boiled with pain.

"You know it, Jake. And you know it's no good." She didn't touch him, but all her intensity came into her voice. "I don't want to do a million things that I can't feel. I want one thing I can feel. And you do too, I know that from the way things went after we met. I want one thing I can feel, Jake. You." She stopped, and when she said the rest the control in her voice pushed tears into her eyes. "Don't you want me, Jake?"

She was tearing him open. She was trying to come into his new life. He held on, closing his eyes as if the darkness were hurting them.

"Not now. Go away now. I'll see you later."

"Jake, will you? Will you later?"

"Get the hell out of here..."

Her gasp stopped him. She had touched him again, to make sure he could feel her, and then she gasped when she felt the gun in his pocket.

"No!" she said. "That's it, isn't it?"

He found his voice the way he wanted to hear it. It came even and smooth and sounded as if he were standing next to himself.

"You know Keel, don't you? He's in the same business, and you know Keel. Why the shock all of a sudden?"

"I don't want Keel, I want you!"

"I'm busy, Ann. Later... I know where you live," he added, and it sounded very smooth to him, like in a movie.

"Jake, please, come with me now. We can leave. We won't be alone together, Jake, and that's how we can leave, don't you see that—"

"Later," he said, like a record, because he couldn't talk any other way. And then he knew she was crying even though there was no sound, and before it tore him open again—he thought about this very clearly—he lifted his hand and hit her in the face.

A big star of pain exploded in his shoulder, making him tremble. It kept bursting, next to him, it kept shining all the time he could hear her feet running away and the way she breathed, running away down the road through the trees. He had reached such perfection in this that he walked to her car to make sure where she was. She had run past the car and down the road. Dickie would be at the main house with one or two friends and that's where the girl was running; which was as expected. But her overnight bag was still in the car. She was hysterical right now; she'd come for it later. In the meantime—now, as a matter of fact, because the car and the girl would come in handy later—now for the business. It was a very small, surprisingly small matter to do this job now. That's the advantage of this new technique. Turn himself off and do a million things. Of course, one at a time, and each one—by comparison—very small, even unimportant. He walked into the cabin.

CHAPTER 25

He left the lights off and walked into Loma's room. He walked past Loma's bed to the dresser, and picked up the comb that was lying there. He took that with him and walked out of Loma's room.

In the bathroom he turned on the light, to complete the enactment, and stood in front of the mirror with the comb in his hand. A clever thing, and so simple it had to work. It was nothing for Spinner to be in Loma's room. He borrowed a comb. And the proof was that Loma had made no move. Had he been asleep? Very good. Had he been awake and done nothing? Very good.

And now Spinner saw a man in the mirror and Spinner and the man stood looking at each other, one very calm face which showed nothing, then the mirror man's arm raised to comb his hair. Spinner twitched just slightly from the grinding in his shoulder, so the mirror man dropped the comb because that wasn't the thing to take back to Loma's room anyway. Spinner watched the mirror man reach into his pocket and come out with the gun. He would take that back to Loma. The mirror man didn't show what happened but Spinner's pain hurt him badly. Any moment the set face in the mirror might show the pain. Spinner closed his eyes. Now only Spinner knew that there was a stiff grinding inside the shoulder, but before he would concentrate on himself— Walk, Spinner.

He had the gun in his hand and walked back to Loma's room. He should walk faster, because the pain glowed and it seemed harder to keep it to himself. Spinner walked into the room, then stopped in the dark because he couldn't see. There was Loma on the bed, and Spinner stopped. It felt very dark around him, which made him feel safe. He would raise the gun, which was simple.

Raise it, raise it! If the pain weren't there, how much simpler the whole thing would be. But the big, sharp star of pain felt like a glow that got brighter. Could Loma see it? Quick. Go through it again, fast and precise to prove that he was doing exactly what he must do: I am a machine which can move, can do anything which the brain tells it to do because what can stop a machine with a brain, nothing can hurt a machine with a brain— Spinner gritted his teeth. He should feel nothing. He lifted the gun. But this pain?

It was like the star bursting and throwing the gun on the floor and turning, running out, was all one thing to him because it was all himself, Spinner himself. He ran out into the open. Now he was no longer running away from Loma's room. He was not running away from anything, but toward something.

The car was there, empty. Her bag was there; she hadn't come back. Spinner ran down the road through the woods, and he thought his lungs would burst.

He ran for the light in front of the main house where some people were standing. Spinner could hear them talk, saw someone holding a glass, a girl giggled—Dickie—and then she stopped, and the three men and the two girls turned around when they heard Spinner running.

"Ann!" he called. "Ann, here I am!"

Ann was holding a cigarette. She put it up to her mouth and took a drag, watching Spinner. She let the stub drop to the gravel and exhaled smoke in a thin stream. She watched Spinner without moving out of his way.

He didn't stop till he was up against her and when his arms went around her he started to laugh, loud and full. He also tried to say something, but the laughter was the only clear thing, and his arms around her.

"Ann," he said, "I'm back! I'm here! You see, Ann. You and me now, the way you wanted it, the way I want it," and he laughed and he cried. Then he felt her arms tighten around him, her face close, her kisses, and she was laughing too.

Loma had stayed on his bed. His open door was a square of light but he didn't watch it any more, and since Spinner would not be back Loma returned his gun to his pocket. He had been holding it for quite a long time. It had taken Spinner a while to come in, but he wouldn't be back. Loma stayed on his bed like that till he heard the motor start up and the lights flit past the cabin. Then he got up and collected his things and the gun which Spinner had dropped on the floor, and walked out of the cabin with the help of the cane. He kept the headlights off and drove away.

They got lost on the way to St. Louis because it was still dark and they weren't watching the signs very closely. But it didn't upset them. Spinner drove and Ann, next to him, talked and laughed and finally got them back on the right road.

"It'll be just dawn when we get there. Won't that be nice?" she said.

Spinner said, "Then we can drive off in the daylight and see what we're leaving."

"I won't take but a minute," she said. "I'll just run up to the apartment and right back down."

"I won't even turn off the motor."

"And we'll drive, drive, drive—"

"And when we stop, everything will start new."

They smiled at each other and said nothing else for a while, just thinking about it. Ann leaned against his side and he put his hand into her lap.

"I can type, you know," she said next.

"I haven't got a thing to dictate," said Spinner.

"I mean when we stop. I can get a job typing and help out."

"I thought you said you had all that money saved," said Spinner. "Or am I marrying a pauper?"

"Take your choice," she said. "You want to marry a pauper or me?"

Spinner didn't answer but slowed the car to a stop. Then he bent over and gave her a kiss.

"My answer," he said, and started to drive again.

"You're in," she answered, and Spinner laughed.

"Fact is," he said after a while, "you won't have to type. I got some talent."

"Like what? I mean, what kind that can earn you a living."

"Well, I got a thing from the army says I'm a good mechanic. Trucks and so forth."

"Where are you going to find all those army trucks to…"

"Wait, wait. And then, when I was guest of the state for three years, more trucks. All kinds. I also got a written thing to prove that part of my training."

She laughed. "How about ordinary cars? And bicycles, maybe."

"No bicycles. Tractors, though. On my farm—" He hesitated, and then said, "Did you know I went to agricultural school for a while? Didn't, did you? You thought I was a peasant, huh?"

She squeezed his arm and smiled. "You know, Jake, perhaps a small town would be best. Perhaps you can work a farm. Would you like that?"

"I would like that best," he said after a while. "But you may not like it. You've lived in the city all your life."

"I won't miss it, Jake."

They drove and shared a cigarette.

"You would like that, wouldn't you, Jake?"

"What?"

"Have your own farm—"

He gave her the cigarette and blew the smoke against the windshield in front of him.

"I can't think that way, Ann." Then he laughed. "Besides, all those weeds are there."

"I just like to think about it. And perhaps, after a while—"

"I can't think that way, Ann."

She put her hand on the back of his neck and said, "I bet you didn't know I could cook, did you? And that I'm a good housekeeper."

"I'll find out," he said.

"And that I once learned how to candle eggs. That's a talent you didn't know about, did you?"

"You just hold on to that talent. You may get it into your mind one day, when you bring home a dozen from the store, to candle those eggs."

She smiled and tucked her legs under her. She looked out the window and said, "I'd like to do it on your farm. I'm just thinking how nice it would be, you know?"

"I know. I like to think of it too."

When they drove into St. Louis it was dawn. The main streets had some traffic already but elsewhere the city looked empty. Ann's street had some trees on one side. They looked cool and clean in the morning air and at the end of the street Spinner could see the road they would be taking. He stopped in front of the apartment house.

"I'm leaving the motor running. Two minutes flat or nothing."

"You won't get away," she said, and jumped out of the car.

Spinner watched her run into the building and after she had disappeared he kept smiling at the front door which closed slowly. She would be a few minutes. For a few minutes he would look the length of the empty street toward the road that went out of town. For a few minutes he would just look at it, and then he and Ann would drive out that way. They would drive west. There was more land that way and fewer cities, and after leaving the state and crossing some others, he would know how it was not to be chased, he would soon feel that freedom too. He rubbed the wheel, thinking about it. He could feel it in his bones.

He could see Ann behind the glass door, running. She was smiling at him. She opened the door and Spinner had never seen a woman look so beautiful.

He saw nothing else. He still grasped nothing else when Ann screamed and her face became white with fright.

They wore mufti and uniforms. Two grabbed the girl, two yanked open the doors of the car, and all Spinner saw was Ann screaming and her arms reaching for him.

They had to sap Spinner unconscious, which was the only way they could take him in.

Chapter 26

Loma did not stop until he reached Seattle, as he had planned. The timetable was off, and while still in the vicinity of St. Louis there had been some special precautions; but aside from that Loma stuck to his original plan since it was still good. And because of the way Loma worked and because of his habits, that should have been all as far as the St. Louis job was concerned.

But he went over it again and again, the last part of the affair, the reasons why he had Spinner arrested. They were all good reasons. The arrest made sure of Spinner's whereabouts, an important point in Loma's flight.

It made sure that Spinner would not try to involve Loma further. Arrested for murder, Spinner could prove innocence only by establishing Loma's existence. To do this he would have to call the very same witnesses who had seen Spinner and Loma together acting like friends. And it would keep Spinner away from the St. Louis people, at least as long as it would take Loma to get out of reach.

Having Spinner arrested only made sense. He was going over it again and again, Loma decided, for no good reason. When he got to Seattle, Loma disappeared.

The prosecutor had speckled gray hair and a well-trained voice with full modulations. The attorney for the defense had also gray hair and a voice that fit his performance. There were differences between the two men, but Spinner did not see them. He rarely looked at anyone and when he did, he saw nothing. He ate when there was food and he slept when he was alone in his cell. He answered when he was spoken to but volunteered nothing. He no longer felt any interest.

Everything had collapsed, and after the first shock of his failure it had almost seemed to Spinner like part of a design. He was still angry then.

Until he lost Ann.

He hadn't seen Ann while she had been under arrest, but they released her quite soon. She had not been an accomplice, she had not even been an accessory to Spinner's flight. Ann had been with him for professional reasons.

She had been released very soon and then had come to see him. They had been strained with each other. He hadn't asked her to come. He had started to wonder about her release and about his arrest. He did not know how Loma could have timed his arrest, how Loma could know he would be at Ann's house. Spinner's doubts grew. But before they got too big, Spinner went suddenly dull. He felt bored with thinking about it, which saved him from doubt and which kept him from finding an answer. He turned dull and did not need an answer. All he needed was to be left alone. And after a while Ann did not try to see him any more.

The trial was dull. Spinner's presence threw a pall over the room, a sense of disinterest, and it was difficult to question his guilt. Even the cross-examination lacked drama. The opposing lawyers both suffered from lack of an audience and only rarely worked themselves up to a spirit of personal enmity. But the prosecutor had to cover a number of points.

"Is it not true, Mr. Spinner, that you spent three years in jail for criminally assaulting Alvin Dixon because of a long-standing feud between..."

"Objection," said the defense.

The prosecutor stopped, the judge cocked his head to one side, and defense counsel said, "... on the grounds that the question is irrelevant to the particulars, namely..."

"We know the particulars," said the judge. "I'm sorry, were you through?"

"... and on the further grounds that an answer by the defendant would tend to be self-incriminatory..."

"Sustained," said the judge, and to the prosecutor, "Do you want to rephrase your question?"

The prosecutor decided to save it for his summation.

"Mr. Spinner, I show you Exhibit A, a Garand bearing your fingerprints. You are aware of the fact, Mr. Spinner, that this gun shot and killed..."

"Objection!"

"Sustained. Mr. Prosecutor, if you want to rephrase..."

"Thank you. Mr. Spinner, have you ever been in the army?"

"Yes."

"As part of your training, did you ever shoot an M-1?"

"Yes."

"And in combat, over a long period of time, have you not shot and killed, repeatedly shot and..."

"Objection."

"Sustained," said the judge. "I particularly want the jury to disregard this last—"

The prosecutor did not press the point any further. He would save it for the summation.

"Back to Stone Bluff then," said the prosecutor. He craned his neck for a moment, closing his eyes, because he was tired. "How did it happen, Mr. Spinner, that you drove the getaway car..."

"Objection—"

"Sustained—"

"... that the getaway car *was driven* into a torn-up road?"

Spinner, after a moment, shrugged. He might have thought of an answer but the prosecutor went on.

"Strike that," he told the stenotype man, and said to Spinner, "On the night that Alvin Dixon was killed you had come to town for the first time in about three years?"

"Yes."

"Indeed. Isn't it true, Mr. Spinner, that you could therefore not know of the recent excavations on the south end of Stone Bluff and could therefore not know that the lane where the getaway car got stuck had been made impassable?"

There was some legal activity on that point, especially when Spinner refused to answer, but then the prosecution relinquished the point. It would be simpler to make it again in summation.

"Mr. Spinner," said the prosecutor, "I have here a shoe." He lifted the shoe off the table where the exhibits were kept. "You and all of us have heard detailed, expert testimony about this shoe." The prosecutor was tired and sighed. Then he said, "This shoe was found at the place where you got stuck with the..."

"Objection. Really, Your Honor, I object..."

"Sustained."

"Expert testimony," said the prosecutor, tired as before, "establishes that dirt on this shoe is identical to dirt found near the hedge of Alvin Dixon's lawn, and identical to dirt found in a spot which is in line with the shot that killed Alvin Dixon, and..."

"Your Honor, this dirt on the shoe could have been..."

"Do you wish to make an objection?" asked the judge.

The defense made an objection and got very technical about dirt. There was an argument which developed some heat. Defense got carried away into raising the point that there might have been somebody else, that it was strange indeed—

"You mean, where is the other one?" the prosecutor started to shout. "Where is the other shoe? Mr. Spinner!" The whole thing was out of order, but the prosecutor kept shouting. "Where is the other shoe, Mr. Spinner, would you tell us? Who's wearing the other shoe, Mr. Spinner, could you say?"

The gaveling and the yelling left Spinner completely out of the picture. It was now important to establish order in the court and the activity turned to that. This ended in silence. The heat of the free-for-all was short-lived because there had been nothing behind it, just some personal irritation. It ended so suddenly that the silence was quite complete.

The prosecutor closed his eyes. When he opened them he looked past the judge.

"Will the court direct the accused to put on this shoe."

They gave Spinner the shoe.

The shoe fit.

There was a room in the courthouse which they let Spinner use during the recess, because the jail was too far away. The room had varnish on all the woodwork and lettuce-green paint on the ceiling and wall's. Spinner's guard sat by the window and looked at the trees outside. Under the trees the guard saw a bed of yellow asters. They had just opened.

"Did you notice the—" the guard started to say, but he let it go. He was going to say something about the plants, but Spinner sat with his back turned the other way and was looking at the walls and the woodwork. He was thinking that if he had a blanket he might roll up on the floor and try to sleep. But the lawyer would be sure to come and interrupt him. He always came in some time during recess to interrupt with questions.

Spinner heard footsteps come down the hall and watched the guard get out of his chair. The guard, too, knew about the lawyer's useless visits.

There was a knock, and the guard unlocked the door, but it wasn't the lawyer. The sheriff came in.

"Hello, Jake."

Spinner grunted. He put his hands in his pockets.

"Jake. I haven't come to see you since the start of the trial. There wasn't any point—"

"Even less now," said Spinner and turned his chair so he faced the window. It kept him from seeing how the sheriff controlled himself, how the old man felt sick about all of this.

The sheriff pulled up a chair and tapped on the table in front of him. He tapped with one finger, making a dull, restrained sound. Then he suddenly stopped.

"Jake, turn around. What I've got to say..."

"You don't tell me to turn around, Sheriff," said Spinner, and saying it quietly, with no effort showing, made the cut in his voice that much sharper. "You're not talking to a man that's green, Sheriff. I'm not scared any more."

Since Spinner was facing the other way he didn't see what was happening. The sheriff had not been able to hold back any longer. He was up and now began shaking Spinner back and forth by the shoulders.

"Listen to me! At least listen to me! Maybe it will take a thrashing to knock that idiot stare out of your face and the bullheadedness out of your head. Maybe you think you're sitting there, all through, but if you were, Jake Spinner, you wouldn't know where to get the strength to be bullheaded like that!"

The sheriff stared at the man on the chair, then turned away. When he faced

Spinner again he was ready to try it differently. "I know how you got this way, Jake. I was in on it, that's how I know. I'm going to try and make good."

"Sure."

The sheriff ignored it. He even thought it was just bravado the way Spinner had said it.

"I'm from a different town now, Jake. Stone Bluff is a different town now. Dixon is gone, and we're trying to..."

"Trying to thank me for the favor that killing did you and that town?"

"Why?" the sheriff was suddenly roaring. "Why? Because you're guilty?"

"*You* think so," said Spinner.

The sheriff waved his arms without saying anything, as if groping for the right, convincing word. Then he let his breath out and sat for a moment.

"Jake," he said. "I'm trying to tell you, Jake, nobody thinks— I don't think you're guilty, until there's proof."

Spinner looked at the sheriff for the first time. He did not think the old sheriff was a good actor, so he must have meant what he said. Spinner said nothing, though. He was afraid to think of this too much.

"Jake, you going to listen to me?"

After a moment Spinner nodded his head.

"Here's what the prosecutor brought up," said the sheriff, and he suddenly talked as eagerly as he had wanted to do from the start. "He said you drove down that road, that plowed-up road out of town, because you didn't know it had been torn up, you'd just come back into town and couldn't have known that it wasn't a road any more. You remember he said that?" Spinner had started to nod but the sheriff went on. "And then I remembered. You told me about that road being torn up when I had you in the station. You said Sloan, back in the bar, was telling you they just tore up the cutoff on the south end. You said that, trying to make us go out there and look for the killer. You remember?"

"Yes. I remember—"

"You knew that road was no good long before Dixon got killed, so you wouldn't have taken that road. You knew it wasn't good long before because they had told you, back in the bar. I checked that they told you."

"You checked?" said Spinner, and then he said it again. "You checked—"

"Yes," said the sheriff and he saw what it meant to Spinner, that it meant all this hadn't been false talk of encouragement or a visit to just ease the guilt of the sheriff, or to thank the killer for a killing and tell him his death would be worth-while.

"You mean," said Spinner but he was still afraid, "you mean what you said about thinking I might be innocent?"

"Yes, Jake, yes! Now listen, we got to follow the steps. First Dixon—why he got killed. You could have had reason, and that lawyer today showed how you could. But I also know about Dixon and the trouble he had with

St. Louis. They could have done it, Jake. I'm not good enough to find out for sure, but I've looked as best as I could. St. Louis had reason and they could have done it. If they sent a killer it must have been all cased ahead of time, and taking the south end cutoff out to the highway makes sense. And coming into town for the killing, the man they sent wouldn't know about the road being no good. Now the gun, with your prints—how come it had your prints?"

"I touched it. I threw it out of the car."

"And the killer wore gloves."

"Yes. He..."

"Now the shoe, Jake. Was that his shoe?"

"Yes. He lost— No, I took it off him. He'd busted his ankle. He..."

"So let's say it was his. It was his," the sheriff repeated. He had gotten out of his chair and was pacing back and forth. "It was his. Therefore—" The sheriff frowned with the strain of finding the angle that might make the shoe the killer's, for sure. But he couldn't think. "How about it, Jake? You remember what happened to the other one, the mate of that shoe. One shoe left, maybe he threw it away, maybe left it somewhere or..."

"No," said Spinner. "He never took that one off. He had a clubfoot."

"Oh— You say a clubfoot?"

"Yes."

"Don't you know, man, how big that is? How big that can be? If the mate to that shoe is a clubfoot shoe, how could that shoe back there in court be one of yours? That can prove you didn't kill Dixon, that would prove it no matter what the killer might say!"

Then came a silence, like a great hesitation.

"You don't know where he is? Who he is?" said the sheriff.

Spinner looked at his hands, shrugged his shoulders.

"Anything at all, Jake?"

"I went with him," said Spinner. "It's too late to explain all of it—"

"Perhaps you don't need to say," said the sheriff. "But the killer. Can't you describe him? Can't you try, now that you know that I'm trying to help you. Can't you..."

"All right!" The old hopelessness inside Spinner made him shout. "He is small and frail, as if he hadn't grown up; he is stooped and lined, like a monkey, his mind is the only thing that's alive about him, and that mind is like a machine! Is that a description? It's better than height and weight and color of skin, but is that going to help with a ghost? And he's got a clubfoot and he never does anything except for a dead cold reason from his live-machine brain! Is that going to help? You know what he'd do if he were here? He'd *prove* I did the killing. He'd prove it just because there would be no good reason why not! And his name? Loma, he said, is the name he's using."

Spinner stopped when the door opened behind him and his lawyer came in. Spinner stopped to catch his breath and to shake his head so it would distract him. He did not want to think about this, he had not thought that he would again, and then he sat down on his chair. The lawyer had asked the sheriff a question and the sheriff had started to answer. Fast and eagerly he went over all of it and Spinner sat in his chair, and after a while he just sat and looked at his hands. They felt swollen and useless. Spinner barely listened to the two men.

"You mean to tell me he *knew* that road was impassable?" The lawyer was loud with irritation. "And why haven't I been told about this?"

   "And why haven't I been called to the stand before? I tried right in the beginning—"

"—and this entire second-person theory, why haven't I received the support any normal defense—"

They hacked at each other because they were frightened and it showed in their anger.

"The mate to that shoe a clubfoot? You realize that could be tantamount, could have been if I had been apprised in time for adequate investigation—"

"—got to follow that up. And the Dixon angle. The gangland angle I been telling you—"

It went on for a while and then the excitement died down. When it did there were a few facts at the lawyer's disposal. There were new avenues for exploration—too late almost, too late for a motion—but a strong point for a retrial if that man could be found, or even the shoe.

Spinner stopped listening. He had heard the important thing. *Too late.* He looked at his hands, which seemed swollen and useless.

CHAPTER 27

The prosecutor had his summation prepared by one of his clerks who had nothing to do but to excerpt the unfinished points from the cross-examination. This method was not pure lack of interest on the part of the prosecutor, but he was busy preparing two other cases. Of course, the prosecutor delivered the summation himself. He was not tired now and he felt almost sorry not to have any opposition.

He said, "Ladies and gentlemen of the jury," and his smile was indulgent. "There is a saying, *mana lavat manam,* meaning simply that one hand washes the other. You have borne with me, ladies and gentlemen, and you have shown perspicacity. In return I shall therefore be brief." He paused, turned serious, and in a short while, from professional habit, became quite vehement. "I have shown you motive, *modus operandi,* and the *corpus delecti.* We need no more; you need no more. I will not insult your intelligence.

"The defendant, as I have shown, has nurtured over the years the kind of animosity which in the weak often results in violence. Years of friction between the victim, Alvin Dixon, and this poor man, the defendant, years whose hate was first crowned with just punishment by incarceration— three years in jail which the defendant had used to nurture his hate—so that, upon his release, his unmitigated criminality found culmination and release in the murder of Alvin Dixon!

"You have seen the gun which killed the victim, you have been shown that the gun bore the defendant's prints, you have seen the shoe worn by the defendant, the same shoe which bore dirt from the place close to the victim's home, the place where the killer stood to consummate his intent to murder!

"Ladies and gentlemen, I would add nothing more. Even in the face of defense's valiant attempt to disperse this logic, to cloud the evidence by the spurious introduction of a possible second to the execution of the crime—even so, I will say no more. Because does it help the defense to claim that the shoe lost by the defendant belonged to someone else? Does it help the defense to invoke a ghost? Yes, ladies and gentlemen, it might help and supply comfort in the same way that it might help to blame illness upon the evil eye! The ghost has not materialized as the myth has grown larger. But I refuse to insult your credulity by enlarging a myth. I return you to the facts of the crime, for which, in good conscience, you must return your verdict of guilty as charged!"

The prosecutor bowed, then sat down. It had been one of his shortest summations. He had not needed more.

When defense rose to walk to the jury box, the prosecutor did not even look up. He knew his jury and he knew what the quiet in the room meant, a settled silence which meant it was over. The prosecutor did not envy defense.

"Ladies and gentlemen of the jury," said the attorney. The prosecutor thought that it did not sound very vital. Stubborn, perhaps, but without life. "I cannot make your heavy task any easier than it is. I cannot ease it for you, the way my colleague—"

He had started with a negative, the prosecutor thought. Not very good strategically. And he is hesitating—

The defense counsel had done even more, he had stopped. The silence in the room had grown heavy, but no longer with that sense of conclusion. It was heavy with waiting, with suspense made frightening by a low rush of whispers.

Two guards came down the aisle with a girl between them. The prosecutor could not remember her name, but she had been with the defendant. She looked tense, rushed, and held her large purse tight in both arms. The prosecutor got up. He would have to join them. He walked to the group under the judge's bench and even the whispers died in the room, like a wind leaving.

Spinner had not recognized Ann in the beginning. He had not looked up till she was up front, and all he had seen was the back of the girl and the group around her. Then she had turned to look at him.

Spinner sucked in his breath with his sudden, strong rush of feeling. It had come too fast for him to know what name or direction his feeling had. So he sat in his chair and clamped his hands to the seat with a strength that felt like a tremble inside. He did not want the feeling to grow. If they stopped whispering under the bench, if they stopped charging the air with their hisses and their fast, checked gestures—if the girl would go away—

Ann came toward him, her eyes large and anxious. She walked fast and there was strain in her face. When she talked the pressure made her voice hoarse.

"Jake—" she said, close to his car. "Jake, dear—one moment longer. Hold on one moment longer, please—" And she added then, "You need a miracle, Jake. Please, dear, I'm with you now— Look!"

Spinner thought all their faces looked alike. The tight, hustling bunch at the judge's bench had turned to look at him, two eyes each, mouths silent and immobile now. They stepped apart.

There was a small table behind them. And on top was the black, lumped, massive-heeled shoe of a clubfoot.

When it was over and Spinner and Ann walked to the girl's car, he was silent and still did not know what to feel.

"Jake," she said, "aren't you glad?"

He smiled at her, but only because she was looking at him.

They drove south, and Spinner saw the flat land getting rounder and the fields and trees slanting up against hillsides. It was a bright day, and early. They would still have daylight when they reached the farm.

Ann said, "Can't you believe it, Jake?"

He shook his head, not knowing how to say what he felt. "Why," he said. "Why? Why did he do it?"

Ann reached into her pocket and gave a small white paper to Spinner.

"He sent you this," she said. "With the shoe."

Ann hardly knew Loma but she knew what it said on the note and that Spinner would understand it.

It was very short: *To Jake Spinner. For no good reason. Loma.*

THE END

PETER RABE
BY DONALD E. WESTLAKE

Peter Rabe wrote the best books with the worst titles of anybody I can think of. *Murder Me for Nickels. Kill the Boss Goodbye.* Why would anybody ever want to read a book called *Kill the Boss Goodbye?* And yet, *Kill the Boss Goodbye is* one of the most purely *interesting* crime novels ever written.

Here's the setup: Tom Fell runs the gambling in San Pietro, a California town of three hundred thousand people. He's been away on "vacation" for a while, and an assistant, Pander, is scheming to take over. The big bosses in Los Angeles have decided to let nature take its course; if Pander's good enough to beat Fell, the territory is his. Only Fell's trusted assistant, Cripp (for "cripple"), knows the truth, that Fell is in a sanitarium recovering from a nervous breakdown. Cripp warns Fell that he must come back or lose everything. The psychiatrist, Dr. Emilson, tells him he isn't ready to return to his normal life. Fell suffers from a manic neurosis, and if he allows himself to become overly emotional, he could snap into true psychosis. But Fell has no choice; he goes back to San Pietro to fight Pander.

This is a wonderful variant on a story as old as the Bible: Fell gains the world, and loses his mind. And Rabe follows through on his basic idea; the tension in the story just builds and builds, and we're not even surprised to find ourselves worried about, scared for, empathizing with, a gangster. The story of Fell's gradually deepening psychosis is beautifully done. The entire book is spare and clean and amazingly unornamented. Here, for instance, is the moment when Pander, having challenged Fell to a fistfight, first senses the true extent of his danger:

Pander leaned up on the balls of his feet, arms swinging free, face mean, but nothing followed. He stared at Fell and all he saw were his eyes, mild lashes and the lids without movement, and what happened to them. He suddenly saw the hardest, craziest eyes he had ever seen.

Pander lost the moment and then Fell smiled. He said so long and walked out the door (page 47).

Kill the Boss Goodbye was published by Gold Medal in August of 1956. It was the fifth Peter Rabe novel they'd published, the first having come out in May of 1955, just fifteen months before. That's a heck of a pace, and Rabe didn't stop there. In the five years between May 1955 and May 1960, he published sixteen novels with Gold Medal and two elsewhere.

Eighteen novels in five years would be a lot for even a cookie-cutter hack doing essentially the same story and characters over and over again, which was never true of Rabe. He wrote in third person and in first; he wrote emotionless hardboiled prose and tongue-in-check comedy, gangster stories, exotic adventure stories set in Europe and Mexico and North Africa, psychological studies. No two consecutive books used the same voice or setting. In fact, the weakest Peter Rabe novels are the ones written in his two different attempts to create a series character.

What sustains a writer at the beginning of his career is the enjoyment of the work itself, the fun of putting the words through hoops, inventing the worlds, peopling them with fresh-minted characters. That enjoyment in the *doing* of the job is very evident in Rabe's best work. But it can't sustain a career forever; the writing history of Peter Rabe is a not entirely happy one. He spent his active writing career working for a sausage factory. What he wrote was often pate but it was packed as sausage—those titles!—and soon, I think, his own attitude toward his work lowered to match that of the people—agent, editors—most closely associated with the reception and publishing of the work. Rabe, whose first book had a quote on the cover from Erskine Caldwell ("I couldn't put this book down!"), whose fourth book had a quote on the cover from Mickey Spillane ("This guy is *good.*"), whose books were consistently and lavishly praised by Anthony Boucher in the *New York Times* ("harsh objectivity" and "powerful understatement" and "tight and nerve-straining"), was soon churning novels out in as little as ten days, writing carelessly and sloppily, mutilating his talent.

The result is, some of Rabe's books are quite bad, awkwardly plotted and with poorly developed characters. Others are like the curate's egg: parts of them are wonderful. But when he was on track, with his own distinctive style, his own cold clear eye unblinking, there wasn't another writer in the world of the paperback who could touch him.

The first novel, *Stop This Man*, showed only glimpses of what Rabe would become. It begins as a nice variant on the Typhoid Mary story; the disease carrier who leaves a trail of illness in his wake. The story is that Otto Schumacher learns of an ingot of gold loaned to an atomic research facility at a university in Detroit. He and his slatternly girlfriend Selma meet with his old friend Catell, just out of prison, and arrange for Catell to steal the gold. But they don't know that the gold is irradiated, and will make people sick who are near it. The police nearly catch Catell early on, but he escapes, Schumacher dying. Catell goes to Los Angeles to find Smith, the man who might buy the gold ingot.

Once Catell hides the ingot near Los Angeles, the Typhoid Mary story stops, to be replaced by a variant on *High Sierra*. Catell now becomes a burglar-for-hire, employed by Smith, beginning with the robbery of a loan office. There's a double-cross, the police arrive, Catell escapes. The next job is absolutely *High Sierra,* involving a gambling resort up in the mountains, but just before the job Selma (Schumacher's girlfriend) reappears and precipitates the finish. With the police hot on his trail, Catell retrieves his gold and drives aimlessly around the Imperial Valley, becoming increasingly sick with radiation disease. Eventually he dies in a ditch, hugging his gold.

The elements of *Stop This Man* just don't mesh. There are odd little scenes of attempted humor that don't really come off and are vaguely reminiscent of Thorne Smith, possibly because one character is called Smith and one Topper. A character called the Turtle does tiresome malapropisms. Very pulp-level violence and sex are stuck onto the story like lumps of clay onto an already finished statue. Lily, the girl Catell picks up along the way only to make some pulp sex scenes possible, is no character at all, hasn't a shred of believability. Selma, the harridan drunk who pesters Catell, is on the other hand real and believable and just about runs away with the book.

An inability to stay with the story he started to tell plagued Rabe from time to time, and showed up again in his second book, *Benny Muscles In,* which begins as though it's going to be a rise-of-the-punk history, *a Little Caesar,* but then becomes a much more narrowly focused story. Benny Tapkow works for a businesslike new-style mob boss named Pendleton. When Pendleton demotes Benny back to chauffeur, Benny switches allegiance to Big Al Alverato, an old-style Capone type, for whom Benny plans to kidnap Pendleton's college-age daughter, Pat. She knows Benny as her father's chauffeur, and so will leave school with him unsuspectingly. However, with one of Rabe's odd bits of off-the-wall humor (this one works), Pat brings along a thirtyish woman named Nancy Driscoll, who works at the college and is a flirty spinster. At the pre-arranged kidnap spot, Pat unexpectedly gets out of the car with Benny, so it's Nancy who's spirited away to Alverato's yacht, where she seduces Alverato, and for much of the book Nancy and Alverato are off cruising the Caribbean together.

The foreground story, however, remains Benny and the problem he has with Pat. Benny doesn't know Pat well, and doesn't know she's experimented with heroin and just recently stopped taking it because she was getting hooked. To keep Pat tractable, Benny feeds her heroin in her drinks. The movement of the story is that Benny gradually falls in love with Pat and gradually (unknowingly) addicts her to heroin. The characters of Benny and Pat are fully developed and very touchingly real. The hopeless love story never becomes mawkish, and the gradual drugged deterioration of Pat is beautifully and tensely handled (as Fell's deterioration will be in *Kill The Boss Goodbye*). The leap forward from *Stop This Man* is doubly astonishing when we consider they were published four months apart.

One month later, *A Shroud for Jesso* was published, in the second half of which Rabe finally came fully into his own. The book begins in a New York underworld similar to that in *Benny Muscles In,* with similar characters and relationships and even a similar symbolic job demotion for the title character, but soon the mobster Jesso becomes involved with international intrigue, is nearly murdered on a tramp steamer on the North Atlantic, and eventually makes his way to a strange household in Hannover, Germany, the home of Johannes Kator, an arrogant bastard and spy. In the house also are Kator's sister, Renette, and her husband, a homosexual baron named Helmut. Helmut provides the social cover, Kator provides the money. Renette has no choice but to live with her overpowering brother and her nominal husband.

Jesso changes all that. He and Renette run off together, and the cold precise Rabe style reaches its maturity:

They had a compartment, and when the chauffeur was gone they locked the door, pushed the suitcases out of the way, and sat down. When the train was moving they looked out of the window. At first the landscape looked flat, industrial; even the small fields had a square mechanical look. Later the fields rolled and there were more trees. Renette sat close, with her legs tucked under her. She had the rest of her twisted around so that she leaned against him. They smoked and didn't talk. There was nothing to talk about. They looked almost indifferent, but their indifference was the certainty of knowing what they had (page 93).

The characters in *A Shroud for Jesso* are rich and subtle, their relationships ambiguous, their story endlessly fascinating. When Jesso has to return for a while to New York, Renette prefigures the ending in the manner of her refusal to go with him:

Over here Jesso, I know you, I want you, we are what I know now. You and I. But over there you must be somebody else. I've never known you over there and your life is perhaps quite different. Perhaps not, Jesso, but I don't know. I want you now, here, and not later and somewhere else. You must not start to think of me as something you own, keep around wherever you happen to be. It would not be the same. What we have between us is just the opposite of that. It is the very thing you have given me, Jesso, and it is freedom (page 131).

And this opposition between love and freedom is what then goes on to give the novel its fine but bitter finish.

Rabe kept a European setting for his next book, *A House in Naples,* the story about two American Army deserters who've been black market operators in Italy in the ten years since the end of World War II. Charlie, the hero, is a drifter, romantic and adventurous. Joe Lenken, his partner, is a sullen but shrewd pig, and when police trouble looms, Joe's the one with solid papers and a clear identity, while Charlie's the one who has to flee to Rome to try (and fail) to find adequate forged papers. In a bar he meets a useless old expatriate American drunk who then wanders off, gets into a brawl, and is knifed to death. Charlie steals the dead man's ID for himself, puts the body into the Tiber under a bridge, then looks up and sees a girl looking down. How much did she see?

In essence, *A House in Naples* is a love story in which the love is poisoned at the very beginning by doubt. The girl, Martha, is simple and clear, but her clarity looks like ambiguity to Charlie. Since he can never be sure of her, he can never be sure of himself. Once he brings Martha back to Naples and the vicious Joe is added to the equation, the story can be nothing but a slow and hard unraveling. The writing is cold and limpid and alive with understated emotion, from first sentence ("The warm palm of land cupped the water to make a bay, and that's where Naples was" – page 7) to last ("He went to the place where he had seen her last" – page 144).

A House in Naples was followed by *Kill the Boss Goodbye*, and that was the peak of Rabe's first period, five books, each one better than the one before. In those books, Rabe combined bits and pieces of his own history and education with the necessary stock elements of the form to make books in which tension and obsession and an inevitable downward slide toward disaster all combine with a style of increasing cold objectivity not only to make the scenes seem brand new but even to make the (rarely stated) emotions glitter with an unfamiliar sheen.

Born in Germany in 1921, Rabe already spoke English when he arrived in America at seventeen. With a Ph.D. in psychology, he taught for a while at Western Reserve University and did research at Jackson Laboratory, where he wrote several papers on frustration. (No surprise.) Becoming a writer, he moved to various parts of America and lived a while in Germany, Sicily and Spain. His first published work he has described as "a funny pregnancy story (with drawings) to *McCall's*." The second was *Stop This Man*. In the next four books, he made the paperback world his own.

But then he seemed not to know what to do with it. Was it bad advice? Was it living too far away from the publishers and the action? Was it simply the speed at which he worked?

Fortunately, with his twelfth book, *Blood on the Desert*, Rabe gets his second wind, goes for a complete change of pace, and produces his first fully satisfying work since *Kill the Boss Goodbye*. It's a foreign intrigue tale set in the Tunisian desert, spy versus spy in a story filled with psychological nuance. The characters are alive and subtle, the story exciting, the setting very clearly realized.

My Lovely Executioner, is another total change of pace, and a fine absorbing novel. Rabe's first book told completely in the first-person, it is also his first true *mystery,* a story in which the hero is being manipulated and has no idea why.

The hero-narrator, Jimmy Gallivan, is a glum fellow in jail, with three weeks to go on a seven-year term for attempted murder (wife's boyfriend, shot but didn't kill) when he's caught up in a massive jailbreak. He doesn't want to leave, but another con, a tough professional criminal named Rand, forces him to come along, and then he can't get back. Gallivan gradually realizes the whole jailbreak was meant to get *him* out, but he doesn't know why. Why him? Why couldn't they wait three weeks until he'd be released anyway? The mystery is a fine one, the explanation is believable and fair, the action along the way is credible and exciting, and the Jim Thompsonesque gloom of the narration is wonderfully maintained.

And next, published in May of 1960, Rabe's sixteenth Gold Medal novel in exactly five years, was *Murder Me for Nickels,* yet another change of pace, absolutely unlike anything that he had done before. Told in first person by Jack St. Louis, righthand man of Walter Lippit, the local jukebox king, *Murder Me for Nickels* is as sprightly and glib as *My Lovely Executioner* was depressed and glum. It has a lovely opening sentence, "Walter Lippit makes music all over town" (page 5), and is chipper and funny all the way through. At one point, for instance, St. Louis is drunk when he suddenly has to defend himself in a fight: "I whipped the bottle at him so he stunk from liquor. I kicked out my foot and missed. I swung out with the glass club and missed. I stepped out of the way and missed. When you're drunk everything is sure and nothing works" (page 164).

Nineteen-sixty was also when a penny-ante outfit called Abelard-Schuman published in hardcover *Anatomy of a Killer,* a novel Gold Medal had rejected, I can't think why. It's third person, as cold and as clean as a knife, and this time the ghostly unemotional killer, Loma and Mound, is brought center stage and made the focus of the story. This time he's called Jordan (as in the river?) and Rabe stays in very tight on him. The book begins,

When he was done in the room he stepped away quickly because the other man was falling his way. He moved fast and well and when he was out in the corridor he pulled the door shut behind him. Sam Jordan's speed had nothing to do with haste but came from perfection.

The door went so far and then held back with a slight give. It did not close. On the floor, between the door and the frame, was the arm.

...he looked down at the arm, but then did nothing else. He stood with his hand on the door knob and did nothing.

He stood still and looked down at the fingernails and thought they were changing color. And the sleeve was too long at the wrist. He was not worried about the job being done, because it was done and he knew it. He felt the muscles around the mouth and then the rest of the face, stiff like bone. He did not want to touch the arm.

...After he had not looked at the arm for a while, he kicked at it and it flayed out of the way. He closed the door without slamming it and walked away. A few hours later he got on the night train for the nine-hour trip back to New York.

...But the tedium of the long ride did not come. He felt the thick odor of clothes and felt the dim light in the carriage like a film over everything, but the nine-hour dullness he wanted did not come. I've got to unwind, he thought. This is like the shakes. After all this time with all the habits always more sure and perfect, this.

He sat still, so that nothing showed, but the irritation was eating at him. Everything should get better, doing it time after time, and not worse. Then it struck him that he had never before had to touch a man when the job was done. Naturally. Here was a good reason. He now knew this in his head but nothing else changed. The hook wasn't out and the night-ride dullness did not come (pages 7-9).

It is from that small beginning, having to touch a victim for the first time, that Rabe methodically and tautly describes the slow unraveling of Jordan. It's a terrific book.

There was one other novel from this period, a Daniel Port which was rejected by Gold Medal and published as half of an Ace double-book in 1958, under the title *The Cut of the Whip*. Which brings to eighteen the books published between *1955* and *1960*. Eighteen books, five years, and they add up to almost the complete story of Peter Rabe's career as a fine and innovative writer.

Almost. There was one more, in December of 1962, called *The Box* (the only Rabe novel published with a Rabe title). *The Box* may be Rabe's finest work, a novel of character and of place, and in it Rabe managed to use and integrate more of his skills and techniques than anywhere else. "This is a pink and gray town," it begins, "which sits very small on the North edge of Africa. The coast is bone white and the sirocco comes through any time it wants to blow through. The town is dry with heat and sand" (page 5).

A tramp steamer is at the pier. In the hold is a large wooden box, a corner of which was crushed in an accident. A bad smell is coming out. The bill of lading very oddly shows that the box was taken aboard in New York and is to be delivered to New York. Contents: "PERISHABLES. NOTE: IMPERATIVE, KEEP VENTILATED." The captain asks the English clerk of the company that owns the pier permission to unload and open the box. The box is swung out and onto the pier.

They stood a moment longer while the captain said again that he had to be out of here by this night, but mostly there was the silence of heat everywhere on the pier. And whatever spoiled in the box there, spoiled a little bit more.

'Open it!' said the captain (page 11).

They open it, and look in.

'Shoes?' said the clerk after a moment. 'You see the shoes?' as if nothing on earth could be more puzzling.
'Why shoes on?' said the captain, sounding stupid.
What was spoiling there spoiled for one moment more, shrunk together
in all that rottenness, and then must have hit bottom.
The box shook with the scramble inside, with the cramp muscled pain,
with the white sun like steel hitting into the eyes there so they screwed up
like sphincters, and then the man inside screamed himself out of his box
(page 12).

The man is Quinn, a smartass New York mob lawyer who is being given
a mob punishment: shipped around the world inside the box, with nothing in there but barely enough food and water to let him survive the trip.
What happens to him in Okar, and what happens to Okar as a result of
Quinn, live up to the promise of that beginning.

But for Rabe, it was effectively the end. It was another three years before
he published another book, and then it was a flippant James Bond imita-
tion called *Girl in a Big Brass Bed*, introducing Manny deWitt, an arch and
cutesy narrator who does arch and cutesy dirty work for an international
industrialist named Hans Lobbe. Manny deWitt appeared twice more, in
The Spy Who Was 3 Feet Tall (1966) and *Code Name Gadget* (1967), to no
effect, all for Gold Medal. And Gold Medal published Rabe's last two books
as well: *War of the Dons* (1972) and *Black Mafia* (1974).

Except for those who hit it big early, the only writers who tend to stay
with writing over the long haul are those who can't find a viable alternative. Speaking personally, three times in my career the wolf has been so
slaveringly at the door that I tried to find an alternative livelihood, but
lacking college degrees, craft training or any kind of useful work history I
was forced to go on writing instead, hoping the wolf would grow tired and
slink away. The livelihood of writing is iffy at best, which is why so many
writing careers simply stop when they hit a lean time. Peter Rabe had a
doctorate in psychology; when things went to hell on the writing front, it
was possible for him to take what he calls a bread-and-butter job teaching
undergraduate psychology in the University of California.

It is never either entirely right or entirely wrong to identify a writer
with his or her heroes. The people who carry our stories may be us, or our
fears about ourselves, or our dreams about ourselves. The typical Peter
Rabe hero is a smart outsider, working out his destiny in a hostile world.
Unlike Elmore Leonard's scruffy heroes, for instance, who are always iron-

ically aware that they're better than their milieu, Rabe's heroes are better than their milieu but are never entirely confident of that. They're as tough and grubby as their circumstances make necessary, but they are also capable from time to time of the grand gesture. Several of Peter Rabe's novels, despite the ill-fitting wino garb of their titles, are very grand gestures indeed.

9 781933 586113